THE BLACK SHEEP
and the
HIDDEN BEAUTY

THE BLACK SHEEP
and the
HIDDEN BEAUTY

DONNA KAUFFMAN

BRAVA

KENSINGTON PUBLISHING CORP.
http://www.kensingtonbooks.com

BRAVA BOOKS are published by

Kensington Publishing Corp.
850 Third Avenue
New York, NY 10022

All Kensington titles, imprints and distributed lines are available at special quantity discounts for bulk purchases for sales promotion, premiums, fund-raising, educational or institutional use.

Special book excerpts or customized printings can also be created to fit specific needs. For details, write or phone the office of the Kensington Special Sales Manager: Kensington Publishing Corp., 850 Third Avenue, New York, NY 10022. Attn. Special Sales Department. Phone: 1-800-221-2647.

Brava and the B logo Reg. U.S. Pat. & TM Off.

ISBN-13: 978-0-7582-1727-1
ISBN-10: 0-7582-1727-7

First Kensington Trade Paperback Printing: January 2008
10 9 8 7 6 5 4 3 2 1

Printed in the United States of America

This one is for Sarah and the Gang.
(Leah, Michelle C., JuJu, Hey April, Anna, Beth,
Kim, Michelle A thru Z, Debbie, Ruby!, Vicki, Diane,
the girls of summer:
Chelsea, Molly, Emmy, MaryBabs,
Erin and the Katie/Kaity's,
and, of course, Billy the ManSlave.)
Thanks for keeping me sane.
Well, mostly, anyway.

Chapter 1

He found himself watching her. Again.

Not his type. And yet, more and more often, Raphael Santiago was making excuses to leave his offices in the main house and wander down to the paddocks. He'd stroll the fence line. And watch her. He'd reasoned that it was his fascination with the horses, and yet he'd been on Dalton Downs property going on two years now, and it had only been in the past several months that he'd found them suddenly intriguing—a time frame that just happened to coincide with when she'd taken over as stable manager and head trainer.

He never lingered, never spoke to her. He'd wander on along, stopping by Kate's office, or head on down to Mac's place farther back on the property, if it was after work hours. Yet he missed very little.

She was graceful in movement, yet strong and controlled. Gentle in tone and demeanor, yet brooked no argument from the half-ton beasts she trained as easily as if they were puppies. She fascinated him, when she shouldn't.

She wasn't his type. Not even close.

He walked along the worn path to the outer barns, careful not to step in anything that would make him regret not changing out of his Italian, hand-tooled shoes, wondering what the hell he was doing. Given that he was headed toward the stables used by employees only, it wasn't to see Kate. Or Mac.

No, he was walking all the way out here because of another man. Not that he had any claim on her. They'd done nothing more than exchange the occasional nod. And it wasn't as if he kept tabs on her personal time, but Dalton Downs was private property, so he'd have noticed if she'd had regular company. And, to his knowledge, this was her first visitor since coming here. Which he gave less than a damn about. Or would have.

Except he'd been heading down to Kate's office, hoping to catch Mac about some questions on one of their case files, denying it was just another excuse to watch her, when the guy had shown up. She'd been surprised to see him, and, from what he could tell of her expression, not entirely happily so. In fact, she'd darted a gaze around, as if concerned to be seen talking to him.

She'd ended her training session with the horse immediately, a poor wretch of a thing she, Kate, and Mac had recently rescued, and handed him over to one of the help, before giving the newcomer a fast, tight hug. Next thing he knew, she was leading the older guy out to the employee barns, away from the hustle and bustle of Kate's teaching program. And, perhaps, the watching eyes of her coworkers.

Rafe certainly hadn't intended to follow them. What she did and with whom was her business. He had more than enough of his own to handle at the moment.

But something simply hadn't seemed right about that brief episode. That look on her face, perhaps, in that split second before she'd smiled and waved hello to her guest. Something. All he knew was that whatever that something was, it had made the hairs prickle along his neck. And the next thing he knew, he was picking his way along the path to the outer stables, trying not to ruin a pair of three-hundred-dollar shoes.

Mac would chalk it up to wanting sex. Kate would scold him for potentially disrupting her program. His mother would have a coronary if she knew he'd spent more then forty dollars for a pair of shoes.

But none of that mattered at the moment. Something wasn't

right here. And if there was one thing Mac, Finn, and Rafe firmly believed in, it was following gut instinct. Maybe that was what had called to him about her all along. That, despite appearances to the contrary, something wasn't what it seemed with Elena Caulfield. It was almost a relief to have an actual reason for his otherwise unusual fascination with her.

She wasn't his type.

Not that she was particularly hard on the eyes. And he admired a woman who didn't mind getting her hands dirty. But from what he'd come to learn about her, she spent a good chunk of her day with at least some part of her person covered in mud or muck. Or worse. And didn't much seem to mind. She wore little or no makeup, as far as he could tell, and pulled her dark hair straight back in a simple, single braid that swung halfway to her ass. An ass even he couldn't make out in the baggy overalls she favored.

Long hair. That part was nice. And he'd have been lying if he said he hadn't spent at least a few minutes wondering what it would look like all loose and wavy. He was a man, after all. But it was clear she wasn't all that caught up in the more conventional rituals of being female, something Rafe unapologetically enjoyed in the women of his acquaintance. Tomboys had their appeal to some men, but he liked a woman who reveled in her femininity.

So his fascination had been something of a mystery to him.

Not any longer. It had merely been instinct that something was off.

Maybe now he was finally going to get the chance to figure out what that something was.

He slowed as he drew closer to the paddock. It was empty, so they'd already gone inside. He'd let them get a good head start so as not to be completely obvious. It was why he'd walked over rather than taking one of the Dalton golf carts.

He ducked through the fence, not wanting to swing the gate open and announce his arrival with a metal squeal. The big, sliding barn door had been shoved along the track just enough to allow a person to duck inside. He glanced back toward the main barns, but no one had followed him. In fact, a quick glance back at the stables and up to the house proved that no one was paying the least bit of attention to what was going on out here. So he moved closer to the edge of the door, careful not to let the sun cast his shadow across the opening. And listened.

"How you doing there, old girl? Elena taking good care of you?"

It was the man, and Rafe assumed he was talking to her horse.

"She's feeding well, not putting on too much weight." This from Elena. "So far, I think we're doing okay."

Her voice was low, soft, with a cadence that was naturally soothing. Rafe began to see how she seduced the headstrong animals she worked with into doing what she wanted. A man hears a voice like that, he might be inclined to do the same.

"That's good. Really good. I know how worried you are. Although, I have to be honest, Lenie. Given that concern, I'm still having a hard time understanding why you left—"

"Kenny, I know you worry, too, but I've explained my reasons the best I can. Besides, it's good here. She's doing great."

"She is. But what about you?"

"I'm—fine. It's a good job, I'm good at it, they seem happy with me, and it's the right place. For both of us. For now."

"But you're going back, right? Back to the track? Your dad would be so proud of all you've accomplished and you know he'd hate it if you gave up on your dream."

When she spoke again, her voice was a bit deeper, perhaps a bit tighter. With what emotion—anger, regret, or grief—Rafe couldn't be sure without seeing her expression.

"Right now the only thing that matters to me is making sure Springer has a foal that lives, and that she stays healthy before, during, and after. That's why I came to you. You're the closest thing to family I have. I trust you. But, as much as I appreciate you coming all the way out here, it would really be best if, from now on, as she gets closer, I brought her to you when the time is right. They're doing right by me here and I don't need or want to worry them with a problem horse."

"I know, honey, and I appreciate that. Just as I'm sure you're so overqualified, they're jumping for joy to have you. I'd imagine, though, given the work they do here, with those kids, the last thing they'd worry about is you taking care of what's yours. I saw that poor thing you were training when I got here. A charity case if I ever saw one—"

"That's something else I took on, for Kate. It's not my regular—"

"I know." His voice gentled. "I'm just saying, it's what they do here, they mend things. Animals. People. Souls and spirits. I guess . . . I just worry that you need mending, is all. I never saw that in you. Always so sure of yourself. Then, after Geronimo and that horrible tragedy—"

"I was going to leave anyway, Kenny. Even if everything else hadn't happened. It—I wasn't going to advance there. I just . . . I wasn't sure what my next step should be. Then I found out about Springer, and it all seemed like a giant signal to just step back, take some time. So I did. No regrets."

There was a long pause, then, "Okay. I just—if you needed to talk, about anything—"

"I know. And thank you. Just help me keep her okay and you'll be doing more for me than you could possibly know."

He chuckled then, and there was a rustle of clothing. A hug, perhaps. Without peeking around the door and giving himself away, Rafe couldn't be certain.

"I'd have been upset if you hadn't come to me," Kenny said a moment later. "But I'm available for more than vet care if you need the ear."

"Understood. And appreciated."

Their voices drew closer and Rafe realized they were heading his way. He'd been so caught up in the conversation and the information it was revealing, he hadn't exactly thought out his escape route.

Too late to duck away, so the only alternative was to stroll in as if that was his intention all along. He slid the door back a bit more, the resulting grind of metal on the metal tracks abruptly stopping the conversation inside.

The sun at his back made both Elena and Kenny shield their eyes as he stepped into the darker interior of the barn. They stopped walking as well, waiting for him to come further inside.

Elena spoke first. "Can I help you, Mr. Santiago?"

"Yes," he said, not having a clue what he was going to say until he said it. "And it's Rafe, please. I was—I'm interested in talking to you."

Her expression grew wary as she looked past him. Expecting to see what, or who, he wasn't sure. But he was too busy scrambling to come up with a reason for his sudden arrival to worry about that.

She wore the same denim overalls he'd always seen her in, with a faded yellow bandana tied loosely around her neck, and her boots caked in God-knew-what. She'd pushed up the long sleeves of her pale green tee, which was covered in the red, dusty clay that passed for dirt in most of Virginia. As he stepped closer, he noted that she had a fair share of dust on her forehead and chin, too, as if she'd dragged her dusty sleeve across them a time or two.

Not exactly an enticing picture . . . and yet, standing closer like this, he found himself wondering how she'd clean up. All that riding she did, he'd bet there were some Class A legs inside those baggy overalls. She could probably do a pair of killer heels some justice, too, he thought, though from what he'd seen, he doubted she even owned a dress, much less heels.

"About?" she queried, making him realize he was staring.

His gaze found hers then. Brown eyes, he noted. Not the cute, puppy-dog kind. The old-soul kind. The kind that saw way more than made him comfortable.

Distinctly aware of the older man's attention focused on him as well, he was even less on top of his game than usual. He paused for a too-long second, then blurted out the only thing he could think of. "Riding lessons."

To her credit, she tried to maintain her professional demeanor, but he couldn't help but notice her quick scan of his attire, which, admittedly, was about as far from barn clothing as you could get without being in a tailored suit or tux. "You . . . want riding lessons?"

"Yes," he said, trying to sound like he meant it. "I want riding lessons."

God help him.

Chapter 2

She'd felt him watching her, earlier, when she'd been working with Bonder. It wasn't the first time, either. Far from it. He was steady about it, open. But in the two months she'd been at Dalton Downs, he'd never spoken to her or approached her. Considering he looked like six feet of raw sex dressed up in beautifully tailored clothes, she doubted very much it was lack of confidence on his part.

So, she couldn't quite figure out what it meant. She doubted it was any kind of personal interest. He wasn't the ruthlessly overgroomed type who took longer to get ready than most women, but the man knew how to dress. He somehow managed to be casually suave and rugged as hell all at the same time. If she cared about things like that, she'd have felt downright shabby whenever he was nearby, with her worn overalls, ancient boots, and shirts that rarely stayed clean ten minutes after she put them on.

He was too polished, too perfect, too . . . everything to want a woman who spent her days reeking of horse sweat and barn muck. Which left a big question mark hanging over what the draw actually was. That very ambiguity should have unnerved her, at least a little, what with everything she had going on. But the truth was, his attention always left her feeling energized and aware, and not in a bad way. Just a way she had no business thinking about.

Not that it mattered. A woman would have to be dead not to respond to those dark eyes of his, the honey-colored skin, the thick, black head of hair, and that naturally broad-shouldered, tapered-waist-and-hips kind of physique. She, on the other hand, rarely commanded such attention. Her staring at him made sense, though she avoided the temptation at all costs. Being noticed and noticing others was definitely not high on her priority list here. Doing her job, providing a safe, quiet place for her and Springer—that was all that mattered.

He was also the only one of the three Trinity men who hadn't formerly spoken to her during her tenure here. Mac came by all the time and chatted her up on his way to see Kate. Nice guy, clearly devoted to her boss, and making a point to keep an eye out for his woman's interests. Elena respected that, and she liked the guy.

Finn Dalton owned the place, but you'd never know it. A bigger flirt she'd never met, but in that completely harmless way that made you laugh rather than feel awkward or threatened. He even chatted up the horses. But she'd also noted he knew everyone by name and made time as often as possible to talk with everyone from management to the part-time stall muckers. He was gone more often than not, but his presence on the property always livened things up and put everyone in a good mood.

Which left Raphael Santiago, the enigmatic but reserved third partner in the other enterprise operated on Dalton Downs property, one that, had she known of its existence, might have kept her from pursuing the job opening here. Ultimately, she was glad she hadn't, regardless of the heightened awareness it forced her to maintain. What she'd told Kenny was true. This was exactly the right place for her and Springer right now.

At least, until now.

"Lessons," she repeated, knowing she sounded less than sharp, but he'd so completely taken her off guard, it was surprising she was stringing her words together coherently.

"Lessons," he replied.

"So . . . I should be getting back on the road," Kenny abruptly interjected. He put his beefy arm around her shoulder for a quick hug, which broke Elena's fixed stare and gave her a merciful second or two to get a grip. Up close and personal, the final partner of the "unholy" Trinity, as she'd heard Kate jokingly refer to them, was . . . a lot. Of everything. Even his voice was a lot. Smooth, rich, with the barest hint of an accent. It was every bit as seductive as the rest of him, and no matter the reason for the attention, she, apparently, was far from immune to it. Horse sweat and barn muck be damned.

She jerked her gaze off of him and, instead, found a smile for the man who had been her father's closest friend, as she scrambled to regain her mental footing. "Thanks again for coming all the way out. I'll call you next week to set up a checkup schedule for our girl."

Kenny held her gaze steadily with his own and she did her best to return it without faltering. The man didn't miss much. Which bothered her as much as it reassured her. She needed him right now, more than he knew, but she couldn't risk bringing him in any more than she already had. She already had too much to worry about as it was.

"You do that," he said. "She looks good, Lenie. You're doing a fine job." His gaze flickered sideways to encompass their guest, then returned to her. "You want to walk me out? Anything else we need to discuss?"

She knew he was offering her an out if she felt she needed one. Did he feel the crackling intensity in the air, too? Or was he just protecting her in that general way men of his generation did? She shook her head, though she was thankful for his sensitivity. It felt odd, but in a good way, to have someone looking out for her for a change. It had been a very long time since anyone had. "I think we're good. Unless you need an escort out, I—"

He smiled, shook his head, and gave her one last hug. "I can find my way. You take care of business here."

"Thanks, Kenny." She pressed a kiss to his fleshy cheek, not minding the scratch of white stubble there. It reminded her of her father.

He nodded his good-bye to Rafe, who nodded in return, then headed out of the barn, back toward the main stable where his truck was parked. It wasn't until he'd cleared the building, and she was left alone with all that was Rafe in the cool, dim interior of the stables, alone and away from, well, everyone, that she wished she'd considered Kenny's escape offer a bit more thoroughly.

Putting as professional a smile on her face as she could, even while damning herself for feeling, even for a moment, like a two-bit farmhand in the presence of all of his immaculate gorgeousness, she brazened it out. "Riding lessons. Did . . . Kate send you down?"

"Kate? No," he said, a flash of confusion crossing his handsome face. "I managed to find my way down here all by myself." The hint of a smile, so unexpected, as she'd never seen so much as a glimmer of one on him before, was really just too much.

She needed a fan. Or a good, stiff breeze. Or . . . something. Dear Lord. It was ridiculous, the impact he was having. Awareness overload. And yet, there didn't seem to be much she could do about it. He was probably used to it.

"Well . . . okay, then," she managed, hating being so flustered. She'd worked with and around men her whole life and had managed never to come across as a brainless twit. "I—I'm not sure if you're aware, but I work more with training the horses. Not so much with people. Perhaps one of Kate's instructors—"

"You're very good," he said, rather abruptly. "With the horses, I mean. I've watched you."

I know, she wanted to say. *Boy, do I know.* "Thank you. I love working with them, but it's always nice to hear that from an outside source."

His gaze had shifted beyond her to the barn and stalls lining the aisles. "I'm about as outside a source as there is. I know nothing about horses." Apparently realizing that might sound insulting, he added, "But even a rank amateur can see that you handle them very well."

He was making small talk. Which didn't quite fit with the image she'd developed of him. It made her wonder what was really going on, why he'd suddenly approached her. For lessons, of all things. Her defenses finally shifted more firmly back into place. "They are complex and intriguing creatures." *As are you*, she could have added, but didn't. He might wear his clothes with an elegant nonchalance that exuded an unspoken confidence, but there was that raw edge to him that was far more wild mustang than refined thoroughbred. Complex creature, indeed. "But, even so, they're easier to figure out than people." She hadn't meant to give voice to that last part and braced herself as he swung his gaze back to hers.

"I'll agree with you there," he said, looking directly at her again. "People are easily the most complex creatures on the planet."

Her body tightened under his steady regard. *Intense* was an understatement with him. Even up close, his eyes were midnight black, with a laser-like intensity that bore into hers in a way she'd never encountered before. She'd definitely be wise never to underestimate him, in or out of his element.

"No matter how long you know somebody, you never truly know it all," he finished.

"No," she said, damning the tight note in her voice. Just as with the four-legged animals she trained, the first rule with any animal was *show no fear*. But the second rule was *show no overt aggression*. A delicate balance at times. So she let her gaze casually, or what she hoped was casually, drift out toward the surrounding paddock, breaking his visual hold on her. Or at least hers on him. "I don't imagine you ever really do." Something she fervently prayed held true for her where he, or anyone else at Dalton Downs, was concerned.

And then it occurred to her . . . was that why he was out here? Had he, or someone here, managed to find out something more about her past? Wouldn't Kate have confronted her directly, though? She wasn't sure how the hierarchy worked here with Trinity and Kate's separate enterprise, but Kate didn't strike her as the type to let someone else handle her personal business, much less dictate her hiring practices.

"But I came out here to talk to you about horses, not people."

She tried not to slump in relief. "I'll be glad to help you in any way that I can."

She glanced at him in time to see him set his jaw a little. As if he wasn't quite sure how to broach what he wanted to say next. Nerves? She wondered what on earth a man like him could have to be nervous about. Couldn't be her. She was quite comfortable in her own skin, and made no apologies for her lack of feminine wiles, but she was also well aware that nerve-inducing she was not.

"Good," he said, then shifted his weight a little before continuing. "You can teach someone to ride, can't you?"

"I—I suppose I could. If it's just the basics you want, I can probably handle that." Though any of Kate's instructors would be better suited. Of course, maybe he didn't want to ask a favor of them. She was the new hire, after all. "Can I ask why you've decided to take lessons?" She knew Mac and Finn both rode, as she'd seen the two of them, and Kate, head out before. She assumed, with his constant attention on her and the stables, that he rode, too, but apparently not.

"I never had the chance to spend much time around horses growing up. None, actually, if you don't count summer camp. I figure it's time I changed that."

It struck her then, as she finally calmed down enough to look at the situation, and him, more objectively, that for all his apparent interest . . . he wasn't exactly really enthusiastic about this whole idea. "Is it . . . job-related? Because your partners ride?" she asked, before thinking better of it. In the end, it didn't really matter why he wanted to learn. In the Dalton Downs hierarchy, he ranked somewhere on the level of her boss, or higher, so from a professional standpoint it behooved her to do what she could to make him happy. Kate might not have sent him over here, but she'd very likely expect her employees to accede to any of the Trinity partners' wishes.

Thankfully, he didn't seem put off by the question. Quite the opposite. "Finn grew up on horseback, probably rode before he walked, and yes, Mac learned last year, mostly so he could impress Kate. They go on these weekly picnic rides now and—whatever, that's not important. I just thought it was a skill I should have, and, being as they're right here, I've probably put it off too long as it is."

Elena tried not to smile. He was awfully chatty all of a sudden. His gaze moved from her to the occupied stalls nearby, then back to her. It was the first time she'd ever seen him as anything other than the enigmatic, intense, controlled man who observed her while she worked. The very idea that he was at all nervous about learning to ride charmed her. Just a little.

"Are you all planning a horseback ride or event of some kind? I only ask because if there is a deadline by which you have to be a decent rider, or if there is something specific you need to learn, that would factor in to how we'd go about setting up your lessons."

She thought about her newly adopted work program with Bonder. And Springer's demands on her time. And all the other horses she was responsible for taking care of, and wondered when she'd have time for this. Not that she had a choice.

"No time frame, no event. Like I said, I just want to expand my horizons a bit. In my line of work, you never know what skills might come in handy."

Which begged the question: what was it, exactly, that he did? She didn't know much about Trinity, Inc., and, frankly, the less she knew about them and vice versa, the better. But now that it looked like she was going to be stuck spending time with him, perhaps it was best to do a little digging. Information was power, after all. A brand of power that, in the wrong hands, could definitely be used to harm her. But in her hands, could only help her. At the very least, it would help gauge just how safe and secure her chosen little hidey-hole really was.

"I know I've been here for a little while now, but I'm afraid I don't know all that much about what you do. I know you, Mac, and Finn run some kind of foundation, so I take it Trinity is some kind of charitable organization, but—"

"We help people. But we're not a charity, or a foundation."

"Okay." She paused to see if he would elaborate, but he said nothing more, and she took that to mean her line of questioning was over. Perhaps for the best. Information was fine, but in hindsight, the more he offered, she supposed, the more she owed in return. Maybe the less they had to talk about, the better.

As if to prove her point, he said, "How long have you been working with horses? I understand you work with racehorses as a rule."

She stilled briefly, surprised that he knew about her past. Not that it was a secret. Kate knew her work history when she hired her. Maybe it was common knowledge around the grounds—she really didn't know, as she made a point not to engage in small talk with any of the other personnel. Still, it was more than a little unsettling to think that he'd been checking up on her, or asking about her. Her guard increased. "I do. Or did. It's a tough industry to get a break in, though, and I wasn't moving along the way I wanted to in my former situation." It had been her stock answer to Kate. And Kenny. And anyone else who wondered why she'd left the industry. Still, she found it hard to maintain direct eye contact in the face of his rather intense focus. She doubted he missed much, and, after dealing with Kenny's surprise visit, her guard was in need of a bit more shoring-up before handling this kind of test.

"I'm guessing there aren't too many women in your line of work."

"Not too many, no." Before she could deftly change the topic back to him and the classes he wanted, he continued.

"So, have you given up on it completely then?"

She forced herself to maintain steady eye contact, but it cost her. She could only pray he didn't see anything in her gaze that was less than forthright. "No, just taking a break. My horse is expecting, so I thought it was a good time to step out of all the chaos for awhile, regroup a little, and think about where I want to go from here."

"How is she doing? Everything going okay?"

Her guard, already on alert now, leapt even higher. This was precisely the conversation she didn't want to be having. She wondered if he'd overheard any of her talk with Kenny. Kate knew about Springer's condition, of course—it would have been impossible to conceal. But Elena had been somewhat circumspect in sharing the rest of her horse's background. Other than letting Kate know that she wanted to use her own vet, an old family friend, as her horse's time neared, she hadn't shared any specifics.

Kate had seemed fine with everything, not suspicious in any way, but now Elena couldn't help but wonder if there might be some ulterior motive for Rafe's surprise visit. She was probably just being paranoid, but better to be overly cautious than simply to take everything he said at face value. She couldn't afford to be less than vigilant where Springer was concerned. Too much was at stake.

"She's doing very well. It's much calmer here and I have more time to spend with her."

"You worked for a good-size outfit, then? You mentioned it was chaotic," he added, when she looked surprised by the question. "So I just assumed that meant it was a big operation."

She had to relax and respond as if this was just a normal, getting-to-know-you conversation, which it likely was. She just didn't want anyone getting to know her, that was all. Especially this man, with his dark eyes and overwhelming intensity. He made her nervous and made her pulse race, all at the same time. "Yes, one of the premiere stables in the mid-Atlantic."

It wasn't anything he couldn't learn from Kate, but she really needed to get him off this line of questioning. She just wasn't sure how to do it without appearing rude.

"You'd think they'd have a pretty good setup for a pregnant horse. Assuming they breed horses."

She tried to maintain a casual air, but the longer he pursued this line of questioning, the harder it was to believe it was simply innocent. Kate had, of course, asked her about her previous work experience when hiring her, but how much Rafe knew, she had no idea. Elena had been as up front and open as possible when Kate interviewed her, and had told the truth. Just not the whole truth. Whether or not Kate had contacted her reference at Charlotte Oaks, she didn't know. She hadn't asked anything specific about Elena's former employer, much less mention that she knew about the famous resident who'd had an all-too-brief stay there, and Elena certainly hadn't brought it up.

Kate had asked questions pertinent to her skills and training and her decision to work outside her chosen field, but she'd seemed satisfied with the answers. After two months here, she'd thought things were going quite well, but . . . maybe not. Maybe Rafe or Mac, or even Kate, had pieced things together, and now they'd come digging.

She ruthlessly shoved that thought from her mind. She had to maintain a steady demeanor. "Yes, the owners were breeders first, racehorse owners second. But the two go hand in hand. No one wants the offspring of an untried mount, no matter how much promise he might have."

"Meaning you gotta play to win."

Her lips curved a little, despite the nerves jumping around in her stomach. "Something like that, yes."

"So why leave? Wouldn't they have taken care of your horse during her gestation?"

He was like a pit bull with this. It was unnerving. And he was unnerving enough, just standing so close. "They had a nice setup there, yes, but it was geared toward racehorses, which mine is not. And those facilities are for the horses they own. I was just an employee."

"Still, it seems like the level of care available would have been superior to anything you could get out here. I mean, it's not like they'd refuse to help if she was in trouble, right?"

She tensed. She really had to divert this line of questioning right now. So, she made an abrupt decision to go on the offensive. "I know you said she didn't send you down here, but has Kate said something to you? About me? Or Springer—my horse?" she added, when he frowned.

"What do you mean?"

"It's just—I hope you'll pardon me for saying this, but you really don't look all that excited about the prospect of getting on a horse. Is there another reason that you came down here? All these questions about my horse—"

His lips twitched, but the amusement didn't go anywhere near his eyes. "Perhaps the interest wasn't so much in your horse, but in you."

Even knowing he was just deflecting her question—there'd been no evidence that he was coming on to her—his claim still made her pulse jump. "I wouldn't think I'd be your type," she answered, this time with complete honesty. Why not?

He cocked his head, and now there was interest in those midnight eyes, but she couldn't be certain exactly what the source of it was. "Perhaps," he said, at least being honest about that much. "But, as you said, people are complex animals, and who can explain the reasons for attraction?" He moved slightly closer, hardly discernible, except she suddenly had a hard time breathing. "Watching you work out there, with that abused horse, was fascinating. You have a way with them that I find intriguing. And so it follows that I find *you* intriguing. Does it have to be any more complicated than that?"

He was standing far too close—at least, that was the excuse she used for taking a slight step back. "I—I suppose not."

He didn't allow the escape, minor though it was. A small

step and he was even closer to her than before. "Besides, if I wasn't here for riding lessons, or because I wanted you . . . then why else would I be here?"

She didn't even hear the rest of whatever else it was he said. She was still hung up on the *because I wanted you* part. Dear Lord. Where was that fan? Or a nice bucket of ice, maybe. When he turned it on, the heat was so intense, she felt scorched clear down to her toes. She had muscles quivering in places that she'd normally have to be naked to have quivering, and he hadn't so much as laid a finger on her.

And, God help her, in that moment, she certainly wanted him to lay fingers and a whole lot more on her.

Trying desperately to shake herself free from such a spell-binding haze, she broke away from his intent gaze and turned to look out over the paddock beyond the open barn door. She didn't care if she was being obvious, or rude. If she thought she could have fanned herself without him seeing, she would have. Her cheeks were probably bright pink. And other parts of her—well, she didn't want to think about what other parts of her were doing. Instead, she was eternally grateful for her baggy bib overalls at the moment. Her nipples were so tight they hurt.

"I don't know," she managed, her voice more of a croak than anything, which further mortified her. He was probably vastly amused, or, at the very least, used to having this effect on women. The thought didn't help much, though, and she kept her gaze carefully averted while she once again scrambled to shore up her defenses. "That's why I asked. Me being the new hire, maybe Kate is concerned about something?" She steeled herself and made an attempt at a casual glance in his direction, though it cost her. His gaze was still connected to her like a tracking beam on a heat-seeking device. She swallowed, but her throat was too dry to manage it. "If that's the case, or if you, Mac, or Finn are worried about something, you can ask me straight out."

So much for rule number two about not showing aggression, but she couldn't help it. She wasn't one to sit and wait for the axe to fall. She liked to take control when she could. Years of harnessing the energy of fifteen-hundred pounds of bull-headed horseflesh likely had something to do with it. "There's no need for pretense."

There was no outward reaction to her challenge; his gaze didn't so much as waver. All he said, was, "What would Kate have told me?"

"What?"

"I asked after your horse's welfare, and you responded by asking if Kate had talked to me. What would she have told me?"

Elena was nonplussed for a moment, trying to mentally backtrack over their conversation, but at this point he had her so discombobulated, she couldn't think fast enough. "I, uh, I wasn't sure what you knew about me and what you didn't."

"Not much. Just that you worked with racehorses and left a pretty nice place to bring your pregnant horse here, to a very small place in the middle of nowhere."

He was worse than a pit bull. Pit bulls could take lessons from him. "Hardly the middle of nowhere. The farms here, if you can call them that, are more like mansions with acreage and stables. And tennis courts. I think I even saw a private golf course on one."

His lips might have twitched the tiniest bit at that. At least he didn't mind spunk. Which was a good thing, because she was feeling a mite more spunky, the longer he dragged this out. She wanted to demand that he tell her what his real motives were, but she'd pushed in that direction about as hard as she could without jeopardizing her job. And she needed to stay here. Pit bulls notwithstanding, in every other way, Dalton Downs was perfect for her needs. Being back out on the road again was not.

"You might have a point there," he said. "But, with the occasional exception, this isn't exactly race country."

"True, but it's not unfamiliar territory for me, either. My father was a show horse trainer. I was raised in this kind of environment, at least the working side of it. So, if you're questioning my background or abilities, the type of control and basic training Kate is looking for with her school horses is well within my field of expertise."

"As I said earlier, even someone who knows nothing about horses can see you know your stuff. I wasn't questioning your abilities." He studied her face. "Are you always so defensive over a little conversation?"

So much for going on the offensive and taking control. All she'd managed to do was encourage more of it. Great. But she couldn't back down now. "When I understand the nature of the conversation, no." She turned to face him, forcing herself to hold his gaze steadily, despite what it did to the butterflies in her stomach. And the painfully tight points of her nipples. "I apologize if I seem rude in any way—I really do. I didn't mean to. I guess I'm just trying to understand the dynamics here. You and your partners have power at Dalton Downs, and a strong connection to my boss. I haven't been here long enough to learn the politics of who's who and what's what. I like my position here—I'd like to keep it. I have no problem fitting in some lessons for you. But if there really is anything else on the table here, then I'd appreciate it if you'd say so, so I don't inadvertently step on anyone's toes. Or jeopardize my job."

He seemed to ponder that, and she braced herself for his response, already mentally kicking herself for being so outspoken. But she had a horse to protect, and herself to protect, and she couldn't afford to sit back and find out too late that there was something going on she wasn't aware of. Call her paranoid, but better paranoid and safe than paranoid and—she didn't want to go there.

"Your job doesn't rest on you giving me lessons, if that's what you're asking."

"And the personal interest?"

The twitch of the lips was more of a real smile now, one that made it all the way to his eyes. And wasn't that just lethal. She swore it made her knees go wobbly.

"Don't worry," he said. "I can handle rejection."

She couldn't help it—she smiled back. "Not something that happens all that often, I'm guessing."

He lifted a shoulder, but didn't respond.

She still didn't believe the interest wasn't just a cover for something else, so she called him on it. "If you'd like, I can find you another trainer."

"You said you could teach me to ride."

Pit bull. "I can. But my job here is to train horses, not people. Kate has a whole crew whose job it is to teach people. If you're still interested in riding lessons, that is."

He studied her for a prolonged moment. "You don't make anything easy, do you?"

"I don't intentionally make things hard, if that's what you mean."

And there it was, a real smile. Enough of one to show a flash of white teeth and crinkle the corners of his eyes. It . . . humanized him. And did things to her body that she really didn't need to know about.

"I'm not a natural," he said. "With horses."

Honestly, it was a good thing she knew he was just messing with her and not serious about all that "because I want you" stuff, but she sure as hell wished her body would get the memo. "I still don't see what that has to do with me."

"If I'm going to learn to ride, then I'd like someone who is very comfortable with horses."

"Everyone who works out here—"

"I've watched everyone out here."

He kept his gaze on hers with such ease, but also with a directness that was unnerving. Okay, a *lot* unnerving. And then there was that hint of a smile, always hovering now, making her foolishly wish he was serious about this verbal foreplay, even if just for the briefest of moments.

"And I've watched you."

She swallowed, again, and folded her arms across her chest, even though she knew he couldn't possibly see how deeply he was affecting her. He probably flirted like this the same way some men breathed. It was second nature to a man who looked like him, when he wanted something. She just wished she knew what he really wanted so she could stop wishing that what he really wanted was her.

"I've never seen anyone as comfortable and in command with horses as you."

"Says the guy with no horse experience."

"I asked you. Would you like me to ask someone else?"

She wondered what he'd say, or do, if she said yes. She wondered why she wasn't jumping at the offer to get out of this situation entirely. "Despite your earlier reassurances, I'm thinking turning down a personal friend of the boss isn't going to do me any favors."

"Kate has nothing to do with this. In fact, she doesn't even know I'm asking."

That tidbit surprised her. Of course, he could be lying. But she didn't think he was.

The twinkle resurfaced, as did the eye crinkling. He was intensity personified, which she was clearly struggling to resist. She really didn't need him to be charming, to boot.

"In fact," he went on, "what with the double duty you're already pulling with the new horse, she might not be all that happy with me for asking at all."

It was his voice, she decided, as if he was hypnotizing her or something. She was looking straight at him—like she could look anywhere else, even if she wanted to—and she could swear he was telling the truth. Maybe she was paranoid. Maybe he really just wanted lessons and to kill some down time flirting with the new girl. Hell, for all she knew, maybe he nailed every female who came to work there as a matter of course.

But being paranoid was what had kept her and Springer safe this long. She couldn't afford to be any other way. Which certainly didn't explain why, every time she opened her mouth around this man, she couldn't seem to help but continue the verbal foreplay he'd so effortlessly begun. Like, even if she didn't have bigger things to worry about, she'd want the attentions of a guy who was more interested in racking up notches on his bedpost than caring who he notched them with. He'd all but admitted she wasn't even his type.

Her forehead began to throb. What she really needed was to go lie down somewhere and give this pheromone fog presently poisoning her every chance to dissipate and leave her the hell alone.

But, instead, she smiled right back at him, and said, "So, you're essentially trying to get both of us in trouble."

His lips curved. There was a flash of white teeth. "It looks that way, yes."

Poisoned, surely that was it. "So, now I either say yes or I say no, and you go bother one of my staff and distract them from their duties, which will just get me in trouble anyway."

His grin was brief, but downright lethal. "Interesting how that works."

So, he was even more dangerous when amused. She'd have to remember that. "When did you want to begin?"

He looked briefly surprised. Hunh. Well, it was good to know she could get him off balance. At least she had some leverage, slender thread though it may be. Then she had another thought that had her swallowing a grin of her own.

If it was leverage she needed, well, maybe she just needed to get him up on the back of a horse first.

Chapter 3

"Riding lessons? You?" Donovan MacLeod laughed. Hard. "Don't start. I'm actually doing this for you and your significant other."

"Right. So when you get thrown on your ass, it's all my fault."

"You learned to ride. How hard can it be?"

"Very funny." Mac stood at the edge of the patio, staring down the sloping back hill to where the stables were. "But why don't you just come out and admit that what this is really about is you wanting to get her naked?" He turned and grinned. "Which, when you think about it, is also a form of riding lessons. Just without the crop." His gray eyes gleamed. "I assume, anyway."

Rafe didn't take the bait. "I'm serious about this. I think there is something else going on where she's concerned. Or I sure as hell wouldn't be getting on the back of some damn horse."

"Oh yeah, spending time with her will be a real sacrifice. She might not be your usual fare of perfectly put-together arm candy with a law degree. But she's got thoroughbred legs and an incredibly fine—"

"Hey," Kate said, as she stepped out onto the porch. "The only ass you're allowed to make Neanderthal comments about is mine." She glanced at Rafe. "Although he's right. I've seen her in riding pants. I'd kill for her ass."

Mac put his hand proprietarily on Kate's backside. "Your ass is spectacular."

She grinned at him. "You just want to get laid."

"Well, yeah, but I could probably manage that without lying, so you know I mean it."

"Men and their logic." When Mac went to take his hand away, she immediately pulled it around her shoulder. "But I'll take it, I'll take it." Tucked under Mac's arm, she looked at Rafe. "When Elena told me you'd asked for lessons, I almost choked. You hate horses. What's going on?"

He'd known this was coming since the moment three days ago when he'd apparently lost what was left of his mind and propositioned Elena. In more ways than one. Which hadn't remotely been his intent when he'd walked out to that barn. He'd been regretting it ever since. Never more so than right this second. "I don't hate horses. They're beautiful animals. I just don't see the need to climb up on the back of one. But that's not the point here. The point is, I think something else is going on with your new manager. Either she's in trouble, or running to avoid it. But something's not right. And I don't want her troubles becoming your troubles."

Mac glanced down at Kate. "He's just jealous because he's around us too much. Now he's hot for a barn chick who isn't his normal glamazon type, so he's projecting some sort of crisis so he can write it off as a work-induced fascination."

Kate listened to Mac with an indulgent smile, then turned a quite serious expression to Rafe. "What makes you think she's hiding something?"

"Hey," Mac said, obviously put out by being brushed off.

Kate leaned up and kissed him on the jaw. "I love you, but you're reacting like a guy, and not like a business owner. If something is going on, then I need to know about it. My kids and my camp come first. I like Elena. A lot. In fact, she's the best thing that's happened around here in awhile." She looked back to Rafe. "Almost too good to be true. I've been saying that since the start. I'd really hate for there to be something to that."

Mac rolled his eyes, but accepted defeat and turned to Rafe. "When did this amazing insight take place? You've evidently had your eye on her since she got here and that was only a few months ago. I was wondering when you'd finally get over yourself and make a move."

"I'm not 'making a move,' " Rafe said, though that was precisely what he'd done. He could tell himself that this was about Kate and protecting her interests, and therefore Dalton Downs' interests, but that didn't remotely explain why he couldn't stop thinking about Elena Caulfield. "Maybe the reason I've been noticing her is because my instincts have been telling me something isn't right. And after what I overheard the other day, I think that's more important than whatever attraction there might be."

Now Kate's eyebrows lifted. "Might be?" She avoided Mac's elbow nudge, keeping her now openly speculative attention on Rafe. "So, what, you think women who work in barns and muck out stalls aren't good enough for you?"

"Don't go all feminist rant on me. I never said that. She actually struck me as a sharp, intelligent woman who handles very large animals like they're small children. I have a lot of respect for that, but I can't help it if I'm more attracted to women who dress and act like women."

Kate's smile turned knowing, and grew wider. She looked up at Mac. "Okay, maybe you have a point."

Mac just grinned. "Guys know these things."

"What?" Rafe demanded. "What's wrong with being honest about what you like and don't like?"

"Because what you like is Elena, and it's making you crazy because you just won't admit it to yourself," Mac said.

That much was true, but not for the reasons he meant. Well, mostly not for those reasons. Elena was more earthy than his usual choice in female companions, but something about the way she'd held his gaze, and handled his attention, had definitely gotten to him. In ways he didn't want to understand, but his body certainly had. Which was the last thing he was going to share with either of the two people presently staring him down. "It doesn't matter whether I'm attracted to her or not. What is important is that she's got more going on than simply taking on a job that will let her mare gestate in peace."

"And you came to this amazing conclusion because her vet came out to see her horse. Her pregnant horse," Mac said.

He'd started to tell Mac the story before Kate arrived, but hadn't gotten further than mentioning Kenny's visit. Rafe turned and picked up several folders he'd stacked on the patio table. "You didn't see her face when he showed up." He slid two copies of a report out from the top folder and handed one to each of them. "I did."

"You're putting together reports on her?" Kate looked up, alarmed. "Rafe, I'm glad that you want to make sure she's on the up-and-up. So do I. But I need her, and I don't want you to go pissing her off by digging into her background and—"

"First off, she has no idea I'm digging. I'm a little better than that."

Mac spoke up, finally serious. "He's a lot better than that." He squeezed Kate's shoulder, then opened his own report. "What did you find?" He was all business now, and Rafe finally relaxed a little.

"Thank you," he said, to which Mac just looked up and grinned unrepentantly.

"Oh, I'm far from being done razzing you about this, but if you really think something is up here, then at the very least, I want to hear about it."

"Good." Rafe turned to Kate. "How much of a background check did you run on her?"

She frowned. "I did the standard check. Her report came back clean. And her references were all in order. Why?"

"Don't worry, she doesn't have a criminal record or anything, but did you make contact with her previous employer?"

She nodded. "I always run references, yes."

"Who did you talk to at Charlotte Oaks?"

"I don't recall his name off the top of my head. He was the head trainer there, or one of them. John something-or-other. It's listed on her application if you want me to check. As I recall, he didn't gush, but I gathered he wasn't exactly the chatty type anyway. He gave her a solid recommendation, though. Said she was a hard worker, showed up on time, did what was asked of her. It was enough for me."

"Did you ask him about her departure? Was it questioned in any way? The timing of it?"

"What do you mean?" Kate asked. "Because of her horse being pregnant? I didn't ask him about that and he didn't mention it. I'm sure if he'd had any issues with her leaving, he'd have said something. I didn't get the impression she left them in the lurch or anything. In fact, she just seemed like another employee. It's a good-sized operation, from what I could tell."

"But she left a good-sized operation because her horse was pregnant, when you'd think she'd stay and let them help take care of her. Especially if there were any concerns."

"Were there?"

"I haven't been able to track it down, but from what I overheard, her horse had trouble the last time she was pregnant."

Kate's brow furrowed. "She didn't mention that part to me."

"I know. She didn't want to jeopardize you taking her on."

"Well, she has her own vet, as you know, so maybe it wasn't as big an issue as you think."

"A vet she was surprised to see show up, and who she wasn't entirely comfortable having here. She even made a point to say she'd bring her horse over to him in the future."

"Maybe she's worried about stepping on toes, using her own vet instead of ours."

"Maybe. But even the vet was concerned that she'd left Charlotte Oaks, that she should have stayed for her horse's sake. And then he made some reference to something bad happening there, which might have had something to do with her leaving."

Kate's frown deepened. "Nothing that I heard about. Again, I didn't ask more than the standard questions, but they certainly didn't have anything negative to say."

"Maybe they didn't know."

Mac opened his file. "It says she left there last October. She's only been here since early March, barely two months. What did she do in between?"

"She thought she had something lined up working for a friend," Kate answered, reading over Mac's arm. "But that didn't pan out, so she stayed with some other friends, worked for a family friend of hers briefly, but there was nothing available long-term until she heard about the spot here."

"Which means she left Charlotte Oaks without a solid game plan in place," Rafe said, "with a pregnant horse who could need special care. Why do that?"

Kate shook her head. "She said she'd known for some time she wasn't going to progress there, that the good-old-boys club was just too tight for her to break in. When her horse got pregnant, it seemed a good time to leave so she could find a place less hectic for her mare to gestate while trying to figure out what to do next. To be honest, it seemed quite plausible at the time. And nothing surfaced to say otherwise." Kate looked at Mac, then back at Rafe. "I'm usually a pretty good judge of people. She's a hard worker, a self-starter, and better with horses than anyone I've ever seen."

"You also think she's too good to be true. Your instincts are good ones, Kate—don't ignore them."

"You know there are a million reasons why she might have wanted to get away from that facility with her horse when she did. As I said, it's a big operation and she was one of many junior trainers trying to get a leg up and not succeeding as well as she'd hoped. Who knows what else may have added to her decision to leave when she did. Maybe there was harassment, maybe she was involved with someone and it didn't work out.

Or maybe it's just what she said it was—a dead-end job, and she had a horse who could use some peace and quiet for a while. If a surprised look about her vet showing up unannounced is all you're going on, then I'd have to say—"

"You don't think it's odd she didn't mention the problem pregnancy when she took the job?"

"Not really. Maybe she didn't want to hurt her chances by making me worry she was bringing in a potential problem. She'd already missed out on her last job opportunity. Maybe that was why she was surprised to see her vet. She'd told me she had an old family friend who would take care of her horse, but nothing about there being a problem. Maybe that look you intercepted had to do with her worrying that he'd say something to the wrong person about her horse having problems with her last foal before she could let him know what was what."

"What did she say about that lost job opportunity?"

"She didn't say specifically, but I gathered it didn't turn out to be what she was looking for. She turned it down, not the other way around. She gave me a reference, but, to be honest, I didn't call that one. She'd been with Charlotte Oaks long enough and her employment there was steady, problem free. And, frankly, I really liked her and didn't want there to be anything to keep me from hiring her."

Rafe and Mac shared a look.

"What?" Kate asked. "You know I wouldn't have hired her if there was even an inkling of a problem. My camp kids mean more than—"

"I know," Rafe said. "Let me ask you this. I'm guessing she intentionally bred her horse. I mean, it's not like a dog who gets accidentally knocked up by the local mongrel. So, she breeds her horse, even though she's contemplating leaving. A horse who had problems with the last pregnancy. Does that make sense? Why make such a huge career transition and do something like that with your horse at the same time?"

"I don't know. Maybe she had a chance to breed her for a

good deal and so she went for it. Hard to say. Maybe her mare is hard to breed and she couldn't afford to pass up the opportunity. I really don't know."

"There just seems to be a lot of that with her. Stuff we don't know."

Kate sighed, and Mac rubbed her shoulder as he tucked her closer to his side. "Don't worry. He'll figure this out without screwing anything up." He kissed the top of her head. "I promise." He looked at Rafe. "Don't screw it up."

"I still don't understand why you're so concerned about her," Kate grumbled at both of them. "I want to go on record as saying I really hate this."

"I know," Rafe said, not exactly loving it, either. "Did she mention how she heard about the job here?"

"Horse community grapevine. You'd be surprised how effective it is."

"I can see racing circles keeping up with racing circles, and the same with show horses, but you're not really involved in either."

"But we're sitting smack-dab in the middle of show-horse country, which her dad was linked to quite heavily, back in his day. She probably has all kinds of contacts because of her family background, and her vet friend is in the area, too. I didn't question her specifically. I mean, clearly she heard about it somehow, as she showed up and applied—why does it matter how she heard?" Kate tilted her head up and eyed Mac, who still looked as skeptical as Rafe felt. "I swear, you guys. You know, not everything or everyone is a 'case file.' Elena told me this was just the right thing for her and Springer at the right time. She was also the right thing at the right time for me. She has every intention of resuming her career goals at some point. And, frankly, I have every intention of trying to get her to change her mind and stay. So unless you can give me a real concrete reason why I shouldn't, then I want this over and done with." She eyed them both. "It's my business to run."

"Understood," Rafe said, looking at Mac, knowing he was

probably thinking the same thing he was. That Kate was sharp, and great at her job, but she was human, and sometimes she let her soft heart get in the way. And, much as he'd like to let this whole thing go and never take a single riding lesson, he couldn't ignore the fact that his gut instincts were still clamoring.

"So what aren't you telling me?" Kate asked. "There has to be something more going on. How much am I going to hate it?"

"Ever heard of a racehorse named Geronimo?"

Kate looked nonplussed. "Geronimo?"

Mac nodded, still skimming the report. "Sure, he won two legs of the triple crown, then broke everyone's heart by missing out on taking the third by half a length. Definitely a crowd-pleaser. A damn shame what happened to him, just doesn't seem right that—" He broke off and looked up. "Oh, shit. Really?"

"Really."

Kate looked up from her report. "Really what? Why oh shit?" She looked between the two of them. "What happened to Geronimo?"

"He's the famous racehorse that died in that fire," Mac said, then went back to skimming the report again.

"He was retired, put to stud, and bought by a new owner," Rafe filled in while they scanned the info. "Not much there yet on that part, but I was focused on Elena and just started digging on the farm itself. Should have gotten this the first day."

"Gene Vondervan," Kate read aloud, then gasped and looked up. "Owner of Charlotte Oaks racing stables. Elena worked for the stables where Geronimo died?"

"Where and when," Rafe confirmed.

"But, wait a minute," Kate cut in, "a whole lot of people work for Charlotte Oaks. Surely if there were any concerns, or if she was involved in any way, negligent in any way, there would have been consequences. At the very least, she wouldn't have gotten the reference she did."

Rafe shrugged. "From what I overheard, it seemed like her

vet thought her leaving might be connected. She didn't mention it when you hired her?"

"No," Kate said. "She didn't."

"The fire was when?" Mac said, still skimming the report. "Last summer, right? But she didn't leave until fall. Doesn't sound like a direct connection there."

"Maybe." Rafe honestly didn't know. Yet. "It just seems odd that she wouldn't mention it. Like she didn't mention her horse having potential medical issues. Geronimo's death has been out of the current news loop for some time, but in the big scope of things, it's still recent news."

"In the race world, maybe," Kate said.

"No," Mac said, "it was a big story everywhere. He was a pretty special horse who had captured the hearts of a lot of people."

"Then how did I miss it?"

Mac smiled and tugged her in for a fast, hard kiss. "Because you don't follow the news unless it's published in a medical journal."

She pushed at him and started to argue, then stopped, looking a bit sheepish. "Okay, so you might have a point there. But she couldn't know that." She looked to Rafe. "She probably just assumed I knew, that it was old news and not worth mentioning?" But even her tone conveyed her skepticism. "Even so, what does it matter?"

Rafe and Mac looked at each other and Kate made an impatient sound. "Would you two cut that out already? It's like you're sending silent smoke signals or something." She looked pointedly at Rafe. "Was there anything else about this that I should be worried about? I mean . . . except as gossip or prurient interest?" She looked down at the report. "Did they ever decide how the fire started? I don't see anything here except that an investigation was launched by both local authorities and insurance investigators for both the farm and the horse. Sounds normal enough, in a situation like that." She looked up. "Is it all wrapped up now?"

"I'm still digging. But no, not from what I can tell. Not entirely."

"Anything odd in that?" she asked.

"Not specifically, no. Insurance cases can take a long time when the cause hasn't been nailed down beyond doubt."

She looked like she wanted to argue further, but in the end, she just let out a deep sigh. "You're not going to stop digging, so I might as well not hold my breath. But I want to know everything you find out so I know when to call you two off."

Mac lifted his hands. "I'm off. This is Rafe's baby. I have the Peterson case you were so hot for me to take."

Kate glanced at Rafe, as if waiting for him to comment on her interference, but he said nothing. "Right," she said at length. "Well, I need to get back to my job. I'll leave you two to yours."

"Speaking of being hot for me," Mac said, as she moved to leave. He snagged her arm and tugged her around, neatly, right into his arms.

She went willingly, with a teasing grin.

"I think you forgot something." Mac's voice had taken on an entirely new note.

One that made Rafe wish he was standing anywhere but three feet away. "Get a room, you two."

Kate went to pull away, but Mac held her more tightly. "Shh, don't mind him. Jealous, remember?" He planted a quick kiss on Kate's lips, that was immediately followed by a longer one that had Rafe looking anywhere but at the two of them.

Kate disentangled herself first. Rafe couldn't tell if the pink in her cheeks was from embarrassment, or desire. Probably a little of both. She shot him a sheepish smile as she waved and started down the flagstone path off the back of the patio. "Still officially hating this," she called out.

"We know," Rafe and Mac said at the same time.

When she was gone, Rafe turned to Mac. "You think I'm right to pursue this? We're agreed?"

Mac nodded. "Too many things are just a bit off. My radar

is pinging, too, though I couldn't tell you what for exactly, but yeah, more information couldn't hurt. Just . . . keep Elena's attention on you. Make sure she doesn't connect any of this to Kate."

"I know. I'm in the hot seat, got it."

Mac grinned then. "Actually, more like a hot saddle."

"Very funny. Now, if you want my opinion on the Peterson thing, then let's get to it," Rafe said, trying to shift things back to business as usual. "I've got things to do."

"Horses to ride. Women to . . . check up on."

"Woman. And she's my riding instructor, and Kate's employee. End of story." Rafe's gaze was briefly drawn down to the paddocks, where Elena was outside working with the abused horse, Bonder. All the camp horses were in, the students done for the day. All but one student, anyway. His first lesson was in a half an hour. Daylight was slowly fading toward twilight, and though the rings were lit, he'd rather his first time on horseback not be after dark.

Rafe caught Mac looking at him from his peripheral vision, and realizing he was staring, shifted the direction of his gaze away as casually as possible.

"Right," Mac said knowingly. "End of story."

Chapter 4

Elena ran her hand along Bonder's neck, then gave his shoulder a good pat. "You did good today, big guy. You almost make me think you're glad to be here." She dug a few raisins out of the little box in her pocket and offered them to him on the flat of her palm.

He nibbled them off, grumbled a little bit, then backed further into his stall and swung his head away while he chewed.

She smiled. "Good night to you, too," she murmured, then brushed her hands against the seat of her overalls before walking down the row of stalls and back out into the paddock. "One ornery male down, one to go." She glanced up the hill toward the main house, but there was no sight of Rafe. Their lesson was to start in ten minutes. It had been a long day with a particularly heavy class schedule and lots of horses to maneuver around and keep happy for the kids. It was satisfying work—more than satisfying, she thought, as she replayed some of the kids' reactions today as they spent time around these magnificent beasts.

In the few months she'd worked for Kate, it had never ceased to move her, the way the animals brought out so much in children who were otherwise so closed off, mostly due to forces of nature and genetics well beyond their control and largely otherwise untreatable. Kate wasn't performing miracles here, in that she wasn't curing anything, but she was certainly enriching the lives of these kids, giving them windows of opportunity to express and enjoy themselves in ways that conventional therapy methods could not. Oftentimes, the look on a child's face, or better, on their parents' faces, made it clear how vitally important her work really was.

It was invigorating, but also exhausting. A whole lot of emotions were being expended into the air of Dalton Downs every single day, and it did zap a person, even if it was for the very best of reasons. Today had been one of those days. She'd debated even working with Bonder, not wanting to risk him picking up on her less-than-sharp reflexes, or worse, her tension. Tension that really had nothing to do with the day she'd put in, and everything to do with the man about to invade her world. But the day she'd put in made hiding those feelings a little tougher. And she needed all the stamina she could muster to make it through their lesson.

She'd finished a little earlier than anticipated when Tracey had offered to take on the last two horses so she could get out to see Springer before her lesson. Word had gotten out about Rafe's lessons, but no one had dared tease her about it. For one, they didn't know her well enough yet, and two, she was technically their boss. The barn help, anyway. The instructors were more her peer group, but she'd had little time to bond with any of them, and not much inclination. Better to stick to what she was here to do and make as few waves as possible, even friendly ones. Which was a shame. For the first time, she was surrounded by women, women she'd enjoy getting to know better. But when people thought they were your friend, they naturally wanted to stick their noses in your business. Something she couldn't risk at the moment. So she was cordial, pleasant, professional, but didn't invite more. It wasn't such a sacrifice. She'd been doing it all her life.

Still . . . there were times when the echoes of laughter and shared conversation beckoned to something inside her, a part of her she hadn't really ever nurtured, and it made her wonder what it would be like to be one of them.

She shut that mental path down. It was pointless and she wasn't the type to feel sorry for herself. Besides, she had new things to worry about. For all her caution, now she had someone not even pretending to be her friend wanting to stick his nose in her business. All she had to do was keep him so preoccupied with horseback riding that he had little or no time to ponder anything more than his rein grip and foot position in the stirrup. And nothing having to do with the person teaching him how to sit a horse right.

"I'm ready when you are."

Elena whirled around and found Rafe standing just inside the barn door. Her pulse kicked up a notch, and not just because of his sudden appearance. Even dressed casually, he was rather riveting in safari-style khakis and a deep green polo shirt that set off his dark complexion and eyes. Then there were those broad shoulders and the centerfold-quality chest. She tried like hell not to let her gaze wander down to where it was tucked in at his perfectly tapered hips. And failed. Spectacularly.

He cleared his throat and, cheeks heating, she jerked her gaze to his. But not before wondering what those khakis might do for his rear view. "I—I'm sorry, I didn't know you were here." Great—she was already stuttering and they hadn't even started yet. Having a few days to regroup and prepare for the impact he so effortlessly had on her hadn't helped in the least.

"I was out at Kate's office, so I came in from the other side." He walked around, glanced out into the ring, then back in the stables.

Eyes on the goal, she schooled herself, *attention on the class. Not the way those button-flap pockets show off his incredibly fine ass.*

He turned abruptly back to her. "I know I don't know much about horses, but I'm assuming it usually helps to actually have one in order to learn to ride one."

Caught staring twice in as many minutes, she felt the heat in her cheeks climb and wondered what it would take to get a grip where this man was concerned. Then he stepped closer and she realized his easy banter wasn't as easy for him as he was making it sound. Not if the taut lines bracketing both his mouth and his eyes were any indication. That, and the fact that it looked as if the hands he'd shoved into his pockets were balled into fists.

Her smile came more naturally then. *Just wait till you find out what class number one consists of.* Reclaiming a sorely needed piece of her fickle control, she walked past him without pausing, motioning for him to follow her farther into the building. "This way. I'll introduce you to your new partner."

They walked past Bonder, who was still facing the rear corner of his stall, and on past a few of the other horses used for classes, before finally coming to a stop at the next-to-last stall. Still smiling, she turned and gestured toward the chest-high door with a flourish. "Mr. Santiago, meet Petunia. She's going to be your riding buddy for the duration. I just know you two are going to hit it off."

Petunia was the oldest horse at Dalton Downs, but far from retirement. Well, kind of far. A year or two, anyway. She was the gentlest mount they had and would pretty much put up with anything. They used her with the frailer kids, as well as the ones with more unpredictable behaviors.

It wasn't that she thought Rafe needed such an easy mount; she was just, well, being a bit perverse. But he didn't have to know that. For all he knew, this was standard.

"Petunia? What kind of name is that for a horse?"

"I don't know—you'd have to take that up with Kate. From what I understand, Petunia belonged to her former college roommate, who was the one who got Kate interested in working with challenged kids. When Marti died, Kate inherited her." It was a story everyone who'd spent any time with Petunia or Kate knew about. Except, apparently, Rafe. "She's one of the favorites here."

He didn't do much more than glance at the horse. "Why is she still in the stall? Shouldn't she be saddled and ready? I know your time is valuable—"

"Oh, you won't be riding her today. First class is always meeting your horse, along with learning grooming, saddling, and the basic maintenance you'll be responsible for as part of your classes."

"Is that really necessary? Surely the kids who come to class don't—"

"Those who can, cherish that part of their time. And believe me when I say, those who can't wish they could."

He did have the grace to look properly abashed. "Point taken, and my apologies. It's just, as a fully functioning adult, I thought perhaps we could just move on to the actual riding part of the program. I don't plan on buying my own horse, so—"

"Did you just get in a car and drive it the first time you saw one?"

Rafe stared at her for a long second, but said nothing. Finally, he turned his attention to Petunia. Then he frowned and stepped closer. "Is she . . . *sleeping*?"

Elena glanced at Petunia, who was, indeed, dozing. Her head was drooping low, and one front fetlock was relaxed and resting against the other. "She's had a busy day, but trust me, she's always up for a new adventure."

Rafe's expression was dubious at best, but he didn't comment.

"Today I'm going to teach you how to halter your horse, lead her from her stall, properly cross tie her, and put on the saddle. If all that goes well, I'll teach you how to mount up and we'll adjust the stirrups and girth strap so you'll know how to set them properly for your next class." Most of which wasn't necessary, as the barn help would be more than happy to saddle up any mount she requested, especially for one of the Trinity three. Even if he hadn't been one of the Dalton Downs honchos, she was certain he'd have no problem getting any woman on the property to do pretty much whatever he wanted. But since the man said he wanted to learn to ride, the least he should do is learn to appreciate what he was riding.

"So, you're saying I have to saddle her every—" He stopped when Elena folded her arms. "Okay, okay." He looked back at Petunia, clearly not thrilled with this whole endeavor, and Elena wondered again why he was really down here.

"So," he said, looking from her to the horse. "Where do we begin?"

"First, you talk to her."

"Talk to her," Rafe repeated.

"Yep." He hadn't minded her being spunky yesterday. She hoped that held true today. "Crazy as it sounds, most people who want to learn to ride these amazing animals, want to do so because they admire them, like them, or just plain want to be around them. This is usually a fun part of the lesson program."

"Fun."

She laughed and Petunia twitched her ears, lifted her head, and blinked at them. "Yes," Elena said. "Fun. Is it that hard to believe horseback riding is fun? Or is fun a foreign concept to you altogether?"

"No, of course not."

Which, from the look on his face, was blatantly untrue.

"Okay. When was the last time you had fun?" she asked.

"I have fun every day."

"From what I can tell, you work every day."

"Exactly. I love my work. It gives me great satisfaction. I enjoy it. Hence, fun."

"That's not the same thing."

He shrugged. "You define it your way, I define it mine."

"So why are you down here? When you could be having *fun* working?" She reached out and stroked Petunia's blaze and nose. The mare bucked her head up a little, nickering in pleasure as she pushed against Elena's hand. Elena noted that Rafe had flinched when Petunia swung her head up, but held his ground. If anything, he'd looked as if he was going to step between her and the horse. Interesting reaction. And it warmed her a little. Unless he was just hard-wired instinctively to protect those he viewed as weaker than himself.

They'd see about that.

"Can I ask you something?" she asked.

He shifted his gaze to her. "Why ask permission now?"

She smiled at that. At least he was learning that *demure and retiring* wasn't exactly her style. Best he understand that early on. "Are you sure you're not doing this on some kind of dare from your partners?" It was the only explanation she'd come up with in the past few days. He didn't seem any more enthusiastic today than he had when he'd asked—demanded, really—that she give him lessons. "No offense intended," she added quickly. "I know how guys can be. I've worked around them my whole life."

"And how is that?"

"I worked with my father growing up—he trained show horses, then branched out into a field that also happened to be dominated by men. Not by choice, that part, it just happens to be the way the racing world is. I guess not many women take after the thundering thoroughbred types, preferring the show ring to the racetrack."

"I meant, how is it that you think men act? But, regarding the thundering thing, women ride horses, too, right? Professionally, I mean. I see them in the Olympics and—"

"Steeplechase and show jumping is hardly the same thing."

"I know, but it's still thundering, of sorts."

"It is, but that field is male-dominant, too. I suppose that women like me, those who enjoy the thundering aspect, as you put it, would lean more toward those routes. They're more acceptable, for one, and available through established channels. There's also barrel racing and the whole western rodeo aspect of that type of racing as well."

Rafe glanced at Petunia, then reached out and stroked the side of her neck. For someone who didn't seem particularly interested in getting up close and personal with his horse, she was pleased to see that his touch was confident, almost casual, as if he'd done it a thousand times before. Petunia leaned a bit closer to him.

Maybe he was just good with anything female, Elena thought, and found herself looking at his hands. They looked strong, with wide palms, solid, long fingers, and she found herself abstractedly wondering what they'd feel like stroking the length of her—

"So why don't you race?" Rafe asked, intruding into her reverie and thankfully pulling her back to the moment literally at hand.

"What? Oh, me, race?" She shook her head. "No. I enjoy riding, but I'm too big to be a jockey. Not that I really wanted to be one, anyway. I enjoy working with the horses themselves. All animals, really." She smiled. "I thought about being a vet when I was little, but it turns out I don't do too well with the sight of blood."

His lips curved just a little and, too late, she remembered that part about his charm being more lethal when he was amused. "That would certainly put a damper on things."

"Pretty much. One of the farms I spent time on as a child was run by a woman who did all kinds of rescue work with animals. She was amazing. And I thought that's what I wanted to do when I grew up, heal wounded animals. Turns out the wounded part was a little hard for me. I ended up following my dad's footsteps more instead."

"You said he was a show-horse trainer."

"He was. A very good one, in fact. He worked hard to build his reputation, but we moved around a lot as a consequence of his popularity."

"What about your mother? Did she work with horses as well?"

"Not at all. In fact, she didn't even ride." When Rafe lifted his eyebrows, she explained further. "My mother and father met on one of the farms where he worked. He trained the horses, she worked in the main house as a housekeeper." She held his gaze steadily now. She was quite proud of her parents, but not everybody who heard their story reacted the same way.

"My mother worked as a maid in a hotel in New York City. Amongst other things," Rafe responded.

Apparently her surprise showed on her face, because his resulting hint of a smile was sardonic at best. "Why are you surprised?"

"I don't know. I guess I wouldn't have pegged you as being from a blue-collar background." Which wasn't entirely true. She'd noted before that for all his casual elegance, there was something edgy about him that spoke of a life not completely without challenges. She just wasn't sure what those challenges had been. "And given that I, of all people, should know better, that was horribly hypocritical of me. I'm sorry." Her smile was more than a little abashed. "My mother would have had such a lecture for me right now."

He did smile then, and it wasn't any less powerful this time around than it had been in the barn the other day. His entire aura changed when he did that. He looked like someone who not only understood the concept of fun, but would enjoy getting you into trouble when he had it.

"I've received that same lecture more than once," he said.

He was already sorely testing her sense of balance. Their chance bond was as unexpected as it was unwanted. At least on her end. She didn't mind him being more approachable, but she could ill afford to let herself become any more attracted to him. For one thing, she hadn't yet determined if he was friend or foe. But even if it was the former, she couldn't risk it. Letting anyone get close right now would be a major risk. Besides, her time here was limited, so what was the point? All she had to do was resist temptation. Very potent temptation.

Putting Springer at the very forefront of her mind, she worked to keep the conversation cordial, but professional. "I guess I had that reaction because you seem so . . . refined." She gestured to his clothes. "Even in khakis and a polo shirt you look more dapper than most men would in a tailored suit."

That got a choked laugh from him. It wasn't exactly a joyful sound, but it was nice to know he had it in him.

"*Dapper*. That's rather . . . stuffy, isn't it?"

She merely raised an eyebrow.

"I'm not remotely stuffy," he protested, but she could see the wheels turning, analyzing, wondering. As if no one had ever mentioned that to him before. She had a hard time believing that.

"Maybe *stuffy* isn't the right word," she said. *Guarded*, she decided, was closer to it, but thought better than to say it out loud. "So, it looks like neither one of us was born with the silver spoon." She glanced down at her own battered overalls and boots and brushed at the ever-present mud and dirt that caked the front of her pants. "One of us just looks more the part than the other," she said with a self-deprecating smile. "So, what about your father? What did he do?"

"No idea. Never met the man."

"Oh." And maybe her heart tilted just a tiny bit. It was only natural, she told herself. She was a sucker for all things orphaned or in need. Not that he was either of those things, but still, she couldn't imagine a life without the strength and wisdom both her parents had given her. "I'm sorry for that."

He lifted a shoulder. "Don't be. My mother is a hell of a woman. I think she did okay by me."

Elena couldn't help but think so, too. As much as she wanted to distrust this man and keep her distance, he wasn't making it easy. She hadn't expected to have anything in common with him, and she still felt they were diametric opposites, probably in more ways than not. She hadn't gotten all that far away from her roots, whereas, while he might have had a rough beginning, he'd certainly gone a long way toward polishing off any rough edges from his upbringing. He was downright burnished, in fact. "I'm sure she's very proud of you. With good reason."

"We all have our lives," he said. "All paths lead somewhere. Mine hasn't turned out so bad."

All paths lead somewhere. Elena couldn't help but wonder about her own, and wished she could say the same. "Where is your mom now?"

"Florida. She's retired, although someone needs to tell her

that. Woman volunteers more hours a week than most people put in at a paying job."

That last part sounded familiar. "Maybe that's her way of relaxing. My mother was happiest when taking care of others, no matter what my dad and I said."

"You two would get along famously," he said dryly. "She's worked so hard her whole life, she should be out playing golf or something now."

Elena laughed. "I couldn't imagine my mother on a golf course. My dad could have probably gotten her out there, though."

"Where are they now?"

"Gone. Car accident, almost nine years ago now, during a freak ice storm."

"I'm very sorry," he said, quite sincerely. For all his dark intensity, he had a very warm, soothing tone to his voice. It made a person want to lean closer.

She nodded and shifted away. It was an easier physical shift than the mental one she really needed to make. "Thank you. I am, too. I miss them very much." She put on a smile. "Well, I suppose we should get on with the lesson, huh?"

Thankfully, he didn't press any further. It was going to be difficult enough being around him and keeping her guard up. The less they shared the better. It was just . . . a lot harder than she'd expected it would be. In less than twenty minutes, he'd already learned more about her than the people she worked next to all day, and had for the past two months.

She turned back to the horse. "Continue to stroke her neck," she instructed. "Talk to her. Get her used to your touch, your smell, the sound of your voice. It's important that you not only trust her, but that she trusts you."

Of course, Petunia wouldn't really care if Rafe were the demon saint from hell. She was notoriously easygoing, but Rafe didn't know that, and regardless, it was good procedure.

Sensing that Rafe wasn't completely comfortable with the whole meet-and-greet routine, much less in front of her, she said, "I'm going to the tack room to get a few things. You two continue to get to know each other." She didn't wait for him to respond, but ducked back down the row of stalls to the tack room located in the center of the two-aisle building, along with her small office.

She already had the things laid out in the parallel aisle and grabbed the halter and lead rope from where they lay next to the western saddle and saddle pad she'd slung over the bench rest. She could have just as easily set up the gear in their aisle, but she wanted him to have the experience of leading the horse, however briefly, before saddling her for the first time.

She walked back through to the other side, but paused at the corner between the tack room and the aisle where Rafe stood at Petunia's stall door, and watched the two get acquainted.

As she suspected, without her presence, he was less guarded. Earlier, when he'd stroked Petunia's neck, his touch was very natural. She suspected he liked animals well enough, but maybe he just hadn't been around one this size before. At least, not up close and personal. Or maybe he was just a tactile sort, and touching came naturally to him, she mused. She cursed the thought when her gaze drifted to his hands, presently stroking along Petunia's neck, and her body reacted to the renewed image of what those wide palms would feel like stroking her.

Petunia moved forward a bit more, lowered her head, and nuzzled his shoulder, bumping him a little with her nose. A definite sign of affection from the old mare. Of course, Rafe was probably used to females asking for more attention. She should have gotten him a gelding instead.

What, you're jealous of an old horse now? She shrugged off the notion as ridiculous, which it totally was, and stepped into the aisleway. What did she care what kind of relationships Rafe had with the opposite sex? She was his riding instructor, nothing more, nothing less. *Nothing less* was all she could afford to be. That *more* part would only get her in trouble.

And she was in enough trouble already.

Chapter 5

Rafe had never touched a horse before. The closest he'd ever come to being near one was on the opposite side of the paddock fence. He'd always been perfectly okay with that.

It wasn't that he didn't like animals, he did. Small animals. Smaller than he was, anyway. He stared at Petunia, who was looking at him with soulful brown eyes from behind ridiculously long eyelashes. "You look innocent enough," he said quietly, "but I've met plenty of women who looked equally innocent, only to bounce me on my ass at the first turn."

Petunia made a sort of whuffling sound and edged closer to her stall door, swinging her muzzle toward him and nudging his shoulder. He accommodated the request by stroking her neck.

"Sure, sure," he said, "flirt with me now. But the first second I do something you don't like, we both know who is getting tossed to the curb, don't we?"

He swore she bobbed her head in agreement, which made him smile despite himself. Probably just rubbing at his hand, but he couldn't help but think she had an understanding of what he was talking about.

He ran his hand along her neck, toward her haunches. "Just don't embarrass me in front of the teacher, here, and I promise I'll bring you a carrot or something next time, deal?"

Petunia shuffled her feet, nudged him again.

"What, you don't like carrots? I thought that was a horse thing."

She stepped back, shook her head so her mane tossed, and nickered. If he didn't know better, he'd swear they were actually communicating. Which was ridiculous, of course. But there was something about those huge chocolate-brown eyes, and the way she looked at him . . . He shook his head. Crazy.

Petunia stamped her front feet a bit impatiently, and took a few steps back.

"So, what, I have to guess now? Flowers? Chocolate? What's it going to take? Dinner and a movie?"

"I see you two are getting acquainted." Elena walked up carrying a long length of coiled rope with a heavy clasp on one end, and what he supposed was the halter that went around Petunia's head on the other. "We're going to slip the halter on first." She hung the rope over the horse's neck and handed him the green nylon halter.

"I thought you said 'we.' "

She smiled. "We, as in, I'll explain how to do it while you slip it on and fasten it. From the looks of things, you already have Petunia half smitten with you anyway, so I don't think this is going to be a big trial for you."

So, she'd been watching his lame attempts to woo the damn horse. He wondered if she'd overheard what he was saying, too. Refusing to be embarrassed, he took the halter from her and studied the arrangement of the nylon straps. "I'm guessing this end slips over the head first?"

Elena nodded. "Then you snap it together there," she said, pointing to a metal locking mechanism on the side. "You adjust it here," she added, pointing to the buckles on either side.

"Isn't there supposed to be a bar or something that goes in the mouth?"

"That's a bridle, but you won't be needing one of those today. This is enough." She opened the stall door and stepped inside with Petunia, then motioned him in as well.

"Shouldn't we walk her out here where there's more room?"

"There are some common safety procedures you should always be aware of when you're around any horse, but you'll have to be in a stall with them from time to time, so best to understand tight quarters as well as open. Petunia is very easygoing, but don't get lax just because she likes you."

Elena said that last part with almost a slight air of resentment, though with some dry amusement thrown in as well to temper any actual attitude. So, she hadn't expected him to make such fast friends, which meant she wasn't going to make this easy on him. Although, to be fair, the horse she picked was clearly not a handful, so she wasn't trying to get him maimed or killed, either. Or scare him into thinking he might be. In fact, he couldn't quite figure her out. But it was only their first session. He had time.

She went through a quick rundown of how to move around a horse, where not to go, where not to stand—which mostly had to do with the rear feet—as well as being careful of horses who can swing their heads around and try and nip at you. He'd looked at Petunia when Elena had made that comment, and he swore the horse gave him an innocent "who, me?" blink.

After a quick demo of her instructions, he stepped into the stall beside her. Despite the fact that the interior of the stall was roomy, they all seemed crowded into the front corner by the stall door, which, despite Petunia's relaxed manner at the moment, did little to smooth over his reservations about this whole thing.

He lifted the halter, but Elena blocked the move with her hand. "You're not through making friends yet."

"What?"

"You just invaded her personal space. Never do this unless invited or instructed to do so by me or one of the stable hands, okay?"

"Why is it I think this isn't standard procedure?"

"You don't feel comfortable around big animals. I'm adjusting your lessons accordingly."

"What makes you think that? About the large animals?" It was completely true, mostly because he'd simply never been around any. The neighborhood he'd grown up in was big on rats, the occasional stray dog, but that was about it. Still, he hadn't thought he'd telegraphed that in any real way. Well, other than his overt lack of enthusiasm for being up close and personal with Petunia. But that was just being smart. She was a whole lot of horse.

"Body language," Elena replied. "You're doing fine, actually, but you're not entirely comfortable, which is understandable. The more you're around horses and get used to the spatial differences between you two, and become comfortable with—while not losing respect for—her power and size, the more swiftly you'll progress. Remember, I said it was about trust. And that goes both ways. If you're tentative, in manner or movement, she'll sense it and react to it."

Elena beckoned him closer, but Petunia chose that moment to shift her feet a little, so he stayed just inside the closed stall door. "Seems to me we'd all be more comfortable out in the aisle. Shouldn't I earn her trust a bit more before we get this . . . intimate?"

Elena smiled and he thought he caught a flicker of . . . something else before she quickly looked back at the horse. And that something else, if he wasn't mistaken, had been a purely female reaction. He hadn't intended the double entendre and he almost wished he hadn't noticed her reaction. She might not be his type, but she did rather command a person's attention. Clearly she'd gotten his. He'd told himself he was only thinking about her night and day because he'd been doing research. He'd also told himself that he'd made the ultimate sacrifice of getting on horseback because that had been the only way to earn her trust enough to get her to talk freely. Strictly doing his job. Going above and beyond, even.

Standing here now, listening to her voice, which managed to be both soothing and no-nonsense, and looking into eyes that were quick to crinkle at the corners, yet easily held his own when challenged . . . yeah, he was finding his rationale a little harder to hang on to.

His body was finding it even more difficult. But he was a man, after all, so he could hardly be faulted for noticing things like how her braided hair swung halfway down to her ass, or how, when she reached up to stroke Petunia's neck, it pulled the backs of her overalls just tight enough across her hips to showcase that very same ass in what was a surprisingly flattering way.

But he didn't need her looking at him as if she was thinking any of those same things in return. Temptation, in this case, was not a good thing. He had enough to handle just trying not to get stomped on by a thousand pounds of horseflesh. Not to mention that he was, in fact, here to do a job. He couldn't afford to be noticing things, or noticing her noticing things, either.

"Keep doing what you were before," she instructed, motioning to the horse. "Rub your hand down her neck, along her flank."

And all he could think, looking at the amused spark in Elena's eyes, was what it would be like to run his hands along *her* long, lean flanks.

Trying like hell to rid his mind of that little visual, he stepped closer and reached out once again to stroke Petunia's neck. She swung her head around, and though he instinctively shifted his shoulder back out of reach of her mouth, he left his hand on her neck. "Easy now," he said quietly. "It's true, I have no idea what I'm doing, which you have undoubtedly figured out, but my intentions are honorable."

Petunia made a snorting noise, and he could have sworn he heard Elena swallow a similar noise. He didn't dare look at her, though. This entire experience was proving humbling enough as it was.

"So, how about I promise to try not to hurt you. And you don't take a chunk out of my shoulder when I'm not looking. Deal?"

Petunia's ears flickered, but, all in all, she didn't seem all that interested in his proposition.

"Just keep at it," Elena coached. "She'll get used to the sound of your voice, to your touch, your scent."

Jesus, she was trying to kill him. Shifting to accommodate the sudden lack of room in his khakis, he kept his focus on the horse. "Scent?" he asked, damning the slight roughness of his voice. Did she have any idea the effect she was having on him? Probably not. He didn't even fully understand it. But tell that to the rest of him, which was having no problem at all responding to her. *Think about the horse,* he schooled himself. *And only the horse.* Not about touching Elena, stroking those long legs, and finding out what her scent was like. Would she be sweet? Musky?

"Everyone has a distinct smell, their own natural scent," she said.

He might have groaned a little. If she said one word about taste, he wouldn't be held accountable for his actions.

"And that scent is layered with shampoo scents, soap scents, laundry scents. And then there are other things, like smoke, alcohol—"

"I don't smoke. And I don't plan on drinking and riding, so—"

"I wasn't saying those things were necessarily bad, just that she'll come to know your scent and identify it with you. She may sense you coming before she even sees you, just by the cologne you wear."

"I don't wear cologne," he said.

She glanced at him, looking briefly surprised. "You don't?"

Which meant, he gathered, that she'd smelled him. Wonderful. This was turning into one big pheromone fest. And they hadn't even gotten the horse out of the damn stall yet. "Just the regular laundry and shower stuff." And how in the hell had they gotten into this, anyway? He was supposed to be finding out more about her, not the other way around.

"Hmm," she said, looking mildly embarrassed, but smiling

all the same. "Remind me to ask what detergent or shampoo you use, then. Smells nice."

His body leapt in response to her softly spoken compliment, urging him to do something—anything—about it. Hard to keep telling himself she wasn't his type when the sexual tension between them was clouding the stall in a thick fog.

Petunia took that moment to nod her head and whinny softly. It might have just meant she was suffering from a sudden lack of attention, but it looked like she was agreeing with Elena about his scent, which made Elena laugh. It was a rich, full-bodied sound that invited a person to join in, and brought an unbidden smile to his face.

"Well, at least I'm doing something right," he said, not wanting to be charmed by her. Needing not to be. Despite Mac's suggestions—and his own body's response—to the contrary, he had rules about how he did his job. Rules that didn't include getting involved with his subjects.

"You're doing pretty well, actually," she responded.

He was pretty sure she meant with the horse, but neither of them was looking at Petunia. "You sound almost surprised by that."

She lifted a shoulder. "Maybe. A little bit. As I said before, for a guy who wants to learn to ride, you just don't seem all that excited about the actual prospect of being around a horse. And it's hard to ride one without encountering that minor detail."

"I suppose I thought it would be like signing up for a trail ride at a vacation resort. You line up, climb on a horse, and meander along a bit until you figure it out. I thought I would be coming down here, hoisting myself up, and trotting around the ring a few times while you told me how to do it right. I guess I didn't realize there would be so much more to it." *Or you.* "I didn't think—"

"That maybe the horse cared who climbed on its back?"

"Well, they're used to it, aren't they? Does it really matter who climbs on once they get used to being ridden?"

"They're highly sentient creatures. It matters."

"I didn't mean any disrespect."

"Tell that to Petunia." Her lips curved then, and the dry smile put them back on an even keel.

"I already promised her carrots. At this rate, she'll have me catering meals."

"Apples."

"Excuse me?"

"Her favorite treat. Preferably Granny Smith. Take a bite, then give it to her."

"Whole?"

Elena nodded. "No cooking or catering required." Then she grinned. "She probably won't even hold you to the movie offer."

He swore he felt his cheeks warm slightly. "Thanks. I'll, uh, keep that in mind."

She shrugged. "Just trying to give you an edge."

"I need an edge?"

Her grin turned a shade wry. "Maybe you're not used to needing one. But it wouldn't hurt your chances."

"What you're saying is, that women aren't all that different, no matter the species. So when you come calling, have something in hand."

Her eyes twinkled. "It certainly never hurts."

And how was it he'd never noticed the light scatter of freckles across the bridge of her nose? Their implied innocence was so at odds with her knowing eyes and full-bodied laugh. But then, she was a study in contradictions when it came to his reaction to her. What was one more thing?

Somehow they'd come to stand closer to one another than he'd realized. She was stroking Petunia's neck, and their fingers accidentally brushed across one another. She pulled her hand away, and stepped back. Other than that flash of embarrassment when she'd mentioned noticing his scent, it was the first time he'd seen uncertainty in her expression or demeanor.

"Okay, enough fraternizing," she said, and he wasn't sure if she meant him with the horse . . . or the two of them with each other. She nodded toward the halter. "Time to get that on her if we're going to get anything else done today."

"You're the one who insisted on me making friends first."

"Here, take the rope." She handed him the end with the clasp. "Then you're going to loop the rope over her neck and hook it, making a loose collar and leash, to give you some control over her movement while you put the halter on."

She moved behind his shoulder and reached past him to show him how to work the rope and slip it around the base of the horse's neck. He was paying attention, but he was also noticing that she had a nice scent, too. Dammit.

"Now, transfer the rope to your other hand, and carefully slip this end over Petunia's muzzle." She turned the halter so it was facing the right direction, but keeping it in his hand.

He felt himself leaning closer, breathing in her scent. Which was dangerous, given his current state of mind—and khakis, but an impulse he seemed helpless to curb. She was wearing overalls that had seen better days. Months, even. And by rights she should smell like a barn. Only she didn't. And, standing this close, he noticed how smooth and soft-looking her skin was. For someone working such a physical job, exposed to the sun and wind, he'd expect her to look a bit more . . . weathered. Then there were those freckles sprinkled across the tip of her nose. They were cute, and she wasn't the cute type. She was no-nonsense and wore her confidence as easily as she did those ancient overalls. What she was not was freckles and soft skin and a slightly lush bottom lip that just begged a man to taste it. Bite it. Just a little.

"Confused?"

If she only knew. He turned just as she went to lean in to move his hand on the harness. The result was his nose, buried in her hair, right where he'd wanted it moments ago, and knew he had no business leaving it. He should be immediately backing up, putting the appropriate space back between them. In his mind, that's exactly what he did. In reality, though, he took full advantage of the accidental contact and breathed in the scent that was all Elena.

And, he belatedly realized, she was letting him.

Of course, she was more or less trapped between him and a whole lot of horse, but she could have shifted away, or given any signal that she wasn't enjoying the incidental moment of intimacy.

Like he was.

Even then, his strategic, work-mode brain didn't kick in. The one that should be telling him to use the moment to his advantage. It was true, he didn't use sex or seduction as a means to an end, but he didn't rule out a little flirting. It was a very human, natural form of communication that men and women did on street corners and in elevators every day. Done properly, it lowered defenses and put a potential contact at ease. As long as it was harmless and he could keep his emotional distance, no harm, no foul. But this wasn't that. This . . . well, he didn't quite know what this was. Whatever it was, it didn't feel all that harmless.

Which was, in the end, what convinced him to put an end to the moment. One of the main rules of his job was, never stay in a situation you don't understand any longer than absolutely necessary. At the moment, he felt totally out to sea and that was definitely not a typical place for him to be.

"I think I got it," he said, and shifted away from her to slip the rope over Petunia's neck, then guide the halter over her muzzle.

Elena reached up and helped him secure the nylon strapping. "Buckle the sides there, and I'll get the back."

He fumbled with the unfamiliar rig for a moment as her continued presence deep in his personal space continued to mess with his equilibrium on almost all fronts, then finally got it all snapped into place. He rubbed Petunia's muzzle and shifted so that his attention was fully on the horse. And not on how badly he wanted to sink his hands into her hair . . . and his tongue into that sweet mouth of hers. "Thanks for putting up with that," he murmured to the horse. "I'll get better at it." He caught Elena's look from the corner of his eye and was drawn right back to the fire. "What?"

A brief smile played across her face. And a mouth he really had to stop noticing. And looking at. And wondering.

"Nothing," she said.

"Are you surprised she's not taking a chunk out of me? Is she some secret demon horse who's suddenly going to unleash fury on me so I'll stop this insanity and abandon the lesson idea?"

Elena laughed that laugh again and it made something inside of him quiver, like a tuning fork finding the perfect vibration. He really had to get them out of this stall.

"Nothing like that. Petunia is a total sweetheart. Any horse can act up, but a demon she's not. I wouldn't do that to anyone."

"Especially a friend of Kate's, you mean?"

"Anyone," she reiterated, then her eyes danced a bit. "I care about the horses too much for that."

Rafe had to smile at that. "Ah. It's all about the horses, then."

"Most of the time. They're pretty straightforward, as a rule."

"Unlike people, you mean."

"You like putting words in my mouth, don't you?"

He absolutely refused to go there, but his mind provided the visual for him, anyway. It took great willpower not to look at that bottom lip, that mouth, and imagine what it would look like, wrapped around—"Actually, I'm not assuming anything," he said, damning the rough edge to his voice. "That's why I'm asking."

"Horses can fool you some of the time. People are better at it—that's all I'm saying."

She was clearly making a reference to her already voiced doubts about his real reasons for taking lessons. Her forthrightness was to her credit.

"Are you?" he asked, figuring he could be just as forthright.

"Am I what? Better at fooling people?" She didn't look panicked or concerned by the question. In fact, thus far, he didn't have any indication she wasn't exactly what she claimed to be. Then again, being as sharp as she seemed to be, he didn't doubt she knew exactly how to handle herself, and, perhaps, him. Keeping him on the defensive was an excellent offensive tactic, one he often employed. He couldn't help but wonder if it was intentional.

"Have I seemed anything other than direct and honest with you?" she asked him.

Yes, she was very good. If he wasn't paid to be cynical and doubt every word a subject said, he'd be inclined to take her at face value. But there were too many unanswered questions as yet.

"No," he said, with all honesty. "No, you haven't. I just wondered where the cynicism came from."

"Maybe you're more optimistic than I am," she said. "But then, that's why you're in the business of helping people, I suppose, while I stay in the barn with the four-legged beasts."

"You're giving me far too much credit there."

"Only an optimist believes he can make the world a better place."

"He can. And I think I do. But I'm not as altruistic as all that."

She paused in adjusting Petunia's harness. "What are you saying? That you're in it for the money? I know you said Trinity wasn't a charity, but I guess I thought it was because from what I hear, you and your partners don't take money from your clients."

"We don't."

"Sounds pretty altruistic and charitable to me."

"I make an income, a good one—I'm a salaried employee of the company. But you're right, what I do or don't do doesn't change my bottom line in terms of income."

"So what motivates you, if not money, or making the world a better place?"

"Revenge."

Her eyes widened.

Good—for the first time, he had her off balance. He didn't realize how badly he'd lost command of the situation until he regained a piece of it.

"Revenge? I'm afraid I don't understand. I thought the point of Trinity was to help people in need."

"It is. We do."

"What does that have to do with revenge?"

"It's . . . complicated. Our company name, Trinity? Short for Unholy Trinity."

"So I heard," she said, with a hint of a dry smile. "Something to do with your partners and the exploits of your youth, right?"

He nodded. So she had been checking up on him. Either that or the barn help had nothing better to do than gossip about him, Mac, and Finn, which he found hard to believe. "Well," he said, smiling, "let's just say some things never change."

"You grew up together?"

"We've been friends most of our lives." And how in the hell had she gotten him talking about himself again? "As for the rest, let's just say I take greater pleasure in righting wrongs to make a point than I do in the more altruistic sense of making the world a better place by doing so. Although, as a byproduct, it's certainly not a bad one. But we're not exactly missionaries here." He smiled at her mildly disapproving expression. "Does that make me a coldhearted bastard?"

"I don't know you well enough to say."

As a dodge, it was a good one. He began to wonder who was the one gathering intel here, him or her?

Petunia grumbled and shuffled her feet, clearly affected by not being the center of everyone's attention.

"Everyone has motivations for doing what they do," she went on to say. "As long as no one is getting hurt, who am I to say which ones are appropriate and which ones aren't?" She glanced up at him. "No one gets hurt, right?"

She didn't look remotely vulnerable. Quite the opposite. So why was it he felt like she was asking him if he was going to hurt her? "Only the bad guys," he said, curling his fingers into his palm to keep from reaching up and tucking that stray strand of hair presently clinging to her cheek.

Her mouth quirked at his response, but her gaze seemed to continue to seek something out in his own. Just as he was about to break the silence . . . or reach for her, after all, she broke the silence. "Keep hold of the rope, with slack, but not too much," she instructed, shifting smoothly back, once again, into instructor mode. As if their little moment hadn't even happened.

But it had happened, and he wasn't being quite as successful shaking off its effects as she apparently was.

She stepped behind him and opened the door. "You want to walk her to the center of the building and over to the other aisle. Stay just to the front of her forelegs, but to the side of her head."

"Not out in front?"

"You can direct her with the rope, but I want you to stay where you can see if she's reacting negatively to anything. You don't want to be five feet ahead of her and have her spook and rear and yank you on your ass, or worse."

"Got it." He looked at Petunia. "No ass-yanking."

Elena laughed. And he knew he was in deep, deep trouble.

Because making her laugh was not his objective. And yet, he found himself wondering how to make her do it again.

Chapter 6

Elena was still grinning as she stood behind the open stall door and watched Rafe lead Petunia out. She had no worries about the horse misbehaving. Barring Rafe doing something totally bizarre, Petunia would go through the motions on autopilot, as she'd done a million times before.

The one she needed to worry about misbehaving was herself. In any near vicinity, Rafe was potent enough. Up close in any personal proximity, he was downright intoxicating. He was intensity and charm, humor and the kind of focus that made her want to smooth her hair back and moisten her lips. Hell, if she were honest, he made her want to do a whole lot more than that. There had been a few moments where she could have sworn he was thinking the same thing—then the mood would shift, or Petunia would interrupt. For which she should be eternally grateful.

Even if Rafe wasn't the enemy she'd feared—and she wasn't certain about that yet—he wasn't an ally, either. Of any sort. Couldn't be, not in her current circumstances. She just hadn't counted on that bothering her so much.

She closed the stall door as soon as the horse was out, then walked on ahead of them, toward the crossover to the other aisle.

"What if she doesn't go?"

Elena paused and turned, only to find them still standing just outside the stall.

Rafe looked from Petunia to her. "I'm guessing giddyap is just something they say in movies?"

She laughed. He was so dry, and, up until today, had struck her as somewhat of a hard-ass. A really suave-looking hard-ass, but a hard-ass all the same. And, in some ways, he was. That unholy part wasn't so hard to believe. His ready humor had been unexpected—it was that part of him, far more than his smooth good looks, that was working on her. "Well, it works when it's accompanied by a swift nudge with your heels or a squeeze of the knees. But you have to be mounted for that to happen."

Even fifteen yards away, she saw the quick flash of teeth, and that awareness in his dark eyes. And mentally kicked herself for the double entendre. She hadn't meant it. She didn't flirt. Not normally, anyway. In her world, a woman had to all but bind her breasts, chop off her hair, and lower her voice two octaves to get taken seriously. One bat of an eyelash and she'd be seen as nothing but a saddle tramp.

But she wasn't in that world any longer. And men like Raphael Santiago didn't stroll across her path very often. She had no experience with someone like him. He didn't fit into any mold she was used to. And seeing as she still didn't know if he had ulterior motives, she couldn't afford to make any rookie mistakes. If she was going to even think about flirting, or what that might lead to, she'd be better off starting with someone a hell of a lot simpler than this man.

And since she had no business flirting with any man at the moment, that took care of that.

"I would love to be mounted," he said, and she wondered if she was imagining the amusement in his voice. "But someone thinks I need to learn to take her out for a walk first."

She folded her arms. "Given that you're standing still at the moment, I'm thinking I was right."

His lips curved. "You may have a point."

For a suave hard-ass, he had no qualms about making fun of himself. It was far too charming. "In cases like this, it's okay to step ahead of the horse and lead. As soon as she starts walking, though, shift back. She's used to this routine—she knows where to go."

"And if she doesn't start to walk?"

"You can encourage her." She made a clicking sound with her tongue. "Like that, or just cajole her a little. That shouldn't be a stretch for you."

This time she knew she hadn't imagined the flash. "Are you saying you think I have experience cajoling members of the opposite sex?"

Elena smiled. So, she was officially flirting, and he was definitely flirting back. But it seemed that the most innocent conversation between them was going to have mixed overtones, and she wasn't sure how to stop that. And to be perfectly honest, she didn't really want to. It felt good. She had no business engaging in it, but that didn't make it feel any less pleasurable. Maybe even more so because it was taboo. "I was saying that you're probably good at getting them to do whatever you want them to."

"Unless they happen to be my riding instructor."

If you only knew. It wasn't lost on her that he hadn't denied her characterization of him, either. She really needed to stop the banter with him. Really.

With a little pat and a few softly spoken words Elena couldn't hear, Rafe walked forward, and Petunia fell into step beside him. He gave her a half shrug when she silently applauded, which was cute and endearing and had her turning away before she opened her mouth and something else completely inappropriate popped out.

Rafe and Petunia made it to the other aisle without further incident, and it didn't take long to run him through the procedure of putting her in cross ties. She kept it all business, at least outwardly, and shortly afterward they had the horse saddled and ready to mount.

Despite having no idea what was expected of him in this situation, he kept his motions steady and his tone smooth at all times. Which was working like a charm with Petunia. Unfortunately, it was working with her as well. She already knew, despite his apparent qualms, he'd be a natural on horseback. He had an easy rhythm to his stride and was comfortably in command of his body. He would adjust to the rhythm of the horse's gait easily, as he had just walking Petunia over, neither letting her lead nor rushing her.

Which naturally led her to imagine how equally skilled he'd be at putting a woman at ease during sex. And God, she really wished she could be thinking about anything other than mounting and riding at the moment.

"So, chief, is there enough time left to take a trip around the ring? Seems a shame to waste all this preparation. Not to mention that we've gotten Petunia's hopes up now."

He had a point. Petunia looked at her and blinked a few times, looking quite winsome. *It's okay,* she wanted to tell her. *I'd want him to ride me, too, if I were you.* "Okay, okay," she said, relenting. "Take the rope." She instructed him on how to unhook the cross ties, then said, "Lead her out to the paddock." She didn't wait for him, but turned and headed in that direction.

He didn't say anything about her defection. A quick glance back showed he just went to work. Attempts to throw him off stride were clearly not going to work, just as he was making it very difficult not to like him, or at least respect him. He spoke his mind, and didn't necessarily agree with her methods, but beyond that he'd followed her instructions and done as she'd asked.

Figured.

Once out in the paddock, she walked over to the fence and waited for them. "Drape the rope over her neck," she told him, using hand gestures to show how he should do it. "Then hook it around, so it makes one big loop. You'll use that as your reins."

"I don't need a bridle thing?"

"Not with Petunia."

His expression was wry. "You gave me the easiest horse here, didn't you? Did you think I'd be that bad?"

"I thought you'd prefer things not to be any more difficult than they had to be."

"Well, you might have a point there."

She tried not to smile, tried to think business, but as she closed the distance between them and walked around to where he stood beside Petunia, she felt a pull just this side of magnetic. Being close to him made it hard to think clearly. She shifted her focus to the horse, and only the horse, and pointed to the stirrup. "Hold the pommel with your left hand, left foot in the stirrup, and up you go. Right leg over the back end, one smooth lift as you push up on your left leg." She held her hand up when he went to do as she'd directed. "Talk to her first."

If she thought he'd roll his eyes or give her grief, she was wrong. Instead, that wry curve reappeared at the corner of his mouth as he casually leaned forward and stroked his hand down the side of Petunia's neck. "What?" he asked, amusement clear in his tone.

She realized she was staring at his hand, the way he was stroking the horse's neck, and quickly pulled her gaze away.

But not before he said, "I'm not entirely green. I do understand the benefits of putting my partner at ease before I, you know . . ." A twinkle entered his eyes that was either a trick of the sun descending in the sky, just low enough now to send its rays slanting into the stable interior . . . or utterly wicked. She went with the former, but only until he added, "Mount up."

Had he really said that? Or had she just mentally filled in the blank? She resisted the urge to fan herself. Or look at his hands again.

"You did say we were going to be partners, right?"

"What?" she asked, faintly.

"Petunia and I," he clarified, clearly enjoying himself. "You said I should think of it as a partnership."

"Yes. Right. Exactly."

With that half smile playing around his mouth, and that devilish light still in his dark eyes, he turned his attention to the horse, leaning forward and whispering something too low for her to make out.

Petunia's ears twitched forward and back and she dipped her head a little, as if agreeing with whatever he'd said. She was a sweetheart of a horse, easily the most agreeable mare on the farm, but it seemed to Elena that there was a bond forming there that she didn't normally see, especially with first-timers.

"Probably seduces any member of the opposite sex, without even thinking about it," she grumbled beneath her breath.

"I'm sorry, what?" he asked, ever-so-innocently while looking anything but.

"I said you don't want to think about it too much, just do it."

"What do you know—that's my motto, too." And then he flashed her a grin that shot her pulse directly into the red zone, turned, and popped up on Petunia's back as if he'd been riding his entire life.

She scowled. In some ways, he probably had.

She looked up at him, shielding her eyes against the setting sun, to find him staring back at her from behind a pair of black sunglasses he'd slid on.

He touched the brim of an imaginary Stetson. "Once around the ring, ma'am?" His southern drawl was atrocious.

And adorable as hell. She wouldn't have thought *adorable* was going to be an issue where he was concerned. As it was turning out, everything was going to be an issue with him. Breathing was an issue.

Rather than respond directly, she stepped up and showed

him how to use the looped rope as a set of reins. "Balance your weight, center it. Feet in the stirrups." For the first time, she noticed he was wearing rather beat-up hiking boots.

He must have noticed the direction of her gaze, because he said, "Sorry, probably inappropriate footwear."

"No," she said, "they're fine, I just—" She broke off as she realized what she was going to say, which was that she was surprised he owned a pair of worn-out anything. He was always so immaculately and sharply dressed. But that was a leading comment she definitely didn't need to make. "Never mind."

"What?"

"Nothing. For what you're doing, they'll be fine. If at some point you find yourself doing any amount of trail riding, you might want to invest in a good pair of boots." She glanced up. "Western. Although I could teach you how to ride English if you prefer."

"Which is easier?"

"Western, like you are now."

"Then let's go with that." He smiled a little. "For now."

With the attention to detail she'd noticed in the clothing she'd seen him in so far, she could easily imagine him in a nicely cut, proper English riding jacket. For certain, those tight English riding pants would show off . . . well, what wouldn't they show off was more like it. Not that he couldn't do some damage in jeans and chaps, it's just that he wasn't the scruffy cowboy type. Far more lord of the manor. With a little Latin flair.

"Okay, now what?"

Now I need a fan, and something cold to drink, and an extended period of getting myself seriously under some kind of control, she thought. She motioned to the rope. "Hold it with some slack. Click a little, with your tongue, then nudge her with your heels or knees. She knows what to do."

"How do I steer?"

"Tug a little on the left rein for left, right for right. Pull back and release to slow her down and stop. You don't have to yank, just a steady pulling motion until she slows down to where you want her, or comes to a complete stop."

"Sounds simple enough."

She smiled. "Should be. Let's see how you do."

First, he leaned forward and spoke gently to Petunia, making her ears twitch forward and back. Then, he straightened and, after a gentle nudging with his heels, they moved smoothly along the fence line. She wished she could say she was surprised, but by now, she wasn't.

"You'll get used to her rolling gait. Just keep your weight centered, stay relaxed, knees with even tension, which is to say, very little. She'll be very sensitive to the tension she feels in your body, which is mainly telegraphed by how tightly you hold the reins, and the pressure you exert with your legs against her sides."

Not that he appeared to need this little bit of instruction.

She let them go around the ring once at a steady walk, then said, "Okay, now, slow her down. You can pull back slightly on the reins."

He pulled Petunia to a stop right beside her.

"Pretty good," she said.

"Pretty good?"

"Okay, you were very good." Probably needed to hear that after every performance, she thought, knowing she was being less than charitable, but reaching for anything that would give her an edge against the effect he seemed to be having on her so effortlessly. "For a beginner."

He took the comment in stride, but didn't tip his imaginary brim again.

"Next class we'll work on turning around and coming in to the center of the ring. After that, we'll work on speed. Trotting, then cantering."

"No galloping?"

"No galloping."

His dark eyebrows lifted in mild surprise. "How about outside of the ring?"

She smiled dryly. "Let's not get ahead of ourselves, okay?"

"Well, the idea is to eventually ride the horse in something other than an endless circle."

"Yes. But this isn't like the movies. I hate to break it to you, but trail riding rarely involves galloping."

"Do you?"

"Trail ride?"

"Gallop your horse. In or out of the ring."

"Neither at the moment—she's pregnant."

"But otherwise?"

She folded her arms. "Why do you ask?"

"You normally work with racehorses. I assume it's rather like guys who work around race cars. Or Lear jets."

"You think I'm a speed junkie?"

He looked down at her from his higher perch, a thoughtful expression on his face. "Actually, I don't know what to think about you."

"I could say the same," she responded, before she thought better of it.

He held her in silent regard for a long moment. He seemed quite relaxed, but Petunia stepped a little restlessly, proving there was more tension in him than he was showing. "Could I interest you in grabbing a bite to eat? Later, once you're free?"

The offer shouldn't have caught her so off guard. They'd been circling each other almost from the moment he'd entered the stables. But it did. "I—I have chores. Then my horse . . . I have to see to her." She was stuttering. She never stuttered. "I'd feel more comfortable if we kept this purely a professional relationship."

"Okay," he said, a little too easily.

Perverse creature that she was, she wished he'd at least been a bit more put out by her immediate refusal.

"Doesn't mean we can't share a meal, does it?" he went on, making her feel inordinately better, which was a double warning sign.

She didn't want him pursuing her. On any level. No matter how good it made her feel. She couldn't risk enjoying even something as simple as having her ego stroked. Much less any other part of her. She tried like hell not to look at his hands again.

He grinned a little. "We can discuss a strategy for helping me show Mac up when we ride together for the first time."

She laughed in surprise. "So, that's it, then. This is all just some kind of macho contest."

"Where men and horses are concerned, isn't it always?"

She chuckled. "Most of the time, yes. And yet, somehow I don't see you as the cowboy type."

"What do you see me as?" He laughed a little and shook his head. "Never mind. Maybe I don't want to know."

He caught her gaze and held it. The combination of that twinkle in his eyes and the laughter was downright lethal. Her nipples ached, her thighs were all twitchy, and there were butterflies dancing in her tummy.

"Or you can tell me over dinner."

She'd never wanted to accept an invitation more. She had no doubt that if the two of them were alone anywhere outside of a business-only situation, dinner wouldn't be all they'd be having. Reason enough to end this little banter session. "I'm afraid I can't."

She thought he might continue to press, and was surprised to find, even knowing better, she almost wanted him to. Maybe he'd find a way past her defenses, find a way to make it okay to take what she wanted and damn the consequences. Only the consequences, in this case, were huge. And didn't involve only her. Knowing that didn't make the ache go away, though. If anything, it only intensified. Her desires had always been career-oriented. She'd never wanted anything purely for the sake of having it.

But she'd be lying if she said that, right then, right there, she didn't want him. Just for now. Or at least until he could make the damn ache go away.

"Okay, then," he said, easily enough. Damn him. "Class over, I presume?"

She broke eye contact, praying that nothing of the thoughts going through her head showed anywhere on her face. He was far too astute as it was. "For this round, yes. You can dismount here. I'll take care of the rest." The faster she increased the distance between them, the better.

"No, that's okay. I'll do what's expected," he said. "Not fair for you to do my work."

"First-timer's pass," she said. "We've gone a bit longer than I anticipated and I still have a list of chores to get through. It will go faster if I take care of her this go. You'll definitely be in charge of that next time."

"So, you're willing to have a next time?"

Do I have a choice? she wondered, but didn't say it out loud. Not that she thought Kate would lean on her to help out her friend, but Elena wasn't a novice when it came to work politics. In her previous field, she'd learned quickly that getting ahead sometimes meant doing things because you might benefit later from the favor. Even if the short-term risks didn't seem worth the effort.

"You're a quick study," she told him. "A few more lessons and you'll have the basics down. Enough to trail-ride with Finn and Mac, anyway, if that's your goal."

"Okay," he said, then hesitated for a second, as if he was going to say something else, but apparently changed his mind. "I appreciate you taking the time."

"For a friend of Kate's, not a problem." Best he understand her motivation was purely professional, just in case he had other ideas. Especially if they were anything like the ideas she was having.

His wry grin reappeared. "So, how do I get down from here without blowing what little horse cred I built up tonight?"

She laughed again. He really had to stop making her do that. This would all be a lot easier if he'd stayed an enigmatic hard-ass. "Hand on pommel, body weight forward, swing your right leg behind you, kick your left foot out of the stirrup, and slide to the ground."

"What do I do with the rope?"

She stepped forward and showed him, this time far more aware of his hands, his thigh brushing her shoulder, than she wanted to be. He slid off far too easily, and before she could step back, landing him once again deep inside her personal space. Right where she wanted him most, and least needed him to be.

He smiled as he handed her the rope, his knuckles brushing the inside of her wrist. A sensitive spot she hadn't known she possessed until that exact moment.

"Not too bad," he said, that smile flirting at the corners of his mouth—a beautifully sculpted mouth.

A mouth she had no business looking at.

"At least I didn't end up on my ass."

"Not this time, anyway," she said, intending to create distance. But neither of them stepped away.

There was a tremendous pull in that tiny space between them, the kind of pull that made it almost impossible not to lean forward, or pray he did first, allowing her to indulge, just for a moment, without any of the guilt of having taken the initiative.

This close, she saw that his eyes weren't black, but a brown so dark they almost matched his irises, but with just enough color in them to create that gleam, that twinkle. His skin was incredibly smooth, despite the hint of five o'clock shadow, with such a gorgeous golden tone to it, she imagined it would always be naturally warm to the touch. And yet the angles of his jaw, the hard line of his nose, his chin, the thin white scar that ran length-wise, just above one eyebrow, all combined to make him more rugged than pretty. Made her want to touch. Taste.

"Shouldn't you hold on to this?" he asked, grabbing the lead rope from her suddenly lax grip. That teasing glint was back in his eyes, as if he'd been able to read her every thought. And, mortifying as it was to contemplate, maybe he had. She wasn't skilled in these kinds of games.

It took enormous willpower not to snatch the rope back from his hand and drag poor Petunia away. "Thanks," she said, as casually as she could manage. As if just looking at him didn't make her want to get naked and do things she hadn't thought about doing, much less needing to do, in a long time. "I can take it from here."

He stepped the tiniest bit closer and for a second, she wasn't sure what his intentions were. She went still rather than move away, her breath trapped in her chest. But he only moved between her and the horse, so he could stroke Petunia's neck and murmur a few good-byes.

She felt supremely foolish until he turned to her with a half smile and a knowing look that suggested maybe he'd been using the horse as an excuse to get closer. Not that he needed an excuse.

"We still haven't discussed your fee."

Had his voice always been that deep? That smooth? Her gaze dipped to his mouth, unbidden, and she had to fight the urge to wet her lips.

"Elena?"

The way he said her name, with that hint of an accent, made her inner thighs twitch, made her wonder what her name would sound like when his voice was rough with desire and . . . then she realized she was staring at him like a half-starved wolf and jerked her gaze downward . . . to anything other than him. Twisting the rope in her hands, she stuttered her reply. "Uh . . . oh. Don't—don't worry about that. Favor for a friend, as I said." She glanced up, smiled briefly. "Or my boss, whichever way you want to say it."

"No. Kate isn't involved in this. I'm taking up your free time, which you don't seem to have much of as it is."

She wondered just what he knew about her time and how she spent it, but assumed he was just being polite. Hoped so, anyway. What with all the hormones raging about, she'd forgotten all her initial suspicions. "Don't worry about it."

After one final stroke to Petunia's neck, he stepped out from his spot between the two of them. "We'll talk about it next time then."

She smiled, mostly in relief. "If you insist, but—"

"I do," he said.

"Fine. Next time, then. When did you want to—"

"I'll find you." Then he tipped his imaginary brim, grinned, and walked away.

She was still standing there, Petunia in hand, staring after him, until he was lost in the gathering shadows around the main house.

"He's trouble," she murmured, stroking Petunia's mane.

The horse nickered softly and shook her mane, making Elena smile. "You think so, too, huh?" She rubbed Petunia's muzzle and, on a long sigh, turned and led her toward the stables. "Yeah, we're both in for it, aren't we?"

Chapter 7

"Turned you down flat, is what I heard."

"It was a strategic request. I'll get over it, trust me." Rafe walked over to where Mac was sifting through a pile of folders on the corner of Rafe's desk. "And how the hell did you find out, anyway?"

"Barn gossip."

Somehow, he couldn't picture Elena chatting with her younger charges about their lesson. More likely she'd mentioned it to Kate, so it wouldn't come back to her that she'd spurned the advances of her boss's friend. "Since when do you skulk around the barn? Don't you have better things to do?"

"Yes. And I'm not 'skulking around.' Kate is down there all the time, so it only follows—"

"Pillow talk. Great. And stop pawing through my files."

Mac smacked him on the shoulder with a folder. "Lighten up. I tell you, where women are involved, the fastest way to find out if there's anything worth investigating is—"

"Unlike you, I can manage to resolve a case without falling into bed with my subject."

Mac didn't even blink. "I'm going to pretend you said that because you're sexually frustrated after being turned down. You know I didn't go after Kate for—"

Rafe lifted a hand. "I know. And I'm not sexually frustrated." Which was the truth, but by a slim margin. So, he might have taken a cold shower after his lesson with Elena, but that hardly amounted to frustration. "Just because you two can't keep your hands off one another does not mean the rest of us can't behave in a civilized manner even if we're not having sex five times a day."

"Two, maybe three," Mac said, pretending to look humble. "But I appreciate the vote of confidence. And I was only going to suggest a little wining and dining on your part. With Elena, I mean. That is, if you can get her to agree to go out with you. Even I have some principles." At Rafe's look of disbelief, Mac simply grinned, then suddenly widened his eyes and pulled a folded manila envelope from the inside of his jacket pocket as if just remembering it. "Oh yeah, thought you might like to take a look at this. It came earlier. I snagged it from the FedEx guy for you."

Rafe snatched it from his hands. "You opened it?"

"Of course I did." Mac pretended to look wounded. "When did we stop sharing everything?" He adopted a hurt tone, but it was totally ruined by the twinkle in his eye. "Lately I feel like we're drifting apart. You never talk to me anymore. It's because I've gained a little weight, isn't it?"

Rafe tried to scowl, but when Mac turned and said, "It's these jeans, isn't it? They make my ass look fat. You can tell me the truth."

Rafe couldn't help it—he cracked a smile and took a shot at Mac's head with the envelope. "Yes, it does look fat, now that you mention it. It's a wonder Kate can bear to see you naked. I could put you in touch with my tailor."

"Very amusing."

Rafe grinned. "I know. And you have to understand, with your head on Kate's pillow every night, I'd rather play it safe if you don't mind."

Now Mac did look hurt. "You think I'd compromise—"

"Not intentionally," Rafe said. "But you aren't always objective where Kate is concerned, never have been. Even you'd admit that."

Mac perched on the corner of Rafe's desk. "Fine." He nodded at the envelope he'd given Rafe. "So, I guess you don't want me to tell you about the fire marshal's report?"

Rafe snapped the envelope open and slid out the documents. "At Charlotte Oaks?"

"What other fire would there be?" He settled his weight. "They were looking for arson. Several different angles came into play."

"Insurance."

"Several different kinds, actually. In addition to who might have benefited—or not—from the loss of the racehorse—"

"Wait—if he died in a suspicious fire, surely the insurance companies aren't paying out on any insurance claim on his life."

"By arson or an act of God, like lightning, no. But—"

"But what? Stables don't combust spontaneously."

"They do when kerosene tanks explode."

"So, it was ruled an accident?"

"Investigations aren't complete yet. Both the local departments and the insurance companies still have their men on the job. But it looks like they're hitting dead ends and the official result will be inconclusive evidence, ruled an accident."

Rafe stopped flipping through the extensive report—one he'd only gotten his hands on by calling in a few favors—and looked at his partner. "You read the whole thing?"

Mac shrugged. "Most of it. But listen, there was another angle besides the life insurance policy itself."

"Such as?"

"Collecting on the life insurance while he was still worth something."

"He was a retired champion, put to stud. So his worth was established."

Mac nodded. "Initially. His progeny, had he had any, would have been worth a pretty penny. And if any had gone on to do anything on the track—" He flipped his thumbs toward the ceiling. "So, when he suddenly goes up in flames—the only fatality in that fire, by the way—the very same night he shows up at Charlotte Oaks, it naturally raised some insurance suspicions."

"You mean about his viability as a stud?" Rafe flipped through the report again. "Says they investigated his medical records to see if there was any reason he couldn't reproduce." He looked up at Mac. "I guess that makes sense. If he was impotent—"

"No babies, no money," Mac finished.

"And?" Rafe skimmed the documents.

"He had good swimmers."

"Did they take any samples for future use?"

"No, just the samples for medical evaluation. They would have, eventually, but he'd only just gotten there."

"So, no insurance fraud there. What's the hang-up with the life insurance?"

"Divorce."

Rafe looked up, eyebrows raised. "Divorce?"

"Gene Vondervan, owner of Charlotte Oaks, was served with papers a week after his purchase of the horse went through, which was a couple weeks before the horse was delivered from Kentucky."

Rafe tapped the papers against his hand. "That sounds potentially messy."

"Divorces between people with a lot of money and assets usually are."

"So, now we have potential sabotage as a means of reducing assets?"

"Or just plain vindictiveness if one party didn't want to share with the other."

"Seems rather extreme, especially from someone who has made his fortune from horses. Is there anything in there about the horse being central to their divorce settlement?"

"I don't know. Nothing in that report other than the notation that the owners are in the middle of divorce proceedings, warranting further exploration."

"What was the deal with the kerosene tank?"

"It was in an adjacent storage shed, but it looks like the final report will be inconclusive as to whether it was tampered with."

"Why is it taking so long to get the reports done?"

"Apparently the Vondervans are complicating things, tying it up in court, hiring independent investigators. As you said, people with money . . ."

"Anybody else hurt besides the horse?"

"No, which is suspicious in and of itself. A brand new multimillion-dollar acquisition, there should have been all kinds of people around him."

Rafe looked at the first page of the report. "Says here the fire started around three in the morning. How many people would have been out there at that time?"

"At least four. Because of the intense media coverage surrounding his retirement and subsequent sale, he was put in an outer set of stables that weren't currently in use. They were installing a full security and monitoring system, as they have in their main stables, but it hadn't been completed yet. According to the report, after he'd been brought in, checked out, and settled in his stall, they'd assigned one of the head trainers and a few stable hands to stay with him that first night."

Rafe looked up. "Same guy, by any chance, that Elena listed as her reference? John?"

Mac shook his head. "Different trainer. JuanCarlo something-or-other. From the report, Geronimo had traveled well from Kentucky and hadn't had any issues with his new surroundings. Other than the media coverage, it was all a relatively smooth nonevent. He had a pretty full schedule that first week, both with media, further medical evaluations, etcetera. Which, of course, never happened."

"So, no other horses, but at least four lives, were at risk. If it was arson, that's a potentially hefty price tag. Which makes the fact that apparently none of them were there at the time of the explosion pretty suspicious. Any reason the crew responsible for watching him would have done this? Any gains to be made there?"

"Other than, assuming arson, they were being paid by the person who wanted Geronimo dead, no. But they've all been interviewed. They were found guilty of negligence and are all facing possible civil suits from Vondervan, who terminated their employment, but none of them are currently under suspicion with the police."

"They really think it was an accident, then?"

"I wouldn't say that, or they wouldn't still be hounding away at this. But the Vondervans' investigators are making sure they have a lock-tight case otherwise, and, as yet, it doesn't appear the locals can put one together that's beyond doubt."

Rafe gave up reading the file. "What is the story on why nobody was there when the tank blew?"

"The trainer was called down to the main stables."

"At three in the morning?"

"Supposedly a horse cut himself pretty badly kicking at his stall door. The trainer on duty in the main stable was relatively new and wasn't sure if it warranted calling in the vet, so he called the other guy down."

"And was the horse hurt?"

"Yes. Needed stitches. They called the vet in, so it's documented."

"And I'm assuming Geronimo's trainer stayed at the main stable while the vet was in transit? What about the other three on duty with Geronimo?"

"Standard 'while the cat's away, the mice will play' story. When they found out the trainer wasn't coming back up for a bit, apparently they slipped off to play cards with a few of their coworkers."

"Leaving the horse completely unattended."

Mac nodded. "He was settled in for the night, and no one was around. I guess they figured no harm, no foul."

Rafe nodded. It all made sense, everyone accounted for. But his radar was still pinging for some reason. "So, what do your instincts say? An accident, and it's just lucky no one else was hurt? Or premeditated sabotage?"

Mac turned away from the window. "I'm really not sure what to think at this point."

"Come on, your gut must be telling you something."

"Sounds like everything points toward an accident. There are some coincidences, with people being gone at key moments, but coincidences do happen."

"So, you're buying an accident, then."

"I'd want to see them keep on digging, find out more about the divorce settlement, make sure there aren't any additional players we don't know about who might also have had a stake in Geronimo's well-being. But, at the moment it feels soft to me. Nothing off enough to really get my juices flowing."

"What about Elena?" He lifted the report. "Any mention of her in this?"

Mac smiled. "I was wondering when you'd get around to that."

Rafe didn't rise to the bait. "Yes or no? She is the only reason we're even looking into this," he reminded Mac.

"You're no fun." At Rafe's scowl, Mac just laughed. "No, no mention other than showing up on the employee list. She worked for the trainers, exercising the horses. Her job didn't have anything to do with Geronimo and never would have. As far as I know, and none of the reports filed to date have mentioned anything different, she never had any contact with the horse."

"Was she interviewed by investigators?"

"Only in the employee roundup. Nothing beyond that."

Rafe fell silent, wishing like hell his instincts were quieting with this new information. Unfortunately, they weren't. It's not like he wanted her to be involved in anything that would jeopardize her working for Kate, but none of this had a good feeling to it.

"What's rolling around in there?" Mac asked, making a knocking motion in the direction of Rafe's temple. "Has Elena done anything to make you suspicious? Did you find out anything new during your lesson?"

"No. Nothing specific. If anything, she came across as a very direct person who doesn't hide anything or pull any punches. It's just . . . I can't shake the feeling that something is off about all of this."

"Is it because you're finding out she's more your type than you'd expected and you don't want any nasty surprises later if you let yourself get into this?"

Rafe was all set to shoot Mac's smug-assed theory down . . . only it made a hell of a lot of sense. "Maybe," he said, clearly surprising Mac. "What? I'm just being honest. She's . . . different. Still not my type," he added, "but not like anyone else I've ever met, either."

"Well, well, well." Mac folded his arms, his grin going from smug to shit-eating.

"I don't even want to hear it, okay? It's a case to me at the moment. Nothing more. Not at this point, anyway."

"After the reams of grief I had to endure from you over Kate, if you think I'm not getting some back, you're crazy." Still smiling, he snatched the file from Rafe and slapped it on his desk. "All's fair in love and war." He walked to the door. "Rafe and Elena, sittin' in a tree . . . wait, sittin' on a horse. Yeah, that's it." He was humming as he walked down the hall. "Hey, what rhymes with *horse*?"

"Go to hell."

Mac's laughter echoed until the door at the other end of the hall snapped shut.

Rafe started to pick up the file, but wandered over to his office window instead, his gaze drawn unerringly down to the stables. He wished he could say for certain it was just his self-protective instincts kicking into gear. But something was all wrong about this Geronimo thing. He felt it. Too many coincidences. And too many coincidences, no matter how logically explained, usually meant trouble. Trouble that seemed to have more to do with the Vondervans, and nothing to do with Elena, but he couldn't make that go away, either.

He punched the intercom that linked most of the main buildings on the property. This one went to Mac's office. "Hey, what do you think about the timing of her leaving?"

"What do you mean? It was a couple months later. A bunch of employees left after the fire."

That got his attention. "Really?"

"File's right there. Might try reading it."

"Why bother when you already have? For a guy who wasn't going to get involved—"

"Kate's involved, peripherally anyway, so maybe I'm a little interested."

"And? How many employees left?"

"Well, Geronimo was a beloved champion, and when his death hit the news, Charlotte Oaks was inundated with media attention from all around the world. Mostly within the horse-racing industry, but there are a lot of soft hearts out there. And this was a huge human-interest story. The stables became a media madhouse. And then, with all the talk of arson, investigators crawling all over the place, media trucks everywhere, things got hairy. But when word broke about the negligence on the part of the employees, the media had a field day with that. Some employees left right then, to keep their good names intact. Which might have been enough for Elena by itself."

"Except she didn't leave right away."

"Seven or eight weeks. Not all that long, really."

"How many employees left of their own volition?"

"The farm as a whole employs seventy-some-odd people. According to the report, at least a half-dozen left within the first few weeks after the fire. Add to that the four who were fired, and you get—"

"An almost twenty-percent attrition rate."

"Plus, if Elena was worried about her horse's pregnancy, that was another reason to leave sooner rather than later. If she wanted peace and calm for Springer, I'm sure Charlotte Oaks was anything but. From what she told Kate, I think she was on her way out, anyway. Not advancing as she wanted to."

Rafe absorbed that, and, again, it all made sense.

"Feel any better about it now?"

"I want to," he said, quite honestly.

"So, dig some more, make sure. Still can't say I'm feeling it, but I'm not as close to her as you are. You've met her, you seem to respect her and like what you know of her."

"So far. But I haven't even scratched the surface."

"Speaking of which, I heard the two of you were in the stables for a pretty long time the other evening." The intercom crackled a little when he chuckled. "You sure nothing else was . . . scratched?"

"If you can manage to pull your mind out of the gutter for just a moment—"

"Why would I want to do that? It's fun down here. You should think about joining in."

"Thanks. I'll keep it in mind. In the meantime, can we stay on topic here?"

"What topic? So far, we've got nothing."

"Maybe your instincts have just gone soft because all that sex with Kate has addled your brain."

Mac's laugh had Rafe leaning back from the speaker. "If that's the case, I don't want the cure, man. Love is a beautiful thing."

Rafe rolled his eyes. "Oh, brother."

"You know, envy doesn't become you."

"Very funny." Rafe clicked off and started looking through the report again.

A few minutes later, Mac popped up at his door. "You're going to keep on this, right?"

He was serious now, as was Rafe. He sighed as he kept flipping through the file. "Yeah. For now." He shrugged. "I know she says she's here so her horse can rest, but it doesn't feel like she's resting. And she doesn't strike me as the resting type. She's spent a lot of years building her career—seems to me she could do that and find a peaceful place for her pregnant horse at the same time."

"What does it feel like, then?"

Rafe looked up then. "It feels like she's hiding."

"From what?"

"I don't know. But that's what I plan to find out."

Chapter 8

Elena stifled a yawn behind her hand. She still had a good couple hours of work ahead of her, and then some time spent with Springer after that. All she really wanted to do was curl up somewhere and sleep.

But the dreams were back. In the past week, she was averaging three or four hours a night, tops. As tired as she was when she crawled into bed at the end of each day, falling asleep hadn't been much of a problem. Staying asleep, however, had once again become a challenge. The nightmare usually woke her up around two or three in the morning. And there was no sleeping after that.

She should be past it by now. And she had been. Since coming to Dalton Downs and settling in, the nightmares had pretty much gone away, even if her need for caution had not.

She wanted to believe it was just Springer's impending due date resurrecting everything, but she could pinpoint exactly when they had come back. The night of Rafe's first, and so far only, lesson. Couldn't be a coincidence.

She just wasn't entirely sure why. Yes, she'd been nervous about him sniffing around, but other than the inferno-level physical attraction between them, nothing had seemingly come of it. And, apparently, nothing was going to come of the combustion between them, either. It had been over a week since their lesson, and he'd yet to even make contact to set up another one. As far as she knew, he hadn't been watching her in any way, either. And after the way he'd affected her during their initial lesson, surely she'd have sensed it if he was.

But while it was true that the way she'd responded to him had made her feel more than a little vulnerable, it shouldn't have been enough to trigger the nightmares. At least, she didn't want to think so. She'd finally convinced herself she'd come to grips with all of it, even if she hadn't exactly figured out a game plan about what she was going to do after Springer finally gave birth. Now, she felt like she was, if not back at square one, certainly not as safe and secure as she had been feeling.

She'd thought about seeking Rafe out, pinning him down on a second lesson time, just to settle the . . . unsettled air. One way or the other. But what if her prodding pushed him to take another lesson that he might have otherwise never scheduled? She had quite a lot on her plate at the moment. So, far be it from her to encourage him.

But working herself to the point of exhaustion wasn't doing the trick, either. She was going to have to do something.

"All set."

Elena whirled around to find Tracey standing there with Bonder. Crap. She'd forgotten all about her scheduled session with him. She wanted nothing so much as to tell Tracey to take him back to his stall.

But with two sets of puppy-dog eyes staring at her, there was no way she was going to be the bad guy.

"Okay, I'm ready. Thanks for getting him. How was he?"

Tracey rolled her eyes. "Well, he's a real pro at not wanting to come out of his stall. I had to bribe him. Again."

Elena sighed. "I really don't want him getting used to—"

"He settled right down. I, uh, only had to use one."

She looked from Tracey to Bonder, who was still smacking his lips. And whose tongue was no doubt purple in color at the moment. "I thought we agreed we'd switch him to healthier snacks."

"Grape Popsicles aren't the worst thing in the world—" Tracey began.

"But the begging situation it creates is unhealthy, and he's facing enough of an uphill battle as it is."

Tracey's shoulders slumped a little as guilt colored her face, but Elena saw the way she looked at Bonder and relented. A little. "We need to wean him onto something else," she said, as sternly as she could. Which wasn't all that stern, given the way Tracey perked up immediately. "Try apples. Real grapes. Anything that's not processed sugar."

"I will. I promise." Tracey looked up at the horse and stroked his mane. He shied a little, but tolerated the gentle attention.

He was improving, and at a better rate than Elena had hoped, and part of that was due to Tracey's assistance. She had a touch that was both natural and gentle, both of which were perfect for a horse like Bonder. With the classes picking up as the weather grew increasingly warmer, Elena hadn't had as much time to work with him, but the daylight hours were growing longer, so her schedule could expand accordingly.

"You've done a great job helping me with him," she told Tracey. "I really appreciate it."

The girl beamed. "It's my pleasure, really. I know he doesn't look like much, but—" She trailed off, looking up at him again, her heart in her eyes.

"I know," Elena said, sighing a little at the sight of the two mooning all over each other. It was an all-too-familiar feeling for her, but one she wasn't totally happy to see in her young assistant. "I felt the same. Something about this guy is different from the nutjobs that normally evolve from the type of treatment he received."

Tracey looked like she was going to say something, but paused.

"Something on your mind?" Elena nudged. "It's okay, you can speak freely. I'm a good listener."

"It's just . . . I know I'm in school, and so I can't even consider having my own horse right now. I'm grateful just to be here, and thankful to work with Kate's horses. Her program is such an important one and so I know I'm doubly blessed. But . . . has she said anything? You know, about her plans? For Bonder?"

Elena had expected as much, so she wasn't surprised by the direction of Tracey's thoughts. "I haven't given her an update on him recently, but I can ask the next time we talk about him. Any particular reason?"

"No. Well, yes. It's just . . . I like working with him, and I know it's highly improbable he's ever going to be right enough to be a class horse with the kids here, so . . ." She trailed off.

"I'll find out what Kate has in mind for him. But you're right—I don't think he'd ever be trusted with the kids. I have to be honest and tell you that I doubt, regardless of his progress, I'd ever recommend otherwise."

"No," Tracey agreed. "I know. That's why I wanted to know, you know, what she's going to do about him. Well, anyway. Thanks. For finding out. I—I appreciate it."

Tracey had handled Bonder so well, Elena had already planned on asking Kate if Tracey could start assisting in her training sessions when she could work it into her schedule, the idea being to eventually turn some of his basic training over to the younger girl. It would serve Elena's need to lighten her load a little, especially if Rafe ever did come back around—not that she was planning around that or anything—and it would be a good working experience for Tracey. She was a natural with all of the horses—all animals, most likely—and had the kind of fundamental calm essential to working with a horse like Bonder. It was something you couldn't teach a person— she'd simply been born with it.

Not only that, but it would keep Elena from getting any

more attached to the poor beast. More entanglements she didn't need. Of the two-legged *or* four-legged variety.

Now, however, Elena wasn't as sure of her plan. It appeared she wasn't the only one grappling with ill-advised entanglements. Seeing just how much Tracey had come to feel for the horse, she wasn't so sure it was wise to encourage that particular love affair. At least not until she found out what Kate's eventual plans were for him.

"I'll let you know what I find out," Elena told her. "Thanks for getting him ready for me. I'll take him from here."

Tracey reluctantly turned over the reins, and with a final gentle pat, stepped back as Elena walked Bonder out toward the paddock. She also really didn't need to get personally involved with the other employees, especially when it came to forming any kind of emotional ties. Even so, she knew she'd be talking to Kate sooner rather than later.

Once in the paddock, she did her best to switch mental gears from Tracey, her neverending list of chores, and her eventual time with Springer, to working with Bonder. She couldn't afford to be anything less than completely focused with this one. And he knew it.

"Come on," she said in a soft, even tone. "Around the ring a few times—let's see how we're doing today."

She used a lunge line, standing in the center of the ring and working him along the fence. To his credit and her relief, he didn't balk, which was promising. If anything, he seemed almost eager. That was a positive sign, too, as long as his eagerness didn't include being so eager to get back to the coveted security of his stall, that he got a wild hair and dragged her there. You had to really read him carefully. With him, panic was easily mistaken for enthusiasm. Another reason not to be out here when she wasn't one hundred percent, mentally.

As well as another reason not to be too quick to adopt Tracey into the training program. The girl had natural gifts, but she was still young and inexperienced, a combination that could be dangerous around a horse as mercurial as Bonder. She rounded along the far end of the paddock . . . only to discover Rafe leaning against the fence as they came around the other side.

Another male who needed to be read carefully, she thought. Not something she wanted to deal with at this particular moment. She was having a hard enough time working with Bonder.

The man really did pick his moments.

She wondered at his timing, but adopted what she hoped was an open smile as she worked Bonder closer to where he stood.

She moved Bonder off the fence slightly, and nodded to Rafe as they passed, letting him know that she didn't mind his presence, but that by saying nothing, she was hoping he remembered from his last visit during a Bonder session that chatting was out of bounds.

It was as good an excuse as any to avoid conversation, and she shamelessly took advantage. In fact, she'd stay in the ring with Bonder all night if it put off another round with Rafe. She needed more sleep—any sleep—before dealing with him again.

She spent far too much time thinking about him as it was. And the fact that simply laying eyes on him again was enough to set her pulse racing. Not an encouraging sign. Bonder tugged on his lead, pulling her attention back where it belonged.

Another time around the ring, and Rafe was still there. Watching.

He nodded, but there was no smile lurking at the corners of his mouth—a mouth she realized now she'd dreamed about.

When she wasn't dreaming about fire.

She murmured encouraging words to Bonder as he leaned heavily toward the stable gate when they passed, while flickering images of dreams lost played through her mind.

Images of Rafe. Of Springer, and Charlotte Oaks. Of Dalton Downs. And fire. Sirens, screaming in the night. Running, sweating, despite the chill of the night air. Working hard, so hard, not to panic, not to do anything foolish that would draw undue attention her way.

Somehow, in the nonsensical way of dreams, she ended up deep in the woods, though there were none on either farm, as heavy gray smoke clung in the higher branches of soaring pine trees. Screaming when Rafe snagged her by the arm, stopping her headlong plunge with the strength of that one hand. Swinging her around, anger blazing from his black eyes as brightly as the fire had from Geronimo's stables.

She tried to explain, in gasping breaths, that it wasn't her fault, that she'd been long gone by the time of the explosion, but he wasn't having any of it. Then, also in the way of dreams, the reality of events past entwined with desires for the future. His passion was fueled, not by lust, but by confusion, seemingly against his will. As if he'd had to fight against it and wasn't happy that his control had snapped, losing him a costly battle.

Or perhaps those were *her* feelings. She was too panicked by the shock of the fire, too overwhelmed by her response to him, to know the difference. Or care.

Then Bonder suddenly reared his head back, and Elena, too lost in her thoughts to react quickly enough, was a split second too late.

His sudden lunge snapped the lead tight in her grip, yanking her forward, off her feet. She landed hard on her knees and hands, then went sprawling in the dirt as Bonder took off. Had she not let go, she'd have been dragged face first.

From the corner of her eye, she saw Rafe clear the fence in one high hurdle and quickly, instinctively, lifted her hand to warn him off even as she was scrambling to her feet. She took off after Bonder, who was stampeding toward the end of the ring and the stable gate.

She didn't have time to look to see if Rafe followed her command, and could only pray that he had. The last thing Bonder needed in his current state was a stranger chasing him.

"Please, don't jump," she murmured over and over under her breath, knowing the horse wasn't physically fit enough yet to clear the fence. God knew how much damage he'd do to both the fence and himself if he tried.

Just then Tracey came out of the end of the barn and froze, with Bonder pounding straight toward her, with only the stable gate between them.

"Move!" Elena shouted, knowing that yelling right now was not a good idea, but having no choice. She was running full-out behind the horse, with no hope of catching him. It was like watching a train wreck about to happen and being helpless to stop it.

Or watching a fire burn out of control.

Tracey moved, but toward Bonder, not away. She didn't run, but moved steadily toward the gate, her hands raised, palms out, not waving them around, but holding them steady.

At the last possible second, Bonder seemed to falter and pull up just slightly. Even in his panic, perhaps he'd realized it was Tracey and it made him pause long enough to forget why he'd bolted.

"Good boy, Bonder, that's the way," Elena called out, keeping her voice as calm as she could, even as she called out to him. She slowed as she came up along the fence beside him, keeping well clear of his hind legs.

Tracey stopped on the other side of the gate, hands still up, as Bonder dug in and tried to slow down, balking now as the gate drew closer.

Elena whistled for him, which, in his distracted state, made him swing his head, slowing him further, as was her intent. Unfortunately, he was still going too fast to handle the sudden move, and she watched in horror as his front leg buckled slightly.

As Bonder stumbled, Tracey came over the gate, much as Rafe had.

Rafe.

Elena had forgotten about him, but didn't look behind her to see where he was. Her gaze was transfixed on the horse as she moved closer.

Bonder rebounded enough to keep from falling, but it was highly likely he'd given his foreleg a good wrench in the process. Slowed sufficiently by the stumble and recovery, he trotted a few steps past the stable gate, then danced sideways a bit into the center of the ring, scared still, and more than a little disconcerted about what had just happened. She couldn't tell right off if he was lame or not, as he was still pretty highly strung. The adrenaline could mask a number of things, at least initially.

Tracey had already eased inside the ring, talking to him as she drew closer.

"Careful," Elena called out as she caught up, but Tracey was already doing the right things, approaching the horse slowly, using a calm, steady tone, talking continuously, gauging his reaction so he wouldn't bolt again. But it was the grape Popsicle she drew from a Baggie in her jacket pocket and began unwrapping that finally got Bonder's complete attention. He calmed a bit more and ambled closer, head down, eyes not as wild, clearly hoping the treat was for him.

Elena stopped a good ten yards away and let Tracey work. Bonder was still breathing heavily through his nose, but his ears were twitching toward Tracey, no longer pinned back, and he was clearly listening to what she was saying.

"Some ride."

Elena startled at the sound of Rafe's voice, and turned to find him walking up behind her. At least he was moving slowly.

"My fault. I was . . ." She trailed off, looked back at Bonder and Tracey. "It shouldn't have happened."

"You hurt?"

His question surprised her into looking back at him again. "Me? No." She looked down and halfheartedly brushed at the dirt and muck that covered the front of her overalls. Lovely. "Well, my pride a little, maybe, but I'm more worried about his stumble. He's probably given that fetlock a pretty good twist. I only meant to slow him down, keep him from coming in too fast at the gate. Tracey—"

"Pretty bold stunt," he commented. "I was torn about whether to get over to you, or run like hell and tackle her out of the way."

"You'd never have made it."

"I know. Scared the shit out of me. She's either the bravest girl I've ever met, or the stupidest."

Elena smiled at that. "You work with animals this size, you have to be a little of both, I suppose."

He shook his head. "Well, there's crazy, then there's . . ." He gestured to Tracey, who was presently hand-feeding Bonder the Popsicle. "That, I suppose."

Elena smiled. "It takes a lot of that to want to work with a horse like this one. She's got a gift, that one."

"I guess you'd know."

She turned to him, surprised again. "I—uh, thanks. I think."

"I meant the gift, but I'm pretty sure you bring the crazy as well." He lifted his hand, put his finger and thumb close together. "A little, anyway."

She laughed before she could think better of it. Not that she worried about distracting Bonder. But she should be worried about letting Rafe distract her. Again. "I won't argue that one. But thanks for giving me credit for having something to balance it with." She looked back to Bonder. He'd finished his treat and Tracey had recovered the lead line and was presently just letting him stand by the gate and gather the rest of his wits.

"Don't walk him yet," Elena called over to her, keeping her tone steady. "We should have that leg looked at before he puts any more weight on it than he already has."

Tracey nodded, but kept her full attention on the horse.

Yeah. She'd have to talk with Kate. As much as she didn't want to involve herself here any more deeply than absolutely necessary, Tracey had earned some support in this, and Elena wouldn't feel right unless she did whatever she could to help figure things out.

"If you'll excuse me," she said to Rafe. "I need to go see to a horse. We'll probably have to get the vet out here."

"Anything I can do?"

She looked back at him. "No, but thanks for the offer. And the willingness to stick your neck out like that. I appreciate your trusting me—us—to handle the situation. You racing in there would only have made things more complicated and potentially dangerous."

His lips twitched then. "I sort of figured that out."

She smiled in return. "Yes, well, you did the right thing."

He simply nodded, touched his imaginary brim again, which did foolish things to her pulse and had her turning her back on him again, before she did something even more foolish. It had been her mooning over him, or her dreams about him, that had allowed the crisis to occur in the first place.

So why she paused, and turned back one last time, she really didn't want to examine too closely. "Why did you come down here, anyway?"

"Set up another lesson." He nodded toward Bonder. "Preferably not on that horse."

She smiled. "Not to worry. No one rides Bonder. As for a lesson, uh, sure. But I really need—"

He raised his hand. "Go do what needs to be done. I'll catch up with you later."

She nodded, turned back, and walked away. Wondering just how much later "later" was going to be.

And why she was looking forward to it, rather than dreading it.

Chapter 9

It was past nine when he approached the outer stables. The stars were beginning to peek out, making him want to slow down and appreciate their beauty. It was one of the things about living in the Virginia countryside that he never tired of—the vastness of the sky above and the endless twinkling of them that lit up the night. Growing up in the city, he'd never known so many stars existed until he'd gone to summer camp upstate in the mountains. Those were the best times of his youth, those long, lazy days spent with Mac and Finn around Lake Winnimocca. And the nights under that huge, starry sky.

He remembered feeling both incredibly insignificant and, at the same time, somehow strangely empowered. As if the very endlessness of it was a reminder of how big the world really was, and that he didn't have to be trapped into one tiny part of it if he didn't really want to be.

The night sky still had the power to make him feel that way.

He shifted his gaze to the stables ahead, and the glow of light emanating from beneath the wide, sliding doors that made up most of the end wall. There was the urge to turn around, to put off the conversation he was about to have, along with all the subterfuge it would require.

He liked Elena, and was admittedly intrigued by her. She was a no-nonsense woman who was good at what she did and didn't look for confirmation of that fact. She seemed wholly at ease in her own skin, which, he realized, most of the women of his acquaintance, regardless of their beauty, did not. And, by not embracing her femininity, or remotely playing on it, she had somehow managed to seem all the more sensual and attractive. Which should make absolutely no sense, but the fact that he couldn't get her out of his mind was proof enough.

He'd rather believe it was the case that kept her front and center in his thoughts, but he was presently working on a number of preliminary files and found it increasingly difficult to keep his mind on any of them for longer than an hour or two. He'd be studying reports, making notes, and his attention would regularly wander to the windows of his office, which happened to provide a view of the rolling hills behind the mansion, leading directly down to the main stables. Where, as he'd come to discover, Elena spent a good part of her day, always hustling here and there, working with this horse or that, overseeing a delivery or working with the barn help.

It was his attraction to her that had kept him from pinning down another lesson time. He'd wanted—needed—to create more distance. Mentally, anyway. He wasn't used to his thoughts being so clouded, and he knew his judgment would be off because of it. He simply had to find an edge and hold on to it.

In the end, that had meant pushing aside his other case files and digging more deeply into anything and everything he had collected so far about her. He'd read the report he and Mac had discussed, front and back, several times, making more notes each time. The prickling sensation on the back of his neck refused to go away, and in fact, only grew stronger with each subsequent study of the information at hand. Which wasn't to say he'd ferreted out any evidence whatsoever that damned her in any way. Which was both relieving and irritating as all hell. Instincts this strong were rarely wrong. But they were usually rooted in something substantive. There had to be more here than he was seeing. And yet, at the same time, he'd never wanted more to be wrong.

His frustration with himself and the whole damn ordeal

was finally what had driven him down to the paddock earlier today. Keeping his distance wasn't giving him the clarity he wanted. And all the attention to the details of the reports he'd gathered wasn't going to lead to anything until he talked with her again.

But then the incident with Bonder had happened and, once again, he'd been thrown off stride. He'd been both terrified for her, and mesmerized by her. She could have been dragged, trampled, or worse, and yet she'd leapt up, had the presence of mind to direct him to stay back, and had charged right after that crazed idiot of a horse, as if it were nothing out of the ordinary. In fact, the only part she'd been upset about was that her attempts to keep the damn thing from plowing down her young barn assistant might have caused the horse an injury.

He eased open the outer paddock gate and closed it behind him, careful to stay close to the fence as he edged his way to the stable doors. He should probably have changed clothes. Or shoes, anyway. In fact, he could have waited until tomorrow. Should have, probably. But another night spent thinking about the conversation he wanted to have without actually having it simply wasn't tenable.

So he'd asked after her at the main stables, and had been told she was out here checking up on her mare. It was a calculated risk, what with him already preoccupied with her, to talk to her on what was arguably her own turf, but perhaps she'd be more relaxed away from the bustle of the main stables and all the attendant ears that went with it.

He wasn't sure whether to tap on the metal doors to announce his arrival, or if that would spook her horse, so he simply lifted the main latch and slowly began easing the door along the tracks. It made enough noise despite his care, grinding and squealing, that he hadn't gotten it half open when she was already calling out.

"Hello?"

He slipped inside, and seeing her at the opposite end of the aisle, with her mare in cross ties, opted not to close the door behind him, just to save them both the ear-splitting noise.

"You should get Kate to have that looked at," he said, as he walked down the aisle toward her.

She looked at herself, then at the horse, then back to him, confusion on her face. "Look at what?"

He jabbed his finger over his shoulder. "Those doors. I'm surprised you're not half deaf."

"Ah," she said, lips curving in that half smile he'd already learned she sported more often than not. "Pretty standard for metal doors. Not much you can do about it. We're used to it."

He forced his attention away from her open and intelligent face to the stall doors he was passing. He hadn't paid any real attention when he'd come out here the first time, as his focus was on her and the vet. He knew some of the employees kept their own mounts at Dalton Downs, but there were only two others out here that he could see. "Where are the rest of the horses?"

"There are only three out here. The others are stabled with the class horses and Bonder down at the main building."

"Why some here and some there?"

He paused a few feet away by an empty stall door.

"Partly because they do better with the hustle and bustle, partly for convenience."

"And yours?" Even a novice could see that her horse was either incredibly heavy in the middle or hugely pregnant.

"Calm is good for her right now."

"When is she due?"

"Few more months."

He strolled closer, careful to keep to the side. Elena was grooming her horse, using some kind of pick to clean out one of the hooves.

"Did you ride her?" he asked.

"No, just walked her. But it's muddy out there." She glanced up at him. "It's good for her, but to be honest, I think the grooming routine is as therapeutic for me as it is her."

His lips curved. "The Zen of horse maintenance?"

She shot him a quick smile. "Something like that."

"How is she doing? I mean, is everything going okay with the pregnancy this time?"

"So far, so good. I don't think I'll relax until she foals, though."

"Do you have any plans for the baby?"

He'd said it lightly, but he noticed a telltale pause in her motions.

"In what way do you mean?"

"Are you keeping it? Or . . . I mean, I don't know how it works with horses. I didn't know if it was promised to someone else or if you are selling it. You know, like when a dog has puppies."

She recovered easily enough, but, and only because he was watching for it, her casual response seemed a bit forced. "I suppose it could be like puppies. It all depends on why the horse was bred."

He said nothing, waiting for her to elaborate. When she said nothing, just continued to clean Springer's hooves, he nudged a little more. "What's Springer's story? I know she had problems last time, so were you always planning to try again? Or—well, I guess it's not like dogs where accidents happen and they end up with an unplanned pregnancy, but—"

"Oh, accidents can happen, even with horses." She wasn't looking at him, focusing instead on removing pebbles and debris from Springer's hoof, but Rafe's instincts remained on full alert.

He'd intended to prod her into talking more about herself, and figured her horse was a good conversational gambit, only now he was wondering if there was something more there. To the outward eye, she was simply busy working, but she was almost overly focused now, as if trying too hard to appear casual. It could be that he was reading something into nothing, given his fixation with trying to locate the source of his intuition where she was concerned . . . but he didn't think so.

He didn't have time to analyze the situation and ask questions accordingly, so he'd have to follow his gut—he knew he needed to tread carefully, make sure she didn't suspect his line of questioning was anything more than simple, novice curiosity. "I'd think in a big operation like Charlotte Oaks, they would be pretty careful about keeping horses in heat away from the stallions."

"They do. Not too many mares around, anyway. Most of the breeding is done artificially. Usually the mare isn't even on premises, but boarded elsewhere. A racing facility isn't really the most conducive place for a restful gestation."

"Which is why you moved her up here?"

She nodded, then shifted back to work on the hind hoof. "I'd been planning on leaving anyway, so it seemed as good a time as any."

"So, what made you decide to breed her again? Was it because you were planning to go and wanted to take advantage of being on a racing farm with good stock? Is she a valuable horse or something?"

"Not all horses are bred for racing lines. Sometimes babies are just babies."

"So, you do plan to keep it."

"Not sure yet. I'm not making any plans until he or she arrives."

"If you don't want to keep the baby, what do you do? Run an ad? Is it like selling puppies after all, just on a grander scale or something?"

"Or something," she said, that dry smile resurfacing again. "Word of mouth works just fine, too."

"So . . . if you bred her to racing stock and she's not racing stock, would the baby still be considered a purebred? Again, I can only compare to dogs. Not that I know anything about breeding them, either, but I know a purebred is worth more than a mutt."

"Like I said, sometimes a baby is just a baby. Springer is a good riding mount. A lot of people just want horses for pleasure riding. As for purebred, just like dogs, that has to do with the breed of horse, not whether both race. In fact, the mares used to breed racing stock are rarely racers themselves."

"Like Springer? What breed is she?"

Elena straightened and moved around the front of the horse to the other side, away from him. "You're full of a lot of questions this evening."

"Just curious. They are a fairly substantial presence at the farm here, but I really know nothing about them. I grew up in the city. We didn't have horses or farms."

"Kate said something about you, Mac, and Finn going to camp together every summer in upstate New York. Her mom owned it, or something? Weren't there horses up there?"

So, she'd been asking about him. His initial reaction was to be pleased and flattered, as a man would be when a woman he was interested in showed the same in return. Which was the wrong reaction entirely, given his real reason for being down here. Especially in light of this new line of questioning. And yet . . . that was the first thing he'd felt. A good reminder that he wasn't as objective here as he wanted to believe. "Yes, the camp had horses, but I never went anywhere near them."

"They can be intimidating."

"That, and the girls in camp didn't seem inclined to spend a lot of time down at the stables. They enjoyed the water sports more."

Elena chuckled. "Ah. Well, girls in bikinis trump mucking out stalls pretty much every time. If you're a teenage boy, anyway."

He grinned. "I don't think age has anything to do with it."

She looked down at her dusty, raggy overalls. "Darn, and me without my bathing suit."

She was flirting with him. In her own way, but it was damn effective. Either that or she was cleverly getting him off the subject of her horse. Regardless, it was working. Especially since he was now imagining just what kind of figure she had underneath the shapeless overalls she favored.

"What brings you down here tonight, anyway?" she asked,

continuing to take the conversational lead. "Surely not a lesson on horse biology."

Apparently they were finished talking about Springer. He wanted to poke around a bit more, question her about her time at Charlotte Oaks and get more into the specifics of Springer's breeding. There was something going on there, but he couldn't figure out what. But if he pushed too much more, it would be beyond the bounds of polite interest. So he shelved it. For now. At least he had another lead to pursue. He just wished he felt better for having discovered it.

"No. I was just following up on before, when I came out to the paddock to see about working another lesson into your schedule, and—"

"Bonder decided he was done with his lesson."

Rafe wandered to the other side of the aisle when she moved to the rear hoof on Springer's far side and leaned against the post between stalls. "He's pretty much a nutcase, isn't he?"

"You would be, too, if you'd been abused like he was. Kate wants to find out how far we can rehab him. And, frankly, so do I."

"Is he really worth all the time, not to mention the possible danger? I'm guessing he'll never be allowed anywhere near Kate's kids."

She straightened again and walked over to where he was standing. "Excuse me," she said, motioning to the carryall behind him which had the rest of her grooming supplies loaded into it.

"Sorry." He stepped aside, but not as far as he might have. He told himself he just wanted to see her eyes up close, get a better gauge on just how settled she really was with their conversation.

She lifted the carryall by the handle, but paused before putting space between them. "No," she answered, "he wouldn't be. But everyone deserves a chance to get their life back, get themselves back. Even broken-down, abused horses that nobody gives a damn about. Don't you think?"

He was listening, but up close like this, with the overhead light shining across her cheeks, he got caught up in those damn freckles. For someone so forthright and confident, the innocence they projected seemed incongruous. And yet he found them somewhat endearing, and it reminded him that no matter how tough the exterior, everyone was vulnerable in some way.

"Sounds like that ideal might come from some personal place." He held her gaze, liking it more than he should when she stood her ground. Ground that kept her in direct proximity to him.

"Isn't your business all about helping to fix the injustices in the world?"

"As I said before, it's nothing so lofty as all that," he replied.

"Still, whatever motivates you, the bottom line comes down to giving someone a chance for a better outcome than they'd otherwise have. That's what I'm giving Bonder. A chance to regain his health, and exist in a world that he can interact with and take joy from."

"Then he's lucky to have found you."

"Kate found him." Her lips quirked at the corners, and that gleaming light entered her doe-brown eyes, ensuring his rapt attention wouldn't stray even if he wanted it to, which he didn't. "I'm just the glass-half-full sap who can't say no to a head case with a penchant for grape Popsicles. I mean, what's not to love?"

Rafe's smile came slowly. "You're an interesting woman, Elena Caulfield."

"There's an ambiguous compliment. At least I'm choosing to take it as one."

"It was meant as one. I can't say I've met anyone like you."

Her dry smile spread to a grin that was as unaffected as it was honest. And he swore he felt something dip somewhere in the vicinity of his chest.

"You don't hang around the right places," she said. "Horse stables are filled with interesting women."

"No doubt." But there was only one who'd captured his attention. And it was becoming a real struggle to keep in mind why he'd sought her out in the first place.

"Now, if you'll excuse me, I need to see to the rest of Springer's grooming." She stepped around him. "I don't get to spend as much time with her as I'd like to."

"Is that a subtle way of telling me you can't fit in another lesson? Or would rather not?"

She set her carryall on a stool and pulled out a flat, wooden brush with a strap she slid over the back of her hand. She began stroking the sides of her horse with the brush, glancing back at him over her shoulder. "No, it just means I don't get to spend as much time with her as I'd like. When do you want to take another lesson?"

"I'll defer to your schedule. What would be best for you?"

She paused and turned to look at him more fully. And smiled. "How early do you get up?"

Chapter 10

Elena backed down the ladder from her loft apartment over the outer stables, yawning deeply and wishing like hell she'd remembered to set the timer on the coffeepot the night before. The sun was barely peeking over the horizon, and last night the temperatures had dipped down a bit further than they had recently, making for a chilly late-spring morning. She shivered despite the long underwear top she'd donned under her overalls this morning. Teach her to be a smart-ass and offer a dawn class. But then, she hadn't really expected him to take her up on it. He struck her as more night owl than early bird. Serve her right if he stood her up. Her luck, Rafe was probably still tucked in his nice, warm bed. Which was where she should be. Well, not in Rafe's bed, but . . .

No way could she stop the visuals that accompanied that little mental slip. It wasn't a shot of warm coffee, but it did have the added benefit of getting her blood pumping a little faster. Of course, if she were in the same bed as Rafe, she wouldn't need any coffee, just . . . stamina.

"Morning."

His voice surprised her, making her lose her footing on the last rung. An instant later, two strong hands palmed her waist and steadied her as both feet reached the ground. She could have told him that putting his hands on her was not the way to steady her at the moment, but she was too busy trying to rally her thoughts away from imagining him manhandling her like this while they were both naked amongst tousled sheets.

Then he was turning her around, and she was getting her first look at a scruffy, early-morning Rafe. And whatever words she might have found evaporated like morning mist under a rising sun.

Goodness knows, her temperature was rising.

He had on an old, forest-green sweatshirt and an even older pair of jeans if the frayed edges and faded thighs and knees were any indication. It was standard weekend-morning clothing for most men, but until that moment, she'd have been hard-pressed to visualize it on him. Of course, on most men, that combination would have given them a disheveled look at best. In fact, she was feeling incredibly disheveled herself at the moment. Rafe, on the other hand, without even trying, looked like he'd just stepped off the pages of the latest Ralph Lauren ad. She would have resented the ease with which he made scruffy so damn sexy, except she was too busy fighting off the waves of lust the look inspired.

"Need help getting something down from up there?"

She somehow managed to drag her gaze away from his face to look, probably somewhat blankly, back up the ladder. His hands were still gripping her waist, so she had to be forgiven for her dazed reaction.

"Uh, no, I don't think I forgot anything. Except coffee."

"You keep coffee in the stable crawl space?"

She frowned, then realized the source of his confusion. "I live up there. It's an old manager's office that Mac converted to a small efficiency for Kate when she first came. I thought you would know that."

A smile played around his lips. And really, should he still have his hands on her? And why wasn't she moving away? Sure, he had her sort of pinned between him and the ladder at her back, but if she really wanted to get away from him . . . She gave up the pretense.

"I don't know that Kate ever actually used it," Rafe said.

"In fact, I'd forgotten all about it. You're the first manager she's hired."

Elena knew that Kate lived with Mac in his bungalow, situated by the creek down past the lower horse field. *Smart woman*, she thought, knowing which living space she'd have chosen, if given the option. Especially considering the roommate that came with it. "Any wedding plans there?" she asked.

"Does there have to be?"

"No, of course not. I wasn't passing judgment, just wondering. In fact, it's not even any of my business. I haven't been around all that long, but anyone can see they're great together."

Rafe shrugged and finally dropped his hands and stepped back. "Exactly. They seem pretty happy with the status quo."

Figures—mention commitment to a guy, even indirectly, and he bolts. "Power to them, I say. Relationships are hard enough. Whatever's working, works. It was nothing more than good wishes on my part."

"What about you?" he asked.

"What about me?"

"Relationships. You seem to believe in happily-ever-after and saying I do's, so why aren't you married? Or are you?"

She was a little taken aback by that. Not that they'd been doing anything more than a little flirting, but she wasn't the type to even engage in that much if she was otherwise involved. But she could hardly act insulted, as that would imply there was some involvement with him. "No, single. But I've nothing against the institution. My parents had a long, happy marriage, so I've seen it work and work well."

"Not one of the battle-scarred, then."

She smiled a little at his characterization. "Said like a true war veteran."

He lifted a shoulder. "Not in the first person, no. I've avoided most of them. But I've witnessed my fair share."

"Sounds like you made a point of that. Avoiding them, I mean."

"Might have. Nothing wrong with occasionally *not* learning a lesson the hard way."

"How did you learn it, then?"

"Well, none of us—"

"Who is 'us'? Your family?"

"Me, Mac, Finn. Which is as close to brothers as I'll ever have."

"I suppose with a nickname like 'Unholy Trinity,' I shouldn't be surprised that none of you is looking to get shackled. That is how you look at it, I suppose. Shackled. Although Mac seems pretty happy to be, at least, somewhat entangled."

"He is, but trust me, no one is more surprised about that than Mac. Kate, too, come to think of it."

"Why is that?"

"We each came from different walks of life, but none of us, Kate included, came from what would be considered a traditional upbringing. In fact, none of us had what you had."

She frowned. "My dad moved us all over the place—I never stayed anywhere for more than a few years. I had no siblings. I did have a horse pretty much all of my life, but that's hardly traditional."

"I meant your parents. A long, happy union. Role models for what can be. None of us had that."

"I'm sorry."

He lifted a shoulder. "I'm not whining over it, just stating facts. All in all, I think Finn's the only one who'd consider going down the aisle. He's a glass-half-full kind of guy." A dry smile curved his lips. "Of course, he'd have to slow down long enough to actually develop a relationship in the first place, so small chance there."

"So, Mac is happily involved with Kate, who was also, you say, without the role models, and now Finn is a possible candidate for matrimony—or something enduring, anyway, or at least open to the idea. And yet you avoid it entirely. No curiosity? No desire for family? Perfectly happy with the idea of growing old alone?"

She had no business asking him this, but she was truly curious to hear his answer.

He folded his arms and leaned back against one of the post beams. "What about you?" was his response. "What are your hopes?"

She tried not to stare at the way his folded arms pulled the fabric of his sweatshirt tight over his biceps. Or the way it made his shoulders look wider. She forced her gaze up to his. "I guess I would want what my parents had. I mean, who wouldn't, you know? Doesn't necessarily mean marriage, but that kind of life—a long bond. They were each other's best friends. And, I guess, I wouldn't settle for less than that, either. But, to be honest, it hasn't been something I've been focused on."

"That makes two of us, then."

"Yes. Yes, it does," she agreed.

There. Independence clearly stated. *Sexual tension resolved,* she thought. *He's not looking, and neither am I.* So why wasn't she relieved?

Because the sexual tension hadn't abated one whit. Mostly because commitment had nothing to do with lust. She could be as lustful as she wanted, crave his touch, want to know what he tasted like, felt like . . . and have absolutely no intention of settling into any kind of relationship with him. She wasn't a one-night-stand type. But she found herself actually thinking there might be exceptions. Circumstances being what they were, and all, she could be forgiven for simply taking what she could have. Right?

Hardly. In her dreams was the only place she was going to do all the things she wanted to do with Raphael Santiago. And that's the way it was going to stay. Had to stay.

"So," she said, her tone overly bright. "You ready for lesson number two?"

"As I'll ever be."

They left the barns and climbed into the golf cart he'd ridden over in. The sun was just breaking fully over the treeline in the far distance, at the back of the lower fields, making her shade her eyes as he expertly steered the cart over the rutted path back to the main stables. A heavy mist hung in the air, chilling her skin. But, after their heated little encounter, the dampness felt good. Refreshing. Head-clearing.

Once at the big barn, she led the way down the aisle toward Petunia's stall. "It's been a while since your first lesson, so keep in mind that you'll probably need to reestablish your rapport with Petunia."

"Check." He said nothing else, just followed behind her.

She stopped at the tack room door and went inside. "I haven't set anything out, so we need to get her saddle, pads, bridle, everything."

He followed her into the smaller room. "Just point to what we need."

She could feel him behind her, her awareness of him as finely tuned as her senses were to the animals she worked with. Except with him, there was all that sexual energy jacking things up. She cleared her throat, maybe squared her shoulders a little, then made the mistake of looking back at him before reaching for the first of the gear.

Something about the morning beard shadowing his jaw, the way his hair wasn't quite so naturally perfect, made his eyes darker, and enhanced how impossibly thick his eyelashes were. And she really, really needed to stop looking at his mouth. But the ruggedness the stubble lent to his face just emphasized all the more those soft, sculpted lips of his.

Her thighs were quivery, her nipples were on point, and the panties she'd just put on not fifteen minutes ago were already damp. The morning air might have been head-clearing, but her body hadn't gotten the message at all.

"You take the saddle there," she said, trying not to sound as breathless as she knew she did. Dammit. "On the third rail," she added, pointing, when he kept that dark gaze on her.

"What else?" He didn't even glance at the rack.

"Grab one of the pads. Same kind we used last time. I'll get the halter and bridle."

"Okay."

She waited a heartbeat too long for him to move first. He didn't.

So they were officially staring at each other now. The silence in the small space expanded in a way that lent texture to the very air between them. The room was tiny, the temperature warm, with little ventilation. The sun hadn't risen enough to slice through the panels on the roof, leaving the room deep in shadows, with thin beams of gray dawn providing the only light. There was a light bulb overhead, but she'd have to reach past him to get to the switch.

He stepped forward. "Elena—"

"Rafe—"

They spoke at the same time, then both broke off.

He paused. "Yes?"

She really wanted to know what he'd been about to say before she'd potentially made a very big fool out of herself, but went ahead before she lost her nerve. "I can't—I mean, not to be presumptuous here, but I can't—don't—mix business with pleasure."

"Are we?"

She didn't back down. She might not be the most experienced person in the world when it came to relationships, but she knew the way he was looking at her wasn't of the innocent teacher-student variety. "It feels like more than a simple riding lesson to me." *There. She'd said it.*

He took another step closer, and her breath suddenly felt trapped inside her chest. So much for being brazen.

"It is a simple riding lesson," he said. "Not a corporate merger. So what if there is more? I don't really see a conflict of interest here."

"You're a close friend of my boss."

He stepped closer still. It was a small room to begin with. He was definitely invading her personal space. Again.

"And you're not planning on staying here long-term anyway, right?"

"What is that supposed to mean?"

"Meaning that as potential conflicts go, that one is temporary at best. As is anything that may happen between us. No commitments, right?" His voice was all just-rolled-out-of-bed rough.

"What are you saying, then?" she asked, tipping her chin up slightly as he shifted closer. She felt the bridle rack at her back. "What is it you want?"

"I just want to learn to ride." His lips curved then, and her thighs—or more accurately, the muscles between them—suddenly felt a whole lot more wobbly.

His eyes were so dark, so deep, she swore she could fall right into them and never climb back out. And that smile made it dizzyingly clear that horses weren't the only thing he was interested in riding.

It was too early in the day for this. She couldn't handle this kind of full-out assault on her senses. Or on her mind. Or . . . hell, what part of her didn't he affect? He muddled her up far too easily. Muddled was definitely not what she needed to be right now.

But when he lifted his hand, barely brushing the underside of her chin with his fingertips, and tipped her head back a bit further . . . she let him.

"I think about you," he said, his voice nothing more than a rough whisper.

Her skin tingled as if the words themselves had brushed against her.

"Too often. You distract me."

"And that's a bad thing?"

"It's . . . an unexpected thing," he said.

She wasn't sure what to think about that. And his neutral

tone made it impossible to determine how he felt about it. "So, this is . . . what? An attempt to exorcise me from your thoughts?"

His smile broadened as his mouth lowered slowly toward hers. "Either that, or make all this distraction a lot more worthwhile."

She had a split second to decide whether to let him kiss her, and spent a moment lying to herself that she was actually strong enough to do the right thing and turn her head away. Who was she kidding? Her body was fairly humming in anticipation and it was all she could do to refrain from grabbing his head and hurrying him the hell up.

Like he said. It was just a kiss. Not a contract.

His lips brushed across hers. Warm, a little soft, but the right amount of firm. He slid his fingers along the back of her neck, beneath the heavy braid that swung there, sending a delicious little shiver all the way down her spine.

He dropped another whisper of a kiss across her lips, then another, inviting her to participate, clearly not going any further unless she did. She respected that, a lot, even though part of her wished he'd taken the decision out of her hands. It would make all the self-castigation later much easier to avoid. Given his aversion to commitment, somehow she figured he knew that. They were either in it together, or not at all.

He lifted his head just enough to look into her eyes, a silent question in his own. *Will you, or won't you?*

She held his gaze for what felt like all eternity, then slowly lowered her eyelids as she closed the distance between them and kissed him back.

His fingers twitched against the back of her neck when she opened her mouth on his, then pressed a bit harder as he accepted the invitation and sank his teeth gently into her bottom lip, tugging a little, before taking the kiss deeper.

He was as natural at kissing as he'd been at horseback riding. She'd known he would be, and her entire body thrilled at the knowledge that he'd be even better in bed.

He walked her so her back pressed up against the bridle

rack. She didn't mind the leather and bits digging into her back. She didn't even really feel them. Because she was too busy feeling Rafe Santiago slide his tongue into her mouth. And if his skill in teasing her tongue with his own was any indication of just how clever that tongue might be in other places . . . She heard a deep, sensual groan, and realized, distantly, it was her own.

Somehow her fingers had found his shoulders, sinking into the hard muscle she discovered there, before sliding along the back of his neck, and burrowing into all those thick, dark waves. He pressed his hips into hers, growling just a little, as she scraped her nails along his scalp. He fit perfectly between her legs and she pushed back, cradling the hard bulge pressing there as she clutched at his head to keep his mouth on hers.

He dueled with her tongue, controlling the kiss as he drew his thumbs along her jawline, before sliding his fingertips down the length of her neck to her collarbone. Now it was her turn to groan as he efficiently popped the clasps of her overalls, allowing the front bib to drop away so he could cup his palms over her breasts. She moaned as he broke their kiss and began to leave a trail of kisses and nips along her jaw, around to the sensitive spot below her ear, as he gently rolled her hard nipples between his fingers.

She wanted to claw her clothes off, feel his skin against hers. She was still clutching his head as he lowered it to replace his fingers with his mouth. He left wet marks as he suckled her through her shirt. The combination of the damp heat and the waffled weave of her long underwear she wore created an exquisite friction that had her climbing a peak without any further stimulation.

She was pushing her hips forward, seeking that sweet, hard bulge she'd felt moments before, but which his current position prevented her from having. Dammit, she wanted it all. His mouth on her, the hard length of him between her legs, buried deep inside of her. She was all but coming apart at the seams as he continued to drive her wild. She dragged his mouth back to hers so he could press his hips into hers again, and groaned in deep satisfaction when he pinned her tightly to the rack and slid his hands down her sides, over her hips, pulling at her thighs, urging her to wrap her legs around him as he once again took her mouth with his in a soul-deep kiss.

The instant she lifted one leg up over his hip so he could sink the full weight and length of him against her, she peaked and peaked hard. The strength of it stunned her, robbing her of breath, but he kept up just the right amount of sweet pressure so she could wring every last pulsing bit of pleasure from the contact. Breathless as he nibbled the side of her neck, she had no idea what to say as the reality of what she was doing began to crash back in.

"Rafe—"

"Shh," he instructed, taking her mouth again, only this time in a kiss so gentle, it seduced her all over again.

She was powerless against this, against him. It was too good, and he was impossible to push away. Especially when she didn't really want the contact to end. She shut out thoughts of what would happen next and tried hard, very hard, to just enjoy this for what it was.

She kissed him back, her fingers still in his hair, toying with the thick waves as he continued. She'd stop him. At some point. Just not quite yet.

He slowed the kiss, then finally ended it. But rather than having an awkward moment when he lifted his head and looked into her eyes again, he smiled. And she smiled back. And it was somehow normal, and natural, with a little hint of co-conspirator twinkling in his eyes, as if they had these little assignations all the time. And she couldn't help but think how wonderful that would be.

He slid his hands between them and tugged her bib back into place. "Seems I've left your shirt a bit damp." He lifted an amused gaze to hers, and rather than be embarrassed, she laughed. Thinking back to the enigmatic man who'd watched her in silence all those times before they'd actually met, she'd never have thought him playful. And yet he was, delightfully so.

She helped him with the clasps. "Seems so," she said, "but then I'm used to getting a little mussed-up at work."

"Are you, now." A rather wicked, speculative gleam entered his eyes and her body responded instantly, quite willing to go along with whatever he had in mind.

He slid her long braid over her shoulder and toyed with the ends of it, glancing up through those impossibly thick lashes. He flicked the ends across the front of her bib, and though she couldn't feel anything through the heavy denim, just the act alone, and what it implied he was thinking, made her twitchy and needy all over again. It was crazy, what he was doing to her, and worse, that she was simply letting him. She wasn't even trying to level the playing field, allowing him full control of the situation.

But it felt pretty damn good not to be in charge. Not to mention he was taking very good care of her and seemed to be enjoying it. Having always been the caretaker in her world, it was heady stuff, having someone seek out her needs and want to fulfill them. "Rafe, I—"

A sudden gasp from the doorway behind him froze them both into place.

"I'm so sorry. I was just—never mind. Sorry!"

Rafe turned his head toward the still-open doorway, allowing Elena to see past his shoulder . . . and right into the wide blue eyes of Tracey, who was presently backing up, tripping over a bucket out in the aisle, barely catching herself in time before crashing into the stall door behind her.

Face flaming, she righted herself and hustled off.

"Tracey," Elena said, extricating herself from Rafe's arms and stumbling past him. "Wait."

"It's okay," her young assistant called back brightly, too brightly. "I was going to start arranging gear, but I can—you know, there's tons to do. I'll just—" Cheeks still pink, she didn't try to finish the sentence, just headed out to the paddock at a quick trot.

Elena debated going after her, but what, honestly, was she going to say? She didn't know yet what *she* was thinking about what she'd just done, much less how to explain it to the hired help.

"She's in college, right? I'm sure she's seen people kissing before. I doubt we scarred her for life."

Elena turned to find Rafe leaning against the tack room door, arms folded, a supremely satisfied look on his far-too-handsome face.

"I'm her boss."

"Her single boss."

"And you're one of my students," she said, doggedly refusing to give him the edge.

He turned and began looking up and around.

"What are you looking for?"

His gaze shifted back to her. "The sign."

"What sign?"

"The one that says there will be no fraternizing between instructors and students."

"It's the accepted rule in most professional situations."

"Most." He pushed away from the door and walked toward her.

"Besides," she said hurriedly, as he drew closer, "most of the students here are children, so it hardly warranted an actual sign. Most civilized people—"

He walked right up to her and tipped her chin up so her gaze met his. "That is where you made your error. I've never claimed to be civilized."

Her heart was pounding, while other parts of her were rejoicing in the fact that he was touching her again. Traitorous parts. "You're the most civilized-looking man I've ever seen. Even your sweatshirt wouldn't dare wrinkle."

"Surely, given your training, you of all people know that

looks can be deceiving." He stroked her chin with his finger. She had to fight the urge to sigh and rub against it.

Somewhere she found the strength to back away from his touch. "Lesson time is wasting."

He merely smiled. "I was rather liking a different kind of education."

"Yeah, well," she muttered, hating having no retort for that, as she'd clearly been liking it pretty damn well herself. She went to move past him back to the tack room, intent on gathering the gear and getting on with the day as originally planned.

He touched her arm as she passed by. "Elena—"

She also hated just how much she liked hearing him say her name, with that slight accent making it sound incredibly exotic. She'd never felt exotic in her entire life. Of course, she'd just felt all kinds of things she'd never felt before. Also, all thanks to him. All the more reason to get this lesson back on track. She'd think everything through later, figure out what to do about it. When he was far, far away and not looking at her the way he was right now. Like he still wanted to consume her.

And she was still very much of a mind to let him.

"I've got other things lined up, so if you want your lesson, we really need to get Petunia saddled." It had come out sounding more plea than command, but at least she was trying to reestablish some boundaries.

He followed her, but was prevented from stepping into the tack room behind her when she swung around and planted a saddle pad and saddle smack into his arms.

"You remember where Petunia is stabled, right?" She turned back to gather the remainder of the gear, every inch the riding instructor now. Okay, so there were still some inches that were all quivery and tingling, but it was a start, anyway. "Why don't you go and reintroduce yourself. I'll be over in a minute."

"Sure thing, Teach." Amusement was clear in his tone. "I'll get right on that."

She flicked him a quick glance over her shoulder, but just caught the corner of his smile as he edged out of the tack room and headed off down the aisle.

The fact that she had to resist the urge to poke her head outside the door to get a rear view of him walking away told her she still had some work to do in regaining control. Something told her he was far too used to getting what he wanted where women were concerned.

Well, with good reason, she admitted. He was . . . a lot. And it was all good.

She slumped against the rack and took a deep, steadying breath as she replayed, truthfully, what had just happened in here. It had been good fun between two consenting adults. Nothing more, nothing less. Certainly nothing to get all worked up over. Fortunately, Tracey hadn't stepped in any earlier than she had. So, no harm, no foul. Just a brief little interlude that was now over. She was back in control, if not of him, at least of herself. And out there, in the ring, she was the boss. He would see she wasn't some pushover he could just do with whatever he pleased.

She snorted a little laugh, because her body was already responding to even the merest thought of him doing what he pleased. "Oh yeah, you're the boss of you, all right." She closed her eyes, willing herself, almost desperately, to take a quick moment to gather her wits before having to face him and his knowing smile again. A smile that held all kinds of promise. Promises she knew he could keep.

Scowling, she folded her arms across her still-damp-from-his-mouth nipples and pushed off the rack with a bit too much force, almost overturning the whole thing. After juggling the gear back onto the pegs, she grabbed the bridle she wanted and stomped out of the room.

Coffee. She should have started the day with coffee.

Instead, she'd started it with a taste of Rafe.

She slowed. Sighed. And admitted the truth. It wasn't as if

he'd scarred her for life. But spoiled her a little? Perhaps. How could she not be left wanting more of that? More of him?

Leave it to her not only to get tangled up when she least needed to, but with a man who was far too astute for his own good, and hers.

"You sure know how to pick 'em," she mumbled.

Chapter 11

O kay, so maybe that hadn't been the smartest thing he'd ever done, but not because of that nonsense about there being a conflict of interest. Although she had no idea just how conflicted his interest in her really was.

No, playing with Elena Caulfield had been a very bad idea because, rather than making his distraction with her manageable, it had been like striking a match to dry kindling. He'd thought—hoped—the reality would be a letdown compared to the fantasy. Instead, she'd been so incredibly responsive that he'd taken it much, much further than he'd ever intended. Which had only served to whet his appetite for more.

He reached Petunia's stall and hung the saddle and pad over an empty stall door across the aisle before turning his attention to her.

The mare sauntered up and stuck her head over the stall door, checking him out with doleful brown eyes.

"Don't look at me like that," he told her. "It wasn't my idea to drag you out of bed at this hour. I'd just as soon be back in my own as well." Only now he wasn't picturing himself there alone.

Elena's body had been more hard than soft, which hadn't surprised him. What had been a surprise was how swiftly he'd responded to her taut, toned lines. She was both grace and power, and he'd wanted, badly, to learn more of what all that grace and power would feel like, wrapped around him. And then there was the incongruous, almost voluptuous softness to her lips. And her even softer sighs. He usually liked his women soft all over, but, as it turned out, the combination of a strong, lean body and pillow-soft lips was all kinds of enticing.

Petunia made a soft, whickering sound, bringing him out of his thoughts. He drew closer and she dropped her head to snuffle around at his hands.

"I didn't bring you anything," he said, with true remorse. "Not such a good date, am I? Drag a girl out of bed at the crack of dawn and don't even bring her flowers. Which, in your case, I'm guessing you'd just eat, but—"

"She, uh, she likes sweet feed. There's a bucket of it in the rack at the end of the aisle."

Rafe turned to find Tracey walking toward him from the opposite end of the stable. She had a halter and lead rope in each hand and a heavy blush still tinting her cheeks as she gamely offered him a smile. He gave her a lot of credit for that.

"Thanks," he said, sincerely. "I appreciate the inside information."

"No problem. Petunia's a dollface. She deserves the pampering."

"Good to know."

Tracey moved on to another stall door and haltered the horse inside. He had to say something, but this wasn't a situation he'd ever found himself in before. He'd meant what he'd said to Elena, about not being embarrassed, or sorry to be caught in a private moment with her, but he also recognized that, had Tracey shown up a few minutes sooner, there would have been more than red cheeks to deal with. He wanted to make sure she didn't feel she'd been inadvertently put in the middle of anything.

As she opened the door and led the horse out, he finally spoke up. "Listen, about earlier, I'm sorry if we embarrassed you. This early, I honestly didn't think anyone else was around, or I—we, wouldn't have been carrying on like that." Which wasn't completely true, as he'd completely forgotten where they were.

"Oh, no, don't worry, it was my fault. I heard voices, but I didn't know you two were—or I wouldn't have intruded. I—"

"You couldn't have known." He smiled. "I just didn't want you to think that Elena would be that cavalier, and—well, it was my idea." He didn't feel the need to explain himself, but if he'd put Elena at a disadvantage with her staff, he wanted to make that right.

"I haven't worked with her very long, but I consider myself very fortunate that I do," Tracey said, hero worship clear in her blue eyes. "She has the most amazing gift with horses—it's a pleasure just to observe her. I'm learning a great deal." She led her horse into the aisle and closed the stall door behind him. She slung the other halter on a hook by the next stall door, and leaned inside. "I'm coming for you next, Rocky, so no point trying to play invisible."

She turned to lead her horse toward the rear paddock, then paused and looked back at him, cheeks pink again, but eyes twinkling as a grin spread across her young face. "I think Elena is a pretty smart woman. That opinion hasn't changed."

Before Rafe could respond to that blatant endorsement, Tracey turned and was gone. Or had Tracey meant Elena was smart to humor his attentions due to his position in the Dalton Downs hierarchy?

Elena chose that moment to come bustling through the middle crossover, bridle in hand, and spied him still staring after Tracey. She glanced down the aisle to see what he was staring at, then back at him. "Did I miss something?"

Rafe shifted his attention to her. "No. Your young barn helper was just here singing your praises."

"Oh." Elena glanced down the now empty aisle again, a frown creasing her brow. "I really think I should go talk to her."

"I already did."

Elena looked surprised at that. "She wasn't—she didn't act uncomfortable because of . . . you know. Did she?"

"Did she act weird because she saw me embracing her boss? No. In fact, I'm pretty sure she gave you a high five."

Elena's mouth dropped open, then snapped shut gain.

"What?"

"Men."

"Proudly, yes, but why is that a strike against me in this case?"

She paused, as if weighing the value of speaking her mind, then said, "Not that sharing a private moment with me wasn't enough, but having the conquest affirmed by another clearly makes you even happier. It's a guy thing. I don't hold it against you."

He grinned. She was very cute when trying to establish boundaries. Boundaries he had no intention of letting her resurrect. Not if he had anything to say about it. "So, you're saying that the fact that your assistant blushes every time she looks at me, and said you were a smart woman for going after what you wanted—" He pointed to himself. "Me, again. That you don't feel even more justified in enjoying yourself back there? Just a little?"

She walked closer and hung the bridle on the rack next to the saddle. "What I think is that we're wasting precious lesson time."

He sighed in mock frustration. "Women."

She cut him a look and he shrugged, fighting a smile.

"If you don't like the course of the conversation due to its logical, rational content, then it's perfectly okay to shut the conversation down rather than admit I have a point." He smiled. "But, I know, it's a woman thing. No harm, no foul."

In response, she merely tossed the halter to him. "Remember how to put that on?"

He nodded, but didn't bother to hide his satisfied smile. He'd caught the twitch at the corners of her mouth even as he caught the pile of nylon and rope against his chest. He liked that she could dish it and take it. She was sharp. And smart. And he already wanted to taste that smart tongue and those so-very-soft lips all over again. Preferably without interruption this time.

A really bad idea. Probably.

But it didn't make him want it any less.

He turned back to Petunia. "You won't hold my guy qualities against me, will you, *mijita?*"

Petunia responded to his low, soothing tone by pressing her nose against his shoulder and nudging him. He laughed and scratched between her ears before rubbing a hand down her neck.

"Of course you won't. You know I'll take care of you."

He thought he heard an "oh brother" muttered behind him, but it just made the smile spread that much wider.

"Come on, let's get you out in the morning sun," he said, keeping up a steady banter as he slid the halter over her muzzle and strapped it on, then led her from her stall. He managed the cross ties all on his own, under Elena's steady regard, then turned to the saddle and bridle. "Which do I put on first?"

He knew the answer, but he wanted to engage her in conversation again. He wanted to engage her, period. And it had little to do with uncovering more information about her past. Not that he wasn't finding himself more than interested in learning more about her, but he'd be lying if he said it was merely to protect Kate and her young campers.

"Saddle, then bridle."

Elena helped him adjust the stirrups and the straps after he slipped the pad and saddle in place, then instructed him on how to put on the bridle and adjust the bit, while taking off the halter. She let him undo the cross ties, then handed him the reins.

"Lead her out to the front paddock. We'll mount and have our lesson from there."

He nodded and Elena walked out with them. "When do you think I could move beyond the ring for a trail ride?"

She cut him a look. "You've been on a horse a total of one time. Patience."

"I'm not suggesting I'm ready now, I'm asking when you think I will be."

"If Mac is pressuring you, you really need to—"

"No, it has nothing to do with Mac. And I'd rather attempt it on my own first, anyway."

"Well, it's never wise to head out on a trail alone. The terrain here is well known, but any number of things could happen. Even with cell phones and—"

"I know. I was thinking you and I would go for a test drive. As a lesson," he clarified, although who needed the clarification more, he couldn't say.

Initially, Elena looked wary at the request—he couldn't really blame her, given that he hadn't exactly planned on making it until his mouth opened and the words popped out. But before she could respond, one of the other class instructors stuck her head out of the stable office door and called Elena's name.

"Call for you."

Elena turned. "Who is it? I have a lesson."

"Some insurance salesman, I think."

Elena frowned. "I don't have time for junk calls."

"He asked for you by name, said it was something about Charlotte somebody? I'm not sure what he meant. He's on a cell, I think, and the connection isn't great."

At the word *Charlotte*, Rafe's attention went on full alert. As in Charlotte Oaks? What other Charlotte could it be? He looked at Elena, but she was still looking genuinely confused.

"Take his number," she shouted back, "and tell him I'll call him back in an hour."

The instructor nodded and ducked back in the office, shutting the door behind her.

Elena turned back to Rafe, all business. If the call shook her in any way, there was absolutely no evidence of it. "Okay, time to mount up."

"What was that all about?" he asked casually as he approached Petunia and stroked the side of her neck.

"Haven't a clue. I don't know anyone named Charlotte and I'm not in the market for insurance."

"Maybe it's about your former place of employment. Charlotte Oaks, right?"

Elena's brow smoothed. "Right. I didn't put that together." She laughed a little. "See what happens when I don't start the day with my much-needed dose of caffeine?" She glanced at him and the most delightful shade of pink colored her cheeks, but she didn't make any mention of how she had actually started her day, or that he might be the cause of her discombobulation.

Worse was that he didn't mind being the source. In fact, he'd like to be the source again. Preferably soon. In fact, the horse lesson seemed like the worst idea ever at the moment, when compared to how he could be spending the next hour.

"Probably someone who got my name from their employee list. I changed insurance companies to the plan Kate offered recently after I hit the thirty-day mark. I never filed a claim or got so much as a checkup with my old plan, so I can't imagine what they want from me now."

"Hard to say. Guess you'll find out when you call."

She just shrugged and Rafe wondered if she'd even make the return call. He wanted to dig a little more, wanted her to want to dig a little more, but there wasn't much he could do without making more of it than the subject warranted. "My experience with those guys, both personally and professionally, leaves a lot to be desired," he said, sliding the reins from Petunia's neck and putting them both in one hand as he prepared to mount. "Tenacious lot."

"I guess," she said absently, turning her attention to the horse. "You remember how to do this?"

Conversation over, Rafe thought. How was it that each occasion he had to spend time with her only left him with more questions and fewer answers? It was both frustrating and undeniably intriguing. Not that she was trying to be mysterious. Under other circumstances, she'd have struck him as someone who was very direct, with little subterfuge.

But there were circumstances, ones that prevented her from being as forthcoming as she'd likely otherwise be. He'd bet money on it. He just didn't know what those circumstances were yet, exactly.

"Okay, Petunia. Be gentle with me," he said, but just as he put his foot in the stirrup, the office door opened again.

"Elena, I'm really sorry, but it's that guy again. He says it's imperative he speak with you now. I don't start with the kids until nine, so I can take over for you if you'd like."

Elena swore under her breath, then looked at Rafe, clearly torn. But now he saw something more than simple annoyance in her expression. He'd bet money this was no ordinary insurance call, and he was pretty certain she'd come to the same conclusion.

"We can do this another time," he offered, mentally scrambling to come up with a reason to follow her into the office so he could eavesdrop.

"Jackie is a great trainer," Elena said reluctantly. "She can put you through your paces. You'd be lucky to have her."

"I'm sure I would be. I want you."

Her pupils instantly shot wide and her mouth parted slightly. And his body went hard in places that would make it really uncomfortable to mount a horse at that particular moment. He had to remember that he was equally affected here, but it was so out of the ordinary for him, it would take some doing. Besides, he'd only told the truth. He did want her. Right here, right now. Baggy overalls, bare-faced, braided hair, and all.

"Rafe—"

"Does the name Geronimo mean anything?" Jackie called out.

Elena froze. Only for a second, but it was telling. To Rafe, anyway. It surprised him how disappointed he was to see even the slightest proof that his suspicions might be on track. Even if he still had no clue what it was he suspected her of doing. Exactly. Whatever it was, couldn't be good. "Maybe he's an insurance investigator, not a salesman," Rafe suggested, poking a little. "That was the name of the horse who died in the fire where you used to work, right?"

Elena stared at him, instantly wary. "You know about that?"

Rafe shrugged, not wanting her to be suspicious of him, but, for the first time, he felt guilty about his less-than-honest reasons for being out here. "Who doesn't?"

She held his gaze a beat longer, as if searching him out for any other possible explanation before going on with what she'd been about to say. "That happened a long time ago. Surely they've wrapped up all their investigations by now. And what in the world would he want to talk to me about, anyway?"

"Have no idea," Rafe said. *Although maybe it has something to do with why you're white as a sheet.*

His heart sinking, Rafe slipped the reins over Petunia's neck, then turned to Elena. "Come on." He touched her elbow.

She moved her arm away. "Come on where?"

He lifted his hands. "I thought I'd go with you. You look a little . . . unnerved."

Color flooded back into her cheeks, but he couldn't have said whether it was from guilt or anger. "I can handle my own phone calls, but I appreciate the offer." She hadn't said it unkindly, but she was clearly distancing herself from him as fast as she could, without looking panicked about it.

But he was finally—finally—on to something, and there was no way he was letting the ball drop now. One way or the other, he was going to get to the bottom of this. He'd examine later why it suddenly meant a whole hell of a lot more to him than a normal case would. "If they're harassing you for some reason, I might be able to help. I have some experience in dealing with pushy people. In fact, you might say that's my specialty."

"I honestly don't know what they want, but I know how to hang up on someone as well as the next guy."

"If it has to do with the death of that racehorse, and the guy is being that pushy already, I'm guessing it's not a solicitation call." He watched her reaction, but she was already shaken. His comments weren't helping any, but then they weren't designed to. He just hadn't counted on feeling so conflicted.

"I'm not sure how you think you can help."

He smiled. "I'm amazingly resourceful."

"I figured that much out," she murmured, looking more than a little wary. "What I haven't figured out is why."

"Why what?"

She lifted a shoulder. "Why all of it. What happened earlier in the tack room. Your being so willing to help me now."

"I have to have a motive? Other than wanting to taste you? And, having done so, wanting to put myself in your good graces in hopes it will happen again?"

Splotches of color bloomed in her cheeks, but her eyes were still guarded and her mouth a bit pinched at the corners.

"I seem to recall a pretty decent response on your part," he mentioned, cursing himself for putting her on the defensive. He needed to stick close, not have her push him away. "What was your reasoning?"

Jackie called her name again.

Elena waved to her. "Coming!" She looked back at him. "You're . . . a lot."

"A lot. Meaning I overwhelmed you, then? What, with my animal magnetism?"

"Something like that."

"You routinely manage to control beasts several times your size and many times your weight. I'm thinking you could have easily resisted my advances if you were so inclined."

"I went with the moment. Now that the fog has cleared, I'm just wondering about a few things."

"Such as?"

"You made it pretty clear that I wasn't your type, yet you hit on me anyway. Why?"

"Chemistry works in mysterious ways. I try not to over-analyze."

"Something tells me you rarely do anything without giving it some thought."

"Most of the time. There are exceptions." His lips curved. "Notable ones, on occasion."

She didn't respond to that, but she didn't have to. The quick, unthinking way she'd wet her lips was all the response he needed. Why she was being so contrary about the attraction they shared—and it was indeed shared—he had no idea. Whatever was going on with this call had completely yanked her out of her comfort zone. Maybe this was her way of getting it back.

"I better go field this call. I'll send Jackie out. Take the lesson. She's good."

Rafe knew he couldn't push much harder. But he couldn't let her back away, either.

"One thing," he said, when she turned to walk away. She glanced back and he said, "If you were going with the moment, why not just continue and see where that leads? The moment was pretty good."

She paused, then said, "I'm not sure. It's just a feeling I get about you. Your type, anyway."

"I have a type now?"

"Yep. The white knight type."

He laughed. "And that's a bad thing?"

"It is when it prevents you from seeing that not everyone needs your help to handle every little thing. I know some women love to be taken care of like that. I just don't happen to be one of them."

"Point taken. For the record, I didn't offer to help you because I thought you were too weak to deal with it—"

"I believe the term you used was unnerved."

"You were."

"So? Stuff happens. I get unnerved. Doesn't mean I can't go on to take care of business."

"I have no doubts about that. It was only an offer of help. One person to another." He smiled a little. "Not even a person hoping for extra-special treatment in return for said help." He settled his gaze on hers and spoke as sincerely as he could. "Elena, we all need help from time to time. I wasn't patronizing you. In fact, I'm here taking lessons because I needed your help. Maybe I was just trying to return the favor."

She nodded. "Point to you. I'm sorry if I overreacted. It was just, you're right, the call rattled me a little. Mostly because I was still a little rattled from . . . before. And then you offer to help and kind of step in a little, and, well, some men—"

He moved closer. "One thing you should know right off. I'm not 'some men.' "

A light entered her eyes. "That much I've figured out." He shifted closer still, but she stepped back. "I'll send Jackie out. Take your lesson."

"What about the trail ride?"

"One lesson at a time."

"And the next lesson will be . . . ?"

The teasing glint faded as her gaze shifted to her office door and the waiting call. "We'll catch up again at some point, I'm sure."

Not unless you can help it, Rafe thought, watching her all but sprint toward the office. And away from him. He wasn't sure which she'd rather avoid more, him or the phone call she was presently taking.

"That went really well."

Rafe turned to find Mac with his elbows propped on the fence. "This day just keeps getting better and better." He swore under his breath. "And you've been standing there how long now?"

"Long enough to wonder how the hell it is you score so many hot women."

"Maybe because I don't see it as keeping score so much as enjoying someone's company when the time is right."

Mac just grinned. "You're so full of shit. But I bet women eat that stuff up."

Rafe glanced in the direction of the barn office. "Not all women."

"Something to ponder, that's for sure."

He looked back at Mac. "Why are you down here? Assuming it's not to gloat over my abject failure to get anything going on this case."

"Oh, is that what that little dance I just witnessed was? You trying to get something going on a case file? Because, while it definitely looked like you were trying to get something going on, it didn't strike me as—"

"She's in the office right now talking to some insurance investigator about Geronimo. I was trying to get her to take me in with her." He looped the reins over his hand and absently stroked Petunia's mane when she nickered at him. "So, yeah, I was working the case."

Mac frowned. "Insurance investigator? Are you sure? About the dead racehorse?"

"Pretty damn sure. Guy said he was with an insurance company, dropped Geronimo's name, said it was urgent."

"What could they want with Elena? And why now, after all this time?"

"I have no idea, which is why I was trying to talk her into taking me into the office with her. As for the rest, you know as well as I do—better, being a former cop—how long investigations can drag on, especially if there's any hint of arson. Just because the police can't seem to build a case doesn't mean it didn't go down that way. Maybe the insurance team has found something they want to pursue. They're not going to pay until they've exhausted every angle."

"An angle that involves Elena," Mac added. "Not good."

"Neither was the way she went sheet-white when the name Geronimo came up in conjunction with the phone call."

"Hello, Mr. Santiago, Mac."

Rafe turned to find Jackie, the instructor, approaching with a smile. "How come I'm Mr. Santiago?" he said in a quiet aside to Mac.

Through his nodding smile to Jackie, Mac replied, "Because I'm down here being friendly and approachable, and you're always skulking around, all aloof, wearing uptight designer clothes."

"So, I don't happen to dress like I'm still doing undercover work for street gangs," he said, with a pointed look toward Mac's ragged jeans and aged hooded sweatshirt. "Doesn't mean I'm not a nice guy." He smiled and nodded at Jackie as she got closer. "And I don't skulk."

He was trying to think of a way to get out of this lesson, but there didn't seem to be an easy escape route, so he went with it, hoping he could keep it short. He debated on poking around a bit and seeing what Jackie's take on her boss might be, but if she went and told Elena he'd been asking nosy questions, that might not help his case much.

But, at least this way he could keep an eye on the stable office door and see what state Elena was in when she finished with her call. If he timed it right, he could catch up with her after class, scope things out a little.

"You probably have other things to do," Rafe told Mac as Jackie joined them. "Please don't let me keep you."

Mac just grinned and settled his weight against the fence. "Nothing so important I can't stick around and lend a friend some moral support."

"Right." Rafe turned and shot Jackie a quick smile. "Up and at 'em, right?"

She nodded and smiled. "We've found it works better if you're up on the horse for the lesson, yes."

Mac snorted. Rafe ignored him and turned his attention back to Petunia. He leaned in close, stroking her neck and mane. "Don't suddenly turn into a psycho horse on me, okay? Thirty-four years of integrity are on the line here."

Petunia made a little whuffling sound and Rafe wished he could sneak her a bribe or something, but she'd been pretty docile up to now, so he just had to hope for the best.

He checked the straps, then planted his foot in the stirrup and hoisted himself up. Hardly a bobble. He might actually get used to this.

Thirty minutes later he wasn't sure who was more bored from walking in circles, him or Petunia. Mac had left somewhere around lap number fifty. So much for support. The last he'd seen of him, Mac was wandering down in the direction of Kate's office. Probably had her up against the nearest wall by now.

Rafe shut that mental path down. Especially because it wasn't Kate he was picturing up against a wall, but him and a particularly frustrating horse trainer. "How about we speed things up a little?" he called out, more to help rid him of the mental image than anything.

"We're about done for today," Jackie called out. She was a compact blonde with thick, curly hair, a girl-next-door fresh face, and a body she had to have poured into her jeans. On pretty much any other day, she'd have attracted his attention. At least some mild flirtation, anyway, just to hear her laugh. Today his attention was split between watching the office door, and not falling off the horse.

"Just one time around at a trot?" he said. "Then we'll call it quits. Give me something to look forward to next time."

He rounded the end of the ring and started heading back toward his instructor when a motion over by the adjacent stables caught his eye. Elena had exited the building and was getting into one of the farm golf carts. He must have tensed, because Petunia reacted by speeding up a little.

"Careful," Jackie called out. "You want to kick a little with your heels and press gently with your knees."

Rafe heard her in a buzzing-fly kind of way. His attention was fully on watching where Elena was zipping off to. Even if he trotted all the way to Jackie and left the horse for her to take care of, he'd never catch up with her. Unless . . .

He dug his heels in a little and pressed his knees more tightly against Petunia's sides as he grabbed the pommel and leaned forward. "What do you say we have a little field trip?"

Petunia, apparently as bored as he was, thought this was a fine idea, and immediately picked up the pace.

"Pull back just a little on the reins," Jackie shouted. "Gently. Then release."

Tracey was coming out of the barn just then and moving toward the paddock gate, perhaps anticipating the end of his lesson. He wondered if they needed Petunia for another class this morning, and sent silent apologies to Kate and her kids if that was the case. Surely they had enough horses to go around and could spare this one for twenty or thirty minutes.

Instead of heading toward Jackie, he steered Petunia across the paddock toward the opening gate. As if sensing the potential for adventure, her ears perked and she picked up the pace a little more, causing Rafe to grab the pommel more tightly. It was that or risk never having children. Sweet mother of God. He hoped he was just doing something wrong, because if this was what it felt like normally, it was a miracle cowboys anywhere ever procreated.

He spared a thought that perhaps this would have been a wiser move after more than, oh, two whole lessons under his belt, but he was committed to it now. And so was Petunia.

"Hey!" Jackie called, trotting across the ring as he headed through the gate.

"I'll have her back as soon as possible," he shouted over his shoulder.

He nodded at Tracey as he trotted by, not daring to attempt the more suave tipping of the imaginary hat for fear of landing his suave ass in a pile of horse manure. She jumped out of the way easily and swung the gate wider, saluting him as he went past, either oblivious to Jackie's shouts or ignoring them for his sake. Her wink said partners-in-crime and he winked back. He'd remember that.

And then they were free of the ring and heading out across hill and dale, following the direction Elena had gone in her golf cart.

There was a clear cart path worn in the grass from the main stables to the far barns where she kept her horse, the same one they'd taken earlier. It didn't surprise him that she was headed that way, seeking some peace and quiet to deal with whatever that phone call had been about. But the speed with which she was racing out there made him wonder just what exactly had happened. If she'd been on the call the entire time, that was a lot of question-and-answer time for the investigator.

Petunia wanted to go faster—he could feel it with the bunch and pull of her muscles. He wondered how often, if ever, she was allowed more free rein than she could get inside a ring. He wondered if maybe she wasn't supposed to get this worked up. She was older, Elena had said. And more sweetheart than warrior. But she didn't seem labored and she wasn't lathering. In fact, he could swear, if a horse could smile, she was grinning ear to ear.

"Easy there," he told her, leaning over a little, trying like hell to find a way to sit in a saddle that didn't threaten his future as an active bed partner and someday father. "It looks a lot easier in the movies."

They finally, blessedly, got to the barns, and Petunia mercifully seemed to understand that this was where her adventure came to an end. He pulled up, but she was already slowing, and came to a complete stop by the closed paddock gate. It was empty at the moment, so he slid—somewhat gingerly— from her back, then led her inside the ring and put the reins across her neck. He scrubbed her mane and scratched her between the ears. "*Gracias, mijita,*" he murmured. "I'll make sure you don't get into any trouble. And there will be extra sweet feed for you, promise."

She pawed at the ground a bit and lowered her head,

butting him on the shoulder, but settled after a few more strokes.

After making sure the gate was closed properly, he turned toward the barns and headed directly to where Elena's horse was stabled. One way or the other, he was going to find out what was going on. Game time was over.

Chapter 12

Elena paced the length of the barn aisle and back again. "Shit, shit, shit." Springer grumbled a little and stamped impatiently inside her stall. "Sorry, sweetie," she said, pausing by the door. Springer was obviously sensing her tension. She shouldn't have come out here. But she needed time to think. She needed space. And there were too many people around for her to disappear up into her loft. They'd knock first, but, if she was needed, they'd definitely knock.

At least out here, it would take some time to get to her, and she'd see them coming.

"Elena."

She jumped, plastering her hand over her heart as she spun around to find a very dusty Rafe standing in the center of the aisle. So much for seeing them coming.

"What are you doing out here?" she blurted, heart racing. To be fair, it was still racing from the phone call. He was not improving matters any, though. "I thought you were in the middle of your lesson." In fact, though she hadn't wasted any time in getting away from the stables, she had glanced over to the ring to make sure he was otherwise occupied.

"I saw you take off like a bat out of hell. I was concerned. So I took a little field trip."

"Where I go and how fast I get there isn't any of your busin—" She broke off and narrowed her eyes. "What do you mean by 'field trip?' " She angled her body to look past him, but didn't see anything outside the barn door.

"Petunia and I thought walking in circles was getting to be a real drag. So we walked in a straight line instead. All the way out here." He shifted his weight on his feet. "Actually, we went a little faster than a walk. I'm guessing there's a way to do that that doesn't render a guy a eunuch. I'll have to get you to show me that."

Any other time, she'd have fought a smile. At the moment, she was still too freaked out for it to register. All she knew was that she needed him gone. Now. "Jackie let you just waltz out of your lesson—"

"No, she had no say in this. I sort of cajoled her into teaching me—or starting to teach me—how to trot, when I saw you take off. Then Tracey was opening the gate—also not her fault, she was just entering the ring—and Petunia and I just sort of took advantage of it."

"Are they on their way out here, too? Tracey and Jackie?"

"I'm . . . pretty sure Tracey headed Jackie off at the pass."

She raised her eyebrows. "Why would she do that? What could Tracey possibly say to Jackie that would make her think I would want to be interrupted by—" She stopped as visions of the scene Tracey had walked in on earlier swam through her mind. She ducked her chin, and massaged her forehead. "Never mind. And, if you don't want to be a true eunuch, then you'd better not be grinning when I look up."

"So cranky."

"You have no idea."

"I'm guessing the call didn't go all that well."

His voice was closer, which meant so was he. She had to look up, but she really needed more space, and more time, before having to handle him, or handle anything. Dealing with Rafe up close in her personal space was more than she could take on at the moment. "I appreciate your concern." She took what she hoped was a steadying breath, and looked up. "But I'd appreciate some time to myself."

"I make a good listener. What did the guy want?"

"Another time maybe." She stepped back, closer to the stall door and Springer. "It might be a good idea to get Petunia back to the main stables. She'll be needed for classes later."

"That's assuming I can get back up on her and make it back there."

"Something tells me you'll do just fine."

He took a step closer, and she tensed. She tried not to show it, but that much was really beyond her at the moment. The stabilized world she'd thought she'd constructed for herself had just been proven to have very shaky foundations. And she didn't know what to do about that. What she did know was Rafe Santiago was the last person she'd ever reveal that to. He already had a way of looking at her, into her, like he saw far past her defenses, to some other place she was unaccustomed to people reaching. And that was without her handing it over to him.

"Elena, I know something's not right." He said it quietly, but somehow the softer tone wasn't the least bit comforting. In fact, it only served to unnerve her further. He saw far too much, far too easily.

"Whether or not that's the case, I'd prefer to handle my own affairs my own way." She put her hand out when he took another step. "Just because we lost our heads for a few moments this morning doesn't mean I need or want your interference. It's nothing personal, just, I've been taking care of myself for a long time, and I like it that way."

"So you've made a point of saying."

"I don't expect that pattern to change anytime soon."

He stood his ground, kept his gaze steady on hers. "Just because you don't usually need help, doesn't mean you shouldn't consider accepting some when it's offered. I'm guessing that doesn't happen too often."

"Do you do that? Accept help?"

His gaze shuttered a bit and she realized she'd said exactly the right thing if she wanted him to back off.

"That's what I thought. Please, get Petunia back to Tracey. We can set up another lesson later." She turned away.

"Elena, I really think if you—"

She swung right back around. "You know, you're going beyond the bounds of being a nice guy here. In fact, you're being pretty adamant about this. What's really going on?"

It was hardly a blink, and if she hadn't been expressly looking for it, she'd never have noticed it, but there had been a flicker. She pounced on it without thinking twice. She was in survival mode now and he was the enemy. One of them, anyway. "Why are you so dead set on helping me out? For that matter, why are you really down here taking lessons?"

"What makes you think—"

"I'm not stupid. A bit slow at times, perhaps, but not stupid. One of the things that makes me good at my job is being intuitive with the animals I work with, picking up on subtle signals. People aren't so different." She folded her arms. "If you have concerns of any kind, or if Kate does, or Mac, or Finn, or anyone else on Dalton Downs, why not just come out and ask? I'm damn good at my job and I thought things were going just fine, but if there's some other agenda at work here—"

His eyes went hard and flinty, and she had to resist the urge to shiver. "Is there?" Gone were those smooth-as-velvet, dulcet tones. In their place was a flat, steely voice that brooked no argument—something far closer, she realized now, to the kind of tone she'd have associated with him before they'd first spoken to one another.

"What the hell is that supposed to mean?" Then it hit her. His sudden appearance, sniffing around her. Followed by that phone call out of the blue today. "Oh my God. It's you who did this, isn't it?"

"What are you talking about? Did what?"

"The phone call. The investigator. You had something to do with that, didn't you?"

"I have no idea who was on the phone or why they called. But I'll admit I'd be more than happy to listen to an explanation as to why an insurance investigator was so keen to talk to you today."

"You've been checking up on me, haven't you? Snooping, making calls, maybe? To my former employer?"

He folded his arms. "Kate does background checks on all her employees."

"I know," she returned flatly. He wasn't the only one who could do steely. At the moment she didn't know whether she was more terrified of the ramifications of what had happened this morning, or pissed off at him for dragging her back into the situation she thought she'd safely left behind. "I passed mine with flying colors. What changed?"

"Things didn't add up."

She felt the blood drain from her face. So it was true. He did have ulterior motives for being here. With her. It seemed ridiculous now, that she'd wasted even a second thinking otherwise. Of course a man like him wasn't going to be interested in a barn rat like her. The blood came rushing back, flushing her cheeks until they felt hot, as she realized how easy she'd made it for him. Key word being *easy*. For someone who'd made it this far living on her wits, she'd certainly lost them when she needed them most.

"Says who?" she demanded, embracing the righteous anger that filled her, along with the terror that she'd been so close, and now it seemed like it was all unraveling at once. "Did Kate have a problem with me? My past employment? Again, why not come straight to me? And if she didn't like my answers, she could let me go."

"She wasn't the one with the questions. But she is worried about you."

"Worried? What reason did she have to worry about me?"

"You have a pregnant horse with prior problems."

"Which I personally told her about. She seemed fine with it, very understanding, in fact. I have my own vet. You met him. It's not something that is going to affect my work here or create any problems for her. Is that what this is all about?"

"You leave the world of horseracing, a world you profess to love and have fought hard to succeed in, to work at a camp for kids."

"To give my horse some peace and quiet, and because I wasn't sure where I was going to go after leaving Charlotte Oaks. And this isn't just any camp for kids. I resent the implication that what Kate does is somehow inferior to the field I was in. I think she'd take serious offense—"

"You know that's not what I meant. You claim to be taking a time-out, giving your horse some space to gestate in the relative peace and quiet of the Virginia countryside. Despite the fact that the operation you left has far more qualified medical personnel on hand."

"Asked and answered. Horseracing is a crazy, intense atmosphere. Springer doesn't need crazy and intense, or a team of doctors. She only needs me and my vet. What, were you an attorney at some point? IRS maybe? You badger very well."

"You also neglected to mention Geronimo in your job interview."

She tried to keep from flinching at that. "I didn't see what that had to do with anything. It was international news, but it had happened some time ago when I was interviewed. I figured if Kate had a problem or concern, she'd have asked me. As it was, she wasn't even curious about it, didn't even bring it up."

"Because she didn't know about it. Because you didn't think to mention it."

"As I said, it was international-level news back when it happened. I didn't think I had to." She tried to keep her heart from pounding out of her chest, but all of her worst fears seemed to be coming to some sort of fruition all at the same time, and she simply couldn't think straight, couldn't decide what to say and what not to say. But she clearly knew who not to trust. "So, because I didn't mention my horse's pregnancy issues and because I took for granted that the person interviewing me was already aware that Charlotte Oaks was a pretty well-known place, there are official concerns about me?"

"I'm just saying that what you call a time-out can also look a lot like hiding out."

"And you make this brilliant deduction based on essentially nothing, unless there is something you're not telling me. And then, bam, you suddenly need riding lessons. What a coincidence! God forbid you just come out and ask me. I don't think I've ever been more insulted."

"Which is exactly why we didn't ask you directly. I didn't want you to storm out of here. You're the best manager Kate could hope to find."

"If I'm not some sort of nutcase, you mean, hiding out from something nefarious."

"Elena, that's not—"

"And, I'm guessing that riding lessons weren't the sum total of your grand plan, right? Is that where that—" she waved her hand in the general direction of the main stables "—whatever the hell we did factored in? You didn't have to seduce me, you know. I was already starting to like and respect you as a person. A few more lessons and God knows the deep, dark secrets you'd have gotten me to expose."

"What happened between us earlier had nothing to do with my initial reasons for wanting lessons. If you haven't figured it out, I was sort of starting to like and respect the person you are as well. It's why I'm out here right now."

She snorted. "Right. It has nothing to do with the phone call I got earlier, which you were being quite pushy about 'helping' me with. And because you respect me so damn much, you went snooping around in my past. Stirring up stuff. And now I've got investigators wondering if they missed something with me. Thanks. Thanks a hell of a lot." She went to push past him, wanting nothing more than to end this conversation. She'd been badly rattled by the phone call and this little confrontation only sealed her initial instinct when she'd heard the name Geronimo. She needed to leave here. Tonight.

He took her arm gently but firmly as she brushed by and

turned her around to face him. "I started this whole thing because I wanted to protect Kate. And her kids."

"Admirable," she said, trying to maintain the steely façade,
thinking her heart might beat straight out of her chest any second. Did the terror show in her eyes?

"I help people for a living, Elena. I can help you, too. If
something is wrong, you can—"

"What? Trust you?" She tried to yank free, but he didn't let
her. "I can see not confronting me with your concerns in the
beginning, but now you're acting like you're all concerned about
me personally. How am I supposed to believe that when you
just admitted you're suspicious of me? When you had this supposed big change of heart about me, why not ask me straight
out then?"

"I'm asking you now."

His gaze was locked on hers, so intent, so focused. So trustworthy and steady. Still, she wavered. It was too big a thing to
leave to a split-second judgment call. But she was running out
of time. And running out of places to go. Trusting only herself
was getting her just so far.

"Elena, my instincts told me that something wasn't one
hundred percent with you. Yes, I dug around. It's also a big
part of what I do. So I'll lay my cards out first. I haven't found
anything specific, and yet I know this isn't where you want to
be. Something is keeping you from being in the world you've
worked hard to be part of and I don't think it's your horse. I
don't think you're a danger to Kate, but given the way your
face went white earlier when the name Geronimo was mentioned, I am thinking you might be in danger yourself."

"And you're worried that if I'm in danger, Kate or her operation or Dalton Downs is at risk."

He took both of her arms then, pulled her closer. "I'm worried about you. I can take care of the rest, but I can't take care
of you unless you let me."

"Maybe I don't want to be taken care of."

"So you've said. But maybe it's not about what you want, but about what you need. I think you need a little help." He gentled his hold, tugging her another inch closer. "I know it's hard to accept help from anyone. Trust me, I know. Especially someone you don't know well. I wouldn't have thought I'd get caught up in you. I never get involved with anyone, on any side, of anything I view as work-related. You took me by surprise."

"So did you," she said, without meaning to, which only caused his gaze to intensify, something she hadn't thought possible.

"Your gentleness with the animals, this innate strength you have, with them, with those around you, your confidence, your ease with yourself and with everyone else. You command attention without demanding it. You command attention just by being you. You certainly have mine."

She didn't know what to say to that. As a means of getting her to lower her defenses, she had to admit, it was pretty damn effective. Standing this close, looking into his eyes, she saw no sign of deception, no wavering. He was either very, very good at his job, or he was telling her the absolute truth. She wished the stakes on knowing which it was weren't so high.

"I only started this to make sure everything was on the up-and-up, because I take care of what's mine. Mac, Finn, Kate, her kids, even her damn horses fall under my care as long as I'm part of Trinity, which I will be for as long as it exists. I'm loyal, and I'm trustworthy to those who earn it."

"How have I earned either of those things from you? You know nothing of what might be going on with me."

"Call it the same gut instinct that led me to you in the first place." He reached up and tucked a loose strand of hair behind her ear, then very lightly ran his fingertip along her cheekbone and down along her chin.

The brief contact made her shiver, but in a good way. He talked about commanding attention. He had no idea.

"Any doubts I had about you being trouble, or being in trouble, were resolved earlier."

She stiffened then. "Because I let you—"

"No," he said immediately. "I wasn't talking about that, though you have to admit the strength of the attraction between us isn't something to be easily dismissed. I'm certain that interlude we shared was no more normal for you than it was for me."

"No . . . no, that wasn't my typical morning routine."

The corners of his mouth curved. "And that, your ability to find even a shred of humor at a time when I know you're not feeling remotely jovial, is another draw. I get you, Elena."

Three easy little words, but they packed a pretty good punch. *I get you.* It was what she'd been trying to put into place since he'd walked into the barn that day. She'd tried to pass it off as a physical thing, a chemistry thing . . . but it was much more than that. Or she'd have never let him put his hands on her. He got her. "Do you think I get you?" she asked, before she could think better of it.

"I think nothing gets by you, not even me. Especially not me. You pull no punches, and take no bullshit. You intimidate the hell out of me, the way you look at me, and see . . . me. So, yeah. You get me. And that was before I ever got on the damn horse."

She fought the urge to smile then. How did he do that? Her carefully constructed life was literally falling to pieces . . . and he was making her smile. Like she had nothing better to do than stand here and flirt. Only this wasn't about flirting. This was fast-forward relationship building. Something she doubted either of them would have engaged in if the situation had been any different.

"So, what was it that decided you, then? On my being in trouble, rather than being trouble?"

"When she said the name Geronimo, you looked terrified."

"How did that tell you anything?"

"Because what you didn't look, was guilty."

She swallowed hard . . . and wondered if he saw the guilt on her face now. He made it seem too easy—just take his help, tell him everything, and hope for the best. She wished she could do that. More than she'd ever wished for anything in a very long time. "The man on the phone was an insurance investigator. He wanted to know if I had any additional information on the events surrounding Geronimo's death. Seems you, or whoever you had do it, calling and asking them questions about me has made them suspicious."

"So just tell them you don't know anything else."

She shook her head. "These guys have been trying their damnedest not to pay Mr. Vondervan a dime on his insurance policy and have apparently managed to string this out this long. And you throw them a nice bone to gnaw at a little while longer. Prolong the Vondervans' grief, prolong the paperwork. And toss me right back into the arena I purposely left behind." She tugged her elbows free this time, fervently hoping he took the diversionary tactic at face value, even while silently apologizing to him. He did want to help her. She believed him. But she simply couldn't tell him. Couldn't risk that. No matter how badly she wanted to. Maybe because she so badly wanted to.

She turned away, but he stepped around her and took her straight into his arms, pulling her flush up against him.

"Let me go," she demanded.

"I will. As soon as you let me say my piece."

"Fine." She tried not to look him directly in the eye, to focus on some point just to the side of his face, but he wouldn't allow that. Maybe he did get her, because while he was clearly not happy with her at the moment, he was also not walking away.

"I wasn't trying to bring trouble your way, far from it. But if there is no new information, then case closed, right? At least where you're concerned. So why are you so upset? Why the white face?"

"My horse is a few months away from delivering. I don't need them following me here, hassling me, just as a means of prolonging their case. I just told you—"

"I know what you told me." And just like that, he gentled his voice, gentled his touch, but the gaze was somehow even more intense for the sudden shift. "It's what you're *not* telling me. I'm trained for the subtle signals, too, you know. You're spooked." He lifted a hand to her face, and despite every instinct she had screaming at her to move away, she let him touch her again without so much as a tiny struggle.

It was no brief, tingling caress this time. He cupped her cheek, and kept his hand there, his touch warm and steadying. As well as stimulating and electrifying. It was more than she could handle. "I've told you everything there is to say." Her voice was wobbling, but he'd have had that effect on her even if she wasn't hanging by a thread.

Instead he leaned in and kissed her, gently but thoroughly, lifting his head again before she could decide what to do about it.

"You don't listen very well," she said, her voice reedy, her body shaking.

"I listen very well. I hear everything you're saying. And everything you're not. I don't know how else to make you believe I'm in your corner. If you're somehow involved in any of that mess back there, and your only solution is to run, I can offer you a better solution."

"Big talk," she murmured, desperately wanting to have the strength to resist this, to resist him.

"I can back it up."

And that was just it. Looking at him, so steady, so strong-willed, so profoundly sure of himself. So very sure of her. The very depth of need she'd developed for him, so swiftly, was more terrifying than the predicament she was already involved in. That alone was reason enough to step back. "I appreciate the offer, I do," she said quietly. "But there's nothing to tell." She slowly extricated herself from his arms. This time he let her go. And, perversely, her heart fell. "If you want me to resign my tenure here, I will. But I want you to know this— whatever happened to Geronimo had nothing to do with me."

Which, at least, was the truth. "I'm sure I'll be able to make them understand that. I was just worried about Springer. I—I need to go tend to her for a little bit here before heading back, and this is already more drama than she needs to be around."

He didn't look remotely convinced. So it surprised her when he stepped back and tipped his imaginary Stetson again. "I'll get out of your way, then. I should be getting Petunia back as well."

She nodded, but said nothing more. She'd already said far too much.

She watched him turn and stroll down the aisle toward the paddock. Just before passing through the barn doors, he turned. "Think about what I said, *mijita*. About everything I said. The offer to help stands, free and outside of anything between us. You have a resource now. A big one." He turned, then looked back one last time. "And if you're really worried about the welfare of your horse, then you might ask yourself if your current plan is what's best for her. Or what's best for you."

Chapter 13

Rafe looked up at the starless night sky and folded his arms more tightly against his chest. Damn chilly, even for spring. He leaned back against the trailer and kept his gaze trained on the barn. Lights had been on all evening, but it had been a few hours since Elena had gone inside. There had been no sign of her since.

Since she'd driven her truck and trailer around to the far side of the employee barn and parked it in loading position, anyway.

He'd known from the moment she'd left the field office this morning that her story was full of holes and that she was full of shit. She was also not as smart as he'd given her credit for if she'd really believed he'd just back off after their little talk earlier. He'd been up close and personal, and he happened to know what true terror looked like. She'd been pasty-white and, despite her surprising mettle during their confrontation, had looked like a light breeze might take her right out.

Not involved, my ass.

Problem was, now *he* was involved. And not just for Kate. He'd been honest with her on that score. Though if he found out something to change his opinion of who was likely to be the victim here, and who wasn't, he'd do whatever he had to, to see justice done. Through proper channels . . . or his own.

But those eyes of hers had gotten to him. They had told him

in a way she couldn't that there was far more to this story, a story he probably wasn't going to like. His gut told him she was in over her head and didn't know how to get herself out. He didn't know what her options were, but he doubted running was the best one of the lot. More than likely, it was the only one she thought she had. She wouldn't be the first to think so.

Just then the lights winked out inside the barn. A moment later the big plank doors started to creak open. His eyes had long since adjusted to the dark, so it was easy to spot her walking through the barn doors. Even easier to spot the horse she was leading out behind her.

He stayed in the shadows beside the trailer as she loaded Springer on board. He waited until the mare was safely in, and the trailer door securely shut. Only when she moved around the back of the trailer and headed toward the driver's side door did he finally straighten and move into her path. "Going somewhere?"

She let out a little scream and jumped back a full foot. He could see the whites of her widened eyes in what little moon-glow there was, slivering down from between the clouds. "Christ, you scared the—never mind. What are you doing out here?"

"I could ask you the same question."

"My horse, my trailer, my truck. Not breaking any rules or laws, last I checked, and I haven't had a curfew since I was sixteen. Now, if you don't mind." She tried to move around him, but he shifted to block her path.

"I didn't say anything about breaking rules. I asked you if you were going somewhere."

"The answer seems pretty obvious."

"Running is not the answer."

"Says the man who doesn't even know what the question is."

"Only because you won't tell me." He reached out but she quick-stepped back out of his reach. "Elena—"

"I'm not cutting and running, okay? I'm just moving Springer."

"Because?"

"None of your damn business. I'll be back in time to handle my work responsibilities. Now, unless you have some other reason to keep me here."

"Why the Midnight Express? Don't you think someone will figure out she's not out here any longer?"

"I don't know that it really matters one way or the other. To anyone but you, apparently." She gave him her best steely-eyed glare, something he realized a racehorse-trainer likely perfected as a matter of survival.

Well, she was about to find out that he was a horse of an entirely different color. "How were you planning to explain Springer's sudden defection to Kate?"

"When Kate asks me, I'll be more than happy to explain the situation." She tried once again to move around him. Once again, he blocked her path. She sighed and grumbled something under her breath. "It's late, my horse isn't thrilled with me at the moment, and I really need to be on the road."

He didn't budge.

"If I told you it was a matter of life and death, would that make you move?"

"A matter of life and death. Whose?"

"Springer's. What the hell did you think? I think she's having early contractions."

"She's due soon though, right? Why not call your vet to come out here?"

"Because I'm not independently wealthy, is why. Kenny can keep her at his place for observation easier than I can keep a trained medical professional here."

He wasn't sure if he believed her or not, but Springer chose that moment to give her trailer a little kick, and he realized it was a chance he couldn't take. He moved and let her by, but was already halfway around the front of the truck before she could get in and get her belt on.

"What do you think you're doing now?" he heard her call out.

He opened the passenger door and hopped in. "Riding shotgun. Would it be better for you to ride in the back with her? Tell me where to go and I'll drive."

She looked at him with open skepticism. Not that he could entirely blame her. At least she had some decent survival instincts.

"I'm bull-headed and I can be a right pain in the ass when I need to be, but I'm not an ogre. If your horse is in trouble, I'll do whatever I can to help out."

She held his gaze a moment longer, then slammed her door shut and turned the engine on. "I can't ride in the back. Not if I want to keep my bones intact." She glanced over at him. "I suppose short of bodily dragging you out, I'm stuck with you."

He smiled. "You do get me."

"Lucky me."

He pulled the seat belt across his chest and snapped it in place. "You have no idea."

"Suit yourself." She ignored him completely after that, focusing instead on maneuvering them across the rutted gravel path to the main service road. It led to all the Dalton Downs outbuildings and barns, as well as up to the main house, and, along another route, out to the main road.

Her jaw remained tense, her shoulders hunched, even after they left the farm behind. Whatever the real story was, she wasn't faking the worry or the fear. It was etched across every inch of her face. Question was, exactly what was she worried about? Protecting a horse that had miscarried once before? Or something much bigger than that?

Before he could ask where they were headed—not that she'd tell him, but it couldn't hurt to try—she pulled out a cell phone and flipped it open. She pressed a button, then held it to her ear. "Kenny, it's Elena. Yes, yes, I am." She paused. "I know. I'm so very grateful. We'll be there in a couple hours. I owe you." She flipped the phone shut and dropped it in her lap, then went right back to keeping her full attention on the road.

A couple of hours? He thought about prodding her, but she hadn't thrown the fit he'd expected her to when he'd invited himself along. Which made him tend to believe she was telling the truth, at least inasmuch as she was just tucking Springer away somewhere, not taking off herself. She hadn't thrown so much as a gear bag in the truck with her, so that supported her story as well.

Of course, there were other reasons she could be stashing her horse away from Dalton Downs. It was awfully convenient that she had to suddenly move her horse the very same night she'd gotten that upsetting phone call. Even more convenient that the whole episode was happening in the middle of the night. Fewer questions that way. And the ones she did get would be a lot easier to handle after the fact.

Although she certainly didn't seem to be having too hard a time handling him.

"Is Springer close enough to term that delivering early has a decent chance of success?" He knew little about regular childbirth other than sex ed basics. He knew even less about foaling.

"Her track record isn't so good."

Which, he noted, didn't answer the question. "How long do horses gestate, anyway?"

"Almost a year."

"Almost as in, like us humans, or almost as in—"

"You ask a lot of questions."

He didn't apologize. "I was always told that was the best way to learn things."

"Eleven months."

"And viable at what? Ten?"

"Springer lost hers at forty weeks. She had to deliver a dead foal. Almost killed her. So, hard to say. I'm not a vet."

"But I'm sure you've witnessed your share, or been around it."

"Around it? Yes. Actually witnessing it? Rarely. Horses are amazingly sneaky when it comes to giving birth. You can watch them round the clock, step out to use the bathroom or take a phone call, come back and they're down and working it out." She smiled a little. "Middle of the night seems to be a favorite foaling time."

"Well, I'm not female, but I think I could understand the innate desire for privacy."

"When your baby isn't worth a few million dollars, you get to be as private as you want."

He smiled at that. "So, only champion racehorse owners watch their property carefully?"

He noticed her shoulders had relaxed a little, the lines grooving the corners of her mouth and fanning out from the corners of her eyes had smoothed a little.

"No, all horse owners pretty much hover, but more often than not, without a crew of people and expensive web cam setups, you miss the blessed event—or a good part of it, anyway."

"How are you going to monitor yours if you're a couple hours away?"

The grooves and hunched shoulders returned. He wished it didn't have to be that way. "It's more important that she be safe than that I'm there."

"You must really trust Kenny."

"As much as I trust anyone."

"Which means?"

She cut him a look. "Which means I trust myself to handle things when I can, but I'm not a doctor. Kenny is. What were you implying?"

He lifted his hands. "Nothing. So . . . it's good you have friends that will help."

"You say that like you're surprised I have friends."

"No, I was surprised you asked for help. I'm glad you have

someone to turn to that you *will* turn to. You—I guess it seemed as if you'd intentionally cut yourself off from your former world, so that part surprised me, too. My mistake. But don't read something negative into everything I say."

"You barge your way into my life and into my personal problems and then try and lecture me about what I should do. Not to mention the fact that I'm worried sick about my horse. I can't imagine why I'm not being more warm and generous."

He was silent for a moment, mostly because she had a point. When the silence stretched to the point of being strained, he spoke. "You have a lot going on. You're in the middle of a change in personal direction. I understand why you wouldn't want to open yourself up to anything new." He shifted in his seat, looked at her. "But here we are, anyway. I don't expect anything. If you take my help, I still won't expect anything."

She said nothing.

"Okay, look at it this way. If the worst-case scenario is that I think you're trouble for Kate and want you off Dalton Downs property, I'd have done that. I don't need to hang around, or badger you with my offers of help. We both already know that if it's more of what happened earlier in the tack room that I'm after, I could probably have gotten that as well. Maybe even more so if I hadn't nagged at you and pissed you off. And on top of all of that, my job is to champion the underdog. So . . . what else could my ulterior motive be?"

He had no idea if she was pondering what he said, or if she'd just tuned him out entirely, until she suddenly said, "What if you're championing someone else? How do I know *I'm* your underdog?"

"Who else would it be?"

She glanced over at him like he'd sprouted two heads. Of course she wasn't going to hand that information out, but the fact that she'd alluded to having some kind of adversary was a start, if a small one.

"So which am I? Underdog case file? Or . . . something else?"

"Both, in a way, I suppose. I've been hanging around because I'm worried, and I want to know what's up."

"Worried for Kate, you mean."

"Initially, yes. Now I'm worried for you. I want to know more about you, but not just for research purposes. If it would help, talk to Kate and Mac. They can personally vouch for my intent, too."

"Don't be ridiculous. They'll say whatever you want them to say."

"I'm not being ridiculous. I'm just trying to—"

"Help. I know. God, who knew being a good Samaritan could be so exhausting."

He looked at her, then noticed the tiniest of twitches at the corner of her mouth.

"I just don't know how else to go about proving to you that my intentions are good, here."

"I'm guessing the people you normally help, or try to, don't put up as much resistance."

"Sometimes they do. If they've been through something that has taught them that trusting only leads to more bad things happening."

"Is that a veiled hint?"

Now he smiled a little. "Maybe."

The twitch smoothed, and her sigh was a heavy one. "Listen, I appreciate . . . everything you just said. And your persistence is nothing short of—"

"Admirable?"

"I was going to say Chinese water torture, but in the interest of having to spend a four-hour round-trip with you, we can go with admirable."

"So this is where you say thanks, but no thanks. Again."

She offered him a brief smile of condolence. "I am grateful for the repeated offer, I really am. I'm sorry my reactions to things earlier today led you to believe I'm in some sort of serious trouble."

"At least do me the courtesy of not insulting my intelligence."

"Fine. Things might be a little complicated, but up to now, you've done nothing but complicate my life further. On a couple of different levels."

"I apologized for the inadvertent attention I brought your way, but I'm not apologizing for the rest."

"I didn't ask for an apology, did I?"

That caught him off guard. He settled back in his seat, frustrated and annoyed and turned on and . . . a whole lot of complicated things he didn't want to be. "I'll promise you one thing," he said.

"What is that?"

"If you won't let me help, I'll back off."

She glanced over at him, clearly skeptical. "No more digging? No more phone calls checking up on me?"

He didn't respond to that. He wasn't going to lie to her. "But you have to promise me—if something happens to make you think that Dalton Downs or anyone who lives or works there is in any kind of jeopardy—"

"Already done," she said quietly. "You didn't have to ask that."

"No insult intended." He reached out and touched her arm, so she looked over at him. "One more thing. If you find yourself changing your mind about needing help, I'd like to think I'd be the first person you'd come to."

She held his gaze for a fraction of a second longer, then dipped her chin in a quick, silent agreement, before turning her attention back to the road.

He accepted that, settled back in his seat, and let the subject drop. At least for the time being. Another dozen or so miles had passed before he put together what she'd just said. *Already done.* Meaning there had been a perceived threat and she'd already taken care of it?

The only thing she'd done was to move her horse.

He let the ride go on in silence as he decided how best to broach that subject again. "So, how has Springer been doing otherwise?" he asked, at length. "Has this pregnancy gone better than last time?"

"Yes, it has, but she's been in far more peaceful surroundings."

"So you think the move up here to Middleburg was the right thing to do, then."

"Most definitely."

"Can I ask . . . where does Kenny fit into all of this? With you?"

She shot him a look of surprise. "You don't mean is he *with me*, with me, do you? Because, first, you know he's old enough to be my father. And secondly, I'd have definitely never done what we did earlier, if—"

"I'm asking where Kenny fits into your new life versus your old life. Do you keep in touch with people from the world of racing?"

This time she kept her eyes glued to the road, but from what he could see of her expression, the wariness was back in full force. "I came here to get away from the hoopla so my horse could gestate in peace. And to consider what I want to do next with my career. I was already planning to leave Charlotte Oaks before . . . everything. But once all that happened, yes, it made the decision even easier. It was a really stressful time, so when I got confirmation that Springer was pregnant, it just seemed like the right time to step back, and out—for a little bit, anyway."

"And being gone for almost a year, don't you think that will hurt your career?"

"Possibly. It's a setback, to be certain, but I didn't burn any bridges."

"So you still have contacts from your time at Charlotte Oaks, then?"

"You already asked me that." She looked over at him. "This is starting to feel like digging again."

"If I'm digging, it's just to get to know you. You don't want my help, fine. But I'm admittedly attracted to you, and I think there's some mutual interest there. I just want to get to know you better."

She studied him for a moment, then turned back to look at the road ahead. "Yes," she said, at length. "I keep in touch with some people."

"Like Kenny."

"Kenny is one of the better equine vets around. He runs his own operation as well as a top-notch equine medical facility about halfway between here and Charlottesville. He was a good friend of my father. I've known him most of my life."

"Ah."

She swatted at his arm, surprising a laugh out of him. "What was that for?"

"That smug, masculine, 'ah.' Yes, Kenny is family to me. Nothing more. Your ego feel better now? Less threatened?"

He folded his arms, grinned unapologetically. "As a matter of fact, yes."

Her mouth dropped open, then shut again. "Men."

"Thank goodness, right?"

She remained silent on that one.

Still smiling a little, he asked, "Why not take Springer to Kenny and stay there from the beginning, when you found out she was pregnant?"

"He wasn't looking to hire at the time, and I'm not looking for a handout."

"And now?"

"Meaning, how am I going to pay for his services? He knows what's going on with Springer and was a bit insulted that I took the job with Kate and didn't even approach him about any of it. He's like family, and he considers me the same. It's why he showed up at Dalton Downs a few weeks ago. He's kept in touch all through her gestation and when things started to go south tonight, I called him. He wouldn't take no for an answer on me bringing her to him for the remainder of her time. To be honest, I didn't fight him too hard this time around. Pride is a fool's conceit when someone you love is in jeopardy."

"Pithy."

"Truth." A mile or two passed, and she looked over at him. "I do know when to ask for help."

"So it seems." They fell into a more comfortable silence for a short while, then he finally said, "Is that the only reason you're moving Springer away from Dalton Downs?"

She didn't so much as blink, but she didn't look at him, either. Nor did she say anything.

His tone quiet, just loud enough to be heard over the rumble of the engine and the road noise of the big truck tires, he said, "When I asked earlier, that you keep any problems from your past separate and away from the folks at Dalton Downs, you said you'd already done that. Were you talking about this trip tonight? Or . . ."

She was quiet for so long, he didn't think she was going to answer. He'd insulted her more than once tonight, not intending to, but at the moment he was more concerned with finding a way past the sturdy walls she'd erected. If he happened to piss her off again trying, then so be it. Ultimately he was more concerned about figuring out what was going on and, if possible, doing something to fix it, than he was about whether she'd still like him when all was said and done. He cared enough at this point, though God knew why, when she was such a contrary thing. He was more concerned with her being okay than with whether he got what he wanted out of this.

Which begged the question . . . what *did* he want out of this? He was still pondering the rather surprising answer to that, when she interrupted his thoughts.

"I moved Springer for Springer's sake," she said, then paused, then ultimately fell silent again.

"The phone call today—"

She gave an impatient sigh, but he noted her hands tightened on the wheel until her knuckles turned white. "You're like a broken record. Change of subject."

"I was just going to ask where you left things today. Do you have to go back to Charlottesville to answer some more questions?" Then another piece fell into place. "Or is someone coming out to Dalton Downs to save you the trip?" *And was it better all the way around if your horse wasn't about when he or she did?*

And if Rafe was on the right track . . . what did her horse have to do with all of this?

"I have no idea what happens next. They know where to contact me if they want me. Right now my focus is on making sure Springer is healthy and stays that way, that her baby is all right, and also stays that way. And I still have a job to do." She shot him a look. "That is, unless you think otherwise?"

"I'm trying to help you, not get you fired. *Was* trying to help you," he reiterated. "I'm interested in you, regardless. My wanting to know you better isn't going to change whether I help you or not."

"Okay, if this is about getting to know one another, then tag. You're it. Your turn to talk about your past, your life."

Shit. "I'm not all that interesting."

She laughed. "Right. You're the most frustrating, irritating, persistent, intriguing, complex man. What you're not is boring. I can't imagine that the life that led you from a tough existence with a single mom to where you are now, happened all smooth and ripple-free."

"How did this get to be about me?"

"Fair play. You want this to be about us? Us is two people, not just one badgering the other."

"I wasn't badgering, I was—"

"Pretending to get to know me so you could keep digging. Pit bulls are less determined than you."

He sat back in his seat, turning his attention ahead toward the road.

He heard the smile in her voice when she spoke. "Not so much fun when the shoe is on the other foot now, is it?"

"Ask me anything you like. Just be prepared to yawn. Which, considering the late hour and the long drive, is probably dangerous to your health. And mine."

"I'll take my chances."

"Now who's the pit bull?" he grumbled. This wasn't going at all like he'd planned. But then, he'd never planned on anyone like Elena Caulfield.

"So, tell me the story of you," she said, with more enthusiasm than he'd heard all night.

"I spend most of my time working."

"Okay, so tell me more about the work you do. I know you said you help people who aren't always in a position to help themselves, but how did all that come about? How did you three go from summer camp hellions to Trinity, Inc., helpers of the downtrodden?"

Rafe sighed, but knew it was only fair. If he wanted her to open up to him, maybe opening up to her was the way to earn her trust. "We spent summers together at a camp in upstate New York and stayed close during the years afterward."

"Have you been working together since you became adults?"

"No. We kept in touch, but we had our own paths initially. We're about as different from one another as you can get. Finn was, of course, born and raised on Dalton Downs, one of the silver-spoon set, though he never acted like it, much to the chagrin of his father. Mac was the son of the camp handyman, who also happened to be an alcoholic and not the nicest guy in the world."

"And you? I know you said your mom was a maid and you lived in the city—"

"I grew up in the Bronx. I went to camp as a charity case. My mother's employer sent me every summer."

"Generous of him."

"No, he did it because it allowed her to keep working for

him while I wasn't in school. And it made him look like a good guy."

"He wasn't?"

"Can't say I agreed with his business practices, but he gave my mom steady employment, which kept food on our table, so I can hardly complain. But the moment I was able to, I got her away from that."

"She raised a good guy, then. Where did you all end up?"

"Mac was a cop in New York, a detective, then later worked high-end surveillance in the private sector. He has a knack for all things mechanical. The only decent thing he got from his dad. Finn was a lawyer, working for the district attorney's office, until his dad passed and he took over here."

"And you?"

"I put myself through business school, then took some classes in computer science."

"You said you were the research guy. So you're the computer geek of the group?" Her smile grew. "Hard to imagine."

He shrugged. "I'm good with information technology."

Her smile faded. "Which is why you were picked to take me on. Makes sense now."

"Elena—"

"No, I asked to know more about you. I appreciate you being honest."

"Good policy to have."

"There's a pointed comment. So," she went on, before he could respond, "when did you three decide to band together?"

"After Finn's father died. That was about four years ago. Finn inherited Dalton Downs, which was a surprise."

"Why is that?"

"He and his father didn't see eye to eye on, well, pretty much everything. Finn wanted to save the world, whereas his father just wanted to own it. Any way he could. To say that Finn didn't admire his father's business practices is putting it mildly."

"So his father left the place to him anyway?"

"Left it all, yes. I suppose, from what I know of the man, he'd hoped to prove to Finn in death what he couldn't in life, which was that everyone had a price tag, even Finn."

"Well, he took it, so what does that say?"

"He spent well over a year dismantling the empire his father had built on the blood, sweat, and, in a lot of cases, the illegal tears of others, and turned it into a new enterprise. We started a little over two years ago."

"Trinity."

Rafe smiled, hoping the old man was still spinning in his grave. "Yes. Trinity."

"And so you use his ill-gotten gains—"

"To help the very types of people he spent a lifetime screwing over, yes."

"And you all quit what you were doing to come work for Finn?"

"Well, our skills blended together well. Each of us had been working at a common goal, of sorts, in our own way, but it would be fair to say we each felt a good bit of frustration. Working for Finn, through privately funded channels, allows us to get things done more . . . efficiently, seeing as we aren't as bound by . . . societal restrictions."

She glanced over at him, clearly concerned. "Are you saying you work outside the law?"

"No. I'm just saying when you work for yourself and set your own rules, you have a lot more flexibility in how you go about achieving your goals."

"And how do you find your . . . clients? Do you advertise, or—"

"No. As I told you before, we're not a charity. There are always people in need of our brand of help. They're not too hard to find, unfortunately."

"So how do you pick which ones you help?"

"Oh, it's a relatively selfish process. We help those who simultaneously give us the maximum amount of pleasure in winning."

She laughed. "At least you're honest."

"Always."

She was silent for a little while, then said, "You know, I wouldn't have pegged you for the street kid."

"What do you mean?"

"I mean, if I knew that, out of the three of you, one was the street kid, one the rich kid, and one the country kid . . . I'd have picked you as the silver spooner."

He laughed. "Finn would love that."

"Sorry, no offense."

"Oh, none taken. But trust me, there aren't too many Latino trust-fund babies out there. Finn is far more the stereotype."

"And yet you said he wasn't really like that at all."

"No. Not at all. He was just sort of born into the wrong family, though it all worked out in the end."

"He became a silver-spoon Robin Hood."

Rafe laughed at that. "Exactly."

"So who thought up the venture? I mean, it's not your normal business proposal."

"Finn's not your normal businessman."

"Robin Hood, right. True."

It was comfortable between them, and as the miles wore on, he got her to open up a little, too, about her childhood, and growing up on various farms and ranches. She glowed when she spoke of her parents, especially her father, and seemed to relax a little. So, despite his desire to push more in the direction of what had happened at Charlotte Oaks, he found himself encouraging her to continue with her childhood stories, even trading some of his own. Rafe wasn't typically one to talk about himself, or the inner workings of Trinity, much less his childhood, and when he did, he was usually gauging every word. With her, however, it felt natural. Easy. Ridiculously so, in fact.

She slowed the truck down. "We're here," she said, and he watched as the tension tightened her up again.

The more time he spent with her, the more he wanted of her. Preferably without the haunted look in her eyes. He supposed in order to get what he wanted, he was going to have to slay some demons. Whether she wanted him to or not.

She rolled the truck to a stop and unbuckled her seat belt. "You can just stay here. It won't take all that long."

He unbuckled his belt. "I'll come with you. I'll stay out of the way," he added, when she began to argue the point. "You're worried about her. And I'm worried about you."

"I really wish you wouldn't."

"Too late for that." And he got out of the truck.

Far too late.

Chapter 14

She should never have let him in her truck.

Elena walked around the back of the trailer and spoke to Springer in low, measured tones as she opened the doors and slowly backed her out. Right now, keeping her mare safe was the only thing that mattered. And that meant keeping her away from Dalton Downs. She needed to talk to Kenny privately, and wondered how she'd do that with old eagle-ears shadowing her every move.

What bothered her even more was the fact that his presence on the ride over had actually been a blessing of sorts. His persistence drove her batty, but it was hard to deny that he had a steadying, calming influence. Getting her to talk about her childhood, and telling her stories about his, had made what would have been a teeth-grinding, white-knuckle drive a hell of a lot easier to bear.

He was always so in control, so certain of himself and his abilities. It wasn't arrogance so much as assuredness. And that was powerful stuff for her at the moment. It was hard not to be tempted to lean on him. Just for a tiny moment. He was sturdy, and strong. The stalwart knight to Finn's Robin Hood.

She swore silently at her silly, fanciful notions. She'd better get the stars right out of her eyes and keep her two feet planted squarely on the terra firma.

Complicating that, however, was Rafe, who fell into step beside her, making it impossible to clear her head. Fortunately, he said nothing as she walked Springer by a halter toward the paddock and barns, which were situated about twenty yards away. There were only a few lights on around the ring, and the large, square farmhouse sitting off to the left was dark, but there was a welcoming glow coming from inside the stables.

Just as she reached the paddock gate, Kenny slipped out from the crack between the paddock doors. Out of nowhere her eyes welled up, and she quickly scrunched her eyebrows and frowned down at her boots in an attempt to ward off the sudden spate of unwanted tears. She was more stressed-out than she'd even realized. But he was a welcome sight and she was having a hard time keeping it together.

He opened his arms and, after handing the lead rope to Rafe, she stepped right into them and hugged him back every bit as tightly as he was hugging her.

"So," he said, his voice as gruff as it always was. "How is the little hotsy-totsy?"

She laughed and sniffled as she glanced back at Springer. "Better, but I'm still worried."

Kenny released her and took a walk around the horse, then introduced himself to her and rubbed his hands along her neck and flanks. Springer stamped her feet a bit, but tolerated the intrusion. "We'll take a good look. See what's what." He looked up at Elena, then past her shoulder. His eyebrows lifted as he straightened. "He still hanging about?" He stepped past her. "Sorry," he said, sticking his hand out as he walked toward Rafe. "We weren't properly introduced before. Ken Crawford."

"Raphael Santiago."

Kenny looked between the two of them, a mixture of curiosity and surprise on his face. Perhaps a little amusement when Elena sighed. "Friend of Elena's?" he asked, ignoring her expression.

"Student, actually." Rafe looked at her. "And friend."

Elena's cheeks warmed, but so did a little spot inside her chest. She'd been resisting letting him in for what felt like forever at this point, but feeling how good it was to have Kenny there, someone she trusted, made it that much harder not to wonder what it would be like to have that same warmth and trust with Rafe. To have him there to turn to, depend on, good times and bad. *Dangerous thoughts*. She should have kicked him out of the truck right off the bat. Too much time under his influence while she was this stressed-out was only going to weaken her defenses.

It was already getting harder and harder to remember why she had to be defensive around him in the first place.

Tired, she was just tired. So incredibly tired.

She looked back at Kenny. "Yes, student and friend. Actually, he works with my current employer's significant other."

"Ah," Kenny said, but the way he looked at the two of them said a whole lot more. "Well, why don't we get this little lady settled in for what's left of the night. I'll check her over thoroughly, make sure nothing is imminent this evening. She's traveled remarkably well, all things considered, so that is a hopeful sign."

"I can't tell you how much I appreciate this," Elena began, only to be met by Kenny's raised hand.

"Then don't. Now," he went on, "walk with me and fill me in on exactly what you've been observing."

Elena did as he asked, glancing back over her shoulder to see if Rafe was going to follow, but true to his word, he stayed by the truck, out of the way.

True to his word. How she wished she could just go with that. She could use a sounding board. Kenny could help with Springer, but even he didn't know the whole story. No one knew the whole story.

She took one last look at Rafe, then turned resolutely back to Kenny and walked him to the stables, feeling more conflicted than she had in a very long time. She could stash Springer here, where she'd be safe and in good hands. Leaving her here meant she'd quite probably miss the birth when the time came, given the distance. That alone was going to be one of the hardest things she'd ever done, but there were no other options. She had to keep her job, had to keep up at least the pretense that everything else was normal. The investigator hadn't mentioned Springer at all during their conversation, so as far as she knew, no one had yet pieced together that vital connection. Having her here with Kenny was Elena's best chance at keeping things that way.

"So, anything you want to tell me about?" Kenny asked, casting a look in Rafe's direction.

She didn't bother to play dumb. "I wish I knew the answer to that."

"Don't know much about the goings-on at Dalton Downs."

"They're not horse people, not in the true sense, so it's not surprising."

"Heard good things about the program your boss runs there, but that's about it. What is Mr. Big, Strong, and Silent's business?"

She nudged Kenny with her elbow to keep him from staring back at Rafe, indicating they were talking about him. "He helps people."

That earned her a wary look. "What kind of help?"

"Now, now."

"Loan sharks help people. I'm just sayin', how well do you know this character?"

"Not all that well." She paused, fought the urge to look back herself, and added, "Yet."

"Ah. So that's how it is."

She sighed. "I don't know."

"You've got a lot on your plate right now. Sure it's the right time to bring someone into things?"

"Not remotely sure. Also not sure I have a choice."

"Nosy, is he? Or is he just sniffing around hoping for something else?"

"Kenny."

"Hey, he's a guy who looks like he knows his way around the fairer sex, and I'm betting they don't say no too often. You, on the other hand—"

"Am just this aging, cloistered spinster, to hear you tell it."

"I'm just sayin', you're not big on the personal-life stuff and I don't want you taken in by a smooth talker."

"I live in a world filled with men who possess way more than their fair share of testosterone. Trust me, I can handle—"

"That guy? He's not from your world. He's not distracted by racing forms and margins and the final stretch." Kenny paused just outside the stable. "And he looks at you like . . . well, a man both starved for a really good steak, and a man who'd kill to make sure that steak lands on his plate, and his plate only."

"Oh great, I've gone from a washed-up spinster to a steak-house special. I'm not sure I've ever felt so desirable."

"I know you can take care of yourself. Told your daddy that when we caught you out on that big App, kicking the daylights out of him so he'd jump the damn fence. What were you? Six? Still don't know how the hell you even got up on his back."

"Five. And I lured him to the fence with grass, then climbed up and hopped on."

"See? Horses you know. Men? Not so sure."

She smiled sweetly at him. "I talked you into watching my dangerously pregnant horse. Guess I'm not doing too badly."

"I'm pretty sure I was the one doing the talking." But he sighed a little. "Just . . . be careful. Let me worry about your horse, not you, okay?"

She squeezed his arm. "I'll try. And I'm sorry, again, for bringing you into this. I wish I had some other way—"

"Your daddy would come back and shoot me dead if he thought you were in need and I didn't step up."

She smiled a bit more sadly this time. "True enough. Thank you, Kenny."

"Come on, let's get this girl looked at, then tucked into bed."

"Okay."

"Now, tell me more about this fellow. You say he helps people?"

Elena sighed and followed Kenny inside the barn.

An hour later, she was hugging him good-bye and taking one last turn stroking Springer's mane, fighting tears once again. "You better give fair warning on this baby, missy," she whispered fiercely.

"I'll page you the instant she's in real labor. When are you coming out to see her next?"

"I'm going to try for Tuesday. I get done early, should be out here by six."

"I'll get Gerta to put some dinner on for you."

"No need to go to any trouble."

"No trouble. Damn woman cooks like we feed an army here." He glanced out to her truck. "And I'd feel a lot better if you weren't making that long drive alone."

"Make up your mind. First you tell me to watch out for him, now you want him tagging along with me."

"I'm just saying, if Mr. Tall, Dark, and Menacing out there wants to hitch a ride over, we can feed him, too. He looks like he can take care of himself." He looked at Elena. "Maybe he can take care of you, too."

She didn't bother to argue. She just hugged him, perhaps a little more tightly than absolutely necessary. "Thank you," she whispered against his shoulder. "For all of it. I don't know how I can repay you."

He leaned her back, faded blue eyes staring directly into hers. "You don't." He was silent for a moment, then he said, "You sure it's just Springer you're worried about?"

She worked hard not to stiffen up. The long day had taken a pretty big toll, and she was dead on her feet, so she felt the panic more than she showed it. "I just want her to get through the next couple of months and deliver a healthy baby. Then I'll be fine." Which was, for the most part, the truth. At least, she prayed to God it would be.

"Then that's what we'll do." He didn't let her go right away, though. "I'm a horse guy, Elena, so I can help you with her. Not so good with the people stuff, never have been. So promise me if you're needing some assistance, too, that you'll ask for help like you did with me for Springer. She's going to need you, so will the baby. You can't be falling apart."

"Just knowing she's in safe hands helps me."

"Elena."

"I know." She sighed, then paused at the door and stared across the paddock at Rafe. "So . . . if I do need help, what do you think?"

He looked from her to Rafe, then back to her. "I think you look at him much the same way he looks at you."

"That could just be hormones."

He choked on a little laugh. "Could be. From what you told me back there while we were checking Springer out, sounds like he's a man who stands up for the ones he cares about. I understand your concerns about the reasons behind his initial interest in you. But he also sounds like a straight shooter. The only way I see him crossing you is if you come between him and those who have been in his care far longer than you have."

"That's not going to happen."

"Well, then I guess you have your answer."

She was silent for a moment, admitting to herself that in telling Kenny about Rafe, hearing herself describe him, talk about him out loud, had brought her to the same conclusion. "Yeah. I guess I do."

He squeezed her. "It's late. Let him drive back. I'll see you in a few days."

"Okay. If anything—"

"I'll buzz you if she so much as bats her eyelashes the wrong way."

"Thanks." She kissed his cheek. "I'll find some way to pay you back. I don't care what you say."

"Get yourself back on track, and back in your own world. That'll be payment enough."

She nodded, but as she walked away from him, toward Rafe, she couldn't help but think she didn't even know what her world was anymore.

Rafe pushed away from the truck. "Everything okay?"

"For now. Kenny will do a more thorough exam tomorrow. She's just uncomfortable—the baby is moving a lot, Kenny thinks, and it's making her nervous. She handled the ride okay, but he wants her to settle in further before doing anything more invasive."

Rafe nodded. "Are we leaving the trailer here?"

"No, it comes back with me. It's mine, but I loan it out to Kate on occasion, when she picks up new stock."

He fell into step beside her as they walked to the front of the truck. "Speaking of new stock, how is Bonder doing?"

She gave him a look of surprise.

"What?"

"Just—never mind." It was silly to be touched that he cared about the day-to-day details of her world. Bonder had put her on her ass, and he'd witnessed it. Of course he remembered. "He's doing okay. Tracey has taken over some of his training. It's been good for both of them. I think."

He cocked his head.

"Well, it's just, she's getting attached. And I—I'm not sure what Kate's plans are for him. I've been meaning to talk to her about it, had thought I would this morning, then—" She broke off, not wanting to dive back into that subject, or any subject that had to do with why he'd ingratiated himself into her world. It was enough that he was here now, and foolish as it may be, she just wanted the comfort of his company a little while longer, without the real world intruding.

"Maybe tomorrow," was all he said, and the fact that her throat tightened a little in gratitude was warning enough that she wasn't thinking clearly.

She nodded, then went to move around him to open the driver's door.

He put his hand on her arm, keeping his body between her

and the truck. "Let me drive home. It's been a long day for you."

"I can get myself home."

"You could probably slay dragons bareback. I'm not saying you're weak. I'm saying you're tired. Emotionally ragged, as would be expected of someone who's just spent the last—how many hours?—worrying about someone she loves."

Really, he had to stop saying all the right things. She was having a hard enough time keeping her head straight about him.

Well, then, I guess you have your answer.

Kenny's comment floated through her mind.

"Let me take you home, Elena."

He'd said it quietly, without a trace of pity or condescension. *Just one friend helping another.*

"Exactly," he said.

She hadn't realized she'd said that last part out loud. "I, uh—" She wasn't used to this. She was usually the one caretaking those around her, the capable one, the steady one, the one with all the answers.

He gently took her arm and tucked it in his own and walked her around the front of the truck. "You get to be the boss when I'm on horseback, but the rest of the time, just let me be your friend."

He reached for the handle and she stopped him.

He turned to face her, his expression all set to argue. She stopped him with a kiss to his cheek.

His eyebrows lifted. "What . . . was that?"

"Thank you," she said softly.

"For?"

"The offer of friendship."

"It's more than an offer. I'd like it to be fact."

"I—I would, too. It's just . . . people don't become friends with a snap of the fingers. Real friends, I mean. You should understand that better than anyone. Someone who's had friends in his life since childhood."

"I do understand. You can have all kinds of friendships. Some develop over time, some are destined to remain casual." He stepped closer, so her back brushed up against the door of the truck. "And then there are the rare few who just become part of your orbit from the moment they step into it. I like it that you're there. Even if you do drive me crazy."

She stared into those steady, dark, reassuring eyes of his. "Yeah," she said after a long moment. "I'm liking you there, too. Even if you drive me crazy, too." The idea that she was letting him in, letting him get closer, now of all times, was both thrilling and terrifying.

But here he stood.

And when he lowered his head toward hers, she didn't turn away.

Chapter 15

He'd been craving the taste of her since their first kiss. He'd convinced himself he must have embellished the hell out of it, because a kiss was just a kiss, right? No way could one kiss be so different, so consuming, so intoxicating . . . so addicting.

As it turned out he was wrong. Way wrong.

Her lips were so soft, and the way she caught her breath in the back of her throat, that little guttural moan, made him go instantly rock-hard. It was all he could do not to plaster her back against the truck and devour her whole. He wove his fingers into her hair, tilted her head so he could take the kiss deeper, half expecting her to push him away. He had no idea if Kenny was still standing over by the barn, or if he could see the two of them, and he really didn't care, but he thought she might.

Except her fingers were clutching at his shoulders, and when her lips parted beneath his, she drew him in almost greedily. Christ, but he wanted her. Purely and fully.

Somewhere, rationality prevailed and he lifted his head, just a fraction, so he could still feel the warmth of her breath, her skin. "Elena . . . this isn't—I mean, my offer to help, it's not about . . . this."

Her gaze lifted to his and what he found there surprised him. Amusement.

"You're so worried that I'm going to think less of you for wanting more of this. What does that make me?"

He had her pinned against the truck now, and though he'd broken the kiss, he couldn't quite find the wherewithal to sever any additional contact. "You want more of this?"

"I'm not exactly pushing you away."

His lips twitched. "True. But I don't want to take advantage—"

"Of my weakened state?" She smiled dryly. "If I didn't want you manhandling me up against my truck, I'd stop you, even if I had one foot in the grave."

He smiled then, even as he gentled his hold on her. "I believe that."

"Good, then we're square."

"Meaning?"

"If I'm going to let you in, let you help, then why would I do that and cut this off? It doesn't make much sense, now does it? Life is hard enough, right?"

He grinned and shook his head. "I can't keep up with you."

"You can thank Kenny."

"What? What for?"

"He . . . sort of got me to think things through. About you."

"Then I definitely owe the man." She was smiling up at him, and it was like his entire world had shifted to some new position, rotating on a completely different axis, with an orbit that was no longer his own to navigate. It should have scared him more. He ran his thumb along her lower lip, watching her eyes darken under his touch, wishing like hell her dragons had already been slain. He wanted far, far more than either of them could give at the moment, so he settled for resting his hips against hers, lowering his mouth to hers. Another taste—he needed that much.

The kiss was gentle, almost sweet, and he felt his heart catch a little when she wove her fingers into his hair and held his head, keeping his mouth on hers, wanting as much as he did. He sighed when their lips finally parted.

"You matter to me, *mijita*," he whispered roughly. "It's the damnedest thing."

"Yeah," she agreed, her fingers playing in his hair. "The damnedest thing."

"You're going to have to let me all the way in, you know that."

He felt her shudder against him, and his hips moved almost of their own volition. It wasn't how he'd meant the statement, and he knew she knew that, but it didn't stop the rush of images that flooded his brain at the thought of how it would be when—not if—they finally had each other fully.

"Rafe—"

"It's not just me you have now, you know. You've got a formidable team behind you. When you have me, you have them, too." He paused for a moment, let that sink in. "But you can't hold anything back."

"I know," she said, her voice barely more than a whisper. "I know. And I will. In my own way, in my own time."

"Is time something you have the luxury of wasting?"

"Don't push harder, okay? Trust goes both ways. Trust me to know when the time is right." She trailed off, turned her face into his palm as he cupped her cheek.

He looked into her eyes. And what he saw there, for the first time, was fear. Raw fear, not the dazed kind of terror that struck her earlier, when she wasn't prepared. This fear had depth, this fear had history, this was intimate fear, the kind that robbed a person of the ability to reason.

"Just tell me this much. Is Springer safe here? Truly safe?"

Her eyes went glassy then, as if his concern for her horse undid something inside her. She nodded, then faltered. "For now. Yes."

"Are you sure she wouldn't be better under our care and supervision? Will she put Kenny at risk in any way?"

"I'd never do that."

"I know you wouldn't intentionally, but if she's the target—"

"She's not."

She'd said it too swiftly. "Elena."

She bristled a little. "No one cares about my horse except me, and Kenny."

"And me."

That caught at her, but she remained more defiant than pliant. "She's not a target."

"Are you?"

"Not now, Rafe. Not here."

"Elena—"

And just like that, she exploded. "Give me a little time, will you? For once, just stop pushing me! I give you an inch and you want a football field." She shoved at him, but he didn't let her push him away.

In addition to the fear, he knew she was tired, the kind of tired you didn't get from one difficult day. But he'd been on quite the emotionally draining roller coaster ride himself, and though he knew she needed him to be calming and gentle, he lost his grip a little, too. "Fine. You can yell at me all you want if it helps get the nerves and the fear under control. But at some point you're going to have to tell me whatever the hell it was you got involved in so we can stop wasting time avoiding the problem and get started on a solution."

"There is no solution," she shouted right back at him. "I'm not a freaking idiot. If there was something I could have done, goddammit, I'd have done it by now. I did what I had to do, and it's working. Or would be if you'd have kept your over-involved, paranoid self out of it."

"You're not paranoid when someone really is out to get you," he shot back, feeling the sting of that particular barb. He hated the fact that his digging had turned up the heat for her, but, at the same time, if it got her to fix it rather than hide from it, maybe it was for the better. He turned her around. "Get in. And climb over. I'm driving."

"You don't tell me—"

"Get in," he said flatly and lifted her by the waist.

"I can climb in the truck without your assistance. Believe it or not, the world continues to revolve without you helping it every step of the way." She smacked at his hands, but she climbed in. And kept going until she was in the passenger seat.

"Well?" she demanded.

He was seriously pissed off, at her and himself, worried, and still a little more aroused than the situation called for. So why he felt like smiling, he had no idea. Ducking his chin so she wouldn't take a swing at it if she caught so much as a glimmer of humor on his face, he climbed in and shut the door behind him.

Life certainly wasn't boring with her around, that was for sure.

He pulled the truck around, fully prepared to bully her into telling him the whole story if he had to. Tired and scared she might be, but he could literally hear the clock ticking, his instincts were screaming so loudly. She wasn't leaving this truck until he fully understood what was going on. But then he saw her gaze dip over to the rearview mirror as the barn housing Springer faded into the background, and he saw her shoulders slump, just a little, and the way she tucked her arms more tightly around her middle.

He knew what it was like to worry about someone you loved. Worse, he knew what it was like to do everything you possibly could, and still feel helpless to do what needed to be done. He'd spent what felt like three lifetimes watching his mother work herself to death because she wanted more for him. He remembered how frustrated he'd felt, not being old enough, strong enough, or smart enough to do anything to help. He'd vowed that the moment he could, he would. And he had.

He'd helped her, first by being the best that he could be, so that all that hard work hadn't been for nothing. Then by making sure that, after spending the first half of her life with nothing, she'd spend the rest wanting for nothing.

He'd helped a lot of other people since then, but despite the occasional frustration over not being able to solve every problem, he'd never felt that deep well of helplessness creep over him, like it had when he was young. He felt the raw edges of that now. Elena was formidable, and there was no certainty that even he could bully the truth out of her, no matter how hard he tried. But he was far from helpless now. And he had years of successfully solving some pretty intricate, and at times, harrowing, problems. The resulting confidence was sometimes an opponent in and of itself.

"Sometimes you can be a real jerk, you know that?"

Considering his thoughts at the moment, he laughed before he could catch himself. "I was just thinking the same thing."

"Well, at least you're self-aware."

"I try."

"And humble, too."

"Lately, just on horseback. But it's probably a good lesson."

"Undoubtedly."

She shut up then, and so did he, deciding to let her find her own way into the conversation they both knew they had to have. Maybe it wasn't bullying she needed. Or a shoulder to cry on. Maybe what she needed was an ear. With a brain attached. Perhaps he should start using his.

Another mile or two passed in silence, but he stuck it out, despite the dozens of questions on the tip of his tongue. After another ten minutes of silence, his patience was finally rewarded.

"The investigator on the phone," she began, clearly uncomfortable, "was digging for information about Geronimo," she continued. "The fire marshal's report—"

"Was inconclusive in forming an airtight case for arson. I know." At her surprised and somewhat accusatory look, he said, "I read it, okay?"

She huffed an indignant sigh. "Why don't you tell me what you know so I don't waste my breath? Hell, you might know more than I do."

Actually, she had a point. "You know, maybe I can fill in some blanks for you." He lifted a hand when she glared at him. "I'm just saying that my research might have garnered information you weren't privy to."

"Why were you researching Geronimo? I thought you were looking into me? I didn't have anything to do with him."

"Just the fact that an incident of that caliber happened while you were working there, and it was just after that that you left—"

"A few months later," she clarified.

"Still, it was no small thing, so it warranted looking into. And we didn't know if you were involved until we checked into it. I looked into everything that provoked any interest. Or as much as I could. I haven't had that much time."

She folded her arms and stared out the window. "Fine. You spill first, then. What do you know?"

The fact that she wasn't summarily rejecting the topic of Geronimo as being relevant was cause enough for Rafe to conclude he was part of this. Somehow. A major step forward, and a relief to know his instincts had been clamoring for a reason. "Generally speaking, I know that neither the police nor the fire marshal was able to establish foul play conclusively. What I don't know yet is why, if they were unable to prove arson of any kind, the insurance company hasn't been able to—"

"Companies."

"Companies," he nodded, "haven't signed off, one way or the other. Despite the obvious reason of not wanting to pay such a big-dollar claim."

"It can get complicated where big-dollar racehorses are concerned."

"Enlighten me."

"In addition, I'm sure, to policies on the building and property, there were also likely two on Geronimo."

"Two?"

"One for his personal worth, and one for his worth as a stud."

"You mean one for him, and one for his, uh, swimmers?"

"Semen. Yes. Or its viability, anyway."

He smiled a little at her impatient tone. "We're guys. We're sensitive to that sort of talk."

"Right. How silly of me."

His smile grew. "You know, for all your gentle nature with horses, you have a surprisingly direct way of dealing with people."

"Horses respond to gentle. People, at least those in my line of work, tend to respond better to direct and to the point."

"Even more important, given the gender inequity in your line of work, I would imagine."

If his sensitivity to her plight surprised her, she didn't show it. "You would be right. It's fine to nurture the million-dollar studs, but you'd better not allow the ones that climb on their backs, much less the ones who sign your paychecks, to assume that extends to anyone other than the livestock."

"Pineapple theory."

"Which is?"

"Tough and prickly on the outside, sweet and—"

"I get it."

Rafe glanced over at her, and saw from the slight twitch at the corners of her mouth that her attitude was more a front at this point. He liked that most about her. She bounced back. "So, he had a life insurance policy, and some kind of insurance on his ability to procreate. I'm guessing the latter didn't come into play in terms of his premature death."

"I don't think so. At least, not in any of the buzz around the farm."

She'd said it calmly enough, but he noticed, in his peripheral vision, that she was fidgeting a bit, as if unable to get comfortable. She was probably only rarely a passenger in her own truck . . . but just as likely it was the topic at hand. "How much did you know? I mean, how much did the average employee know about what was going on with the investigation?"

"A lot. But no more than you or any other Joe Q. Public who watched any of the major news networks. They were all camped out along the road to the farm for weeks after it happened. Every last little detail they ferreted out was played and replayed, analyzed to death."

"No insider info?"

"It was speculated, when the media endlessly debated the whys and wherefores of the tragedy, that the relationship between Gene Vondervan and his third wife, Kami, might have been somehow related to Geronimo's death."

"Trouble in paradise?"

"To the outside world? No. The Vondervans were very good about putting on a good show. Gene demanded it. He was a tough nut to work for, very demanding, wanted everything to his exact specifications. But to the world at large, his peer group, he wanted to be perceived as the jovial, beloved, benevolent philanthropic guy who happened to own a few million dollars' worth of racehorses. It wouldn't surprise me if he'd had it put in the prenup. Kami definitely complied, but then it was in her best interest to do so if she wanted to maintain the status quo."

"In public. But you're saying in private it was different?"

"Not that anyone saw, but when the wife is young—very young—and blond, and the husband is old, balding, and very, very rich, there's always speculation. And when the networks have hours and hours of airtime to fill and there's the tragedy of a beloved icon dying in a horrific fire, it doesn't take them too long to go in that direction."

"Being that she was wife number three, I guess that plays. How long had they been married when it happened?"

"Over three years, for sure—almost four, maybe. I was there for close to three years and they were still considered newlyweds when I started."

"What happened to wives one and two?"

"From what I heard, his first wife died after a long illness, though I'm not sure what. He remarried almost right away, and it seemed a popular opinion it had just been a rebound reaction to losing his wife. He and Maryann, his first wife, were well known in horseracing circles and she was very well liked. They were married a long time. He had the second one annulled, but I don't know all the details, or even her name, except it was over almost right after it began."

"And Kami?"

She shrugged. "Who knows? It was a few years later, I understand, when they met. I'm not sure where or how. It wasn't the whirlwind wedding the second one was, but pretty much everyone seemed to agree it was a quick romance. I think in their circles she was tolerated more than accepted, mostly because no one wanted to piss Gene off."

"So, what was the public verdict? How does the May-December nature of their marriage have anything to do with Geronimo's death?"

She lifted a shoulder. "How the hell should I know? I really tried to stay out of all that. Gossip was second nature around the barns, so I heard it—it was impossible not to—but I didn't get caught up in it. I was more worried about my future, both on the ranch and in the business."

"Not to mention a pregnant horse."

"I didn't know that, then. I was hoping that all the public cries of negligence wouldn't tarnish the names and careers of everyone who worked there, despite the fact that very few, if any, of us had any direct contact with Geronimo, or his care and maintenance. With the exception of that one incident, Charlotte Oaks had an impeccable reputation, which is why many of us had sought to work there, so we all took it personally when they tried to tear the place apart looking for signs of negligence or worse."

"Did they find any?"

She shook her head. "But the damage had been done, to a degree. In time, it would all be water under the bridge, but my time there was already sort of over. I'd worked my ass off to try and climb the ladder to head trainer, did all I could to get promoted, and was passed over time and again. I knew it was because of my gender—Gene is very old-school when it comes to women—"

"Then why hire you in the first place?"

"I was well qualified, had impeccable references, and they had no clear reason not to. But that didn't mean they had to promote me. I guess I just thought they'd see my skill and dedication and sort of get over the female part. Of course, I couldn't prove anything. The guys promoted over me were also qualified, so what was I to do?"

"Must be incredibly frustrating."

He saw her shift and look directly at him. "If you're even remotely thinking of going the bitter, disgruntled employee route, don't. I would never—ever—intentionally do harm to any animal. Or person, for that matter."

He knew that, but it was good to hear her flatly state it as well. "When did you find out, anyway, that Springer was pregnant? In relation to Geronimo dying, I mean. Had you already bred her when it happened?"

Elena shifted her attention back out the front window, but when she spoke, her voice was still calm, straightforward. "She'd been bred, yes, but I wasn't sure if she was pregnant at that point." She fidgeted in her seat a little then, looking out the side window. And as far away from him as she could get. "You were asking about Gene and Kami and what inside information I had. I don't know what their marriage could have to do with Geronimo, but there was trouble. In private, anyway."

Rafe hadn't missed the less-than-subtle way she'd refocused the conversation. "Was that the basis for the media speculation?"

"I don't think it was public knowledge at that point."

"But it is now?"

She glanced at him. "It was after I left, but there were news stories about papers being filed. I think there was speculation that all the stress of the horse's death and endless investigations had taken a toll, but by then the media had mostly moved on."

"But you're saying there was trouble in paradise before all that?"

Again, she lifted a shoulder.

"I'm surprised no one blabbed that to the media."

"As I said, we were all worried about our jobs. If word got out who the 'anonymous source' was, and it always does, no other owner would hire us. Loyalty is everything in this business."

"I can understand the more highly placed employees not risking it, but more than a few lower-ranked employees left. I'm surprised none of them were paid to talk."

"There wasn't much to talk about. Just the sort of general knowledge that there was greater tension than usual between the two. Maybe that's why the media was digging in that direction to begin with, I don't know, but as I said, Gene was scrupulous about maintaining a tight public image, and they always appeared together in public, seeming supportive of one another about the tragedy and all the investigation speculation. Since the papers weren't filed until much later . . ." She shrugged. "I don't see where any of it really matters, in terms of Geronimo, anyway. I didn't then, and I don't now."

"You mentioned loyalty . . . did your leaving hurt you? In terms of being hired again?"

"The longer the speculation wore on, the more we worried that staying was worse than going. No one at Charlotte Oaks held it against those of us who opted out. In my case, I had extenuating circumstances with Springer, so no one was surprised. I had good recommendations, as Kate knows, and, I guess, you. I don't think it hurt me to leave. In fact, it was probably better to leave when I did, with everything else going on, than to just leave on my own terms."

"So, when the baby is born and everything is okay, the plan is to return to the sport and go back to building your career as a trainer."

"That's the plan."

"You said you were using this time to figure out your next step. Do you have prospects lined up?"

She surprised him a little by smiling. "You gonna call and harass them, too, and cost me the job before I even get it?"

He took the pointed jab. He'd earned it. But he grinned and teased her back. "Well, if it would keep you around Dalton Downs longer, who knows? Maybe I have my own ulterior motives now."

They glanced at each other, connecting gazes for a long moment. It was nice to know that, even in a situation like this, where a lot was at stake, they had already built up enough trust to be able to tease like this and know it was just that, teasing.

"I'm not asking for specifics," he said, though the idea that she was planning to leave in the fairly near future started to sink in a bit more realistically than it had before. "I'm just asking, now that the time is drawing near for Springer, if you've lined anything up."

"I wouldn't leave Kate in the lurch, if that's what you're getting at."

"But you've talked about it."

"I was up front about all of it when she hired me, but we haven't discussed it recently. It's not like I'm going to bolt the minute the foal's feet hit solid ground."

"She's going to try to get you to stay."

Elena smiled again. "She was up front about that when she hired me, too."

"So, you still haven't answered my question."

"Which one?"

"Do you have a job lined up?"

"I've had feelers out all along."

"Nothing concrete?"

She huffed a sigh. "You're such a pit bull."

"Which, knowing that, you'd think you'd just save yourself the time and aggravation and answer me."

She sighed, but there was no animosity in it. "No, nothing concrete."

"And the other?"

"What other?"

"The insider info. Nothing more to the Gene and Kami story? No juicy speculation on what was really going on in paradise?"

She looked over at him. "You know, I wouldn't have pegged you as the *National Enquirer* type."

"I'm not. Far from it."

"Then why all the interest in them? What difference does it make if they're happily married or getting divorced? Do you know something I don't?"

He lifted a shoulder and kept his eyes on the road. "I did know about the papers being filed, but I hadn't had time to do any digging where they were concerned."

"What could it possibly have to do with Geronimo?"

"Well, high-profile divorces between people with a lot of money can get quite nasty. Especially when it comes to splitting assets."

Elena gasped, and Rafe had to smile. For all her straightforward, no-bullshit style, she was still remarkably and quite sweetly naïve about some things. Despite spending most of her adult years in a male-dominated world where women were definitely second-class citizens, being raised in a loving home had apparently managed to shield her from the reality of just how nasty the war between the genders could get.

"You honestly think either one of them would have done

anything intentionally to Geronimo, just because of some kind of divorce settlement?"

Rafe shrugged. "People in love have done worse for less. So, what was the lowdown about those two? How ugly was it behind closed doors?"

Elena huffed and sat face-forward again, folding her arms across her waist. "This is incredibly distasteful."

"Divorce usually is."

"But they weren't divorcing until later—"

"The papers came later. But marriages don't end overnight. Or they usually don't, anyway. If papers were filed a few months later, then chances are things went to shit long before that. And you've already said there was gossip amongst the employees. What was the rumor du jour?"

She stared out the window for a long moment, then settled back a bit more. Clearly, gossiping was not something she did on a regular basis and it didn't sit well with her. Another thing he liked about her. "The story goes that the head trainer had gone up to the main house one afternoon to have a meeting with Gene and overheard the two of them arguing. Doesn't sound like much, I know, but if you knew those two, and the over-the-top lengths they went to, trying to look like the perfect golden couple, you'd realize how out of character it was for them to be seen anywhere while disagreeing, even in their own home."

"Married couples fight, even golden ones."

"True. But these two cultivated their images like politicians running for president. No way would they—Gene especially—have been so careless as to have an argument that could be so readily overheard."

"You're saying they staged it?"

"No, I'm saying it blew up in such a way that it got out of hand before either of them could get a grip. At least that's how JuanCarlo related it."

"He's the head trainer?"

She nodded.

"And he told this to you?"

"I knew him, we got along well. In fact, it was because we did and he respected my work that I was so frustrated when I'd get passed over. But no, I wouldn't have been privy to that kind of personal conversation. Word was he told the assistant head trainer."

"Just how far down the chain were you in this incident?"

"Third. Along with several other trainers who happened to be in the tack shed when we overheard Juan's assistant talking about it with his lead trainer."

"So, a bit more than rumor."

"Well, who knows how embellished or distorted it was, or how many times he'd told the story himself, after hearing it from Juan. But it was enough that I believed some kind of altercation had occurred."

"And no one blabbed this?"

"I can only speak for myself, but I never heard it directly related in the media reports, beyond the typical speculation, anyway."

"What were they fighting about?"

"Trust."

"As in one of them was cheating on the other? Or thought to be?"

"I honestly don't know. Juan didn't hear what they were saying exactly, except it was pretty accusatory, and what the trust issue was about, wasn't revealed. It ended right when he got there. It was news because they'd fought at all. The topic was speculated over, of course, endlessly, but that's all we knew. It was a one-time event. And that was all eclipsed by the fire. I think it was pretty much forgotten after that."

"Okay."

"Okay? That's it? Okay?"

"Well, I have to do some digging, of course, but—" He caught her look. "What? It deserves looking into."

"Why?"

"Because whatever was going on between them might have something to do with the fire."

"Who cares? I mean, what does that have to do with me?"

Now he looked over at her. "Good question. What does all this have to do with you?"

"I had nothing to do with Geronimo's death."

"But it's related. To why you ran. To why you're hiding. To why that investigator wants to talk to you."

"Who said I ran?"

He slowed the truck and looked over at her. "Are we really going to play this game again? You said you were going to let me help. Then you have to tell me the whole story."

"Well, the story has nothing to do with Gene and Kami Vondervan."

"I can't know that until I know what the story is about."

She sighed, folded her arms, then fidgeted in her seat, then sighed again, before swearing under her breath. "I don't really know who it's about. I didn't think it could be them because they owned him, I mean, they'd just bought him, so—"

Rafe began to realize where this was headed, and just how in the dark she truly might be. "Answer me this. Do you think his death was an accident?"

She wrapped her arms around her waist, then finally shook her head. "I know it wasn't an accident."

Holy shit. Now they were getting somewhere. And it was a somewhere he really didn't want her to be. "And how would you know that? Do you know who did it?"

She shook her head again. "No. No, I don't." She looked at him. "I truly didn't have anything to do with it, not even unintentionally."

"I know it wasn't you, Elena." And he did. She was worldly in some ways, and so very not in others. "It's not in you to even see the evil that exists in man, so I know it doesn't exist in you. No matter the provocation."

Relief slumped her shoulders.

Rafe slowed the truck further, but his grip on the wheel could have bent steel. He looked over at her, and for the first time, she looked vulnerable to him. "How do you know it wasn't an accident?"

She turned those huge brown eyes to him, and finally let go of the secret she'd been harboring for so long. "I was the last one to see Geronimo alive. Or . . . the next to the last one. The last one was the killer."

Chapter 16

She'd gone and done it. She should be freaking out that she'd told someone, anyone. And to what amounted to a virtual stranger, by anyone else's measure. But when she looked over at Rafe and found his steady gaze aimed back at her, all she felt was relief.

He slowly pulled the truck and trailer off the side of the road, then shifted in his seat to face her. "You were with Geronimo? Out in his private stable?"

She nodded. "I—I wanted to see him. He's a great champion and I wanted to meet him, look at him up close, talk to him, just—you wouldn't understand. It's my dream to train a horse like him one day, and there he was, greatness, just a few hundred yards away. I was never going to be the one working with him, never going to get the chance."

"So, how did you? Who got you in? JuanCarlo?"

"No one got me in. I let myself in."

"The reports said the security system wasn't fully in place yet."

"No, it wasn't. Gene was still arguing with JuanCarlo over how much was needed and what type of system was best. Then Geronimo was able to be delivered to them ahead of schedule and, well, no, the system wasn't complete."

"And this was common knowledge?"

"Common enough."

"JuanCarlo had that much say in the security of Charlotte Oaks?"

"As head trainer, he had say in what would best protect the horses. Gene owned a number of high-profile racing horses, but none that had ever been a Crown winner, much less one as beloved as Geronimo."

"Even though he wasn't racing any longer, he still warranted the star treatment?"

"And then some. Partially due to his history, and partially because of what everyone hoped would come next. He was being put to stud, and there were high hopes."

"And big dollars, I would presume, for anyone who wanted one of his offspring."

"Yep," she said, but bit her lip against saying anything more.

He looked at her, but thankfully didn't press further. He seemed more interested in what exactly had happened that fateful night, and how her presence related to it. "Walk me through it."

"I was leaving my stables—it was late. Middle-of-the-night late. There was an injured horse—"

"Right, the reports said JuanCarlo was called to the main barns in the middle of the night when one of the stallions hurt himself kicking at his stall."

"Yes. But I didn't know he'd been called down. It wasn't my horse, but I had gone over to look in on the situation, as had a few others. But it seemed they had it under control, so I left, intending to go back to my trailer and to bed. And that's when I saw the lights still on out at the private stable and JuanCarlo's truck parked out front. I decided to go out, see if maybe he'd sneak me in just to see Geronimo."

"What kind of relationship did you have with JuanCarlo?" He lifted his hand. "I'm not suggesting anything, I'm just asking."

"Friends," she said. "Professional friends. He'd worked his way up through the ranks and so he appreciated hard work and dedication more than politics. He saw skill first, and gender second. So I made it my business to try and work as near his team as I could. Strictly business, but we did get along. As I said, that made it doubly disheartening when I didn't get moved up."

"Did you ever think he expected that you'd do something . . . more to earn the promotion?"

She tried not to lose her temper. They were fair questions, ones she'd have likely asked herself, but that didn't mean she had to like them, or their implication. "Like I said, he was a professional first and last. As was I."

"But you thought you could sweet talk him into letting you get a peek at the newest acquisition."

"No, I thought I could appeal to the same drive that had led him to campaign heavily to be the one to oversee Geronimo, that I also have to eventually work with thoroughbreds of that caliber." She folded her arms. "There's nothing salacious to this story, so I'd appreciate it if you could—"

"I meant no disrespect," he interrupted. "I didn't," he reiterated when she gave him a disbelieving look. "It's just, in my line of work, well, it's not unusual for there to be a salacious angle. And it doesn't reflect poorly on you if he was a womanizing jerk who wanted something more than you were willing to give."

"Well, he wasn't. Not with me, anyway. As it turned out, it didn't matter because he wasn't there. He'd already been called down to the other barns to see the injured stallion—I'd just missed him. I went out one way while he was coming in another."

"So who let you in?"

"No one. No one was there."

"Right. The poker game. It was in the news, remember?" he said, when she looked surprised. "All the negligence reports."

"Right."

"So, the reports were correct, then? No one else was there?"

"No," she repeated. "As far as I know, anyway."

"But no one knew you were there."

She shook her head, dipping her chin a little and wishing like hell she didn't have to run the events of that night through her mind ever again. "No."

"So, is it possible there was someone else there? Someone you didn't see? Someone no one knew was there, like no one knew you were there?"

That had her looking up. "I—I don't know. It's not a big barn. I—I don't think so. I called out, but no one answered."

"If you were out there setting a fire, would you have answered?"

She shivered. In all the times she'd relived that night, over and over again, awake and in endless nightmares, she'd never once contemplated that possibility. She'd worried that someone had seen her coming or going, especially the someone who'd started the fire. But she'd never thought they might have been there, hiding, waiting for her to leave. "If someone was there, if they saw me, then don't you think they'd have said something about my being out there? If for no other reason than to shift the suspicion to me?"

"Not unless they were afraid they'd been spotted, too."

"But if I had, it would have been obvious right off that I didn't tell anyone."

"Which might be what got you quid pro quo. You kept quiet, so did they. Perhaps if the fire marshal had been able to build a case, they'd have come forward."

"But he couldn't."

"Exactly. However, the insurance investigators—"

She gasped, and her heart skipped a beat. "You don't think— is that why they called me? You think they finally have proof I was there?"

"Did they say anything that led you to believe that?"

She shook her head. "He just kept questioning me about Geronimo and what I knew about him, and if I'd had contact, but he never accused or even intimated that it was anything more than standard interrogation procedure."

"And yet, he was pretty adamant about talking to you."

"I figured it was because you guys had called and stirred things up that they figured they'd look at me again, just in case. If for no other reason than to prolong paying the claim."

"But you were scared. Sheet-white scared."

"Of course I was. I didn't know what they knew, or why they wanted to talk to me after such a long period of time. It can't be coincidence that it happened right after you started snooping around. They weren't this interested in me when it all happened, so why now if not that?"

"I don't know. I guess we need to find out."

"Rafe, you can't go digging—"

He reached over and put his hand on her arm. "When I was asking after you, I was direct and aboveboard about it, as I had no reason not to be. But the direct route isn't the only way to get answers."

"Still—"

"I know what I'm doing, Elena. And I'm very good at my job."

She held his gaze a bit longer, then finally sighed. "Okay, but I want to know what you're doing. And who you're talking to. Every step of the way. No more surprises."

"No more surprises."

"Good." She huddled a bit more in her seat. "Okay." But she didn't feel remotely okay. She wasn't used to this, used to someone else having any say in how things were going to be handled.

"Come here," he said, reaching over and tugging at her arm.

"What?"

"You're too far away. This can't be easy for you," he said, pulling her across the bench seat, reaching under it and shifting it back as far as it would go before turning and pulling her into his arms, so her back rested against his chest. "Much better." He leaned down and pressed a kiss against her temple. "I know it doesn't count for much, but I'm not liking dragging you through this, either."

It was all so much—unburdening herself, trying to reconcile

having someone else in the loop, then this . . . this overload of sensations with him holding her, caring about her . . . "I can handle this," she said, while not making the least effort to climb out of his lap.

"I know you can. It's one of the many reasons I've been such a pit bull. You're not an easy person to help." He tipped her head back, so their gazes could meet. "Thank you for trusting me, Elena."

She trembled a little, wanted to be strong enough to scoot away, but had the presence of mind to finally admit to herself that this felt good. Having someone on her side didn't just have to mean physical support, it meant emotional support, too. And her world wouldn't come to an end if she admitted she needed a little of that right now.

"It's a lot. This," she said. "And it's good. Almost too good. I'm—I'm not used to it, so I might not always handle it very well, but it's not because I don't appreciate it." She turned a little more, so she could look more fully at him. "Now that you know more . . . if you don't want to get involved, I'll understand. I—"

He shut her up with a kiss.

And that felt pretty damn good, too. How he had gone from complete stranger to this in such a short time, she had no idea. But he was here. And he was staying. And, for now, she liked it that way. Enough to kiss him back.

And despite the fatigue, the stress, the worry—or maybe because of it, or maybe because it would always be that way with them—it quickly got out of hand. And she did absolutely nothing to stop it. There was so much left to be said, so much more to go through, and this felt so very, very good. There wasn't enough of this in her world, and she, quite greedily, decided to take it now that it was here.

Rafe seemed of the same mind as he shifted them both around, sliding to the middle of the seat so she could straddle his lap. Both of them groaned when she settled her weight more fully on him, the rigid length of him fitting all too sweetly between her thighs. His hips lifted and she pressed down as he continued his almost decadent assault on her mouth. She kissed him, dueled tongue with tongue, as they pulled and yanked at each other's clothes.

Safely off the highway, in the middle of the night, in the middle of nowhere, with only the starry sky as company, she shut out everything except this man, and this moment.

Struggling with their clothes, they broke apart. "This isn't . . . even as a teenager, I didn't—" he started, then stopped as he dragged his shirt over his head. His breath was coming in warm gasps as he finally wrestled free and helped her do the same before bracing her face with his hands. "You deserve better than the front seat of a truck. I want you on the softest linen sheets, I want you—"

"You want me now," she told him, then pinned him to the back of the seat and kissed him for a change. She had no experience with this sort of thing, so she just went with what felt right. Considering the deep growl that came from him, and the way his hips pistoned off the seat, she figured she was doing okay.

He reached between them and undid first the button of her pants, then his. She wriggled hers down her hips, lifting up to slide them down further, then froze with a loud gasp as he used her leveraged position to help himself to the very tight tips of her nipples.

"Oh . . . God. You—that is—" She gave up trying to find the words and instead let her head drop back, never so thankful for the roomy interior of her truck cab as when he leaned her back over his bracing arm and took his sweet time paying almost reverent attention to first one, then the other, turgid tip.

She sank her fingers into his hair, keeping his mouth warm and wet where she wanted it.

"I want to taste all of you, *mijita*," he murmured, and she shuddered, hard, at the very thought of his hot mouth taking the rest of her to the places he was already taking her now.

She wriggled her hips, wanting—needing—to feel him there,

too, knowing she couldn't have both at the same time. "You're right," she managed, "a bed would be great right now. Hell, a blanket would do."

"You have one?" he asked, lifting his head, making her whimper a little in disappointment at having that lovely sensation cease for even a second.

"Not one I'd want to get naked on."

"Well, then, we'll just have to make do." And with that, he shifted her from his lap to his spot behind the wheel, only with her back up against the door. He was dragging her pants and panties the rest of the way off without so much as asking permission. Of course, the fact that she was helping him might have negated that requirement. "You have way too many clothes on."

As he maneuvered around, tucking his legs in the well of the passenger side so he could lean down and kiss her bare tummy, she got her first brief glimpse of him shirtless. And she found herself wishing their positions were reversed so she could be the one trailing her tongue across that smooth chest, down that rigidly defined abdomen and across all that taut, honey-toned skin. But then his tongue was marking the same trail and she forgot every last thought in her head except the one begging him not to stop.

"Sweet," he murmured, tracing his tongue lower, closer, teasing the ends of her curls, nudging her thighs apart. "Oh, so very sweet." Then he slid his tongue over her, and into her, and she arched against him as he moved his hands beneath her thighs and teased with brushed fingertips as he held her where he wanted her.

She was climbing rapidly, her nails scraping his scalp as she gripped his head more tightly, keeping him there . . . though he didn't seem to need the direction. And then it was there, hitting her like shock waves, more powerful than the first time as he continued tormenting her, wringing every last bit of shuddering pleasure from her before tugging her down so she lay flat on the seat, and covering her body, or most of it, with his own. She wanted the full weight of him on top of her and kicked at the passenger door in frustration as there was no way to wedge the lengths of them along the seat bench.

He shifted back, fishing his wallet out of his jeans, sliding the condom packet out, before looking at her. She nodded, and that was all he needed to know. "Come here," he said, shifting back, pulling her on top of him, straddling her across his hips, then looking up into her eyes before guiding her down onto him. "Elena—"

"Don't stop now," she told him.

"I just want to make sure—"

She pressed her finger across his mouth, then gave in to the need she'd had almost from the first time she'd laid eyes on him, never once thinking she'd actually do it . . . do this. She traced her fingertips over his lips, so beautifully sculpted, so perfectly suited for her own, then leaned down and replaced her fingertips with her lips as she pressed down and took him inside her.

They both groaned, and prolonged the moment of joining, neither moving, both just accepting and reveling in that exact moment of filling and being filled . . . and then she moved, and so did he. His hands were in her hair and she was clawing at the seats as they took each other on a wild ride. He pushed her up and over again—as she shuddered through her release, he let go with his own.

Both of them breathing heavily, they held each other for several long minutes. Then he finally pulled her up, sprawled across him, and tucked her against his damp chest. The windows had fogged, the air was humid and heavy, tendrils of her hair lay damp against her neck. But he tipped her chin up and looked into her eyes, and all she could think was that she wanted to be able to look into his whenever she wanted to. Like this, intimate and personal, or across a crowded room, when nothing more than a quick smile would say everything that needed to be said between them. It had been like that with her parents, that connection that no distance could diminish. It would be like that with him. She knew it. She saw it there.

She started to speak, to try and find the words, but he tucked her back against his chest then, and she knew there'd be time later. Reality would intrude shortly, and drag her back into a situation she was heartily sick of dealing with. So she soaked up as much strength and serenity as she could, tucked here, safe. For now.

It might have been minutes later, might have been hours, but when he finally shifted them both up, she only knew it felt too soon. She wanted to curl up and keep the world at bay longer, even as she knew they'd already taken all the time that they could.

He kissed her temple, then her cheek, then her mouth, then they both began to dress. Nothing was said, but nothing needed to be said. As she'd known it would be, the silence was easy between them, but that didn't render the reality of it any less profound. It was too soon to think it through, to analyze it, and she was frankly too tired and spent to do it justice at the moment. So she just did what needed to be done. Later, whenever later came, she'd think about this and figure out what it meant. And what she was going to do about it.

She glanced over at him as he settled himself once again behind the wheel. And she would have to do something. Because he mattered now, too.

He didn't start the engine right away, and for the first time, she wondered what he was thinking.

"We need to get back on the road," he said, at length, then looked over at her.

His expression wasn't readable, and that gave her pause. Had she just stupidly romanticized something that was nothing more than a backseat romp? She didn't think so, but what did she know of such things? "Rafe—"

"I know that wasn't what either of us would have wanted."

Now she did tense. Was he saying he regretted what they'd

done? He certainly hadn't acted like it. Before, during, or, most importantly, afterward. "I wanted it," she said, quietly. No more holding back, she decided. It was far too late for that.

"I meant here. Like this. It's not . . . me. Not how I'd have—"

"I know." She smiled then. "At least you weren't wearing anything tailored."

His lips curved a little, too. "True. But that's not what I meant."

She reached across between them. "I know. It's okay. There will be other times." Her smile spread. "And I promise the thread count can be as high as you want."

He laughed then and lifted her hand to his lips, kissing the back first, then the palm, before curling her fingers in to seal it there. It was a simple gesture, both playful and intimate, and because she wanted to hold on tightly to both of those things, knowing what lay ahead, she kept her fingers tightly curled as he started up the truck and pulled back onto the highway.

Chapter 17

They drove for a half-hour before he finally spoke up. "You up to talking about this any more?"

"*This* being us, or this meaning Geronimo?"

"Geronimo." He looked over. "Unless there's something about us you need to talk about."

She smiled briefly. "No. I'm okay with us."

"Good," he said, meaning it, relieved she did, too. It wasn't that he'd worried about that, but who knew what she'd talk herself into, or out of, given enough time. He'd thought—hoped—that maybe she'd drift off and catch a little sleep, giving him time to think all of this through. But she hadn't, and being alone with his thoughts wasn't making things any clearer. Except for one thing. Kate wasn't the only one who was going to do her damnedest to keep Elena Caulfield around.

"Where did we leave off?" she asked.

"You, at the barn, being the last to see Geronimo."

He noted she tucked her hands between her thighs, but otherwise didn't seem to tense up too much. "Do you really think someone saw me?"

"I don't know," he said, wishing he could be more reassuring. "It's an angle, and all angles have to be considered."

She was silent for a moment, then said, "I guess you're right. But I really don't think anyone was there. I think I'd have felt it. Or something. I don't think things would have gone this long without anything happening, only to happen now."

"Still—"

"I know," she said, lifting her hand. "I understand."

"So . . . where were you when the tank blew up?"

"Back at the employee stables."

"How long from the time you left the barn until the time it blew up?"

She flinched a little, and he knew she was replaying the horrific scenes from that night. He wished he could spare her that, but with his observations as well as her own in play now, maybe she'd recall something of importance that she wouldn't have before, something that would help them.

"About forty-five minutes," she said.

"Why did you think it wasn't an accident?"

"Because there was a kerosene heater in the center aisle and the tank was sitting next to it. I assumed it was there because they'd just set the heater up for that night."

"And that was suspicious?"

"No, it wasn't. But they said the tank blew in the attached shed out back. And there was only one tank, according to what they reported."

"Meaning that someone had to have come in after you left and moved the tank from the aisle to the shed."

"Exactly."

"Couldn't it have still been an accident?"

"Yes, but it just didn't add up. The reports had JuanCarlo in the main barn waiting for the vet and the other guys at the trailers playing poker. When the explosion happened, all of them came running. The media reported on every single detail of that night, ad nauseam. So, whoever moved it wasn't one of the people who were supposed to be there."

"Why didn't you come forward with all that?"

She gave him an incredulous look. "Right. I was supposed to volunteer that I just happened to be the last one to see him alive, putting me where it was strictly off limits to go, and with questions of arson flying all around."

"Maybe the same can be said of whoever moved the tank to the shed. Maybe it was still innocent, still an accident, but they didn't come forward for the same reasons."

"Maybe. But if I had told the authorities what I knew, there was no way to prove it hadn't been me. I didn't see anyone on my way out there or back. No one saw me go back to my trailer, either, so I had no alibi, no witnesses. And, like you said, I couldn't be a hundred percent sure it wasn't an accident."

"So you decided to take off and hide out anyway?"

"I didn't decide to leave until I got confirmation on Springer's pregnancy," she told him. "I was going to go anyway, but yes, that pretty much decided it for me."

"And if someone had seen you or they determined you were there?"

"I would have told them what I just told you. Then hired a lawyer, most likely. But it didn't. And I wanted to leave, anyway. Springer decided it for good. I just wanted to put all of it behind me. I had a few options lined up, but they didn't work out, then I heard about the position here and thought it sounded like the perfect place for her, and I would use the time to figure out what to do next."

He glanced over at her. It all made perfect, logical sense. Except his instincts hadn't quieted one bit. "And that's it?"

She lifted her shoulders. "Isn't that enough?"

A nonanswer, but as they were almost back to Dalton Downs, he opted to let it drop. For now. She was still harboring something, but it was only a matter of time now. She'd trusted him enough to tell him this much. He'd figure out a way to get her to tell him the rest.

"So," he said, at length, "all this time, you never told anyone about this?"

"No," she said. "No one."

"Not even Kenny?"

"Not anyone. I was harboring a big secret, yes, but I also knew that I had nothing to do with Geronimo dying or the tank exploding. I also didn't see anyone out there who might have done it. So, it didn't make any sense to put myself at risk when I really had nothing to offer, other than to corroborate the fact that JuanCarlo wasn't out there. But since it was well documented that he was at the main barn when the tank blew, they didn't need my statement for that, either."

"Did the investigator ask you anything about JuanCarlo, or any of the other barn help that night?"

"No. Not specifically. He just went over all the same questions I was asked back when it happened, the questions we were all asked."

"I know you think it's my digging that triggered this, and I'm not prepared to say otherwise at this point, but think hard. Is there anything else that might have triggered his renewed interest? Are you sure it's not anything else? I just don't want us not to see something right in front of us, because we've already concluded it had to be something else."

"All the angles. I know. But I honestly can't imagine what else it could be. Trust me, I asked myself that a hundred times during the call, and after. They've been at this for quite some time now. They're probably grasping at any straw. I don't want to be a grasped straw. But I also don't want the truth of my whereabouts that night to come out now, all this time later. If I would have looked suspicious then, imagine what it would look like now? That's why I was so freaked out. Springer is close to foaling, and I thought everything was fine. Done. In the past. So yeah, it rattled me."

"So, if all they wanted to know was the same old rehash, then why move the horse?"

"I told you, for medical reasons."

"That's it? It was just coincidence?"

She didn't bristle this time, which was good. She was finally seeing that he was only prodding her to make sure there wasn't anything left unconsidered. "She was having some problems. I was already a little concerned, which was why I'd told Kate about having Kenny come out to take a look at her. But after the call, yes, it did rattle me, and now that someone might show up here asking more questions, well, who knows what that might stir up? If, for whatever reason, the media picked up on it, I can't have that kind of stress around Springer, not when we're this close. She's already restless just feeding off my renewed anxiety."

"What about—"

"Kate? Don't worry. If any undue attention comes my way, I'll leave. I wouldn't do that to her or the kids."

It was what he'd expected her to say, but he hadn't expected the pang of panic that accompanied it. It was one thing, earlier tonight, to suspect she was taking off and plan to stop her. Now . . . things were different, and he'd be more than a little pissed off if she tried to pull a stunt like that. But he didn't think this was the time to get all territorial or proprietary. Though he'd be lying if he didn't admit to feeling more than a little of both. "And go where?"

She lifted a shoulder. "Springer is safe, so as long as I don't bring down the wrath of the press on Kate, it doesn't really matter. Somewhere until it blows over, I guess, then I'm not sure. Frankly, I haven't had the chance to think that far ahead."

"You wouldn't go to Kenny?" he asked.

"Depends on how close Springer is at the time. I certainly don't want anyone trailing me to his farm. I moved her there for the express purpose of keeping her out of any media glare."

Rafe slowed as they reached the entrance to Dalton Downs. Neither of them spoke as he pulled around the long, narrow road leading down to the barns. "Where do you want to park this thing? Do you want it out in the trailer lot, or all the way out by the employee stables?"

"We can leave it here for tonight. I'll move it in the morning. Or later in the morning, as the case may be."

"I don't mind parking it out there now."

She shook her head. "You've done enough. This way you just have to hike up the hill to the house." She looked at him. "You do live in the main house, right? I mean, I know Mac has his own little place down past the back fields, with Kate, but . . . maybe it's none of my business."

He smiled. "Since I plan on having you on my million-thread-count sheets, I suppose it would be handy if you knew where they were."

She smiled then, and he was glad the mood had shifted. "Million-thread-count, huh? Wow, you *are* spoiled."

He just grinned. "Care to be spoiled with me?"

She shook her head. "I'm pretty sure it will be a test just to get to my own bed tonight. I'd rather wait until there was a better-than-average chance I wouldn't be snoring two seconds after lying down on your bed. Wouldn't want to tarnish your reputation or anything."

He didn't rise to the bait. "I've done enough tarnishing all by myself, thanks, but I understand. At least let me see you to your bunk."

"You never told me where yours was."

"Right. Well, Mac has the cabin, and Finn has a wing pretty much to himself. We use another wing for our offices."

"And you? You have a wing, too? Are you afraid I'll trail barn droppings in with me?"

"No, no wing for me."

"Hmm, I'm intrigued. Where do you live, then?"

"I, well, I live in the pool house."

"You live in the—" She broke off on a laugh. "I'm sorry, really. It's just . . ."

"No, I know how it sounds. But I like it out there. It's small, but private, and close enough that I can jump in any direction when I need to."

"Workaholic, are you?"

"Always plenty to be done. And I like what I do."

She popped the door open. "Pool house." She glanced back at him and her lips twitched. "You'd make an okay cabana boy."

He opened his own door. "Just okay?"

She lifted a shoulder. "You're a little intense for a laid-back job like that, but you could probably adapt. Maybe."

He slid out of the truck and closed the door behind him, then rounded the back of the trailer and truck just as she slid out.

"So, good night," she said, a distinct huff in her tone.

Did she really think he'd just walk off? He smiled in the moonlight when she turned and bumped directly into him.

"Oh! I didn't see you, sorry."

He crowded her back a little, until her back was against the truck door. "Intense, maybe," he said, his voice low. "But I serve a mean martini."

"I—I've never had one. A martini, I mean."

"Then we'll have to rectify that. Tomorrow evening, perhaps? Or, actually, this evening, given the sun is going to rise in a few short hours. I'll cook dinner. We can even make it a business-free zone."

"You cook?"

"You sound surprised."

"I—I guess I am. And I have no idea why. The great chefs are men. And you're a bachelor, so of course you need to eat, and . . ." She trailed off on a sheepish smile. "I'm babbling."

"You're tired. And worried about your horse. Come on." He turned and offered his arm.

"Come on, where?"

"I'll walk you to your ladder."

"Thank you, but I don't need—"

"I think we're well past what you need and what you don't. I want to walk you out, okay? It's what *I* need."

"Old habits." She held out her arm. "And for the record, I have nothing against it being about what you need."

He grinned. "Good to know. Now let me be a gentleman, will you?"

She snorted a little, but allowed him to lead her toward the far stables.

He sighed. "We men really do have our work cut out for us in the public relations department, don't we?"

"What, you're saying that all your intentions are pure and innocent?"

"Is that what being a gentleman means to you?"

"What's your take?"

He opened the paddock gate for her and swept his arm gallantly in front of him. Then, immediately after closing it behind him, he snagged her arm and spun her neatly around and directly up against him. "It means we ask before we take."

"Take what?"

"This." He lowered his head, but paused just before his lips touched hers. "May I?"

"Rafe—"

"Elena," he whispered, "it's been hours. Let me taste you."

"Just kiss me already."

He took her mouth, but gently this time, almost reverently. His body, which was tired, cramped, and spent, should have been perfectly happy with a nice good-night kiss. So that didn't explain why it roared to life the instant she opened her mouth beneath his.

What had happened in the cab of her truck should have been awkward and uncomfortable, by any description . . . but all he could remember was the way she'd clutched at him, holding on to him so tightly, and the way her body had taken his, holding him there so tightly, too. He wanted more, so much more, already knowing it would be, between them, the way it had never been for him with anyone. She was one hell of a woman.

And she was his.

As the kiss slowly deepened, the battle raged between libido and common sense. It was late, they were both tired, there was another long day ahead of them with little sleep to go on, and who knew what other surprises lay in store. She hadn't told him the whole story—he'd bet on that.

"Rafe," she whispered against the corner of his mouth. "I think you have me bewitched."

"Bothered, and bewildered?" he finished, with a little half smile.

She smiled, looking up into his eyes. "That, too. A lot of that."

She was so easy to talk to, to play with, to spend ridiculous amounts of time in bed with. His hold on her tightened slightly. "Thank you," he said, never more sincere.

"For?"

"Trusting me. I know it's not easy. I hope you know it's well placed."

"I'm counting on it."

"I'm going to bring Mac in on this—Finn, too, if he gets back anytime soon." He'd expected her to stiffen, but she didn't.

"What will they say? Will you tell them about . . . this?"

He smiled. "I won't have to."

"And . . . that's not going to complicate things?"

"They'll have their fun, but they'll also be in your corner, because they're in mine."

"You're sure of that?"

"As sure as I am that the sun is going to rise in a few hours and you need some rest."

As if to underscore his words, she was overtaken with a yawn just then. Both of them laughed. "Come on." He walked her inside the paddock, then opened the door to the barn.

Before they stepped inside, she turned to him and put her hand on his arm. "I don't want to complicate things for you. With Mac or Finn, or with anything else. What I said earlier stands. If you don't want to be involved, I'll understand."

"I'm involved. And I'm not going anywhere. I know it's complicated. That's how life works. I'm not expecting simple."

"That's the problem. You'll have expectations. I don't know that I can fulfill any of them. I don't know what you want beyond right this moment and I can't make you any promises."

"I don't recall asking for any. One moment at a time, okay? You've enough to deal with. We'll take the rest as it comes. Not everything has to be planned out."

"I just—" She stopped herself. "Okay." She smiled a little. "You can tell I'm new at this."

He tugged her close, bumped hips with her, making her eyes widen a little. "You can tell I don't mind in the least." He slid a hand beneath the heavy braid lying on her neck and tipped her head back as he lowered his own. "Maybe tonight you'll have sweet dreams. If I can do that, it's enough." He kissed her then, and put all the promise he felt behind it. Things he couldn't yet put words to. And when she kissed him back, so easily, so honestly, his own barriers began to crumble, ones he hadn't even been aware were there. So that by the time he'd broken the kiss, he felt compelled to say, "Okay, so that was a lie."

She frowned. "What part?"

"That it'll ever be enough." He backwalked her into the barn. "The more I want, the more I want. I want to know everything about you. What your favorite food is, what position you like best in bed, what you're still not telling me about the situation with Geronimo."

"Rafe—"

"I can even claim I'll be patient, but that'll probably end up being a lie, too, though I'd certainly try. I'm a pit bull, as you said, always have been." He kissed her again, until she was making those soft, little moans that made him crazy. Then he was sliding his hands down over her hips and tugging her thighs, urging her to wrap her legs around his waist and let him press the once-again rock-hard length of himself more deeply between her thighs. Sweet almighty, he might never have enough of her. Bewitched, indeed.

And then she was kissing him back, voraciously, digging her nails into his shoulders, hooking her ankles at the base of his spine, urging him closer, and once again, they had way too many layers on between them. Only this time, there was a bed. A mere ladder-climb away.

"Hold on," he told her, wrapping one arm around her back, the other hand closing around the nape of her neck, keeping her mouth fused to his as he stumbled them both closer to the ladder leading to her loft.

He bumped up against it, jarring her loose. She grabbed for his shoulders, her ankles slipping down over his backside.

He leaned them into the ladder. "Invite me upstairs, Elena."

She laughed a bit breathlessly. "You have to ask?"

"I am a gentleman," he said, as he nipped at her earlobe.

"And if I don't?" she teased, tilting her head to allow him even greater access.

He let her feet drop to the ground as he turned them so he leaned back against the ladder with her sprawled across him. His grin felt lazy, and he knew his gaze was just a touch more than a little proprietary as he stroked the side of her face, tucking a stray hair behind her ear. "I'll be taking a very long, very lonely cold shower back in the pool house."

She made a fake moue with her lips. "The horror."

"Certainly feels like it at the moment, but I've survived worse."

"Heroic of you."

"So I've thought."

She smiled up into his eyes. "I have no business getting sidetracked by you, you know, much less letting you get sidetracked by me."

"Sometimes it's the side paths that prove the most rewarding. You coming here to Dalton Downs, for instance."

"But there are better times than others to involve other people on your journey."

"Ask me upstairs, Elena."

"Pit bulls are pussycats compared to you."

He grinned without a hint of remorse. "If it gets me what I want, I can be relentless."

"I'm getting that."

He wrapped his arms around her waist and pulled her snug between his legs. "You could be, but apparently you like to torture me."

"Only on horseback."

"Kinky."

She swatted at him, but she wasn't making any move whatsoever to disengage his tight hold. Which only had him drawing her closer still. "I do want you, Elena." He moved his hips. "Hard to deny that one. But I'll want more than just that."

"Maybe if you only wanted me for my body, this would be easier."

"I don't compartmentalize."

She smiled. "Wear your heart on your sleeve, do you?"

"Typically, never. With you? It's fast becoming something of a struggle."

His direct answer, coupled with his very direct gaze, seemed to catch her off guard. He wasn't flirting now. And she knew it.

"I don't know what to do with that," she said. "Or what to do with you."

"I have a few ideas," he replied, a hint of the teasing smile coming back, but still keeping his gaze focused tightly on her.

"Rafe—"

He tugged her mouth close and kissed her. "I won't hurt you."

"Famous last words."

"Is that what's holding you back? Is that the other part of the story?"

"No."

He wanted—badly—to push, but he'd crossed so many boundaries in the past twenty-four hours, he had to find some control at some point.

"Invite me upstairs, Elena." He went to tug her mouth down to his again, but this time she pressed her fingers across his lips and stopped him.

"I want to. That much is obvious, but—"

He moved his mouth a little and nibbled on the end of her fingers.

"You're incorrigible."

"Unrepentantly."

She slipped from his hold, and reached out her hand. When he took hold of it, she pulled him away from the ladder. "I won't sleep if I ask you up. We're both almost giddy with exhaustion. I think maybe we'd best get at least a little rest."

He wanted to argue, but clearly, as she was yawning again, she had a point.

"I don't snore," he said, trying his best to look innocent.

She laughed. "Go home."

He stepped out of the way and allowed her to start climbing the ladder. "Good night, *mijita*."

"Good night, Rafe." She paused, looked down. "Thank you. For your help with Springer. And for . . . well, for being there."

"Always."

She nodded and he stood there, long after she'd closed the loft hatch. He listened to the creak of the floorboards overhead as she readied herself for bed. Stood there until the creaking stopped and the light splintering through the loft hatch went out.

"Good night," he murmured again, and walked out of the barn, knowing that today had marked a profound change in his life. In him.

He was falling for the last person on earth he'd ever have expected to catch his attention. She was contrary, opinionated, and stubborn to a fault. She was both trouble and in trouble. Worse yet, she planned to leave at the first opportunity.

Perfect. Just perfect.

He grinned like a madman all the way back to the pool house.

Chapter 18

"She moved her horse. In the middle of the night."

Rafe paced inside his office as Mac made himself at home behind Rafe's desk. "Don't prop your feet up on—" He sighed and moved the stack of folders out from under Mac's size twelves. "Yes, she moved her horse. About two hours from here. To her vet's place. Guy named Kenny."

"No last name?"

"He's an old friend, a vet with his own rural practice. Big spread, from what I could tell."

"Name of the farm?"

"Didn't get it."

Mac grinned. "What, no signs anywhere?"

"I was too busy trying to find out what the real story was, okay?"

"And? Stop with the suspense, already—you're killing me. What is the real story? Is her horse in some kind of danger? Someone from Charlotte Oaks think he's the babydaddy or something?"

Rafe started to tell Mac what he'd learned, when it hit him. Mac had just been kidding, but Rafe froze as the last pieces finally slid into place. "Holy shit." He looked at Mac. "That's it."

Mac let his feet slide off the desk and leaned forward. "That's what? What's it? What did I say?"

"I can't believe I didn't figure it out."

"Figure what out? Come on, help a brother out here."

Rafe began fishing through the stacks of files piled on one corner. He finally found the report he was looking for and flipped it open, scanning through the pages. "Dammit. Not here." He kept flipping, scanning. "Fuck. Nothing." He slapped the file back down. "That's got to be it, though. The timeline fits. But how in the hell . . . I wonder if the investigator suspects? Dammit!"

Mac stood up. "Would you tell me what's going on, for Christ's sake? Did Elena have something to do with the death of that racehorse? What could she have possibly done? From everything Kate has said about her, no way would she hurt an animal. Was it an accident?"

"It's not what she's done, it's what her horse did. Or, more specifically, if I'm on the right track here, what Geronimo did to her horse."

"What could he possibly have . . . oh." Mac's eyes widened. "Oh, shit."

"You're damn fucking right, oh shit."

"But, wait a minute—before we get carried away here, no way in hell something like that happens and no one knows about it. I know his security team ducked out briefly before the fire, but still, a multi-bazillion-dollar, half-ton stud just doesn't happen to pop his cork unnoticed. When two horses go at it, it's not just a little slap and tickle in the nearest hay bale— wait." Now he started digging through the files.

"Already looked for it. And I know more than you do about that night. More than the police-interview reports, more than the fire-investigator reports."

Mac abruptly stopped, put the folders back down, and turned his full attention to Rafe. "Okay, fill me in."

Rafe paused a moment before telling Mac what he knew. He'd told Elena he was going to bring Mac into this, but he knew how hard it had been to extend her trust to him. He trusted Mac with his life, but he had to make sure they were on the same page here from the get-go.

"Cat got your tongue?" Mac grinned. "Or maybe it's Elena

who has your tongue? And I'm not speaking metaphorically here."

"Very funny. It's just that she finally talked to me last night and I don't want to do anything to jeopardize that."

Mac looked wounded. "Do you really think I—"

"Of course not. But it's not about what you or I think, it's about what she thinks. I don't want her spooked back into silence."

"I won't say a word to her until you give me the green light. Behind-the-scenes man, that's me. But, for the record, she obviously didn't tell you everything."

Rafe looked at his partner and best friend, torn, for the first time, between two people he cared about. "I know. But she did tell me she was out there the night Geronimo died."

"Out there . . . as in *with* Geronimo?"

Rafe nodded and relayed the story. "I'm assuming—now, anyway—she must have ridden Springer out there. It was the only time it could have happened."

"And no one saw this." Mac's flat tone made it clear what he thought of that probability.

Rafe shrugged. "Apparently not, since it sure as hell would be, or would have been, the front-page story on every major news outlet."

"Which means she omitted revealing her little visit when talking with the police."

"She was very likely the last one to see the horse alive. No witnesses. No alibi."

"Yeah, I can see where that might not be a great thing to share. Worse, even, if her horse happened to get knocked up with million-dollar sperm right before the sperm donor dies."

"Exactly. Then there is also the little matter of a moved kerosene tank."

"But there was only one tank in the reports, which is the one that blew." Mac's eyes widened. "She *handled the tank*?"

"No, she saw the tank. Next to the heater, in the middle of the barn."

Mac flipped open the police report. "I thought it blew up in an attached shed."

"It did."

Mac looked up. "Don't get pissed off, but I have to ask— are you sure she's not involved? Because this is looking pretty damn shady."

"As sure as I can be."

"And which head are you thinking with?"

Rafe gritted his teeth. "The same damn head you were thinking with when you helped save Kate's property."

Mac surprised him by laughing.

"What is so goddamn funny?"

"I thought it might be like that."

"Like what?" he demanded, though he knew damn well where Mac was going with this. Might as well stake his claim now anyway. Let the fun begin.

"You know exactly what. Finn and I knew you had her in your scope a long time before your concerns about her even came up."

"I didn't." Not in a conscious way, anyway. But he had done some thinking about that. And . . . Mac had a point.

"Not like you do now."

"No," Rafe said evenly. "Not like I do now. And, fair warning, you have any problems with any of this, you go through me. If you doubt her in the least, then focus on another case and I'll handle this one."

Mac just grinned. "Glad to see we're being objective and open-minded about all this." He stood up and rounded the desk, clapped Rafe on the shoulder, and stuck out his hand. "Welcome to the club, my friend."

Rafe shook his hand. "What club?"

"The 'your life is never going to be the same' club. Don't worry, it's a pretty sweet club to be in."

"Thanks. I think."

"Oh, don't thank me yet. I have a few years of major ragging on your ass to get off my chest. But at least you'll have a soft pair of arms to cry into every night when I get done."

"Very funny."

Mac laughed. "I know. I can't wait to tell Finn."

"Can we get back to the matter at hand here?"

"Sure. But, fair warning, I am going to question you on this, just like you did me with Kate. I might not have appreciated it at the time, but it did help me stay objective enough to see all the angles. This looks way more twisted than the situation at Winnimocca. I think you're going to need all the objective minds you can collect. By the way, no way can I keep this from Kate."

"I know." At Mac's surprised expression, he said, "I already told Elena that. But maybe it might be better coming from her, or me. Before you start gloating all over the place, okay?"

"I'll give you the rest of the day, since I don't plan on seeing Kate until tonight. But we don't keep things from each other." He caught Rafe's gaze. "A policy you and Elena might want to consider adopting here real quick."

"I know."

"So, does she still think the explosion was an accident?"

"She's not sure. But she made the observation that everyone who should have been in the building came running from other places when the tank blew. So that tends to lead me to believe whoever was there, shouldn't have been there."

"Like Elena shouldn't have been there?"

"Yes. And maybe they didn't come forward for the same reason she didn't."

"And this mystery person didn't see her there, or see the whole match-game moment with the horses? Because that would be pretty hard to believe."

"She said it was about forty-five minutes after she left the stables when the tank blew. Whoever it was had plenty of time to come in after she left. And no one has contacted her, or ratted her out, which you think they would have done if they saw her there. Pin the blame on her."

"True, true. Unless . . ."

"Unless what?"

"Unless they thought she saw them."

"We talked about that, too."

Mac grinned. "Did a lot of talking, did you? Is that all you did?"

"Don't."

"I don't have to. You have that whole 'me caveman, you mine' attitude thing Kate says I had after we finally . . . stopped talking."

Rafe ignored him. "What we have to figure out now, is what the insurance investigator knows."

"What was the deal with that phone call, anyway?"

"It shook her up, but he didn't ask her anything new. It was the timing of it. She's pretty set on the idea that it was because we did some digging, calling Charlotte Oaks about her, that got them interested in her again. She thinks it's just a stalling tactic on their part to drag out the investigation that much longer, not pay the claim."

"And you?"

"The timing suggests she has a point, but with the secrets she's been keeping, we can't be too sure. Apparently the guy is going to come out here to talk to her in person. So that leads me to think there is more going on."

"Is that why she moved the horse?"

"I thought so. In fact, I thought she was running. But it turns out she was just moving Springer for medical reasons."

"You think the horse was really having problems? Or was it because she thought someone might be on to the babydaddy angle."

"Her mare was having problems, but now . . . I'm thinking it was both." Rafe swore under his breath and wished Elena had told him the rest. It definitely changed things. This wasn't just about her innocence now and making sure she didn't get railroaded if the truth came out. Now—hell, he didn't know what to think now. "I don't even know the legal ramifications of her horse carrying Geronimo's offspring."

"We need Finn. He would know where to dig, who to ask."

"It would be helpful. You hear anything from him?"

"Not a peep. But he said this might take a while."

"I sure as hell wish we knew what 'this' was all about."

"Yeah, well, I'm sure he'll fill us in when he can."

"Which does jack for me now. I'll see what I can dig up."

"I'd ask Kate, but her knowledge of horses is strictly about using them with the kids. I doubt she knows anything about breeding them or the legalities of it all. She might know someone who does know, though. She has a lot of contacts."

"Wait on that. Let me see what I can dig up. And I have to talk to Elena first. This is still all supposition on our part."

"You think we're on the wrong track?"

Rafe sighed. "I wish we were."

"Do you think maybe she bred them on purpose?"

"If I believe that, I almost have to believe she had something to do with the explosion and Geronimo's death."

"I don't follow."

"I don't know that I do, either, but it's just too damn big a coincidence otherwise."

"But something like that couldn't happen by accident, could it? I mean, unless he got loose or something, but surely someone would have noticed a million-dollar stallion charging around."

"It was the middle of the night."

"How would one person catch him and get him back in his stall?"

"Well, if it was anyone else, I'd say I don't know. But if that one person was Elena—"

"Our resident horse whisperer . . ." Mac trailed off and fell silent while they both thought over the situation.

"What would the scenario be for her not being involved?" Rafe asked. "If her horse got knocked up by the same stud that miraculously dies in a horrible fire hours later . . . what scenario works where she's still innocent?"

"If it truly was an accident."

"We've already established someone moved the tank. Someone who didn't come forward with that information after the fact. So that brings reasonable doubt."

"Based on her word." Mac lifted a hand. "Playing devil's advocate. Of course she'd say someone else was there, someone she conveniently didn't see, who conveniently didn't see her. Or two horses going at it. It doesn't play well, even if it is the truth."

"That much is the truth. I was the one she told the story to, and I believe her on that and that she wasn't involved with his death. At least she believes that she wasn't."

"Meaning?"

"Meaning, she didn't have anything to do with the fire that she knows of. The facts are still that she was there and her horse got knocked up, and the horse that did it died an hour later. It just seems too probable that those two things are connected, but if she didn't connect them, who did?"

"Okay, accident or planned conception, maybe someone saw what happened. The same someone who was out there for whatever reason, the guy who moved the tank. Maybe the fire wasn't the plan at that point—could be just a barn worker—but then he sees this happen and decides to take out Geronimo, knowing Elena's horse carried the only heir to a triple-crown champion. Wouldn't that make the baby that much more valuable?"

"Yes, but he would have no way of knowing if the mating took or not. Kill the fatted calf too soon and lose everything."

"Maybe it was his only chance."

"So . . . where is he?"

"Hiding, waiting for the baby to come?"

"Why not steal Springer?"

"Maybe that was the plan, but then she left and he didn't

know where she went off to. She moved around quite a bit that first month or so after she left."

Rafe thought about it, then shook his head. "I can't see someone just rashly killing off a famous horse like that, not without some guarantee."

Mac leaned back and folded his arms. "I agree. You got any better scenarios?"

Rafe swore, hating every second of this. "Maybe it is just what it looks like. There was a guy out there, with plans to blow the place up, for some other reason entirely. Elena went out on the spur-of-the-moment—no one knew she'd be there. It could be as simple as that. She came and went, the other plan was already in motion."

"And the miracle conception?"

Rafe shrugged. "All we know is that it was forty-five minutes after she left that the tank blew. And since the tank was moved after she left, then whoever came to set it up could have missed the whole thing, never known she was there. It could be coincidence."

"If that's the case, she's lucky she didn't blow up with him."

Rafe shuddered at the thought. To think he'd never have had the chance to meet her, to know her, to—He looked at Mac as another thought occurred to him. "Except, what do you make of this sudden interest in her? Simple as me digging around, making calls?"

"Could be. Probably is. Is there anything else going on back there that would make you think otherwise?"

"We have the most recent reports and they show a stunning lack of evidence, so it looks like the insurance claims will have to be paid. So it could be them stalling."

"Maybe it was all an accident. The guy was just a worker who put the tank away, maybe damaging it in the process. Maybe nothing was planned."

"Maybe."

They waited two beats, then looked at each other.

"Yeah," Mac said. "I don't think so, either."

"I wish like hell I did. So now what?"

"Now we at least figure out what her culpability is, in terms of her horse carrying a million-dollar baby that may or may not be her property."

Rafe nodded. "First thing."

"And then we figure out if the investigator is snooping around because we snooped around. Or because someone put two and two together about her pregnant horse."

"She's been here quite a while and no one has come looking for her."

"Like you said, she moved around a bit."

"Well, someone at Charlotte Oaks knew she was here the day she started, because Kate called to verify her reference."

"Maybe the someone in question wasn't privy to that phone call, but overheard or intercepted yours."

Rafe nodded. "Maybe so. But how does that translate to an insurance investigator?"

"Two ways. One, either the person who figured this out stands to lose something and alerted the insurance guy, or the insurance guy isn't who he says he is. Do we have any proof of that?"

"No. But we can take care of that when he gets out here. I'll make sure I'm part of that little visit. We'll put Kate on the alert, too."

"What about the other guy? The vet? What does he know?"

"He only knows her horse is having problems. He's an old family friend."

"You sure she didn't confide in him?"

"As sure as I can be. She said she didn't tell anyone about this. But that wouldn't keep him from maybe talking to the wrong person about her pregnant horse. He's pretty well known within the horse set, from what I understand. I'll talk to her, follow up on that."

"Could there be anything more going on there?"

Rafe just looked at him. "He's old enough to be her father."

"Some women like younger men, some women . . ." Mac ducked when Rafe made as if he was going to toss something at his head. "I'm just saying."

"I watched them together. Trust me. Very father-daughter."

Mac just shrugged. "Whatever you say. So, let's go over the conception thing again."

"What's left to discuss?"

"It's just . . . that's the one part of all this that is the hardest to make fit. How long do you think something like that takes?"

"Hard to say, but I would think not very long, once things get going."

"But something like that has to make some noise, cause a little ruckus. No one heard? No one came running?"

"The reports say the private stable was a distance from the main stables, and even farther from the main house. It was closer to the trailers, but not by much. They had music blaring, along with the all-night poker game, so that might have covered it."

"Yeah, I suppose."

"Unless . . ." Rafe drifted off, really not liking where his thoughts were leading.

"Go on."

He sighed, swore a little. "Unless she did have it planned and it was done inside the stables. I don't know how much room it takes, or what kind of facility the private barn setup was, but if it was done intentionally, it might have been controlled somehow. Which would have made it quieter, less likely to be seen."

Mac held Rafe's gaze. "Makes a lot of sense."

"I know. Dammit."

They both fell silent for a moment, then Mac said, "Could she have orchestrated and pulled off something like that alone?"

Rafe looked up. "Doubtful." He perked up a little. "Which is good news—great, even."

"Her having an accomplice is good news?"

"She doesn't have an accomplice."

"How can you be sure?"

"She might be good at avoiding a subject, but she's a terrible liar—her face gives away everything she's thinking. When we talked about that night, she led me through the events, and that clearly took a toll on her. She was tired, already stressed over the phone call, scared for her horse's health, definitely not at her strongest. Probably one of the reasons she finally relented and told me what she did."

"She didn't tell you about the Geronimo hookup?"

"I didn't ask her about it. I didn't know to. I asked her about the fire, and she told me. If there was someone else in this with her, she'd have had to think a lot more quickly on her feet to cover for that. Besides, that puts someone else involved the whole time she's been here, and I highly doubt that scenario. She's damn determined to do things for herself. It was monumental for her to tell me about this."

"Maybe she had her story ready. She's had a long time to perfect it."

"Maybe."

"But you don't think so."

He shook his head. "You know how you were about Kate? How certain you were? That's what my gut says about Elena. It's not in her to do this, any of this. I'd bet money on it."

"You're going to have to be willing to bet a whole lot more than that if this thing blows up and you've in any way helped her to conceal a crime."

Rafe nodded. "I know."

"So, we say she's innocent—how are you going to make it make sense?"

"Do what I do best. Dig. And talk to her.

"You going to tell her what we suspect?"

"I'm going to ask her who she bred her horse to."

"You said she's good at avoiding, terrible at straight-out lying. So just ask her straight-out if Geronimo is the father."

"I want her to tell me."

"You don't want her to run."

"That, too."

"Any chance at all she's playing you?"

"If she is, then I deserve everything I've got coming to me."

Mac stood up and stretched, then smiled and clapped his hands together. "Then we're in."

"*I'm* in," Rafe clarified. "It's sticky—I'll understand if—"

Mac's smile spread to a grin. "Like I said. We're in."

Rafe smiled back. "Thanks."

"Don't thank me yet. Thank me when it's over and we can get on with giving you shit for, oh, a few years ought to cover it."

"You help me get her out of this, you can rag on me as long as you like."

"Then I guess I better make sure that not only do the good guys win, but that you get the girl."

Now Rafe grinned. "Leave that part to me."

Chapter 19

"How's he doing?"

Tracey paused, hoof pick in hand. "A little setback today, actually."

Elena frowned and walked closer, but stayed clear of Bonder's rear quarters. It had turned out that his stumble that day hadn't caused any damage. For which she'd been eternally grateful. Poor thing had enough to overcome as it was. But now she was worried. She ran a close eye over the leg that had buckled, but it looked okay, no swelling, and he wasn't favoring it. "Is it his forelock? Did we miss something?"

"No, nothing like that, his leg is fine. He got spooked pretty badly, though. We'd been out about forty-five minutes and I had him trotting along the back rail, or would have, but—"

"Trotting?" Elena glanced at Bonder, who chose that moment to shake his mane a little. She couldn't help it, she laughed. "All bad-ass now, are ya?" She looked back to Tracey, who had the grace to look a little abashed, but not enough to squelch the excitement and pride that shone in her light blue eyes.

"Well, we've been working up to it, but he seemed so steady today and he's been extremely well-behaved lately." Before Elena could comment, Tracey added, "And no, no more Popsicles. I've been giving him carrots, like you suggested." Her cheeks turned a shade pinker. "Okay, so maybe with a little peanut butter, but it worked. He's a total tramp for peanut butter, as it turns out."

Elena patted Bonder's side. "That's okay—I'm a big fan of the stuff myself. Extra chunky," she told him, then looked back at Tracey. "So, what happened to set him off?"

"We were on our second lap and I was working him up to speed, when some idiot in a monster-size pickup truck came roaring up the lane, heading toward the main house. I managed to keep him steady through that, but then they had to go and blow what sounded like a broken foghorn . . . Anyway, Bonder freaked and all but dragged me back in here."

"You didn't let him turn tail, did you?"

"I almost didn't have a choice. I thought he was going straight through the fence, but I managed to turn him and slow him down. I walked him for another fifteen minutes, then brought him in here. He was still shaken up, very distracted, very jumpy."

Elena moved in then, and stroked Bonder's mane and neck. "Poor baby. Just can't catch a break." She kept talking to him, stroking him, as Tracey went back to cleaning out his hooves. "You're doing really well with him," Elena told her. "You're making amazing progress."

"Well, I spend a lot of my spare time with him." She looked up quickly. "Off the clock, don't worry."

"You don't have to do that," Elena told her, knowing damn well it wouldn't make any difference. It wouldn't have to her, either.

"I want to. I enjoy it. I actually look forward to the time I get to spend with him after I get done with the rest of my chores."

"I'm sure he does, too." She scratched him between the ears. "Don't you, big guy?"

Bonder whuffled a little, then lowered his head and nudged at her pocket.

"Nothing in there for you."

Tracey fished in her pocket and came out with a small Ziploc bag. "Here. He only got one so far." She pulled out a carrot and handed it to Elena.

"What the heck is this?"

"I halve the carrots and layer them with peanut butter."

She laughed. "A carrot-and-peanut-butter sandwich?"

Tracey smiled sheepishly. "Pretty much. He's remarkably easy when you find his weak spot."

"I thought women figured that out about us a long time ago," came a deep voice from behind them.

Elena turned to find Rafe standing a few yards away. She hadn't seen him since last night and, given all that had happened between them, she wasn't sure how she'd feel when she saw him again. Or what conclusions he'd come to today, now that he'd had time to think about what she'd told him. She wondered if he'd talked to Mac . . . and what Mac's reaction had been.

"I, uh, do you two need to talk?" Tracey straightened and brushed her hands against her pants. "I can make myself scarce."

"No," Elena said, maybe a bit too quickly. "Keep on with Bonder." She handed Tracey the peanut-butter carrot. "We'll leave you to it."

She walked past Rafe, toward the opposite end of the barn, hoping he followed until they were out of earshot. And eyesight. It surprised her, the strength of her desire to run to him, to smile into his face and hope he pulled her into his arms for a kiss. Like a normal couple. She didn't know what they were, but she doubted they were that. Too many complications. So she wasn't sure how to act. It was all so new.

He fell in beside her and her entire body responded to his nearness. She wanted to ask him if his palms were sweating like hers were. Not sure if they were far enough away yet, she played it safe and said, "What can I do for you?" all business-like, until his chuckle made her realize what she'd inadvertently offered. She smiled. "And here I thought you were such a gentleman."

They were passing the tack room and, before she could sense the motion behind her, he snagged her arm and neatly spun her inside the dark, dank room. The door shut behind her and he turned her against him before she could so much as draw a breath. "You make me want to do very ungentlemanly things," he said, his voice barely more than a low rasp. A low, amused rasp. "In fact, you provoke a whole variety of inappropriate responses. Ones I'm having an increasingly difficult time ignoring. Though I did try. I really did try."

Tracey was not fifty feet away and she'd already caught them here once, though it was doubtful she'd follow them. Still, Elena should be pushing him back out of here. What she did, however, was take his face in her hands and do what she really wanted to do. She kissed him. Backwalked him up against the wall with such force, in fact, that several saddles came close to tumbling off their perches.

To his credit, he was smart enough to go with the flow. In fact, he was downright brilliant. He accepted her tongue with a smooth ease that told her she was giving him exactly what he'd hoped for. Well, good. But what started as a simple kiss, affirming their status quo, quickly turned into something else completely. She'd thought she was keeping it together, that she was handling this, but it turned out she was far from in control of the emotions he'd stirred inside her.

She kissed him like she'd never kissed a man in her life. She poured everything she had into it. Every single confusing, exhilarating, profoundly life-changing thing he'd ever made her feel was shoved right on out there. Let him deal with it—he'd provoked it, after all.

Not that he was complaining.

Her hands moved from his face to his hair, then rapidly down to his shoulders, where she sank what nails she had to get a better grip so she could kiss him even more deeply. Her heart was pounding so hard she could hear the thrum of it in her ears, and it was quite probable that the moaning sounds echoing in the room were all coming from her. She didn't care. She started pulling at his shirt, suddenly wild to feel his skin again, to sink into that blissful, mind-blowing place where she didn't have to worry about her horse, or the baby, or the fact that someone from Charlotte Oaks was hunting her. She wanted to drown herself in the knowledge that he could very easily—oh, so easily—take her to another place, a place where it was just about sensation, about feeling, about pleasure.

Her fingers fumbled at the buttons, and, suddenly frustrated and completely out of patience already, she gave up and just started to rip his shirt open. That was when one of them came to their senses. And it wasn't her.

"Hold on there," he said, covering her hands and trying to disengage his mouth from hers. When she kept on clawing at the buttons on his shirt, he turned and pinned her against the wall, grabbing her hands and trapping them beside her head. "Wait just a damn minute, now."

"Why?" she demanded, knowing full well she probably looked like a demented animal at the moment and still not caring. "You want this, too, right? You want more, you said. You want it all."

"I—yes, but not like this. What the hell has gotten into you?"

"You. You've gotten into me. And I don't know how to handle it. My whole world is turning upside down and I can't make any sense of it anymore. I'm feeling things I have no business feeling about a man I just met. I'm confused as hell, scared as hell, and I don't know what to do about it."

He turned her around, gently this time, and cupped her face with his hands. "You trust me. And trust this." He leaned in and kissed her, only this kiss wasn't an assault on her senses . . . it was a promise. When he lifted his head, he kept his face close to hers, their gazes locked. "I know it's crazy. Insane, even. But so what? I'm right where I want to be. You?"

She could only nod.

He pulled her into his arms, tucked her against his chest.

"I feel like such an idiot. I should be handling this better. I always handle things."

"If it makes you feel any better, I don't have the slightest idea what I'm doing, either." He leaned back enough so she could look up into his face. "I just know I'd rather be doing this, with you, than just about anything else on earth. So I'm going in that direction, see where it gets me. It can be that simple, Elena."

"Nothing in my life is that simple. Not now."

He traced the contours of her face with his thumbs. "It will be. We'll get it there." He slid his hands down her arms, and wove his fingers through hers, then held on.

For whatever reason, that undid her like nothing else could.

Her heart was still pounding, her mind still reeling, but his gaze, and the way he held her hands, the size of his body, almost cradling hers, protecting her like a shield . . . it calmed her, soothed her in a way that at any other time would have had her scrambling to get away, as she didn't need any saving or soothing. But she'd be lying to herself if she said it didn't help her in that moment, to find a center in the storm, to feel safely buffeted for the first time in days. Weeks, even. Maybe forever.

"I'm not going anywhere," he said, "so stop trying to scare me off, okay?"

"Is that what you think I was trying to do? Wait—my kissing you is scary? Am I that out of practice?"

His lips twitched. "Your kisses, under about almost any other conditions, would have had you naked and me buried deep inside you in about five seconds flat."

She gulped. "Oh."

"Yeah. Oh."

"That's . . ." She had no words for that.

"Intimidating as all hell. As are you. And yet, glutton that I am, I keep coming back for more."

"Gee, I'm feeling better by the moment, here."

He squeezed her hands in his. "You are strong, Elena. I know that if anyone can handle everything you're presently dealing with, and somehow take care of every part of it and make all of it turn out right in the end, it would be you. I have no small amount of respect for you. Or I wouldn't be here. I am not your white knight and I won't pretend to be. I'm just a man who wants to be with you, and can, coincidentally, help you out of a jam you happen to be in."

He lifted their joined hands and dropped a kiss on one of her knuckles, then another.

"My hands are dirty," she said, stupidly and distractedly. She didn't know what to do with this, with him.

His response to that was to loosen his hold and turn her palm to his mouth. Then he kissed her there, too, before curling her fingers inward to hold on to it, another promise delivered and now sealed.

"To the rest of the world, we're two bad-asses who don't need anyone, okay?" he said, his voice a shade rougher now. "But right here, right now, you and I? We know different."

"I scare you," she said.

"*Terrify* would be accurate."

Her lips curved, just a tiny bit, and she sniffled again. "Good. Just so the playing field is even."

"Exactly."

She felt his fingers tighten slightly around hers, felt the warmth of his body, the strength that poured effortlessly out of him, doing nothing more than standing there. And she wanted to wrap herself in it, just for a moment or two, just long enough to draw strength from it and get her bearings back. Would that be so wrong? So horrible a thing?

Except it wouldn't come without a price. That price being expectation. If she took from him, he'd expect her to give in return. Rightfully so. Could she do that? She wasn't sure what was more terrifying, that she'd fail . . . or how badly she wanted to succeed.

"What do I offer you?" she asked, not realizing she'd spoken out loud until he responded.

"You offer you."

She snorted. "A stressed-out person who is more comfortable with horses than people and is in a fairly serious amount of trouble, or might be. Yeah, I'm a real catch. Any man should be so lucky."

He grinned. "That is exactly what you offer. Right there. Blistering honesty, absolutely no artifice, and not a shred of concern about what others might think of you. I've watched you walk into a ring with a psychotic horse and tame him with gentle words, sweet caresses, completely confident that you can and will succeed. And I find myself wanting to discover what it would be like to have all that confidence and gentleness aimed at me. Which, if you knew me—and you will—you'd find absolutely hilarious."

He used their joined hands to stroke his knuckles down the side of her face, and his voice softened further. "You provoke me, *mijita*, you make me wonder about things I've never wondered about. You make me think about you every damn second of the day. You've only just come into my life, and yet I find myself wondering what you'd think about this or that. I'll want to get your feedback on something I'm mulling over, because I know you won't bullshit me and I know you'll give a thoughtful, well-reasoned response without caring if it's what I want to hear or not. I've never met anyone like you."

"You need to get out more."

He barked a laugh, then his gaze grew quite serious. Which was quite terrifying, because she knew there was no hiding from him. He saw through all of her bullshit. It was like being naked at all times, vulnerable at all times. It should unnerve her, and it did. But, as he'd more or less just said about her, it was also comforting. To know there was one person who got her. Who would always get her. No matter what.

He kissed her knuckles again, then leaned in and kissed the tip of her nose. Something about that simple gesture, so sweetly innocent in its promise, so at odds with the man she was coming to know, made tears spring to her eyes. "Rafe," she whispered shakily, "I don't know what to do."

"Tell me the rest of the story, Elena. Let's get this thing resolved so we can get on with this."

"This?"

He squeezed her hands. "Yeah. This."

She swallowed hard, but his steady gaze helped. "There is something I kind of omitted yesterday. About Springer."

"She's pregnant with Geronimo's baby, isn't she?"

Elena's mouth dropped open, but no words came out. She finally closed it, swallowed hard, but still didn't know what to say. So she just nodded.

"Planned or unplanned?"

"Un," she said, shaking. "Very un."

"No one saw?"

She shook her head. "I didn't know what to do, so I went home, went to bed, thinking I had time to figure it out since it might not have taken. Then—then the fire, and Geronimo dying and . . ." She didn't know what else to say. "Everything I've said is the truth. I was already planning to leave. I waited to see if she was pregnant, still not sure what I was going to do, or who I was going to tell, if she was. But the media glare was insane, the investigation was going all over the place, speculation was pretty rampant, and I didn't have anyone I knew I could trust . . . so—so I left."

"I talked to Mac this morning."

"And?"

"He's digging, I'm researching. I'm trying to find out what the legal ramifications are of you having a horse carrying a baby after unauthorized, unpaid-for stud service—not to mention who provided that service. I want to know the strict legal aspects. Mac is digging to find out more about what's happening with the insurance investigation so we're better prepared when whoever it is shows up to talk to you." He looked at her. "A conversation I'm going to sit in on, so don't buck me on that. Two sets of ears and an outside observation can only help."

"I was going to ask you if you would, so thank you." That obviously surprised him, which made her smile. It felt good to smile. "I'm not a complete hard-ass."

He grinned and nudged her with his hips. "I happen to think your ass is damn near perfect."

She bumped him back. "You should know." Then her smile grew. "Are you blushing?"

"I never blush. I'm pretty sure it goes against the guy code."

"I don't know," she said, tilting her head to see his face in better light.

He'd just caught her in a fast kiss when a knock came on the door.

"Elena?" came a slightly raised whisper. It was Tracey.

It was a measure of how far she had sunk into this burgeoning relationship that, even with the sudden intrusion of the real world, it took her a few more lingering moments to end the kiss and surface. "Yes—" The word had come out like more of a croak. She cleared her throat, even as she caught Rafe's glinting smile. "Yes?"

"Sorry, but there's someone here to see you. Says it's urgent."

They both tensed. "Who is it?" she asked.

"Same jerk who came by in that truck and spooked Bonder. I guess he went up to the main house first. Now he's down here. He didn't give his name."

"Where is he now?" Rafe asked.

Any other time she'd have been mortified to have been caught—again—in such an unprofessional, compromising situation. But the real world had returned with a vengeance, and she wasn't prepared yet.

"Out at the barn office. Kate's there."

"Good," Rafe responded. "Have her keep him there for a few, will you?"

"Do my best."

"Tracey?" Elena called out, but there was no answer. She turned to Rafe. "What do we do?"

"Do you have a laptop in your loft? One with Internet access?"

"Yes, I have a computer—no, I don't have access. I use the office computer when I need that, which is rare-to-never."

He tucked her hand in his and turned to the door. "Then we'll just have to be a bit stealthier."

"And do what?"

"We're going to head out through the rear paddock, circle the ring till we get to the grove of trees that runs all the way up the hill to the house, and use that for cover."

"What, we're suddenly *Mission: Impossible*?"

"I want to know more about this guy before we talk to him."

She was following him without realizing it, but paused then, tugging on his hand. "How are you going to get any more information on him than you already have without talking to him? Why don't I talk to him while you run whatever checks you want?"

"You don't go in there alone."

"Kate is in there alone."

"He doesn't want Kate."

She tried not to shiver a little at the thought, but she still felt hunted. "I can handle it."

He tugged her against him and kissed her. "I know. So just imagine how amazing it's going to be when you add me to the mix."

"Relentless."

"I believe I mentioned that."

She smiled. "I know. It makes me a little nervous."

"What, you don't think I can handle this?"

"No, because I believe you can. And worse, I like it."

Chapter 20

Rafe opened the door leading to the side entrance of the suite of offices he shared with Finn and Mac.

"I still don't understand why we're in stealth mode here. Why not just confront the guy and find out what he wants?" Elena asked.

"Always better to go into any battle with more information than your opponent. As of now, all you know is that he's an insurance investigator—or says he is—and he's hot on your tail because of some renewed interest supposedly spurred by our contacting your employer to ask a few questions. Something isn't adding up here."

"What do you mean?" She closed the door behind her and looked around. "Wow. Very nice."

Rafe absently looked around the room, trying to see it as she did, recalling how he'd felt about it several years earlier when he, Finn, and Mac decided to join ranks and form Trinity. Finn had revamped his father's expansive home office and library into one main deliberating room surrounded by three smaller satellite offices. They rarely closed the doors, however, and they all wandered freely in and out of each other's space all the time. Hell, most of the time one or all of them weren't even around.

The offices had once been a stultifying fortress of mahogany, wainscoting, and rare Persian rugs. The floor-to-ceiling custom

bookshelves had been filled with specially bound leather vol-
umes, dotted with rare and expensive collectibles and artifacts
that Finn's father had prided himself on collecting. At times
through less than humanitarian means. But then, no one
would ever call Harrison Dalton anything so benevolent as a
humanitarian, despite the number of charities that had borne
his name.

Finn had deconstructed the space immediately and turned it
into something more befitting their individual tastes. The central area was a study in warm tones, soft fabrics, and leathers,
with low tables and subtle lighting, intended to put the occasional client at ease, though it was far more common for them
to travel to see their clients than to bring them in. The idea had
been to make it warm, inviting, and not intimidating. Dalton
Downs was that all by itself.

"Mac?" he called out, but there was no response. "He was
just here. He was supposed to be digging up whatever he could
find out on the insurance companies that covered Geronimo."

Elena had wandered over to an end table next to the couch.
"I think he left a note."

Rafe crossed the room. "Why didn't he call down to the
barn?" He picked up the note and scanned it quickly. "Looks
like he got called away on that Peterson deal. Took off to the
airport about twenty minutes ago." He picked up the stack of
papers that had been left underneath the note. "This was all he
could dig up, but the note says there is nothing new there in
terms of any late-breaking news in their investigation. He also
didn't find any trail leading anyone to you, or out here."

"That's good news, right?"

"Yes, and no. It doesn't explain who the guy is in Kate's office."

Elena wandered to the open door of the first office to the
right. "This is . . . interesting."

"Mac's office."

"I take it he decorated it himself?"

Rafe smiled. "You know he was a former cop, right?"

"Which explains why it looks like a precinct."

"He's not too big on frills."

"I see that." She peered in at the standard-issue desk, the huge dry-erase board that filled most of one wall, the giant magnet board that filled the other. The remaining wall was lined with several metal file cabinets and a tall bookcase crammed with every manner of book, binder, or pamphlet that Mac had ever used. Shelved in no particular order and looking like a librarian's worst nightmare, Rafe knew Mac could put his hand on any specific title blindfolded.

Elena walked to the next door and laughed. "Let me guess. Finn."

"He had a stunted childhood—what can I say?"

Finn's space was more amusement park than office, but then Finn was anything but traditional in his approach to business.

"That's the biggest foosball table I've ever seen."

"He had it specially made. Actually, one of our clients constructed it for him, as payment. He was a game developer whose ideas were ripped off and we helped him regain control of his patent."

She poked her head further in. "Oh my God, is that—"

"Ms. PacMan? Sadly, yes. When he first got that one in, he played it until all hours. The sound effects haunt me to this day."

He watched as she took in the mini basketball court, the massive flat-screen television, specially built-in xBox 360 gaming console and seating area, and the vintage Las Vegas blackjack table—reputed to have been used by the Rat Pack themselves back in the day—before turning back to him. "So . . . he plays games all day?"

"Says it helps him think through things. And considering he's about twice as productive as Mac and me, who slave twice as hard, we can't really call him out on it."

"Whatever works, right?"

"Right."

She took a step closer and peered around him. "Which leads us to your space."

Rafe stepped aside, more curious about her reaction than he'd thought he'd be. In fact, he'd never once cared what anyone thought about the way he chose to live, or dress, or the environment he worked in.

"This is definitely you." She walked all the way in, and turned to take in the whole room.

Bemused by the certainty in her tone, he followed her inside.

"You designed this yourself, didn't you?"

"None of us is the hired-decorator type."

"But yours could have been done professionally—no one would think otherwise." She turned once again. "You have as good an eye for interior design as you do for clothing."

"Thank you. It was an acquired skill, I can assure you."

She smiled, as if surprised that he'd so readily accepted the compliment.

"It means something to you, doesn't it? Comfort, casual elegance. I mean, it's not contrived or overdone, and it totally suits you. But you don't take this for granted."

"No," he said, quietly. "Not one square inch of it."

"So, if I were to play armchair psychologist, I would say that you probably weren't raised around pretty things. Maybe *pretty* isn't the right word, but—"

"Beauty. And you're right. There was a distinct lack of beauty in my world. I vowed to make up for that. I wanted to create a space that was pleasing to the senses—soothing, I guess. I don't apologize for that. I still see plenty of ugliness."

"I'm sure you do. And who would ask you to apologize for working to change something so fundamental?"

He didn't respond. He'd never felt defensive about his choices. In the past, with other women, he hadn't cared much one way or the other what they thought. He didn't seek to impress, but was simply comfortable in the knowledge that whoever was in his company would always feel comfortable in his surroundings.

He'd had women in his pool house home, but she was the first woman he'd brought into his office. Oddly, he felt more exposed here than he did in his personal space. He spent a moment wondering what that said about him and his priorities.

Elena ran a hand over the backs of the soft leather side chairs that fronted a low table, all arranged facing a small, slate fireplace. His desk was on the other side of the room. It was constructed from warm cherry, an average size, with a functional computer center set up to one side. Bookcases lined one of the walls, and while not the wild chaos of Mac's, neither were they filled with the pretentious leather collections of the elder Dalton.

"Who painted that? Anyone I should know and am shamefully undereducated about?"

She was looking at a landscape that hung over the fireplace.

"No, no one most people know. It was payment from a client. My first for Trinity, actually. She's showing in several West Coast galleries now and doing okay—for a starving artist, anyway."

"She?" Elena turned and pretended to study the sculpture next to the lamp on the end table.

Rafe smiled. "Yes, she. No, we weren't involved."

Elena looked up, her widened eyes claiming total innocence, but the blush in her cheeks saying otherwise. "I wasn't intimating. Besides, it's certainly none of my business."

"It is if you think I make a habit of mixing business with pleasure."

"Do you?"

Rafe didn't take offense. It was a fair question. He crossed the room to stand next to her as they both studied the oil painting. "What do you think? I'm asking sincerely."

She favored him with an assessing side glance, then looked back at the painting. "I think you don't see women as conquests, but rather as temporary companions. It's not a game to you, but you don't strike me as someone looking to put down roots with anyone, either. Which makes it easier not to have too many rules or boundaries." She looked at him again, and found his gaze already on her. She held his easily. "I think you're with who you want, when you want, and it doesn't much matter why she crossed your path or how long she remains in your orbit." She smiled. "But I do bet they're always stunningly beautiful. In keeping with your new world aesthetic."

It should have disconcerted him, how easily she'd summed him up. And how correctly. But, frankly, he'd have been more surprised if she'd missed the mark. Her intuitive skills were one of the things he most admired about her.

She smiled. "So, do I still get you?"

He was reaching for her before even being aware of his intent. It just seemed both natural and necessary for him to have her close, where he could touch her, taste her, take in her scent. But she smoothly sidestepped him and wandered over to the bookcase, seemingly oblivious. Somehow he doubted she missed much.

"So," she said at length, reaching out to touch the spine of a book, then thinking better of it and rubbing her hands off on her overalls first. Tilting her head to read the title, she went on. "How do you explain me?" She lifted her head and pinned him with a bemused look. "I'm all kinds of wrong for this world of beauty you've created."

"Why would you say that?" Although he knew perfectly well why. She was exactly correct. She wasn't anything like the women who typically caught his attention. But he wanted to hear her put it into words, see what her view of herself was.

To that end, she just laughed and gestured to the stable hand clothes she had on. "I wouldn't know a designer label if it was stamped on my forehead. Thread-count means nothing to me. I don't have the faintest clue about what makes great art or literature. I'm perfectly happy with some fried chicken or barbeque. Five-star cooking would be lost on me." She swung her braid around to the front and tugged on it. "Hell, I use the same shampoo as my horse."

Rafe smiled and walked over to her. "Lucky horse."

"My idea of beauty is watching a young thoroughbred pound around a mile-and-a-quarter practice track just as the sun tops the trees and starts to burn off the morning fog. Smelling the sweat flying off his neck, seeing the fierce will in his eyes, hearing one set of hooves pounding into the soft track."

"Sounds like a sight worth seeing." He stopped in front of her. "As are you." He reached up, stroked a finger down the side of her cheek.

"Rafe," she said quietly, "who are you kidding here?"

"I'm not kidding anyone. Least of all myself."

She sighed a little. "I wish I had your conviction."

"You've got enough on your plate. Don't overanalyze this."

"It's because I do that I have to closely consider every step I take. Professionally and personally." She held his gaze. "I guess what keeps tripping me up is . . . why me?" She held up a hand to stall his response. "I mean, I know there is chemistry."

He grinned. "Hard to ignore that part."

"But chemistry isn't everything. We're so different." She gestured to the room. "And if I needed more proof of that, I'm currently surrounded by it."

"Are you really that uncomfortable here?"

"It's a little intimidating. I spend my days around horse-stall muck. This . . ." She looked around. "It's lovely, and inviting. And I can't help but feel that I shouldn't touch anything for fear of mussing it up."

Rafe followed her gaze, and, through her eyes, began to see what she saw. His gaze came back to her, and as the matter became more necessary with each passing moment, he reached for her again. She resisted when he took hold of her arms and gently tugged her closer, but not enough for him to reconsider. She kept her eyes studiously focused on his chin, so he dipped his head down to catch her gaze with his. "Maybe I need a little mussing up," he said.

She snorted. "You spent your life building this world for yourself, and there is absolutely nothing wrong with that. It's gorgeous, and you deserve every comfort you've worked for. It's just . . . it's not the world I'm accustomed to."

"Would it be so horrifying to think about adjusting to it . . . just a little?"

She lifted her eyes to his, clearly wary. "I'm not Eliza Doolittle. I'm happy in my mucky world."

"Anyone who spends five minutes with you sees that. Speaking of which, I've spent some time in your world. Willingly."

"You were just digging for dirt."

He conceded that. "In the beginning."

"Are you trying to tell me that if you were convinced that things were fine with me and all my problems were solved, that you'd continue to pursue your riding lessons?"

"If you'd asked me that the day of my first lesson, I'd have said no."

"But now you have a sudden burning desire to ride?"

"Now I want to know more about your world. And if that means getting up close and personal with those half-ton crazed beasts you love, then, yes . . . I want to learn to ride them."

She took a moment to digest that, and, in the end, didn't question his sincerity. He took it as a sign of progress. What the hell he was progressing toward, he had no earthly idea, which was why he was taking his own advice and not over-analyzing it. All he knew was he was right where he wanted to be.

"So . . . what expectations do you have of me? You're willing to learn to ride—what will I have to learn?"

"I have no idea. You look around and feel out of place. I look at you here, and wonder how I can convince you to hang around for awhile." He ran his hands up her arms. "I like you here. But then, I'm admittedly liking you anywhere I happen to be." He leaned in closer, dipped his mouth closer to hers. "It doesn't matter where that is, or whether we're surrounded by the finest hand-tooled leather chairs, or hand-tooled leather saddles. You fit in, because you fit me."

He kissed her then, sliding his fingers into her hair, then down the length of her braid, where he slid the elastic band free and began to unwind those thick, dark tresses.

"Rafe—"

"Let me," he murmured. "You run your hands through my hair and I love the way that feels. Let me do the same." He continued to unweave the heavy plait, punctuating his words with kisses along her jaw, to the soft underside of her chin. She sighed and tipped her head back, and he was torn with the twin desire to grin in victory . . . and pull her down to the carpet right where they stood and bury more than his hands in her hair.

He shook the heavy waves free, then finally slid his hand to the nape of her neck, sank his fingers into her hair, and tipped her mouth up to his again. She groaned deep in her throat as he raked his fingertips along her scalp, his kiss growing hungrier with every little sound she made.

Her hands were on his shoulders, but rather than push him away, she dug her nails into the muscle there and kissed him back, her appetite every bit as voracious as his.

Whatever restraint he'd had, whatever pace he'd thought to take with her, slowly seducing her into his world, into his bed, disintegrated along with his carefully maintained control. Every inch of him was rock-hard and aching. His need to taste her, to breathe in her scent, to touch, revel in the earthiness that so intoxicated him, felt suddenly vital.

With one hand still cupping her head, keeping her mouth fused to his, he let his other hand explore, first sliding down to solid roundness of her shoulder. He found he didn't mind that there were hard angles to her, and muscle, both necessities of the life she led. But when he released the catch of her overalls so the front bib fell open, and slid his hand further down, past the ridge of her collarbone, he found her soft places, too. He loved the way the swell of her breast fit him perfectly as he cupped his palm there.

She let out a soft moan, and pushed against him in primal response as he rubbed his fingertip across the tip of her nipple until it became a rigid nub, pressing it against the soft cotton of her faded t-shirt. She didn't wear a bra, which only pushed him closer to the edge.

The taunting of her hips grinding into his, begging him to sink every aching inch between those long legs of hers, and the need to take that taut little nub between his lips and teeth and tease and taunt her until he drove her wild, sent him right to the edge of restraint.

He flicked open the catch on the other shoulder, and tugged at her t-shirt, pulling it up. She kept her fingers deep in his hair, his mouth mated to hers, as he tugged and yanked and eventually bared her to him. There hadn't been much time for this in her truck, so he wanted to revel in it now. Her skin was smooth and soft, with a hint of a natural glow, and a scattering of tiny freckles that beckoned him to trace each and every one with his tongue. But the full, plump perfection of those nipples demanded all of his attention.

She growled when he closed his mouth over the first one, cupping his palm over the other. His hips bucked forward of their own volition, his body seeking its place inside hers with rapidly growing insistence. But he couldn't have both. Yet.

He slid his hands to her hips, sliding her overalls down further, baring her to her hips, where a scrap of something yellow caught his attention. But her hands were back in his hair, urging him to keep his focus—and his tongue—on her nipples. He grinned at her demands, which only served to jack him up even higher. Feeling somewhat primal himself, he backed her up against the bookshelf and slid his hands behind her thighs, pulling her legs up around his hips. She gripped the shelves over her head, arching her back; he took every advantage of the invitation and suckled, licked, nipped, and savored her sweet breasts until he thought they'd both lose their minds.

Her thighs were so tightly wrapped around him he could barely breathe. Strong and muscled from years of gripping something a hell of a lot more powerful than he was had him all but dying to strip her down and let her ride him as naturally and beautifully as she did those powerful beasts. He might die from the pleasure of it, but, at that moment, he was pretty damn sure it would be worth every last breath.

He slid his hands inside her overalls and down over the soft silk of her panties, teasing his fingers along the edge of the elastic as far as he could reach, while still enjoying the way her nipples teased his tongue.

She started bucking almost immediately.

"Rafe . . ." It was one word—raw and demanding. And far be it from him not to give the lady what she wanted.

He swung her away from the bookshelf. She grabbed at his head for balance, burying his face in her breasts as he blindly staggered them to the soft leather couch that fronted the fireplace. They bumped up against the back of it, then went sliding over the thickly padded backrest and landed on the cushions with her finally where he wanted her, beneath him, legs parted, welcoming him between them.

Except there were way too many clothes still in play.

Once again, her demands paralleled his as she worked her fingers between them and tugged at the button of his pants. They were both working toward the same goal. He was tugging down her overalls and she was tugging at his pants when a short buzz sounded, followed by Kate's voice echoing through the office.

"Rafe? You in there? I have a very . . . aggressive individual in my outer office asking after Elena. Tracey seems to think you're aware of this and that Elena is with you. What are you planning to do about this?"

At the first word, Elena had frozen beneath him.

Shit. Clearly Mac hadn't had the chance to say anything to Kate, mainly because he'd asked him not to yet. Dammit. "You don't happen to have a gun on you, do you? Because, at the moment, I'm perfectly fine with you shooting the bastard."

Elena started to squirm, trying to slide out from under him. He pinned her down. "Kidding," he whispered to her. "Mostly. I let Mac take care of shooting people and he's not here at the moment."

Still keeping her half-naked beneath him, he lifted his head and spoke in the direction of the intercom. "Let him cool his heels for a few minutes. Next time he can make an appointment."

"There's going to be a next time? Something you want to share with me?"

"Yes, but not at the moment. Trust me, I'm handling it."

"I'll just bet you are," Kate muttered under her breath, but it came through loud and clear.

"Oh, God." Elena started struggling anew.

"Thanks, Kate," Rafe said.

There was a pause, then, "Elena?"

Cheeks a flaming red now, Elena nodded, then seemed to realize that wasn't going to convey anything, and choked out, "Yep. I'm here."

There was another static-filled pause, then, "Ah. Really sorry."

"You know," Rafe put in, "you and Mac aren't the only ones who—"

"I said I was sorry," Kate said, hurriedly cutting him off. "What can I do to help?"

"Stall the guy and get the info off his truck plates for me."

"Will do."

"Let me up," Elena whispered fiercely. "At this rate, I'll be lucky if I still have a job by sundown. First Tracey, now this."

Rafe didn't budge. "I was kind of enjoying you right where you are."

She squirmed. "Not kidding."

He sighed and levered himself off of her, then helped her up, catching her to him when she would have turned her back.

"I know that was awkward. I'm sorry. I really am. But—" He held tight when she tried to turn away. "Regardless of awkward outside interference, please don't ever hide from me." Her shirt was still pushed up, her breasts bared, her overalls hanging down around her hips and her hair a wild tangle around her face. He'd never seen anything so fantastically beautiful in his entire life. "You're breathtaking."

"Let's not get patronizing."

He tugged her hips forward, so they met his own. "Still doubt me?"

She visibly swallowed, and he couldn't help but smile when her hips instinctively moved a bit on his before she moved back.

"I don't think I can do this," she said.

"Do what, exactly?"

She waved a hand between them. "This." She started to straighten her clothes, but he brushed her hands away.

"If you must, allow me. After all, I was responsible for getting you half-naked—it's the least I can do."

"I wasn't exactly beating you off with a stick." She tugged at her shirt.

He sighed as she covered herself. "A crime, really."

"Please." She untangled the buckled straps of her overalls and hooked them over her shoulders, but he stopped her when she started to pull her hair back.

"Leave me with something."

She just rolled her eyes. "You'd think you're starved for it or something, when I happen to know it was just yesterday that we—"

He stopped her with another fast, hard kiss. "That was light years ago. I think I'll always be starved for you." He was kissing her again and she was responding, then suddenly she pushed him away and shook her head.

"I swear, I have no restraint around you. It's crazy, is what it is. I've never behaved so unprofessionally in my life." She flung her hand in the direction of the intercom. "That was my boss, for God's sake."

"Who is living with my partner, so I seriously doubt she's going to have a problem with us having a relationship."

His use of the "r" word rattled her a little, but, to her credit and his supreme satisfaction, she didn't back down. Instead, she squared her shoulders—and damn beautiful shoulders they were—and looked him in the eye. "Fine. But no more naked time during business hours. It just confuses and distracts."

"But—"

"Aha, see? You should see your face. It's like I told you there's no Santa. We have to get a grip on this."

"I'd be lying if I said that wasn't a disappointing rule, but . . . okay."

Now she looked wary. "Okay?"

He tucked his hands in his pockets. It was either that or he'd have them in her hair again. And then he was pretty sure some level of nakedness was going to occur and rules just barely established would already be broken, and, well . . . he curled his hands into fists. "Yes, okay." Then he grinned. "But the rule applies to you, too."

She backed up a step. "No coercing, no seducing."

He shrugged, enjoying himself now. "Okay."

"I mean it."

"It's your call. Anything else? Any other boundaries I should respect?" He took a step closer, grinned when she took another step back.

"Boundaries? I don't know," she said, looking a little disconcerted now, and a little nervous. He liked that last part. "Just . . . keep your hands off of me. I can't think when you're touching me, and thinking—keeping a clear head—is imperative. I mean, we've got an investigator stomping around out there and am I doing something about it? No. I'm in here about to do the horizontal tango with you. You see my point?"

He couldn't help it, he glanced down. "Both of them." He caught her hand before she could smack at his shoulder, and tugged her closer.

"See? You already can't play by the rules."

He lifted his hands, held them up. "Sorry. I'm working on it. You're very compelling."

Her eyes narrowed. "We have a deal, then?"

"I don't want you to walk out of my life, so you have leverage."

"Good to know."

He moved an infinitesimal bit closer, hands still raised. "But so do I. Have leverage, I mean."

"Rafe, I mean it—"

"No, no. Hands off. I'll follow your rules."

"Good," she said, looking entirely unconvinced. "We have much more important things to worry about and I can't afford to have you muddle me up."

"Understood. No muddling."

She cocked her head. "I see wheels spinning already. It's the pit bull part of you. I don't trust that part."

"You should—it's what makes me reliable."

"Reliably relentless and incorrigible."

He grinned. "Yeah, but I thought you liked that about me."

"I'll like it even better when we put it to use figuring out who that guy is outside."

Chapter 21

The intercom beeped, then Kate's voice filled the room again. "Okay, this is what I've got. His card says he's Stephen Johansson with Intrepid Insurance and Securities. Drives a bronze Ford F-250 pickup, North Carolina plates." She read off the numbers. "He won't say why he's here, other than it's private business and that Elena is expecting him. He's still pacing in my outer office. I've given him coffee and told him I'm trying to track Elena down, that she might be out on a trail ride. What else can I do?"

"Nothing," he said at length. "Thanks, Kate. I'll take it from here. Just—don't let him leave."

"I'll do my best."

Rafe strode over to his desk and sat down, spinning his seat over to the computers, where he immediately began rapidly tapping out something on the keyboard.

"What are you going to do?" she asked, walking over to his desk.

"See what else I can find out about our Intrepid Mr. Johansson."

"Intrepid Insurance doesn't sound familiar to me."

"That's because it's not one of the companies listed in the reports."

Elena's eyebrows lifted. "Meaning?"

"Meaning he's either a phony, or there's another policy at play here."

"On Geronimo?"

"That's what we need to find out."

He was pretty focused on whatever he was typing in, and she didn't want to interfere, so she turned and walked to the other side of the office. Only, one look at the couch they'd just been sprawled on and she wanted to drag him onto his desk and finish what they started. So much for her hands-off rule.

She snuck a surreptitious glance in his direction. His expression was set, his fingers flying over the keyboard, his attention so tightly focused on the monitor that she doubted he'd notice anything short of a house fire.

Something shifted inside her, as she continued to watch him. It was that focus, that intensity, that she so readily responded to. Sure, it was an obvious thing to react to physically, but now, standing here, thinking about it more clearly, she began to understand the depth of the connection she was forming with him. He was like that with everything that interested him. Whether it be her body, or just the discussion at hand. He was alert, always, to every nuance, every word, every sound, breath, scent, and texture of the world around him. No wonder he scared the living hell out of her. It was intimidating to be on the receiving end of such focused attention.

But she also identified with it. She was much the same, only she'd felt hers was more an intuitive connection. With her horses, anyway. People she didn't deal with as much. Maybe that was why she couldn't seem to keep her head around him. He was the first person who called to that intuitive part of her. He didn't let her get away with anything. No subterfuge, no avoidance. And he gave the same.

She paced to the other side of the office, and tried not to think about what would happen when this was all over. If she wasn't in jail, or worse, that is. She wanted to go back to the career she'd spent a lifetime working to build. Working here was great—rewarding, even, in ways she hadn't expected. But what she wanted, what she craved, was that thundering excitement that only came with working around young thoroughbreds pounding their hearts out along an oval track. She couldn't get that here.

Oddly, the rush she always felt when she thought about that, when she imagined her return, allowed herself to want it, think about how much she missed it, didn't come.

She turned to look at him again, sitting there behind his beautifully appointed desk, in his personally designed office, dressed, even casually, like he could pose for a menswear ad just by looking up and smiling into the camera. This man who grew up with nothing, who had fought to put beauty into his life, who respected, above all else, the need to nurture the soul, his as well as others . . . he made her heart pound.

She sank down onto the couch. She shouldn't be so stunned by the revelation, but she was.

Ducking her head, she fumbled her cell phone from one of the pockets of her pants and flipped it open. *Focus, dammit.* She needed to feel productive, and at the moment she was anything but. She punched in Kenny's number, then frowned as the line continued to ring and no one picked up. She finally flipped the phone shut again.

"Who are you calling?"

She looked up to find Rafe staring at her. "Kenny. With all this going on, it's past the time I told him I'd call to check in on Springer."

"And?"

"No answer."

Rafe frowned. She didn't want him to frown. She wanted him to shrug it off and go back to tapping the keyboard and finding out why an investigator from a heretofore unknown insurance company suddenly had such a dire need to speak to her.

"He's a practicing vet, right?"

"Right. He's probably with a client." Except Kenny had

texted her early this morning with his surgery and appointment schedule for the week and promised her that he'd keep his phone on him twenty-four/seven so she wouldn't worry.

She glanced at the clock on the fireplace mantel. He didn't have any surgeries today. And his last appointment had been several hours ago. She supposed he could have been called out on an emergency. She checked her phone, but, as she already knew, no messages awaited her. She was just being paranoid. For all she knew, he was in the shower.

She glanced back at Rafe, but his attention was back on his monitor. She tried to take that as a good sign, and worked at shoving aside the panic fluttering in her stomach. Other than Rafe, Mac, and Kate, no one from Dalton or Charlotte could possibly know where she'd stabled her horse. It was just all the jumbled nerves caused by the investigator showing up. And the fact that she'd been half naked on this very couch not twenty minutes ago.

"Finding anything?" she asked, rising from the couch and walking back over to the desk.

"Come here, look at this."

She walked around the desk and stood behind him. "What am I looking at?"

"Aerial shots of Charlotte Oaks. Before." He clicked the mouse. "And after."

She'd seen them before—they'd been all over the news back when it was news. "Okay. I don't see anything new or different. The stables are there, then they're gone." She still flinched at seeing the black, scorched earth, and her heart squeezed at such a tragic end to such a great champion.

"Right. Now, look at this." He clicked again, and another photo popped up.

She bent over his shoulder to get a closer look. "Wait, that looks like—but it can't be. If the investigation is still going on and the claim hasn't been decided on, then how . . . ?" She let the sentence trail off as she studied the aerial shot again. But no matter how long she looked at it, the facts didn't change.

New stables had been built on the burn site. In fact, everything from the fences to the scorched earth itself had been replaced and rebuilt. "With the new design and different paddock layout, you'd never know it was the same spot." She peered even closer. "Are you sure that's the same spot?"

He clicked a few buttons and the screen zoomed out slightly. He pointed. "See, there's the main stables, the track." He shifted his finger. "The main house. The orchards, the vineyard."

She nodded. "Wait, where did these photos come from? Some new media report?"

"There are Web sites now that let you access satellites and zoom in on pretty much anything you want, as long as you have an address."

"No way."

"Way." He clicked open another screen and typed in the address for Dalton Downs. Fifteen seconds later, a very distant topographical image popped up. With a few clicks, he zoomed in closer, then closer still, and *voila*. There was the house, the stables, the whole thing.

"That's just . . . well, it seems wrong, doesn't it?" she said, peering closer. "Like you can just spy on anyone."

"Well, most of these sites, the photos are archived, so you're not seeing things live, or even all that recent, in some cases. Just a snap from whenever the satellite last passed over the spot, or even longer ago than that. Usually months, at least."

She pointed. "But there's my truck, on the far side of the employee barn. I never park it there, but I did today because I wanted to load a few things to take to Kenny's this week." She gasped and pointed to the main stables. "And there's the investigator's pickup truck. Rafe!"

He looked over his shoulder, up at her, eyes crinkling at the corners. "I said *most* Web sites. We happen to have access to something a bit more . . . immediate."

"I know Finn is loaded, but you don't have your own satellite, and with all the heightened security in our country, I sincerely doubt the government allows—" Her eyes widened. "You are not jacking into some government satellite, are you? Because I don't care how much trouble I'm in, that's just—"

"Calm down. I assure you, it's all legit."

"But how?"

"Let's just say when you mentioned Finn's capacity for wealth, you might have overestimated what a decent satellite costs these days. Or, for that matter, leasing a private company that puts them up there for a living."

"Overestimated? How could I possibly—" She cut herself off and straightened. "Never mind. I don't think I want to know." She turned her attention back to the screen. "So, the new barn. How could they rebuild if there are still ongoing investigations?"

"That's just it. As far as I can tell, there aren't any. The reason Mac couldn't find anything new is because there isn't anything new."

"Files closed, then? They paid the claim?"

"It would take me a day or two to get copies, but it looks that way, yes."

"Then who is that guy presently wearing a path in Kate's office carpet?"

"I don't know."

"Did you find anything out about his company?"

"It exists, but from what little digging I could do in this short a period of time, that's all I can tell you. Nothing pops up on this guy personally. I will find out more, but it will take a little bit more time. Nothing is coming up linking this firm with anything else we have to date, either. No connection to Charlotte Oaks that I can find, or Geronimo."

"Can you find out who hired him or his company? Or do you think he's just doing this on his own? Maybe he's freelance investigating for some media outlet."

"Possible, but that's not where my gut is headed with this one."

"If the police have signed off on the case, and are unable to prove arson, and the insurance companies have called it a day, then what else is there to look into?"

Rafe looked up at her, and dread filled her.

"The only thing left is someone finding out about Springer," she said.

"I hate to say it, but it's the only thing that connects them to you, and the only thing that wouldn't be covered under any of the previous investigations."

"But how? Who?"

"I don't know."

She stepped around him to look at the photos again. "They sure built this pretty fast. Wouldn't you all have found something about the claims being paid?"

Rafe frowned and looked back at the monitor. "You know, you have a point."

"What if the claims weren't paid? I mean, what if they just decided to go ahead and rebuild? It's been months and months—maybe they got tired of waiting. Gene isn't the most patient guy in the world, and maybe he stopped caring about the payoff."

"Possible. Were those stables in demand?" he asked.

"Actually, no. They weren't in use the entire time I was there, until Geronimo came. Maybe he just wanted to get rid of any reminders of the fire. He is all about image."

"True." Rafe continued to study the photos, zooming in closer. "The other reason to rebuild is if you're afraid they'll find some evidence."

"After all this time and that many people digging, surely they'd have found anything that was left to find."

Rafe lifted a shoulder. "Just thinking about—"

"—all the angles," she finished for him.

He looked up and they both shared a brief smile. Then he shoved back and stood, taking her in his arms and leaning against his desk.

She raised her eyebrows, but he was unrepentant. "Screw

the rules. Things aren't looking so hot and I feel better when you're right here."

She let him tug her further between his legs. "I have to admit, you have a point."

He pushed her hair back and looked into her eyes for a long moment, then sighed and tugged her the rest of the way into his arms, so she was tucked against his chest.

"Now what?" she asked quietly. "Do we go talk to him?"

"I'd feel better if we knew more about why he was here."

"Maybe we should just confront him."

"Maybe, but nothing about this feels right."

She shivered a little and he ran his hands up and down her back. "I'm really hating this."

"I know," he said, continuing the soothing strokes. "I'm not real keen on it, either. I wish Mac was here—we could use the double team."

"I know. I'd feel a lot better if I could talk to Kenny."

"Why don't you try him again?"

She slipped her phone out of her pocket and punched in his number. Whatever the real story was with Mr. Johansson, she'd feel a hell of a lot better if she could just hear Kenny's voice and confirm that Springer was fine. She listened, and listened. No answer. She looked up at Rafe. "I think I need to go out there. Tonight. I need to see her. With my own eyes. I know you think I'm probably overreacting, but—"

"Actually, I don't."

Her heart sank at the same time her stomach tightened. She wanted to throw up. "Meaning?"

"Meaning whatever is going on here involves information that neither the police nor the other investigators got hold of before closing their files, and that was after some pretty intensive work. Johansson is a wild card since we don't know what claim he's investigating, or for what policy . . . or policy holder."

"So, what do we do about Mr. Johansson?"

"Nothing. Yet." He kissed her on the temple, then gently moved her aside so he could sit back at his desk again. He immediately began tapping at the keys.

"You think he's just going to wait around while we take a few hours to go check on my horse? What about Kate? You can't just stick her with—" Then she realized what he was doing and bent over his shoulder. "You're using the satellite thingie to view Kenny's farm?"

She watched as he manipulated the pointer until the satellite cam moved in on the general farm location. A cold chill skated over her. "You know, I always thought the whole Big Brother thing was really overexaggerated. Not so much anymore."

"Which is why Finn thought it was smart for the good guys to have the same access as the bad guys." Rafe kept working and manipulating the map until he could zero in on the right spot.

"Just what kind of trouble are these people in who come to you for help?"

"All kinds. Business scams, legal trouble, deportation issues, security issues." He glanced up, smiled. "Or a horse with a big secret and a history-making one-night stand."

Things were pretty damn scary at the moment, so the fact that he could make her smile, even now, maybe especially now, made her heart teeter dangerously closer in his direction. "Are you calling my horse a slut?"

He looked back to the screen. "If the horseshoe fits . . ."

She swatted at his shoulder, which he abruptly covered with his hand, trapping hers against him. He turned his chair and toppled her into his lap.

"We suck at following rules."

"Yeah, I know." He turned her face to his and kissed her soundly.

And, well, she kissed him back.

When he finally broke contact, he kept her face close to his, his palm cupping the back of her head and neck. When he spoke, he spoke softly but directly. "I think we need to go out to Kenny's place."

"What?" She was still a little dizzy from the kiss.

He sighed, then turned the chair so they were both facing the screen. "Look."

She shifted in his lap, and her heart, which was racing in a good way just a moment ago, stuttered and skipped a beat or two now. In a very bad way. "Oh no. Oh my God."

His hold on her tightened at precisely the same instant she tried to shoot off his lap. "Don't go tearing out of here."

"But Kenny's truck is gone. His big trailer is gone." She looked at the screen again. "All of his trailers." She fumbled for her phone, but it was in the pocket presently trapped between their bodies. "I have to find out where he is. Maybe someone came by there, too, and he took her and his other horses and—" She was babbling now, and made a concerted effort to stop, to rein in her panic, and try as best as she could to think clearly. Only it was impossible.

"I'm going to call Kate and tell her to inform Mr. Johansson that you're unable to meet with him today."

"I don't give a damn about Mr. Johansson, I have to get out of here—"

He wrapped his arms around her, stilling her for the moment. "*We* have to figure out what is going on a little more before we run in any direction. From what we can tell, there is no one at the farm. It would be a wasted road trip at this point, and quite probably put us off the playing field. And it's possible that's what they want."

"They? Who are they?" She tore her gaze away from the abandoned farm, and looked at Rafe. "I can't just sit here and wait. I can't."

He tightened his hold on her again when she renewed her struggle. "I didn't say that, just that we need to be smart about the next move we make. Now, think about this. No one related to the original investigations seems to be linked to this new interest in you. No one except you, me, Mac, Kate, and Kenny know where Springer was moved to, and only you and I know why she was moved. Unless you told Kenny that part of the story."

She shook her head. "No, he just knows she's pregnant and that I'm worried about her. He knows her history with her last foal. He's just doing a favor for a family friend."

"He knows you're in trouble, though."

"He knows I'm at a crossroads in my life, but he doesn't know why. He knows that I was at Charlotte Oaks, working on the farm where Geronimo died. And he knows I'm not working in the racing field at the moment. I swear I haven't told him anything else, but yes, he might be worried about me."

"Worried enough that he might talk to someone else about it? Maybe the wrong person? Unknowingly?"

She wanted to state that, absolutely, he'd never do that, but when Rafe put it in that context, she couldn't be sure. Maybe she should have told him more, but she hadn't wanted to put him in any kind of jeopardy, not when he was being such a good friend and going out of his way to help her. "I—I can't be sure. But who would he say anything to?"

"Would he have called anyone at Charlotte Oaks? Does he have any connections that way?"

"I doubt it. He's well known in the horse world in this area, but mostly with show horses, that kind of thing. He's not really connected to the racing world." Which is why she'd felt okay about bringing him into this at all. "And if he was just worried about Springer, enough to take her somewhere, why are his other trailers gone? I don't see a single horse out, either. So, either they're all in stalls where we can't see them, or they're gone, too. Why is the whole place so empty? He couldn't have moved them all himself."

"We don't know that. When was the last time you spoke to him?"

"Last night when we left. He texted me this morning that

he'd be in surgery all morning and that Springer did well through the night. I was supposed to call him an hour or so ago."

"So he's had all day, then."

"I just don't see it. He was fine last night, his normal self, nothing remotely out of the ordinary."

"Things can change fast."

She thought that was the understatement of the century. Just look at the two of them. "If something happened, even suddenly, for him to take such drastic measures, he'd have contacted me." She gasped. "What if someone else came and took Springer? Kenny could be somewhere on the property, hurt." *Or worse*, but she wouldn't let her mind go there.

"Why take his other horses?"

"Maybe they don't know which one she is."

"The pregnant one?"

Elena dipped her chin. She was panicking and not thinking clearly, and doing no good for anybody. "You're right, of course." Her heart was thundering and it was all she could do to keep it together. "I—I can't sit here, Rafe. She's—" She stopped when her throat closed over. "I've done everything I could to keep her and the baby safe. All this time, and now we're so close and . . . I don't know what I'll do if anything happens to her. Maybe I should have kept her here. I should have told you sooner what was going on. I should have—"

He turned her back to him, taking her face once again in his wide palms and keeping it there until she focused on him and not her blind panic. "You *are* doing everything you can. You've done nothing wrong, made no wrong moves. Sometimes things aren't always in your control."

"So . . . what are you saying? We can't do anything to help?"

"I'm saying that we're going to go find where Mr. Johansson goes, and follow him."

"What? What does he have to do with—"

"He's the only new cog in the wheel. And he is the only one

connecting you with Geronimo. And he's here, and your horse is suddenly gone. I say that, right now, he's our only connection to what is going on."

"You think he stole her?"

"I don't know who he is, or isn't. Or what he's capable of. All I know is, he's all we have." He turned his chair slightly so he could stretch one arm across his desk and push a button on the console. "Kate?"

A few seconds later, there was a responding beep from the intercom, then, "Here. Our Mr. Johansson is losing patience."

"Send him on his way. Do you think you'll need help with that?"

"No, he's agitated. Very agitated. But I can handle it. What can I do for you? Is Elena okay? Elena?"

She couldn't answer, didn't know what to say. She'd dragged this whole place, these people who'd been nothing but kind and generous to her, directly into her mess.

"Take his card, tell him we'll be in touch, and you'd appreciate it if he'd call first next time. Then watch him leave, and let me know which way he heads out."

"Will do. Anything else?"

"I don't suppose you have a spare helicopter I can use. Finn is still hogging ours."

"Sorry. Other than my trusty golf cart, horseback is the only alternate mode of transportation I have at my disposal."

"Thanks. I'll keep that in mind."

"I'll be back in a minute."

Rafe shifted her off of his lap and stood, keeping his hand on the small of her back as they stepped out from behind the desk. "Come on."

"To?"

He walked over to a wooden file cabinet that had a key pad on the side and punched in a series of numbers. When it sprang open, he took out a black gear bag and slung it over his shoulder. "We're going to go find your horse."

Chapter 22

Where was the company helicopter when he really needed it?

It was damn near impossible to follow someone on a rural country road, so Rafe had had to give Johansson a pretty decent lead. He had no idea how closely the investigator had looked at the vehicles parked up at the main house, so he'd taken one of the farm pickup trucks instead. A nondescript green Ford wasn't likely to draw too much attention. Elena had wanted to take her truck and the trailer, but he'd quickly talked her out of that idea.

As if she were reading his mind, and he wasn't too sure she couldn't, she chose that moment to grumble, "I still say it wouldn't be all that unusual to have a truck and trailer behind you out here."

"All true, but they're not really all that great in high-speed chases or quick maneuvers."

"Do you think we'll really be doing that?"

Despite her relative calm, he noted she had her fingers curled into white-knuckled fists in her lap. "I like to keep my options open."

"He's not exactly racing off somewhere. We're barely going over the speed limit."

Which made following the guy even more of a pain in the ass. He had to lag back to the point of ridiculousness to keep

Johansson from pegging him or Elena in the rearview mirror. It would almost be worth having the trailer hooked up, just as an excuse to go slower. Not that he planned on mentioning that to her.

"I'm still really torn about heading toward Kenny's instead. Whatever went on out there couldn't have happened without leaving some kind of tracks or trail of some kind, right? And what if Kenny is still out there? What if he's hurt? I'll never forgive myself if something happened to him because of me."

She wasn't thinking anything he hadn't already thought about. "I . . . took care of that."

She swung her gaze to his. "You what? How? When? And who?"

"When you went into the barn to get the harness and lead rope, I made a few calls."

"I might need them. Why didn't you tell me you had someone checking on him? I've been sitting here worried sick."

"Because you hadn't mentioned it and I didn't want to bring that possibility up if it hadn't occurred to you yet. No need for you to worry more than you already are."

"Thanks, but I'm a big girl. And I'd really appreciate being in on whatever is going on. It's my horse, my friend, my life we're talking about here."

She was right, but that didn't mean he liked it any better. "You know how it's a learning curve for you to let someone help you? Well, I'm not used to working alongside the people I'm helping."

"You work with Finn and Mac."

"That's different—they do what I do. You don't."

"We're a team, in this together, as you so often point out, so I think I deserve a different consideration from your usual client. Actually, I don't just expect that, I demand it."

"I wasn't patronizing you."

"No, you were protecting me for my own good. Same thing, in my book, even if your motives were pure."

"Well, I wouldn't go that far. A lot of my thoughts about you are anything but pure." He smiled at her, but she was in no mood to be teased.

"We need to keep everything open and on the table."

"Okay."

"Okay." He caught her wary gaze from the corner of his eye, but she knew when not to push. "When will you hear anything? From whoever it is you have checking the farm out?"

"Not sure. But I will tell you what I find out. I'd planned on that, anyway." Maybe not every little detail—that depended on Aaron's report. But he'd keep his word and tell her what she needed to know. People always thought they wanted to know everything. He'd been on enough cases to know that that wasn't always true. She didn't want to trust him to judge for her, and he respected that, but he wasn't about to expose her to more grief than she already had. And if she found out later and got pissed at him, well, that was a risk he was willing to run.

"Cell service is spotty out here, so—"

"Which is why we carry satellite phones."

"Oh." She settled back in her seat, looked back at the road. "Good."

"We thought so."

She was silent for a minute, then said, "How many people is 'we'?"

"You mean besides me, Finn, and Mac?"

She nodded.

"Depends. No other actual company employees. Everyone else is freelance, or on permanent retainer."

"How many is 'everyone'?"

"It varies according to the case and the kind of help we need. We've worked with dozens of different people since we started."

"I guess that makes sense." She went back to staring daggers at the back of Johansson's truck.

"So, in the spirit of keeping everything on the table, how did Springer get knocked up by a million-dollar race stud?"

She flinched at the sudden question. It took her another mile to come to terms with telling the story, but she finally started talking. "Springer doesn't come into heat regularly. Usually she's late. This time, however, she was early. When I went out to see Geronimo that night, I rode her out there."

"Did you normally ride your horse back to your quarters when you got off work?"

"No. I usually walked or took one of the staff golf carts. But I'd had one of the hands bring her down after the rest of the horses had been put up so I could get the farrier to look at a problem I thought she was having with one of her shoes."

"Is the farrier on staff?"

"They have one on rotation with two other big spreads in the area. He wasn't scheduled that day, but I knew he'd be stopping by on his way back from Green Hills because of Geronimo's arrival."

"Did he check him out, too?"

"I don't know, but I don't think so. It was more just to be there, be part of the excitement of the day. A lot of people in the area found a reason to stop by that day. But I'd heard through the grapevine that he was coming by, so rather than wait for his regular visit, I had Springer down for him to look at. Which he did."

"So he was gone when you rode her out to Geronimo's barn?"

"Yes. Everyone was gone. I had her in a stall near where I was working, but there wasn't anyone else over there, or any horses stalled there, either, that night. So I didn't know she'd come in season."

"What happened when you got out there?"

"I rode her into the paddock and left her ground-tethered while I walked in and looked for JuanCarlo."

"Who wasn't there."

"Right. Geronimo started making some noise in his stall, which, I realize now, was probably because he'd scented Springer. I thought it was just a typical temperamental stallion being a little ornery. He'd had a very long day, after all, and was in a new, unfamiliar place. But that directed me to his stall." She paused for a moment, then sighed and said, "He was stunning. Truly stunning."

He could hear both the pain and the longing in her voice, and for a moment, Rafe hated himself for making her relive even a moment of that tragic night. If it hadn't been so important, he'd have told her to stop right then.

"He, uh, he was in the back of his stall, and had no desire to come over and see me. I remember wishing I'd brought something out with me, some kind of treat. Of course, I wouldn't have dared."

"Why?"

"Even though he wasn't racing any longer, he was still on a highly monitored diet. There would have been all kinds of tests run on him once Gene took possession, just as a routine precaution, so . . ." She shrugged. "I just wouldn't have done it."

"So, I'm guessing when you couldn't cajole him over, you went into the stall? Wasn't that ridiculously dangerous? Wait," he said, stopping himself. "I forgot, you're the horse whisperer."

"I knew better. I was just—I knew I'd probably never get another chance. You have to understand, for someone like me who has dedicated her life to working with those magnificent beasts, knowing the chances of even crossing paths with a horse a tenth as talented as Geronimo is incredibly slim. This was a chance of a lifetime for me."

"He was going to be housed on your farm—surely you'd have had the chance to get close to him."

"He had nothing to do with my program. At best, I'd see him from a distance. I certainly wasn't ever going to get up close and personal with him like I happened to be in that moment."

"So you sweet talked your way into his stall."

"More or less. It was bigger than I'd imagined, so I had plenty of room to maneuver around him." She dipped her chin. "It all happened so fast," she said, her voice hardly more than a whisper. She shook her head slowly. "I still can't believe—I was so stupid. So stupid."

He reached over, touched her knee, and she jerked her gaze to him. He glanced away from the road long enough to connect with her. "You know that what happened with him and Springer had nothing to do with his death. You couldn't have prevented what happened to him that night, whether you'd gone out there or not."

She nodded, but didn't look any less miserable. "He swung his head around and his ears twitched, he snorted, then the next thing I knew, he was bolting for the door. It was all I could do to dive out of the way to keep from being trampled. I took off for the paddock after him, and, well, do I really have to go into detail?"

"And no one saw or heard this?"

"It can be a noisy thing, depending, but Springer didn't really freak out or anything. The paddock was private, in the rear of the stable, and, like I said, it was over almost before it started. Afterward he was fairly docile and though it took me a few minutes to get close enough to throw a lead rope around his neck, leading him back to his stall wasn't all that hard." Her shoulders slumped a little. "At the time, it felt like eons. I don't think I've ever been so scared in my life. I kept waiting for lights to flash, sirens to go off, for half the farm to come running." She shook her head slowly, deep in reverie.

"No one came."

She continued to shake her head. "No one. I honestly couldn't believe it. I waited to make sure he was okay, then I panicked and took Springer back to her stall in the employee barn. I stayed with her until I could be sure she was okay, then I finally went home. I'd just turned out the lights when all hell did break loose. At first, I thought it was my fault, and that something had happened to Geronimo. Then I heard the sirens. I was already outside by then, and I saw the smoke."

Rafe had kept his hand on her knee, rubbing slowly. Now he tugged at her elbow until he loosened her hold on herself, and slid his hand into hers, giving her a reassuring squeeze. It didn't feel like nearly enough, given what he was putting her through. Her skin was pale, her palm chilly and damp.

"I—I didn't even have a chance to figure out what I was going to do if Springer ended up pregnant. If I told JuanCarlo, or, God forbid, Gene himself, I'd lose my job for sure. Which would have been understandable and I'd have dealt with that—it was only fair, on negligence alone. But I wasn't too sure they wouldn't take Springer from me, too. For sure they'd have taken the baby, and I would have obviously let them, but I don't know the legalities of who would have gotten what. I did know they were powerful and rich, and I was not. It was such a nightmare—all the way back to my trailer I was praying it wouldn't take and maybe no one would be the wiser." Her grip tightened in his. "I had no idea that the nightmare hadn't even begun."

"You never told anyone any part of this?"

"No one. Not one word."

"How did you explain the pregnancy when it was confirmed?"

"I trailered her out of there, took her to a different vet, not one we dealt with, for the test. They didn't ask, I didn't say."

She was trembling now, and Rafe wished like hell he had an answer for her problem, but the more she talked, the worse things looked.

"I've never had anything in my life I had to hide, and I'm not sure I'd have kept myself from running to JuanCarlo or Gene straight off and telling them, just to clear my conscience.

I doubt I'd have even made it until I could run the tests on her. But in less than an hour, before I'd even collected my wits about me, the explosion happened. Then the media descended like vultures, and there was speculation of arson almost immediately. Though I knew I hadn't been responsible, there was no way I could say anything without fear of being tarred and feathered before they even bothered to find out if I was innocent. I was scared. Scared-out-of-my-mind scared. Scared enough to keep my mouth shut. So I sat, and prayed it hadn't taken. And then it did . . . and I just didn't know what to do. I couldn't lose her. She's been with me for ten years. She's the only family I have left."

"Did anyone there know that Springer was pregnant?"

She shook her head. "I left before it was noticeable and never mentioned it, but it wouldn't have mattered, really. It wasn't that we didn't breed our personal mounts—that's a private decision. I owned a mare and she wasn't being raced, nor was she being used in the Charlotte Oaks program in any way, so what I did with her in that regard was my business. But there was no way I could have bred her, even off premises, and not had someone there know about it. I would obviously have had to say something at some point, and questions would have been asked, just in regular conversation."

"Which is why you left the racing world altogether."

"In part. I didn't want to have that conversation with anyone there."

Good at avoiding, he thought again, but bad at lying.

"But it was also time for me to go."

"Which is what you told Kate when you took the job here."

"Yes. I also told her Springer was pregnant, but I didn't want to spook her by mentioning her problems right off. I knew Kenny would be there for me, so it wasn't going to adversely affect anything here."

"And you weren't worried she'd mention it when she called your references?"

"No, not really. Why would that come up? But even if it had, it had been a while since I'd left and I wasn't too concerned that anyone would put it together. I hadn't mentioned exactly how far along she was." Her eyes widened. "Maybe she did mention it though, maybe that's how—"

Rafe shook his head. "No, she didn't—she mentioned that early on when this whole thing started. And I didn't mention it, either, if that's your next question. That wasn't on my radar at that point."

She sat back in her seat, shoulders slumping a little. "I just can't figure out the connection. Why me? Why now? I mean, even you calling and doing some additional background checking shouldn't warrant all this. And I can even maybe, understand the insurance guy, but not this thing with Kenny." She hugged her middle. "I can't stand this. I really can't."

"I know. I'm not liking it much, either. What do you plan to do after the foal is born?"

"I don't know," she whispered. "Legally—"

"It's Gene's. If I'd paid the stud fee, the baby would be mine."

"Which is how much?"

"More than I'd earn in a lifetime. Even if I won the lottery and Geronimo were still sitting pretty in his stall, I don't know what would have happened if I'd come forward and told the whole story. I have no problem giving the baby up— it's Gene's, by all rights. But with the way things turned out, the entire world is mourning him, and with suspicion running rampant, while I have a horse carrying his only offspring—I have no idea what would happen if I came clean. To me. Or to Springer."

"Elena—"

"Don't say it. Okay? Just drive. I don't want to think about it right now. My only concern is to find Springer and make sure she's okay. Is there someone you can call about your guy? I'm really scared that something has happened to Kenny. Would he be there by now?" She rocked in her seat a little, hugging herself tighter. "Everything is falling apart. I thought I had it under control, and now it's all unraveling, and people I care about might be getting hurt. I'll never forgive myself—I just wanted to make sure Springer got through this okay."

"I know." He tugged her elbow until he loosened the death grip she had on her middle, and pulled her hand into his, weaving their fingers together, holding on so she could feel the strength of his conviction in his touch and in his words. "We're going to find her. And we're going to figure this out. I'll find out what your legal standing is. We have all kinds of contacts—"

She looked instantly panicked. "No one else can know—not until she's foaled, not until—"

"No one is going to know. The nature of our business means we only work with people who know how to be discreet about their work. And, trust me, they want to work with us."

"I know, but this is pretty high-profile stuff. The temptation to leak it would be huge. I just—I'd rather not involve anyone else."

"Who said anything about mentioning Geronimo by name? Listen, you've trusted me this far, trust that I know what I'm doing in this, too. It's not just something I want to do, it *is* what I do. And I'm damn good at it."

"I'm not trying to insult you—really, I'm not. It's just I've spent so long protecting her, protecting . . . all of this. It's hard enough to bring you in. Hell, I didn't even bring Kenny in, and look what's happened to him."

"Mac is due back tomorrow and we'll sit down and talk about it, all three of us. Kate, too, if you'd like. After this little road trip today, I hope we'll come out of this with more information." He tightened his grip on her hand when she went to pull away. "It's my decision, not yours, to put myself in the middle of this. Mac and Kate, too. No guilt trips. You're carrying a big enough load as it is."

"There's no one else at fault here but me—of course I feel guilty."

"You can save it, where I'm concerned."

She started to say something, then stopped. Eventually she relaxed a little in her seat. He had no idea what was going on inside her head. What he did know was that she still had her fingers entwined with his. For now, that was enough.

Silence grew between them, more from necessity than strain. It was broken a few minutes later when his phone chirped. He'd let go of her hand to retrieve the phone from his pocket, when brake lights suddenly blared ahead of them.

"Shit." He slowed and glanced down at the incoming message at the same time.

"Is it your guy? About Kenny?"

"Hold on," he said, looking up again, frowning. "There's no turnoff here. What is he doing?"

A split second later he got his answer. Johansson had abruptly put his big truck into a swerving one-eighty and shot off in the direction they'd just come from. Rafe didn't even get a good look at the guy. His side windows were tinted. Which meant he didn't know if the guy got a good look at them, either. Could be why he'd pulled the stunt in the first place, but the way he'd taken off like a bat out of hell told Rafe otherwise.

"Are you going to follow him?"

"It's a bit trickier now. If I turn right now, the jig is up that he's being followed and we lose whatever leverage we had."

"Or? You can't just let him take off like that."

"Or, we continue on until another car passes in the opposite direction, then turn around."

"What if we can't catch up? It's not exactly a superhighway out here, in case you hadn't noticed. One slow car and we're screwed now that he's running."

"Which works in our favor. As I recall, there isn't another crossroad going that direction for a good ten miles. Plenty of time to catch up."

She folded her arms and tucked herself back into her seat, some of her defenses sliding automatically into place. "You'd better pray this as-yet-unseen car we're waiting for is also being driven like a bat out of hell."

"We'll catch up to him." He grinned at her. "Trust me."

Chapter 23

"Where is he? I don't see him. Did we lose him?" She grabbed his arm. "What happens if we lose him?"

"We've only been backtracking for about ten minutes. It's a one-lane road with no turnoffs for miles. He's up there, okay?"

"Feels like ten years," she muttered, trying mightily to keep the panic at bay, but this sudden turnabout made that pretty much impossible.

"I had myself half convinced the insurance guy wasn't going to amount to anything. Now this. I feel like we should be heading to Kenny's, but now I want to know why he made that sudden turn. Have you tried to return the call yet?"

"Yes. No reply."

"Why would everything be gone? I don't get that part. Why would anyone want all of it gone? Who would do that? Who would want to do that? If they just wanted Springer, why take everything? It's not like electronics you can just throw in the back of your stolen van, you know? This required serious planning. Long-range planning." She shifted in her seat so she faced him. "Springer has only been there for one day. How could anyone have planned a full-scale abduction of Kenny and every horse on his farm in a single day?"

"How many are there?"

"No, no. You're supposed to say something comforting, like, 'maybe they're all safe in their stalls and we just can't see them.' Even though I know he has more horses on the premises than he has stalls. Or you could say 'maybe he moved them for a different reason. Maybe there was some kind of wild virus at a nearby farm that required immediate quarantine, so he moved them all to be safe.' Why can't you say something like that instead of asking how many horses he has, because you think someone really did come in and steal them, and abduct Kenny, and you're trying to figure out what they needed to pull off a job that size."

"Elena—"

"I know I'm hysterical, okay? I know! Just—just find that damn pickup truck, then pull him the hell over and let me talk to him. I can find out what he knows. He wants to talk to me, remember? We can make this work in our favor. I know we can. We just have to find him, dammit!"

"We will, and I know you're at the end of your rope here, but you have to hang in a bit longer. When we get her back, Springer is going to need you, and you won't be any good to her this way."

He was right. Of course. He was always right. She willed her racing heart to slow, but, in the end, she found her strength in the steady, tight grip of his hand on hers.

They trailed behind the slow truck in front of them for a few more miles, with Elena trying in vain to peer around the side to see who was on the road in front of the truck. By this time, Johansson could be forty miles ahead of them.

"I know we can't see around this truck, but if he'd turned off at any point, we'd have seen him."

"Not if he'd gotten far enough ahead, we wouldn't. Do you know most of the farm properties around here? Are there any with any kind of race interests?" she asked.

"Finn grew up here, I didn't. He'd be the one to know."

"I know he's out on some job, but is there any way to send him a message? I mean, if we can't track Johansson down, then that means he's somewhere out here, most likely."

He glanced at her as if something new had just occurred to

him. "Have you had any contact with neighboring farms in any way? Have you ridden with anyone from another farm? Talked to anyone? Anyone else know you or that you have a pregnant horse?"

She immediately shook her head. "I've deliberately kept a low profile. Even with Kate's own students and their families. I work with the horses and the barn help, that's it." She paused as a thought struck her, then swallowed hard. "But the barn helpers know I have a pregnant horse. So does the farrier and the vet."

"Would they mention it to anyone? Even in passing? Have you talked with anyone about the problems she's had, something that would make talking about her interesting?"

She looked over at him, her heart creeping toward her throat once again. "The horse community is always small, whatever area you're in, so . . . yes, it's possible. But, no, no one other than Kate knows she's had a bad birth history, and without that piece of info, just having a pregnant horse isn't really gossip-worthy."

"What about the fact that you used to work for Charlotte Oaks? Any of the barn helpers, students, families, or Kate's instructors ever pay attention to that? I can see where it would be something that could stir some interest."

"No, I made a point not to talk about that, or where I worked before coming here. They all know I have experience, but I let my work speak for itself. Unless Kate mentioned it to someone, but you said she didn't even know about Geronimo, so I doubt it."

"You have any other ties to this area besides Kenny? You said your dad was a trainer—"

"North Carolina mostly, and that was a very long time ago—and a completely different field of expertise as well. He and Kenny are from the old days. My parents have been gone for some time now, and my dad had already retired from training a while before the accident due to some health issues. Kenny moved up to this area about ten years ago." She fell silent. "Do you think someone from around here somehow pieced things together? It just doesn't make any sense. Where would Johansson fit in, then? Where did you say his agency was based?" A dozen different scenarios tried to form in her mind at the same time.

Rafe wove his fingers through hers, keeping them trapped against his thigh. "I know you're not going to like this, but I have to ask—and you have to push sentimentality aside and try very hard to focus on any real possibility. Do you think there is any way that Kenny is involved?"

"Of course he's involved, I involve—" She broke off as his meaning sank in. Her mouth dropped open, then snapped shut. Her immediate response was to vehemently deny that there was any possibility that her father's old friend was in any way associated with Johansson or anything that happened on his farm.

"Push past the emotional part," Rafe said quietly. "I know it's not something you even want to consider, but, like you said, why would someone uproot Kenny's entire operation if all they were after was Springer?" He rubbed his thumb along the side of her hand. "Is it possible that he figured out whose baby Springer was carrying and, perhaps, got a little greedy?"

She shook her head, adamantly denying it, even as the rationale of Rafe's argument took root and stubbornly refused to be ignored. "He couldn't. He wouldn't have." *Not to me*, she thought. *Not to me.*

"He knew you worked at Charlotte Oaks. He knew about Geronimo. Maybe he figured out the timeline and counted back to the conception date, then put two and two together. He could have run some tests, couldn't he? If he had any idea about the conception situation . . . he'd know that baby would be worth a whole lot of money."

"He wouldn't do that."

"How much do you know about his situation? About him? Could he be having some kind of problem? Be desperate for cash?"

She let her chin drop to her chest as everything inside of her rebelled at the very notion that she could have been betrayed by the only person she'd known, without a doubt, she could trust. She just couldn't see it; even when she tried to be objective, she couldn't see him doing it. Then another thought occurred to her and her head shot back up. "Maybe Johansson found out where Springer was before coming to Dalton Downs. Maybe he went sniffing around Kenny's place and got him worried. Maybe Kenny packed up and got out because he'd been threatened in some way."

"And not told you about it?"

That stopped her, but only for a second. "Not if he thought communicating with me would put me in any kind of immediate danger. I'm sure he'll let me know where he is when he can." There. That was more like it. That was an explanation she could live with, an explanation that made real sense.

Rafe kept rubbing the side of her hand with his thumb. When the question came, it came gently. "What kind of danger would make him pack up his entire operation and skip town?" He squeezed her hand to keep her from replying until he was done. "Why not contact you and let you know the situation and tell you that Springer was in danger and needed to be moved right away? It doesn't make sense that he'd pack up everything."

"What if whatever it was, was sudden and there was no time? I'm hours away. And the reason he packed them all up is because he couldn't leave any of them behind to an uncertain fate. It's the reason people run into burning buildings to save the family dog. No way would he just abandon all of them to save one of mine."

Rafe seemed to ponder that for a moment, his attention on the road ahead.

"Or!" Her mind was spinning now, and she needed a second to let the scenarios in her mind play out. "What if his whole operation was threatened? Not just Springer?"

"What do you mean?"

"Whoever killed Geronimo did it by burning down the entire barn. Maybe that same someone threatened to burn down Kenny's barns unless he turned Springer over to them. It would make sense, then, that he'd move all his horses. He couldn't protect the buildings, but he could protect what he put in them."

Rafe nodded. "Makes sense."

She took enormous relief from those two words. She knew it was a plausible scenario and had to believe in it, but she also knew she was incapable of being objective at this point. Not just because a betrayal of that magnitude would be too hard to take, but if she was right, it meant that there was a better chance that both Kenny and Springer were somewhere safe and unharmed.

"I still come back to why he hasn't contacted you in some way. He has to know you'll be terrified."

"He doesn't know I know he's gone, just that he hasn't been answering his phone. I wasn't supposed to go back down there until tomorrow or Thursday. And yes, he'll know that my not being able to get him on the phone will worry me, but—"

"Enough to know you'd drive out there yourself, and then what?"

"He'll contact me. I know he will. Unless—" A sick ball of dread formed in the pit of her stomach. She turned to Rafe. "Unless it's not just me he's worried about putting in danger by making contact. Rafe . . . what if Dalton Downs has been threatened in some way?"

"If you're right and someone is coming after him, they already know about you. It's the only way they could make the connection and track Springer to Kenny."

"Do you think that's why Johansson was at the farm today? Do you think he's the one who tracked her? Then he gets there and she's gone and he's furious. It would explain why he came hell-bent for leather onto Dalton Downs property."

"Except, what would have tipped Kenny off? If Johansson hadn't been there yet, how would he know to move?"

Just then the truck in front of them braked abruptly, red lights glaring. Rafe braked hard, too, causing Elena to grab at the dashboard.

"Great," she said, as they came to a complete stop. "We'll never catch up to him now. We should have just taken off after him the second he made that one-eighty."

"Actually," Rafe began, as traffic began to move slowly forward, shifting to the oncoming lane as directed by a line of road flares, "maybe it's a good thing we didn't."

"What's going on?" Elena craned her neck, trying in vain to see around the truck in front of them, but as they shifted lanes, she got a glimpse of what had snarled the rural highway. In the distance there were flashing emergency lights and a cluster of vehicles on the side of the road. "Looks like an accident up ahead. Maybe, if we're lucky, Johansson is caught in the backup, too."

Rafe didn't say anything, and something about his silence drew her attention.

"What did you mean when you said it was a good thing we didn't turn around right away? Because we might have been the ones in that accident?"

Rafe split his attention between the road ahead as they continued to crawl forward, and the scene of the accident as it drew closer. They were almost abreast of it when Rafe abruptly pulled off on the opposite side of the road and put the truck in park.

"What are you doing? Stopping to help? They have a half-dozen emergency vehicles here already—why are we—?"

"Stay here," he said, his tone brooking no argument, then got out of the truck.

She immediately popped her door open, but he swung back, as if expecting her not to listen to him.

"Let me check this out first. I need you to stay here. Keep the truck running. I'll answer your questions when I get back."

"Rafe, what in the world are you—" She stopped and slowly panned her attention across the road, peeking in between the passing cars and trucks, trying to see through the emergency vehicles to the accident itself. "Oh my God." She spun back around toward Rafe. "That's not—"

"I'm afraid it might be. We have no idea what's going on, and I need to find out. You stay here. For a bunch of reasons. We're clear on that much, right?"

As badly as she wanted to go with him and find out for herself what had happened, and if that was Johansson's truck presently flipped upside down in a drainage ditch, she understood why it was smarter for her to maintain a nonexistent profile. It was dangerous enough that they'd stopped at all. She had no idea what in the hell was going on with Springer, this agent tracking her, Kenny, or any of the rest of it, but until they had more information, the less she was directly involved, the better.

"I'll stay low. Do—do you think it's wise for you to go over there? What if Johansson is okay and he sees you?"

"He doesn't know me." He motioned for her to get back in the truck. "Yet. Lock the doors, keep your face averted." Then he ducked between two cars and disappeared behind a fire truck.

"Be careful," she said, knowing he was out of earshot, but feeling compelled to say it anyway. She climbed back in the truck and slid down low in the seat. It was a different thing for her, being worried about someone else. Other than Springer, anyway. It didn't make her feel as hindered as she might have thought it would. In her profession, making connections to further your career was a good thing, but making personal connections wasn't necessarily so. Jobs could be fleeting, and most of the men she was around were either competing for the same position, or didn't much care for a woman trying to make it in what they saw as a man's world. And she didn't have time to pursue a social life beyond her immediate realm, which meant her social possibilities were the very men she worked with.

Then Geronimo died, and her realm as she knew it ceased to be. And then had come Kate, and her kids, and Tracey, and

Bonder, and a whole host of people and horses whom she'd pretended were merely distractions from the stress of her life. Something to help bide the time until she could reclaim her rightful place in her world.

Only somewhere along the way, she realized now, she'd started to care. Life at Dalton Downs was completely different from life as she'd known it, at least in any recent years. It reminded her more of the world she'd grown up in, with her father training and her mother keeping house for the family who owned whatever farm they were working for. It had been a transient life then, but she hadn't really minded. Maybe because she didn't know anything different. Which was also probably why the transient nature of the racing life had suited her so well.

She hadn't given much thought to any other kind of life. Until now. She inched up in her seat until she could peer out the passenger window, but her view was completely blocked by a passing panel truck.

Rafe had happened now. And she wasn't sure what she was going to do about that. It wasn't like letting herself care about Springer, who had to follow her rules, her life, her path. Rafe didn't have to do a damn thing.

And yet, there he was, intentionally putting himself in harm's way. For her. She could tell herself he was just doing the same thing he'd do for any of his clients. But that was a lie that wouldn't serve either one of them well, and she knew it.

She tucked her arms closer around her waist and tried like hell not to imagine what was going on across the road, but it was impossible. The fact that there were already emergency vehicles on the scene, in a place as rural as this, told her he'd put a pretty hefty distance between them after making his abrupt change in direction.

They'd never have caught up with him. She'd known that, and still wondered why Rafe hadn't been more persistent in trying to close the gap. It was almost as if he'd been intentionally holding them back. She tried to stop her thoughts from veering in that direction. She needed to trust at least one person right now, and he was the only one she had left.

But the track wouldn't be averted, and she started to wonder if maybe, somehow, for some reason, Rafe was the one involved in this whole thing. Her gut said no. Every fiber of her being said no. She replayed his consistent words of reassurance to her, the way he looked at her, held her, made love to her. *Unless that had been a calculated move to gain that exact effect*, her little voice contributed. A little voice that wouldn't be shut out.

She really hadn't known him that long. They'd been going on fast-forward since he first stepped inside that barn, leaving her little time to think things through. Even then it was doubtful she'd think clearly, given the thick haze of hormones that swirled around them. Had she been a complete fool to trust someone she'd only just let into her life?

But then she thought about Kenny, whom she'd known and trusted since she was a child, and what he might have done. She hated even thinking he might have a hand in all this. Or had Rafe just planted that seed on purpose? And what was she to Rafe, anyway? A bed partner? A potential cash windfall if he could blackmail her out of the baby her horse was carrying? He'd been snooping in her business from the beginning. Who knew what his goals really were, or, for that matter, what Kate or Mac or Finn really wanted from her.

No, she couldn't let herself believe that someone like Kate, who'd devoted her life to improving the lives of such severely challenged kids, would have any part in something like this. But how well did she really know the men of Dalton Downs? The men of Trinity, Inc.? Rafe had called them the Unholy Trinity. Maybe that wasn't such a childish nickname after all.

Her thoughts had spun so far beyond her control that she all but leaped out of her skin when the driver's-side door suddenly opened and Rafe filled the space in the cab once again. "You okay?" he asked, sincere concern lining his rugged features.

Maybe that was it. Could she really have her head turned by a handsome face and some pretty words? She didn't want to think it, but she was human, after all. And under severe stress.

"Is it—was it him?" she finally managed, scooting back up in her seat and pulling her seat belt across her chest, as if that could somehow protect her.

Rafe nodded, his expression flat.

Her heart sank and her stomach knotted, all at the same time. "An accident? Was he going too fast? Blow a tire?" Something, anything. Anything other than what the queasy sensation in her gut already told her was true.

"Too soon to tell," he said. "The investigator isn't out here yet and the county cops are just trying to preserve the scene and still let the emergency guys do their job."

"If the emergency guys are working, then that means he's alive, right?"

Rafe started to talk, then stopped, as if unsure just how much to tell her.

"It's my life, my horse's life, and possibly Kenny's life on the line, here. You're not sparing me at this point by editing things out to protect my feelings. I need to know what's going on. I need to know exactly how dangerous this whole thing is getting. Is he going to be okay?"

"He's trapped in the truck. They're working to get him out." He held her gaze. "It's not looking too good."

She ducked her head, but only for a moment. "Do you think it's an accident?"

"No other car was involved. Skid marks make it look like he slammed on his brakes and swerved, possibly to miss a deer or something, and lost control. Caught the soft stuff on the side of the road and ended up flipping into the drainage ditch."

Barely more than the wheels of Johansson's truck was visible at road level, so she knew the ditch had to be a deep one, which could have caused a pretty severe impact. Not to mention the large rocks that usually lined the deeper drainage ditches, or that there might be water involved, and with him topside down—she forced herself to stop the images there, covering her face when will alone wasn't enough.

She started when she felt Rafe's hand on her thigh. Then he was reaching for her, tugging her across the middle part of the seat until she was in his arms, her cheek tucked against the steady beat of his heart. "I'm sorry," he said, pressing his face against her hair.

She'd just been having serious doubts about him—she should be scrambling across the seat, safeguarding her heart, along with everything else. But she couldn't seem to make herself move. Being held by him felt . . . right. God, she was so tired, so confused, she didn't know what to believe, who to trust, any longer.

"I'm sorry, too. I don't even know what side of good or bad he's on, but—" She leaned back and looked up into Rafe's eyes. "You don't think it was a deer, do you?"

He said nothing, just held her gaze.

She started to tremble. "You know, I was scared before. For Springer, for myself. And for you. I'm past that now. I'm terrified." She studied his eyes. "What's going to happen to Springer? Where do we go now?"

"Mac's on his way to Kenny's place."

"But I thought he was away on some other case."

"Kate contacted him and he turned around, came back to help."

"But—"

"It's what we do. I'd do it for him."

She thought about that, the scope and depth of their friendship, their bond. A part of which he was extending to her. It was something she'd witnessed firsthand between them, and she knew then that this was a man she could trust. She should be thanking her lucky stars he'd come into her life, not doubting him. "I thought you already sent someone to Kenny's."

He framed her face with his hands. "I did."

"But—" Her eyes widened. "Is he—did something happen to him, too?"

"I don't know. But there should have been contact by now."

She tried to scramble out of his arms and back to her seat so they could get back on the road. Sitting in one place was suddenly not an option. "You can't send Mac there if something has happened to him, possibly to Kenny, too. It's bad enough I've involved you. And Kenny. And now this other guy I don't even know. I can't involve anyone else. I'll go out there. This is all my fault, this is—"

He held on tight to her, not letting her go anywhere, turning her face to his. "You'll let Mac do what Mac is trained to do. What you and I aren't trained to do."

"But—"

"Elena," he said, the gentle tone of his voice at complete odds with the riveting intensity of his eyes. "We're in this. We are going to figure it out. Whatever it takes, whoever it takes. When I'm working, I don't stop because things get difficult. In our line of work, difficult is expected."

"But dead isn't."

"No, no, that's not part of the game plan. And it's not this time, either. We're not going off half-cocked here." He stroked the side of her face. "And we're definitely not going away. So stop wasting time pushing."

"Rafe—"

He cut her off. "Even if this were just a job, and you were just a client, I wouldn't be going anywhere. But it is you, and you matter. What the hell kind of man do you think I am, if you believe I'd walk away now?"

She blanched. "I wasn't—I didn't mean to insult you, but you matter to me, too, and I—"

"—am very happy to hear that." He took her mouth then, silencing the rest of her protests with a kiss that left her breathless.

Between the kiss and the events of the past thirty minutes,

with her thoughts careening from worrying that he might be part of whoever or whatever was after her to being scared to death that something might happen to him, she couldn't think straight.

He lifted his head, but before he could move away, on instinct she framed his face in her hands, needing to feel him, needing to look into his eyes, needing to tell him what was going through her mind. "You matter. I'm not used to worrying about anyone other than me and my horse. So, if I'm going to trust you, if I'm going to care, then you can't let anything happen to you. Deal?"

He smiled. "I'll do my best. Besides, I have a vested interest in keeping us both safe and sound."

"Why is that?"

His smile grew. "Because in addition to being relentless, I'm insatiably curious."

"About?"

"What happens next with us. And there's only one way to find out."

Chapter 24

Rafe pulled the truck around the back of the main house. "Shouldn't we have heard from Mac by now?"

It was the first thing she'd said in almost an hour. Judging from the way she'd all but twisted her fingers off in the meantime, her silence had been hard-won.

"Let's get inside."

"Shouldn't we talk to Kate? She might have heard from him."

"We will." He opened his door. "Come on. We'll know more in a few minutes."

Despite the fact that it was a rather balmy spring evening, and the sun had just begun to set, Elena rubbed her arms and hunched a little as if she was freezing as she scooted up the path. He had no business thinking about the myriad ways he'd like to warm her up, but that didn't stop his gaze from drifting down along the curve of her hip of its own volition. Nor did it stop him from catching up with her and steering her away from the main house and toward the pool house instead.

"Where are we going?"

"My place."

"But—"

"I've got an office in there, too. I don't particularly want to deal with any of the house staff at the moment, if you don't mind. In fact, the fewer eyes on you, the better."

She let him open the door, escort her inside, and close the

door behind her before speaking. "You don't think anyone on your staff is involved, do you? They don't even know me."

"They know *of* you. And no, I don't. But there's potentially a lot of money involved in this situation. I'd like to think I could vouch for the absolute loyalty of every employee here, but the truth of it is, we're all human."

"Could you be bought?"

He flipped on the lights, then turned to her. "Could you?"

"I asked first."

His phone chose that moment to ring. He flashed her a brief smile. "I think we both know the answer to that one." He glanced at the screen before flipping it open. "What do you have for me, Mac?"

At the mention of Mac's name, Elena's eyes widened and she immediately moved closer to his side. He debated putting it on speaker, but he had no idea what Mac had stumbled across out at Kenny's place. He had every respect for Elena and the way she'd handled herself so far, but they were far from out of the woods yet, and he needed her to keep her head. Mac wasn't known for his tact, either, so he opted to vet the information first. She could be pissed off at him later.

"Not a whole lot, and what I do have isn't very good," Mac replied.

"Where are you now?"

"Scene of the crime."

Rafe almost repeated the word *crime*, but happened to glance into Elena's eyes and caught himself at the last second. "Which one?"

"Roadside. Johansson. I'm not real sure anything nefarious happened out at Kenny's."

"What about Aaron?"

"No sign of him, but no sign of any struggle, or any damage of any kind. Tire tracks in and out are consistent with the horse trailer and truck tracks that are all over the place here. Nothing out of place."

"And the main house?"

"Hard to tell. He's an organized, orderly guy. Lives alone, far as I can tell. Probably has a housekeeper. It's neat as a pin. Nothing out of order, though. Can't tell if he packed before leaving—there's nothing lying around. No dishes, no laundry."

"No sign of Aaron? No contact?"

"No sign. Phone goes straight to voice mail. No leads there at all."

"And the rest?"

"Johansson. Yeah, he didn't make it."

"Injuries sustained from the accident?"

"I'm sure they didn't help, but it was the bullet straight through his head that killed him."

Rafe tried not to react, but from the way Elena's shoulders straightened, it was obvious she'd picked up on something. He'd do well to remember her sensitivities extended beyond horses.

"It wasn't until they jawed open the side of the truck that they realized the blood wasn't from the impact of the truck flipping on its lid," Mac continued as Rafe stared into a pair of brown eyes that saw way more than they should.

"Did that cause the accident, then?"

"Looks that way."

"Close range, distance, what?"

"Drive-by."

"Oncoming? That would take some doing."

"Passed from behind, is the guess. His window was down."

"Wasn't when he passed us. Tinted like midnight, so I'm thinking he liked it that way."

"The thinking is that someone passed him, rolled down the passenger window, and motioned him to do the same."

"Car? Truck?"

"Level entry, so a truck. Whether he swerved when he saw the gun, or if the other truck swerved in to force the situation, hard to call. No impact with the other vehicle, though, so no trace evidence there."

"They working any other scenario?"

"It wasn't self-inflicted, if that's what you're getting at. And it definitely came from outside the vehicle."

"Possible road-rage incident? Maybe they were playing road tag. Judging from his behavior here earlier, it wouldn't be a stretch."

"Couldn't rule that out entirely, but I'd say it was damn unlikely."

"I just don't want us diverting our attention if this is a red herring."

"My gut says this has to be part of the big picture. We certainly can't afford to treat it otherwise, no matter what the official supposition is."

"I agree." But it helped getting Mac's opinion. Rafe knew he was far more emotionally involved than he'd ever been before, and he wanted to make sure his judgment wasn't getting too clouded. "Get any additional info on him?"

"Nothing more than what we had. Haven't had time to do any more digging. That's your arena, anyway."

"I was on it until we did an aerial of Kenny's place and saw it empty."

"I'm going to head back down there now, maybe lay low for a little bit, see if anything crops up." He paused, then added, "You think there might be a benefit in getting someone to check out whatever might be going on at Charlotte Oaks?"

"You think someone there is behind this?"

"I think it had to start there."

He looked at Elena as he spoke. "Maybe it started with Kenny figuring out Springer's gestation date and, most likely, her suitor. I'm going to check on his financials, see if there might be some motivation there." He sent Elena a visual apology, but she nodded her understanding. He doubted she liked it very much, but she knew the stakes were too high not to check every last angle.

"Doesn't explain why he took the herd with him."

"Elena said it was like rescuing the family dog. No matter how desperate he is, he wouldn't leave what amounts to his family behind."

"No contact from him at all?"

"Zero."

"That doesn't bode well, no matter the reason behind it."

"Yeah," Rafe said, still looking at Elena, "we know."

There was a long pause, then Mac said, "You know, there could be another angle here."

Rafe sighed. He knew Mac would go there, knew he had to. And though it pissed him off, he knew his partner was just covering all their bases. Which was always the smart play. He'd have done the same in a reverse situation. Had, in fact, when Mac and Kate reunited last year under less-than-perfect circumstances.

"Have to ask. You sure she and Kenny aren't in this together somehow? Maybe working some kind of deal, possibly playing both sides, with you—us—coming up the loser if all hell breaks loose?"

"If we're trusting our guts here, the answer is yes. I'm certain." He looked at Elena. "As certain as I have to be."

He thought Mac would call him on it, and perhaps a year ago, he would have. But since the situation with Kate, and her reentry into all their lives, Mac wasn't as quick to judge. Rafe could only hope that was a good thing in this case.

"I'll check in when or if I get more. A shame Finn isn't around. We'd cover a lot more ground if we had the damn bird."

"You hate that damn thing."

"I hate flying in it. I don't hate you all using it for the good of many."

"Well, he's incommunicado, so it's all-terrain for now. I'll be in touch. And when you locate Aaron—"

"Don't even think about asking me to hold him for you. You have enough to keep you occupied. He's mine."

"Kate might get jealous."

"Very funny. But he's my hire, so he's my problem. Besides, the one you want messing up your pretty clothes isn't Aaron."

Given the fact that Rafe was halfway to a full hard-on pretty much all the time around her now, even with everything that was going on around them, he doubted he could fight that one with any real sincerity. "Good point. Just don't mess him up too much. He might come in handy when all this plays out. If we have something on him, he'll be more willing to play for our team."

"I'll do my best."

Rafe clicked the phone off and steeled himself for the barrage of questions he expected from Elena the instant he pocketed his phone. But as she managed to do more often than not, she surprised him by turning and pacing away from him, either in an effort to gather her thoughts, or figure out where to begin the interrogation, or both.

She walked to the windows that lined the front and end of the pool house. All were covered with floor-to-ceiling, wide-panel, vertical blinds, for privacy. At the moment, they were closed, but she shifted one aside at the far end and gazed out. He knew exactly the scene before her.

Past the corner of the pool deck, the backyard sloped gently downward toward the stables and paddock. He knew exactly how much view was afforded by the foliage around the outside of the pool house, because he'd stood in that exact same spot many times, watching her put this horse or that through their paces. Cup of coffee in hand in the morning, glass of wine in the evening. He'd done that pretty much since she'd come to work there. Mac and Finn had been right all along.

She kept her back to him and remained silent. He had no idea if she was truly seeing the vista before her, or if her thoughts were entirely inward at the moment. She'd had to accept and process a great deal today, and despite her few brief lapses into panic, she'd maintained extremely well. He didn't know her well enough to know her breaking point. Maybe she didn't know, either. But from the steady set of her shoulders, he didn't think she was teetering on the brink. Yet.

"Johansson's dead, I gather. And it wasn't an accident." Her tone was flat, unemotional, stating facts rather than asking questions.

"Yes, he is. And no, it wasn't."

For some time now, he'd been juggling the need to protect her and take charge of the situation so she wouldn't suffer any more than necessary. She'd told him not to do her any favors, that she could handle it, but he didn't see the logic in pushing a person too far. Not when he could avoid it. Now, watching her, the rigid line of her spine, the tense set of her jaw, he realized that keeping her out caused her to suffer more than if he was open with her. About all of it. He knew imagination was often far worse than even the harshest reality. She'd already seen a lot. The fire. Geronimo dying. It was far more than most people should have to witness. He should have respected that more. Respected her more.

"It wasn't the accident that killed him, though."

She turned around then.

"He was shot, Elena," Rafe said quietly, though it didn't lessen the impact. "That's why his truck flipped."

Her eyes went wide and she froze to the spot. "Shot?"

He nodded.

"I—from your end of the conversation, I thought maybe someone forced him off the road. But somebody *shot* him?"

Despite the absolute horror on her face, Rafe didn't back down from his decision to be open and honest. "In the head. And whoever it was might have helped his truck into that ditch, but regardless, it wasn't an accident."

She turned back to the window, then back to him, then began to pace. "Shot. Dear God. This has gone too far. Way too far. I should never have kept this a secret." She looked up, terror and not a little panic on her face. "It was so selfish of me to want to keep her, keep her safe, when I should have just told the truth from that night on."

"You have no idea what would have happened if you had. We don't know the forces at play. You did what you had to, to protect the one thing you loved. Second-guessing that now isn't going to get us anywhere."

That seemed to help her regain her grip a little. "Do you think they got Kenny? And—and your guy, Aaron? You don't think he's also—oh my God." That last part ended on a gulp. Arm braced around her stomach, she spun around again and stood in front of the window. Her shoulders began to tremble and he was crossing the room before he thought better of it.

He wanted to treat her fairly, and with respect, but dammit, he hated this, hated her being tortured. He turned her into his arms, pulling her tight whether she wanted to be held or not. Maybe he needed to hold on as much as she needed someone to hold on to. She wasn't crying. The trembling was induced from sheer terror. Her eyes were enormous when she looked up into his.

"Springer—would someone . . . would they—"

"She's carrying the golden goose. I think she's probably the safest part of this whole ordeal."

"I—I don't understand any of this. I don't know who would do something like that. My God, they shot someone. Killed someone." She tried to break free. "I don't care how much the baby is worth, and you know I'd lay my life down for her, but to kill someone? That's crazy. This whole thing is crazy. They can just have the damn baby. I never wanted to profit from this, I just didn't want to lose my horse. I wanted to make sure she'd be safe. Why didn't whoever is doing this just come find me and tell me they knew, demand I give the baby to them? Not do this. Never do . . . Jesus, Rafe, who would do this?"

He turned her chin with his hand so she had to keep her gaze focused on him. "A desperate person. A greedy person. You'd be surprised the lengths people will go to, to get what they want."

"How do we get out of this? How do we make it stop? Do we need to go to the police? Tell them what we know?"

She was digging her fingers into his shoulders, shaking him, as if rattling him would force a solution to their rapidly growing set of problems.

"There are no fast solutions here. And we would be handing the police more questions than answers at this point. I don't see how they could be effective right now. We don't know all the players yet, but we're working on it and we know a hell of a lot more than anyone else." Plus, what he didn't say, was that the police could easily pull one or both of them in for extensive questioning, which would be highly likely given their involvement, and take them both out of the picture for God knew how long. "Mac is heading back to Kenny's to see if he missed anything, and to be there in case anyone else comes calling."

"You think he might come back? He didn't just take Springer, he took all of his horses. And who is helping him? We never talked about that. He doesn't have a rig big enough for all of them."

"I don't know. Whoever wanted Springer, I suppose."

"We can't just sit here. We have to do something."

"Right now, this is the safest place for you. I need to do some digging myself, on all the players, but you running around the countryside isn't going to help, and potentially only puts you at risk. The only places we could be looking would be Kenny's place and Charlotte Oaks." He stopped her before she could say anything. "Mac is sending someone down there, but we're not sending them in until we know what we're sending them into."

"I should be the one to go down there. Or to Kenny's. Anywhere but here. I can't let everyone else run around at my expense while I do nothing. Besides, if one of your own men got involved, who's to say I'm not at risk here? Or that you're not?"

"The staff has been excused for the evening. Mac took care of that. No one is in the main house, and this one is secure. The main entrance is closed."

"What about Kate's instructors and—"

"The ones who don't live on the property will go out the separate entrance for her school. Which is also being monitored. No one goes in or out without approval from Kate." He gentled his grip. "You're safer here than anywhere else at the moment. Springer is most likely being very well taken care of."

"The stress alone—what if she goes into early labor? What if—"

"I know it's hard, but you can't let yourself go there. If Kenny is with her, regardless of why, then she's in good hands."

Elena's eyes widened. "That's it! That's why they wanted him. They're blackmailing him, or forcing him to attend the birth. Maybe they know her history, or maybe they just want to make sure nothing goes wrong with Geronimo's only offspring. That would explain everything."

"Except why they took him, Springer, and every other horse on his property."

She swore. "I know, I know. I can't figure that out, either, but I just can't see him doing this. I've thought and thought about it, all the way back here, and I swear I'm being as objective as I can be. He wouldn't, Rafe. Not this. Not to me, not to anyone. He just . . . it's not who he is any more than it's who I am. For any price."

"Don't take this the wrong way, but you were pushed to do something you'd never otherwise do when this situation happened. Who knows what he's facing?"

She blanched and looked away. "Point taken."

He lifted her chin with his fingertips. "I'm not saying he's dirty, but we have to keep all options open."

She looked into his eyes for the longest time, then gathered herself and said, "I know. I do. But you've talked a lot about gut instincts. That's why I told you what I did. It's why I've told you anything, ever. My gut says I can trust you. Just like my gut says I'm right about Kenny. I won't shut down possibilities, but I won't believe it's true until I see some proof."

"Is that what you've told yourself about me? Trustworthy until proven otherwise?"

"No, I looked at the man you are, with the deep bonds you have, and what they will do for you, and you for them. And what you were all willing to do for me, because it's what you thought was right. That's the only measure I needed."

He took her mouth. Right then. No preamble, no slow lowering of his lips to hers, no choice given. Just a choice made.

The surprise of it kept her still, but only for a second. He mentally braced himself for her to shove at him. He'd have respected that, backed away, though it would have cost him. He knew then how well and truly entangled he'd become. It had never been like this for him. Almost irrational. He relied on instinct, on rational thought. Not on emotion and his hard-on. Or his heart. Life wasn't set up to be fair about those things, and he'd had enough of the unfair part of life.

Then she moaned, just a little guttural sound in the back of her throat. And her hands came up to fist in his hair as she pulled his mouth down even harder on hers. And kissed him back with every ounce of intensity she had in her.

And he knew there was no protecting himself from this. Or from her. Nor did he want there to be.

Chapter 25

Elena was so tempted to sink into that blissful oblivion only he could provide. Escape the overwhelming worry and fear, even if only for a few moments. But, in the end, even Rafe couldn't transport her, and their kiss eased from the powerful thunder she was already coming to crave, to something quieter, and yet perhaps even more compelling in the way it nurtured something else inside her. And that something was hope.

When he lifted his head and looked into her eyes, she said, "We're going to find her."

He nodded.

"And we're going to figure this out."

He nodded again, then took her hand and drew her with him as he walked across the main room and through a sliding partition that sectioned off what turned out to be a small office. Through another sliding screen, she could see his bedroom, and the oversized bed, sitting low to the floor in a teakwood box frame. A detailed latticework headboard, gorgeous wall murals, and sumptuous-looking pillows in decadent jeweled silks combined to make his bedroom look like a combination of crisp Asian beauty and extravagant Arabic splendor. She didn't dare let her gaze linger there, because it made her want things she couldn't have. Not now.

She thought about what he'd said, about wanting to know

what came next with them. It was a seductive thought, and one she couldn't afford at the moment.

Her attention was pulled away when he tugged her over to his desk. What his bedroom was in sensuality, his office was in functionality. Nothing like the warm tones and softly tooled leathers of his main house office, this one was more track-lit, high tech, smooth grays and stealth black, like a compact space station.

"Wow," she said, turning around and looking at all the equipment packed perfectly into the specially designed series of shelves and cubicles.

Rafe slid into a sleek, black leather-and-chrome desk chair and began tapping keys on a curved, consolelike keyboard. A flat screen mounted on the wall in front of him sprang to life. He motioned to a pod-shaped scoop of black padded leather that was tucked into a side corner. "You should make yourself comfortable—this could take a while."

"What is the game plan?" she asked, still nosing about.

"It's getting late in the day. Mac is on his way to Kenny's— we've got someone heading down to Charlotte Oaks. They'll stand by until given directions. With Aaron's disappearance, we're not going to show our hand again until we know more of what is going on."

"And how are we going to figure that out?"

"I'm going to start an in-depth search on Johansson." He glanced at her. "And Kenny."

She nodded. "I understand and I agree. If for no other reason than to eliminate him as a suspect."

Rafe merely nodded in return and went back to his console. Elena paced.

"There is a galley kitchen on the other side of the main room if you're hungry. I'd have something sent over from the main house, but—"

"I know. I can't eat."

"You should. We probably both should. It's been a long day

and it's likely we're in for another one." He glanced over at her. "Other than gathering information, there isn't much more we can do tonight."

"I won't be able to sleep."

"She'll be okay, Elena."

"Nothing is okay. Nothing is remotely okay."

He paused and swiveled his chair so he could face her. "I know. But sleepless and weakened isn't a good place to be, either. Think of it as doing what you can for her by taking care of yourself. It won't happen tonight, but it will happen soon."

"What if we don't find anything? What if Kenny's background doesn't reveal anything, and Johansson is a dead end?" She flinched a little as the double meaning of her words played back in her head.

Rafe suddenly turned back to the console and tapped a few keys.

"What? What did I say?"

Mac's voice came through a speaker somewhere a moment later.

"What's up?"

"I'm just starting the research, but it occurred to me that maybe we should have someone tag along with Johansson's body. See who else might be nosing around, asking questions."

"One step ahead of you. I took care of that before leaving the scene."

"Keep me informed. I don't care what time it is."

"Will do."

He disconnected and shifted his attention back to her. "I might be at this for hours. I know you're going crazy with nothing to do, but I want you to stay here. With me. Tonight. It's the safest place for you . . . and I want you here."

She hadn't thought that far ahead, and her gaze went to his bedroom before she could stop it.

"I don't have a spare bedroom, but I honestly want you next to me. I'll stay more focused, rest better, if you're right there." He waited until she looked back to him. "Are you okay with that?"

Considering she was torn between the need to go leap in the nearest vehicle and go somewhere, anywhere, to start looking for Springer . . . and the need to go curl up in his lap and beg him to tell her he was going to find them some answers . . . his request was an easy one. "I'm very okay with that."

His lips curved just a little, but his gaze remained serious. "Good." For a moment she thought he was going to say more, but instead he turned back to his console and went back to work.

She paced some more, but he had a point—it wasn't serving to calm her, it just made her worry more with each path she wore in his rug. She had to find something to keep herself occupied. She wasn't remotely hungry, but maybe fixing him something to eat, or at least a pot of coffee to sustain them over the next who-knew-how-many hours, would be a start.

"Do you have a coffeemaker?"

"With my own grinder," he said, not looking up. "And yes, I would dearly love some."

"Then I'll see what I can do."

She went to slip through the screened panels, when he called her name. She turned back. "What? You take it black? Or do you have some complicated recipe you want me to follow?"

He pushed back and stood up, walked over to her, but rather than draw her into his arms, he simply reached out and cupped her cheek. "Thank you."

"I should be the one doing the thanking. I'm feeling rather useless at the moment. The least I can do is make coffee."

"I meant—"

"I know," she said quietly, putting off whatever he'd been about to say. She was too close to being undone by the day's events. She couldn't handle much more, even if it was something meant to make her feel good. Her emotions were barely restrained beneath the surface as it was. "Let me—I need to—"

He dropped his hand. "I know."

She nodded, silently thanking him. He did, indeed, get her. A rather profound gift, that. She slipped through the screens and wandered in search of the kitchen, fighting off tears of exhaustion while admitting she couldn't imagine getting through this without him.

Hours passed and midnight came and went, with disheartening results. She'd made some soup in addition to coffee and they'd both managed a bowl and several cups, but their rejuvenating effects had long since worn off. Fatigue was rapidly replacing worry, and her eyelids were drooping as she sat on her perch in his office chair where she'd finally retreated an hour earlier.

It was the cessation of tapping fingers and a muttered oath that had her eyes fluttering open. "What? What did you find?" she asked, shaking off the cobwebs, or trying to.

"Nothing. That's the problem."

He'd finished digging on Kenny a while back, with nothing out of the ordinary coming from his search. The search on Johansson had revealed that he'd had a spotty work record and held a private investigator's license in addition to being bonded to do work for Intrepid. Though he'd portrayed himself as an insurance investigator, Rafe had wondered in what capacity he'd truly been hired, given how things had gone. They'd had less luck digging up any information on any past clients he might have worked for privately. And the lateness of the hour precluded him from pulling more strings and garnering a few favors from well-placed insiders.

Calls to Mac had also not brought any enlightenment, as no one had shown up to snoop there, and his more exhaustive investigation of the property had yielded no new clues. He planned to do more once the sun came up, but at the moment, they were all pretty disheartened.

Silence from Aaron, Kenny, and no new information coming from the morgue completed their disgust and discouragement.

Rafe tapped a few more keys, and the screen went blank and the banked lights beneath his shelves winked out. He pushed back and stood, groaning a little as he arched his back.

She started to climb out of the concave-shaped chair, but he stepped over and offered a hand before she could stand.

He gently pulled her to her feet, then caught her against him as she wavered slightly. "We need some sleep. We'll tackle this again tomorrow."

She nodded, not trusting herself to say anything lest she break down completely. She didn't want to feel hopeless, but nothing, not one tiny thing, had gone their way tonight. She was thankful that nothing obvious had popped up on Kenny, but beyond that, the night had been a complete zero.

Rafe wrapped his arms around her and held her for a moment, hugging her and accepting her arms snaking around his waist with a deep sigh and a kiss to her temple. "Let's go to bed."

He kept her tucked to his side, and they turned toward the screened panels that led to his bedroom. Any other time in her life, this moment would have filled her with anticipation and the kind of pulse-accelerating excitement she could only have dreamed about. Now, all she could think about was getting some rest, and praying to God she could sleep without the dreams haunting her. *Not tonight*, she prayed.

Once in his room, he opened a panel next to the door and pushed a series of buttons. Lights throughout the pool house dimmed and a soft voice said, "Security, activated."

Elena lifted her head from his shoulder, but said nothing about the state-of-the-art system. Frankly, it didn't surprise her, and knowing it was there made her feel safer.

"There is a bathroom through there," he said, motioning to the opposite corner. "I'll grab you one of my t-shirts if you'd like."

"I'd like," was all she said. "Will I set off an alarm if I get up and wander to the kitchen in the middle of the night?"

"It already is the middle of the night. But no, the system keeps unwanted intruders out, it doesn't trap you in."

She gave a shaky sigh of relief. "Thank you."

"Thank Mac. He designed it. I only wish I could be doing more."

"You're doing an amazing amount," she told him, never more honest. "It's at least eliminating suspicion and telling us we need to look in a new direction."

He shuffled her toward the bed and quietly popped the clasps of her overalls. "In the morning."

She could only nod as he let the bib panel fall forward and undid the buttons at her hips. She stepped out of the pool of worn denim, left only in her long underwear shirt and panties. It seemed like three lifetimes ago that she'd dressed and met him for an early morning class that had ended with an almost-tryst in the tack room.

Her thoughts drifted there and clung to those moments like a lifeline, helping her to block out the reality of the moment and spend some time in another place. A place where people weren't being shot dead and her beloved horse and family friend weren't in danger.

She tugged his shirt loose and lifted it over his head. He raised his arms, accommodating her, and soon she had his bare chest at her disposal. To do with what she wanted.

And, beyond the bone-deep fatigue, beyond the sheer terror and almost debilitating fear . . . there was a wealth of desire.

In some recess of her mind, she wondered if this was what they meant by life-threatening situations acting like some kind of sudden aphrodisiac. Her sudden voracious hunger for him was limited only by her lack of available energy. So she took it slow. Sweetly, deliciously slow.

He'd tasted her, taunted her, teased her, on several occasions. Now it was her turn.

Her entire world narrowed down to the smooth expanse of

honeyed skin wrapped oh-so-tautly across his chest. She dipped her head and drew her tongue slowly from his collarbone down the valley between his pecs, and then teased her way over to his nipple.

He drew in a sharp breath when she flicked her tongue across the sensitive tip. His hands came up to her hair, which he slowly unwove from its heavy braid as she continued her exploration.

"Elena," he said, his voice barely more than a rough whisper.

"Rafe," she said, making his name a vow.

He cupped her head and slowly drew her mouth up to his, his eyes on hers as their lips met.

She took his kiss, letting her eyes drift shut as sensation after sensation poured through her. He slowly lowered them both to his bed, where he rolled her beneath him, and continued his sweet seduction. Their clothes didn't come off in a frenzied hurry, but with slow deliberation. As if they both needed to offset the harsh reality of what they'd been through the past twenty-four hours, with something pure and honest.

They took turns slowly exploring each other, delighting in discovering what made them gasp, what made them moan. It was a slow but complete capitulation, where nothing was held back, nothing was hidden.

When she finally rolled to her back, taking his weight fully on top of her, it was as if she'd reached a golden point, a place she'd been trying to get to for a long, long time but could never quite find. That place where life suddenly became more complete and took on even greater meaning.

Without a word, they locked gazes and he slowly pushed into her, not stopping until she'd taken him fully inside of her. She wrapped her legs around him, holding him there, taking a moment to wallow, to revel a bit, in the supreme pleasure and contentment of being joined to that person who was meant to be hers.

And, in that moment, despite all the fears, all the work yet to be done, and the very precarious future that lay ahead, one thing she was certain of: her time spent with this man was going to mean something to her for the rest of her life.

The rest she let go, and willed herself just to feel, to truly live purely in that moment and that moment only. She moved first, pressing her hips up into his, then wrapping her legs around him. He began to move inside of her, so deep, filling her so perfectly. It wasn't wild, it wasn't frenzied; it was powerful and necessary. He slid one arm beneath the small of her back and lifted her hips even higher so he could sink into her even more deeply. Their gazes caught, held, and their thrusts came faster, deeper. She watched him climb, watched as his need for her strengthened, felt his muscles gather and bunch as he drew ever closer. She tightened around him, needing to know she could take him to that place, give him that sweet bliss that he so effortlessly gave her, and found herself shuddering, too, in intense satisfaction as he growled through a pulsing release.

He kissed her, pressed another kiss to her temple, then dropped another one just below her ear, before rolling to his back, pulling her with him, and settling her body alongside his.

She'd never spent the night fully with anyone. It should have been awkward, at least momentarily, trying to figure out how to align her body with his, but it all fell into place as effortlessly as she'd fallen for him. She didn't question it. Her eyes were already drifting shut as she shifted enough to press a soft kiss over his heart before tucking her arm across his body. Then she draped her leg across his, wanting him to feel as cosseted and taken care of as he made her feel.

One thing she'd learned from all this was that it was okay to take. It made giving all that much sweeter.

She had no idea what time it was when her eyes flew open. Nor could she say what had woken her from such a deep sleep. She went to move, then felt the weight of Rafe's arm tucked across her back, holding her against him. She didn't want to disturb him, but she was struggling to orient herself, and her still-muzzy brain took a moment or two to remember where she was, and what she was doing there.

There was a dull throb of a headache beginning as she lifted her head, willing her eyes to adjust to the dark so she could seek out a clock. The time didn't matter—it was still before dawn—but it would help her get her bearings. Bearings put in complete disarray by the man whose bed she was presently sharing.

She thought about that for a moment, partly because it pushed the return of fear and panic to the edges of her mind for a few more precious seconds, and partly because she couldn't help but wonder what, in fact, did come next for them. She realized that the events currently unfolding could end up robbing her of finding out, but that didn't stop her from thinking about what she'd want, if it were up to her.

Slowly, cautiously, she slipped out from beneath his arm and gently shifted her weight off the bed, her eyes adjusting just enough to keep her from stumbling on her way to the bathroom. She took the time to splash cool water on her face, debating whether it was worth turning on the bright lights to search for some aspirin.

There was a small, diamond-shaped window high on the central wall between the vanity and shower. She stepped over to it, thinking the familiarity of the farm would lend some much-needed normalcy to this moment.

The waning moon was just strong enough to light the tips of the apple trees to her left, and lightly gild the roof of the stables, down the hill past the edge of the pool. She wasn't sure when she made the decision; she only knew there was a sense of relief just in the thought of doing it. She didn't question it beyond that, and found herself moving silently back through his bedroom, slipping on the two garments she groped first. His shirt and her overalls. He'd said the house kept intruders out as opposed to keeping them locked in. She could only hope that was true as she slowly turned the knob to the door leading to the pool, and the path that led to the stables.

It was closer to dawn than she realized. As she skirted the pool and stepped onto the path, she wished she'd scrounged for her shoes. But the late-night, or very-early-morning, air felt too good brushing against her skin to turn back now. She just needed some fresh air, a few moments to herself to get her head on straight and mentally gear up for what would likely be the most difficult day of her life.

Once on the path to the stables, she couldn't help but look beyond, out to her stables, to her place. She paused, looking back up at the pool house. In her haste to get some air, she hadn't thought to leave a note, not thinking she'd be gone more than a minute, and not planning on going past the pool's end.

But there was a golf cart right there, beckoning to her. The thought of fresh clothes and her own personal surroundings were a balm to her battered soul in a way that even Rafe couldn't provide, though he'd been a lifesaver. She promised herself she'd make a quick run of it, over there and back, then slip inside to make him a fresh pot of coffee before he woke up and missed her.

The cart moved almost silently through the predawn moonlight, and she quickly slipped inside the barn and up the ladder to her loft rooms. She hadn't realized how fully and completely she'd turned her life over to Rafe for safekeeping until seeing her own jumble of belongings made her eyes go glassy for a moment.

She wouldn't have traded a moment of his help, and she was supremely thankful for his arrival in her world—his confidence, his knowledge, his comfort. But there was something to be said for taking command of a part of her world again, even if just for a moment, to rejuvenate her spirit and her will to push on.

She'd just pulled on fresh overalls and a long-sleeved t-shirt when she heard what sounded like the creak of the big barn door. It often did that on windier days, but the air had been cool and still on her ride over.

Her heart caught as the creak came again, and she realized it must be Rafe, come to find her. She felt awful for giving him even a moment of panic and was all ready to deliver a heartfelt apology when she hit the top of the ladder and froze.

There was a dark silhouette at the base of the ladder, the only entry and exit to her loft. And when he looked up, she stared down into a pair of familiar eyes. But they didn't belong to Rafe.

Chapter 26

"*Hola*, Elena. I've been waiting for you."

"JuanCarlo." It was all she could get out, because she'd looked past his face now, and discovered the gun in his hand.

He gestured with it now. "Come down, we have much to talk about."

She couldn't move, couldn't think clearly, couldn't decide on any course of action, because too many things were racing through her brain all at once. Where was Springer? What happened to Kenny? And how in the hell was JuanCarlo involved in all this?

"I can see by your expression you have questions, too." He gestured again. "Come, we will both learn many things."

She hesitated, not wanting to get within arm's length of him, debating for a split second whether to step back, slam the trapdoor shut, and shove something heavy over it as fast as she could.

"The bullet will reach you before I do," he said calmly, as if reading her mind. "It will also be less painful." Once again, he gestured for her to come down. "Don't test my patience. I've already used this twice, so it will not hasten my journey to hell if I use it again."

"Twice?" *Johansson and*—her gaze flew to the end of the barn, and beyond.

"Your boyfriend is still alive." He wiggled the gun. "But we could change that." His face brightened when she immediately started down the ladder. "Ah, I see we've found your bargaining chip. Well, I believe that will work both ways."

"You won't get away with anything here," she said.

"I'm fairly certain I already have," he said, then shocked her by suddenly grabbing her hair and yanking her against him, her back to his chest. Her scalp on fire, an instant later she also felt the cold muzzle of his gun against her temple. His voice next to her ear made her shudder. "Do not test me more than you already have." His fist was still in her hair, and tears sprang to the corners of her eyes as he gave it a vicious twist. "Now, I will release you, and you will do as I say, when I say. Are we understood?" To underscore the question, he tugged her even more tightly back against him.

"Yes," she choked out.

"Good," he said quite pleasantly, and released her as suddenly as he'd grabbed her.

She staggered forward and landed hard on her hands and knees on the packed dirt floor of the barn.

"Get up. Time is precious. We must go."

She scrambled up, wanting to keep her eye on him at all times. "Go where?"

"Why, to retrieve your horse, of course."

Relief filled her. Springer was okay. "Where is she?"

He frowned and waggled his gun at her. "Don't think to toy with me on this. I'm quite clear on the situation, and the pawns involved. I've removed two. I can remove more."

Two. That was the second time he'd said that. *Kenny!* "Who—" She had to break off, clear the sudden lump from her throat. "Who is the other one?"

Now his eyes widened. "Which do you know about?"

"Johansson," she said, not seeing the point in keeping that information secret. "Who else did you shoot?" She'd said it perhaps a bit too stridently, but her heart was pounding so hard she could hardly hear over it, and hysteria was edging up her throat, squeezing it tight.

Perhaps sensing this, he gave her what she asked for. "Your boyfriend's errand boy."

Mac? No, that couldn't be. "Aaron," she blurted out, as she realized who else it could be.

"Is that his name? Matters little now."

"Is he—"

"Dead? Perhaps. Though I'd hoped not, as I planned to use him for leverage. I've looked into your boyfriend's little business here, and it seems he has a thing for loyalty. I am counting on that going both ways. However, now I have a much bigger piece of bait to dangle. Come on now, we're wasting precious time."

"Where is he? Where is Aaron?"

"Somewhere safe."

"Where is Kenny? Is he with Springer?"

He just looked at her for a moment, then laughed. "Very good. But don't try your amateur tactics on me."

"I'm very serious. Where is he? Where is Springer? Where did you take them? Are they okay?" It all fell into place, or part of it did, anyway. JuanCarlo had access to huge horse trailers at Charlotte Oaks. Between an Oaks rig and Kenny's, the horses could all have been moved in just a couple trips. "Did Kenny help you?"

"Hardly. But then, you know of that very well. I will not tell you again—do not toy with me regarding this, Elena. You and your vet friend have made your good attempt, but it will not succeed." He stepped closer, aiming the gun at her chest, then lifting it to her head. "So let's stop wasting time, shall we?"

"But, I—"

She wasn't given time to finish her sentence before Juan-Carlo grabbed her elbow and shoved her roughly ahead of him. "Walking, no talking. Not until we are clear of this place. Given the ridiculous amount of security set up here, I do not trust your boyfriend and his cohorts not to have wired every last square foot."

He kept insisting Rafe was her boyfriend, and the hairs on

her neck stood up as she wondered how long JuanCarlo had been skulking about. He had to have seen them together, and that had only been for a short time now. "How did you get onto the grounds?"

"You want something badly enough, you find a way." He spun her around and shoved her roughly with the muzzle of the gun. "No more questions. Only answers. Don't play games, Elena. Too much is at stake. For you."

She didn't say anything, but kept walking in front of him. The feel of the gun muzzle against her spine was enough to insure her silence. She hated having her back to him, but she tried to use the few minutes she had left before he took her away from here, to figure things out. It was a struggle just to think clearly. If JuanCarlo was the person behind this, then what was his motive? Unless he was working for someone else, but that someone could only be Gene, and if he knew she had Geronimo's unborn foal, he'd have come for her directly, and probably personally, as it was rightfully his.

People were dying, and people were missing. Horses were missing, namely hers. Which meant whoever wanted the baby had no more right to it than she did. And she had no doubt it was the baby they wanted. Or they'd have gone to Gene, or the police, and reported it.

Something else was going on here.

Think, Elena, think. As they left the barn and entered the rear paddock, she tried like hell to formulate any scenario that worked, but raw terror made clear, linear thought next to impossible. Being on the far side of the barn, her view of the pool house was blocked. Why, oh why, hadn't she left a damn note? She had no idea how long Rafe would sleep, having only spent the one night together.

Perhaps their only night, she thought, then immediately quashed that line of thinking.

Likely he'd be up early, due to their situation. She could only hope he figured out that she'd been taken and hadn't willingly gone off after her horse or something equally stupid. Except she *had* been stupid. Royally, and potentially fatally, stupid.

They left the paddock and JuanCarlo pointed her in the direction of the trees that bordered the far side of the property. "That way."

"It's still too dark—I can't see. And I—"

"Walk."

She stumbled over the uneven ground, thinking maybe there was some way to fake a fall, then wrestle the gun from him, but the risk was too high. She wasn't sure how badly he needed her, and she wasn't willing to find out the hard way.

"Do you have a vehicle on the property?"

"Through the trees," he ordered, not answering her question.

Her eyes slowly adapted to the shadows, but she still had to put her hands out in front of her to keep from getting hit with low branches. Twigs and leaves scratched at her arms and face, but she kept moving. Once they left the property, she knew her chances of survival greatly diminished. She knew who he was, knew he was involved. And he'd already killed. No way was he letting her go.

Which meant she was dependent on Rafe to find her . . . or she had to find a way out herself. Since JuanCarlo wasn't even on their radar, she doubted Rafe would come to the rescue. Which meant her survival, and possibly Springer's, once again depended solely on her.

Chapter 27

Rafe rolled over and laid his arm across his bed. His empty bed. He came wide awake instantly, though it took him a second or two longer to process why he'd been so alarmed when sleeping alone was the norm for him. His subconscious had already adapted to having Elena by his side. Except, at the moment, she wasn't.

He looked to the bathroom, but no light shone. He slid his feet off the bed and stood, trying not to panic, despite what his gut was telling him. Then he noticed his shirt wasn't lying on the floor, and smiled. Picturing her in his kitchen, wearing nothing more than his shirt, made him happy. It was going to be a difficult day at best. So perhaps starting it off with some alone time wasn't such a bad idea.

He stuck his head in his office, but there were no lights flashing, indicating incoming messages. So he wandered out to the kitchen, already formulating his plan for getting her back into his bed for a little while longer.

Only the kitchen was dark.

As was the rest of the pool house. Without wasting another second, he moved swiftly and silently back to his bedroom, checked the bathroom, then immediately got dressed. He noted her overalls gone from the floor, and prayed like hell she'd just decided to get some air.

Exiting the house, he saw right away that she wasn't around

the pool area. He looked down to the barns, the beginnings of sunrise casting it in an otherworldly glow. No sign of movement down there. Then he looked out to the far barn and realized she'd probably run home to get a change of clothes and maybe shower in her own place. He could understand her need for that, but he planned to make her aware, in no uncertain terms, that he really didn't want her traipsing around alone, even on Dalton Downs property, until they resolved this. More than likely he'd meet her heading back; still, a note would have been nice.

By the time he made it to the barn, he was running. His instincts were on full alert and he wasn't taking any chances. Her ladder was down, but he didn't allow himself to feel any relief until he laid eyes on her. He took the rungs two at a time, calling out her name.

No response. *Please let her be in the shower.*

She wasn't. But she'd clearly changed clothes, as he found his shirt and her overalls on the floor by her closet. There had been no sign of a struggle, nothing looked out of place. He couldn't even take time to register her personal space and take in whatever else it might have revealed about her.

He all but leapt off the ladder and raced to the back paddock. Nothing. He slapped his pocket to get his phone and realized he'd left it in the pool house in his panic to find her. Panic was not a normal state for him. Ever. He needed to calm down, think rationally.

He went back to the ladder, and started to look around for clues, but his racing in and back out had scuffed the dirt floor fairly well. Dammit! The dirt was so hard-packed it likely wouldn't have told him much, but if there had been another set of footprints . . .

He raced back to the paddock, where the ground was much softer, and his heart skipped several beats when he found the proof. Proof he really didn't want to see. He'd rather be pissed off at her negligence than scared shitless. But there they were, two sets of footprints. Smaller . . . likely Elena's. And larger. Clearly a man. But which man?

He tracked the prints out of the paddock and a few steps toward the trees, but the dirt quickly gave way to grass, and it was still too dark to see any impressions. It looked as if they'd walked off into the woods.

He swung around, looking back in the direction of the main house. It would be supremely foolish to race off with no form of communication on him. But time might be of the essence, and if anything happened to her because he'd wasted critical minutes retracing his steps, he'd never forgive himself. Torn, he realized that until it grew lighter, there would be no way to track through the trees, and the grove was wide enough, and dense enough, that they could have gone anywhere.

Most likely, though, they'd gone to the edge of the property boundary, which was fenced with rail and both electric and sensory wire, but wouldn't be impossible to circumvent. Plus, it was just another fifty yards or so through another stand of trees, then over a ravine, to the main road.

It was the likeliest route, so that was the one he took. He could figure out where they'd gone over—or under—it after he got there.

It wasn't until he reached the fence line that he realized he was also unarmed. Christ, he was losing it. The fence was intact and the wire hot, so either they were still on the property, or whoever did this had figured out how to circumvent it. Going under the fence was the likeliest route, but digging in Virginia's hard clay and rocky ground was difficult and unlikely to get done quickly or without triggering the sensor wire.

He had no tools for either. Shit, he had no fucking tools of any kind, except his mind, and that had clearly deserted him the first time he'd laid eyes on Elena.

He turned and headed back to the house, taking a beating on his forearms and face as he raced through the trees as fast as he could. Less than fifteen minutes later, he was armed and on the road heading out of Dalton Downs. He stopped at the end of the property lane and dialed up Mac.

He picked up immediately. "What's going on?"

"Everything. Elena is gone, and I don't know who has her, but I do know they've left the property. Fence line outside the apple grove beyond the far paddock."

"How'd they do that without tripping the sensor wires?"

"Beats me—"

"Unless they had help. Or planned this together. You've got to at least consider—"

"Someone took her, Mac. The footprints show it was a man, and that she was walking a few paces ahead of him. Right in front of him. I don't think they were playing follow the leader."

"Shit."

"Exactly. Nothing going on there?"

"Not a peep."

Rafe fell silent and willed himself to think clearly, but found it more of a struggle than it had ever been before. Sick with worry, literally nauseous with it, he fought to rein in the panic. "What about Charlotte Oaks? What have you heard from down there?"

"Nothing. I sent him in to do quick reconnaissance, but nothing out of the ordinary to report. The rebuilding is well under way and the bigger buildings mostly complete, but nothing looked out of the ordinary. No sense of anything awry that he could tell, but he'll know more when he can get in there and listen to the general buzz from the workers, see if anything is being bandied about."

"We don't have that much time. What is your gut on that?"

"I think Dalton and here at Kenny's are the two hot spots. We've got someone in place down there if we need him. My next suggestion for today was to scope out all the spreads between the two places, start looking to where Kenny might have taken his herd. Nothing popped on him at all? Nothing suspicious?"

"Zip. Elena didn't really know who he'd gotten close with, neighbor-wise, since moving up here. She doesn't spend much actual time with him. He's more old family friend than current confidante."

"No way to track who he's talked to?"

"I was going to dig into phone records today. It was too late to do anything about it last night." He thought about that, then said, "I can't go back in there and just sit and pound keys, Mac. She's out there, going through God knows what. We have to figure this out, dammit! Where the hell is she?"

"If we find the horse, we find her. And vice versa. The most common link is, obviously, Kenny. And Rafe, I know you swear she couldn't be in on this, but—"

"If I'm wrong, I have to live with it, okay? But whoever walked her out didn't do it holding her hand. So we handle this as a hostile abduction." Just saying that out loud almost had him throwing up. "We need the fucking helicopter. I tried to raise Finn last night, every which way I could. Nothing. So he's either in so deep he can't risk the communication, or—"

"Let's not go there. One of our tribe is already in danger."

Our tribe. "Thank you," Rafe said, never so sincere.

"I push because I have to, for you, and for her. But I know better than anyone where you are right now, and you have my word we'll do whatever it takes."

"I owe you."

"Shut up. Now listen, I talked to Kate, picked her brain to see if she'd ever had any conversation with Elena about who she might still be in contact with besides Kenny, who could have inadvertently blabbed something, but she said Elena stayed pretty private about herself."

"She told no one."

"I understand, but now, with her gone, maybe we should check all the same, run her phone records, see if there has been any contact with anyone. Maybe we should check at Charlotte Oaks, too. Anything to give us a lead, a connection. If it's not Kenny, then I don't know where else to look. We could contact her old boss, use some story, and see what he might know about who her friends were."

"If this is related to anything or anyone down there, it could trigger—"

"She's already gone, Rafe—I don't think we can afford to play it safe. Maybe someone there knows something, anything, that might give us a lead as to who is doing this. She was there long enough. Someone might have a clue about friends, where she liked to hang out, who with. It's a start."

"Yeah, yeah, okay." He was tapping his foot in rapid-fire succession, hardly able to sit still. He realized now how it must have been for Elena all day yesterday, wanting to race across the countryside to hunt down her horse, but not knowing where to start.

He was staring at the main road, and had no idea which way to turn. It was hours to Kenny's in one direction, and double that distance to Charlotte Oaks in the other. "Call our standby pilots and get me a damn helicopter. I'll head back to the house and start making calls. I want a bird on the platform before the sun clears the horizon."

"Done."

Chapter 28

"Drive," JuanCarlo said from the passenger seat. Elena was behind the wheel of a beige Charlotte Oaks pickup truck, with a madman next to her, pointing a gun at her head. And absolutely no idea where to take him. Gripping the wheel with both hands, she looked directly at him, and tried like hell not to look at the gun. "I don't care if you want the baby, JuanCarlo. It's yours. I just want my horse back. So you have to believe me when I say, if I knew where she was, I'd take you to her. I thought you took her. Or whoever was doing this—I didn't know it was you. The only thing I can figure is that Kenny panicked for some reason and moved her. But I don't know where. I don't know his friends or contacts. We can start with the closest farms, but—"

He jabbed the gun at her. "Liar! Don't lie to me!" He was yelling now, and sounded more unhinged than he had since his surprise appearance. That scared her almost as much as the gun.

"I'm not lying, JuanCarlo. I don't want to die. I don't want Springer to die. It's why I took her away."

"You tried to cheat the Vondervans and all of Charlotte Oaks, so you cannot be trusted." His voice was calmer, but his eyes were still too bright.

"I didn't breed her on purpose. It happened by accident. I saw your truck out there that first night and rode her out, hoping I could talk you into letting me see Geronimo. But no one was there—you were up at the main stables because of that injured horse. So I let myself in. I didn't know my mare had come into season early, and when I let myself into Geronimo's stall—"

"Are you mad? Why in the hell would you do something so foolish? You know better than that. I don't believe you'd be that stupid."

"I *was* that stupid. And I panicked. I took her back to her barn and was trying to figure out what to do. I would have told Gene, I would have done the right thing, but then everything went to hell when the explosion happened."

He said nothing, apparently taking in her explanation, then, "You stayed. After. Why?"

"I was praying she wasn't pregnant—then it would all be moot. I couldn't come forward because there was talk of arson and I was afraid they'd think I'd done it because I was out there, and because of what happened. I couldn't risk that. When I found out she was pregnant, I decided to leave. I'd already decided to anyway, even before Geronimo came."

"I knew nothing of this—you hadn't given your notice or discussed it with me." He jabbed the gun at her. "Don't play me for a fool."

"I wasn't going anywhere at Charlotte Oaks, JuanCarlo. You know that—you're the one who promoted people over me. Not that I would have done anything because of that," she hastened to add. "I just knew I wasn't going to reach my goals there. I hadn't worked out where to go yet, so I hadn't talked to you. Then everything happened and I wanted to be gone before she started to be obviously pregnant."

He fell silent again.

It occurred to her that he hadn't accused her of setting the fire to cover her tracks. Which told her one of two things: either he had set the fire, or he knew who had.

"How—how did you find out? About the baby?"

"It doesn't matter how I found out."

"Maybe it will help me figure out where she might be."

He didn't argue with her this time, or call her a liar, which she took as a sign of progress. If she could get him talking, keep him talking, the more she learned, the better chance she had at finding her way out.

He waited so long, she thought he was going to refuse, but in the end, he said, "It was your own employer who gave you up."

"Kate?"

"No," he sneered. "Your boyfriend."

So, it had been Rafe's snooping that had tipped them off. It didn't matter now. Nothing mattered except staying alive.

"It surprised me," he went on, his tone one of disgust. "I didn't think you were like the rest. Whores, tramps."

"Who are 'the rest'?" she asked before she could think better of it.

"None of your goddamn business!" he barked, reminding her how close to that unbalanced edge he was at all times.

"I—okay. I'm sorry. And I'm not sleeping with my boss. He has nothing to do with my job. I'm not planning on staying on here, so there is no ladder for me to climb. I want back in the race world, just as soon as—"

"You sell that baby to the highest bidder."

"No," she said flatly. "I could hardly do that without revealing my role that night."

"So what was your plan? To keep it, raise it, train it to race, then tell the world?"

She'd never once thought of doing that, but no one else would believe that. It was a logical assumption. "No, I'd have found a way to get him or her back to Gene. But that was going to be between me and him."

He snorted. "Fuck Gene. Why give it to a man who doesn't care what he does, who he hurts?"

"Because he owned Geronimo."

"No. No, he did not." He said this quietly. Too quietly.

She wasn't sure how to proceed without setting him off.

"Drive," he said again. "It is too risky to sit here with the sun coming up. I don't care what direction you go, but go."

His flat tone—and the gun—brooked no argument. She'd been half hoping that if she kept him talking long enough, Rafe, or someone from the farm, would come by and see her sitting in the cab of the truck. She pulled out and headed in the general direction of Kenny's. It was the only connection she had right now.

"Who . . . who would I contact, then?" she asked after they'd been on the road for a few miles. "About the baby, I mean. Who is the rightful owner?"

"It doesn't matter," he said, in that strangely calm way. "You will not be contacting anyone."

Ever again—the words her mind heard tacked on to that, and tried not to let sheer terror seize her once again.

"What are you going to do with the baby, then?" she asked, hoping if she deferred to him as the clear and rightful owner, that would put him at ease.

"None of your concern. It is the only thing to do to make it right, so there will be no discussion."

"Make what right?" She glanced over at him, at the gun, and looked quickly back to the road. *Pretend you're just driving, pretend there is no gun on you, just talk.* "Maybe there is some other way."

"There is no other way!" he screamed suddenly, making her jump. "Don't you think I've tried everything?"

"I'm—I'm sure you have," she said as calmly and reassuringly as she could. She'd always thought of him as a very smart, very focused man. Never once had she thought him crazy, or even close to it. She couldn't imagine what had sent him to the edge, but her bet was that it was a woman. He'd alluded to tramps and whores. It was all she had to go on.

He'd said he wanted to make things right, which meant he was on the outs with someone. Maybe it was something else entirely, but she was betting that someone was the woman in question. "Are you getting the baby back to give to the person who owns it?"

Just asking the question made some of the pieces click into place. Before she could control the reaction, she looked over at him, surprise clearly on her face. Clearly, because he immediately noted it.

"Do not think you understand anything about this!" he roared, waving the gun again.

She looked immediately back to the road, but her hands and legs were shaking now. She was on to something here, but it was obvious that it was that very something—or someone—who'd driven him over the edge. Which meant she had to tread very, very carefully. In all her years dealing with highly strung, half-ton beasts, she'd never questioned her skills, or underestimated their power. She tried to reach for that same balance here.

Which was hard, when her opponent was so very clearly unbalanced.

"I know what it's like to care about someone," she said carefully. "I know what it's like to want them to care back. It's the best feeling in the world and I know I'd want to do anything to have it." She thought about Rafe, about the things he'd said to her, the way he'd made love to her, and then had to shove that away when it made her eyes burn and her throat begin to close over. At least she'd had that much, she told herself. At least she'd experienced the beginnings of something powerful.

"You know nothing," he told her. "Betrayal, lies, that is what you know!"

"If you explain, I'll help you."

He barked a mad laugh at that. "Tramps, whores. I wouldn't be so foolish as to ever trust another one."

"You said I was different from them," she said, recalling his comment, clinging to the hope she was on the right track with it. "I *am* different, JuanCarlo. If I wasn't, I'd have tried that tactic to get ahead at Charlotte Oaks. You know I never did. I never once used that to gain any leverage. I have too much pride for that. You know that about me. It's why I was leaving, because I would never stoop to that. I earn my way fair and square, not on my back. Never that way."

He seemed to think that over, but only said, "Just drive. Quietly. I need peace now."

Elena was happy to give it to him. She needed to think this out a little. All along she'd assumed Gene was the rightful owner of Geronimo, and de facto owner of his offspring, as she hadn't paid for stud. Now she was thinking that a Vondervan was indeed the rightful owner . . . but that Vondervan wasn't Gene. It was Kami.

She forced herself not to glance over at JuanCarlo. She thought about the argument between the Vondervans that he'd told his assistant about, who then blabbed it where she could overhear. She remembered thinking at the time that she was surprised JuanCarlo had gossiped that to anyone, given Gene's obsession with public image, and JuanCarlo's loyalty to his boss. But she'd just assumed JuanCarlo was closer friends with his assistant than she'd realized. Now she wondered if that hadn't been a calculated bit of backroom talking on his part, knowing full well word would get out.

But what would he have to gain by that? A hope that word would spread, as good gossip does, that the supposedly perfect Vondervan union wasn't so perfect? And the reason he'd want the schism made public? Maybe Kami wouldn't leave Gene for him. Maybe it was an affair that had gotten out of hand, with one party wanting more than the other could give. Or maybe his advances had been thwarted, so he was just trying to create trouble for her. Maybe there had never even been a fight. His anger toward the opposite gender suggested he'd been thwarted one way or the other.

But why would he want the baby? She assumed he meant to give it to Kami. As a peace offering? Had his airing of their dirty laundry—real or fabricated—caused her trouble he was now regretting? She remembered the report stating there had been divorce papers filed, but that had been before Geronimo had died, and the Vondervans were still together. She debated tipping her hand, asking him straight out about Kami, mentioning that she'd filed papers, perhaps add her vote of confidence that maybe it was just a matter of time, and see what that got her. But it was a huge risk.

Of course, making amends didn't usually work all that well when the person was willing to kill in order to make them.

Crimes of passion. It was the only thing that explained his extreme behavior. Only he'd taken the heat-of-the-moment reaction and nursed it into a full-blown obsession. Maybe Kami had seen that in him. Maybe he'd always been unbalanced in that way. Elena had been telling the truth about avoiding socializing with her coworkers, so it was a side of him she wouldn't have witnessed, first- or secondhand, as she hadn't been one to even hang out with the crowd.

A county sign caught her attention. She hadn't realized how long they'd been on the road, but they were only one county away from Kenny's place. Another forty-five minutes or so, and she'd be there.

She could only pray Mac was still there, and would know what to do. She hated putting him at risk, but as a former cop, he was her best bet for survival. It was a risk she had to take.

She wondered what Rafe was thinking right now. She doubted he was still asleep. She had no idea how he'd read her sudden disappearance, but she could only hope that he'd at least realized she hadn't left of her own free will. If that was the case, he might well have pulled Mac from Kenny's place. She tried not to let that thought sink what little hope she'd built up. Of course, JuanCarlo might not let her get past Kenny's main gate, but she'd deal with that when they got there. He didn't seem to be paying real close attention to the direction they were heading. She'd have to make sure he stayed that way.

To that end, she risked speaking to him again. "Do you . . .

do you hope that by giving her the baby, it will make things right between you?"

"It can never be right," he said, then seemed to realize what he'd revealed and retreated back to his sulking mood. "I told you, I need peace." He settled back in his seat, seemingly more interested in whatever thoughts were going through his twisted mind, than her. She noticed, peripherally, that the gun was now resting on his thigh. Still aimed at her, but carelessly so.

She wished she had the nerve to do something daring, like swerve the truck, leap from the side door, but too many things could go wrong with that plan. Most of them deadly.

Another fifteen minutes passed without a word. She had no idea how to gauge where he was mentally. He hadn't badgered her about Springer or the baby, or questioned where they were headed. Maybe their sparring had sent him in a different direction mentally, though whether more or less sane and rational, she had no idea. The way he was just sitting there, brooding, she'd bet on less.

She was just trying to come up with another conversational gambit to get him talking, to try and get a better read on him, when she heard a distant sort of thumping sound. It took her a few seconds to place the noise, then it hit her. Helicopter!

They'd gotten Finn to come back. Or something. It had to be. She knew there was enough wealth around, and that Dalton Downs wasn't the only spread with a helipad, but she had to hope that they'd spotted her. Only . . . had they? Would they know she was in the truck? She knew it was a Charlotte Oaks truck, but there was no obvious marking. Gene didn't go for that, claimed it was tacky and crass. But he had had the entire fleet painted a specific shade of tan that wasn't available through regular purchase. She knew it. And anyone who worked at Oaks would know it—but would Rafe or Finn know that?

The sun was well up now, and the skies were clear, but as she tried to scan the sky surreptitiously, she saw nothing. The sound faded and she wondered if she'd imagined it. Maybe she was finally losing it. She'd been through enough at this point that it wouldn't surprise her. But she knew what she'd heard.

She tried to keep from telegraphing her sudden renewed alertness, staying semi-slouched at the wheel, keeping her hands as relaxed as possible. She did her best to scan her rearview mirror, not chancing a look over at the one outside the passenger door.

JuanCarlo was still deep in thought, so she maintained the status quo while trying to figure out what she'd do if there was a helicopter, to signal them. Swerve? Flash her lights? Would they see that? Maybe they'd just been flying over behind her on their way to Kenny's, it being a more direct route by air than by land. Or maybe it was nothing at all.

Then she heard it again, fainter this time, and tried to strain to hear it without being obvious. Then she saw it! A flash of black in her rearview, there in the far distance, then suddenly gone again. It was black, and small, just like the ones she'd seen them use in the past. They were staying well back, she supposed to keep from triggering a reaction from JuanCarlo.

Or maybe it wasn't a Dalton Downs chopper. What if it belonged to someone else involved in this? The Vondervans, maybe? Maybe it was Gene, tracking down JuanCarlo.

And then they passed the sign for Kenny's county and, of course, that he noticed.

"Where are you headed?" he demanded, suddenly alert, and very angry.

"You said to drive, and so I just started driving."

"Where?" He swung the gun up and pressed it directly against her temple, making her jump and swerve a little at the swiftness in his change of mood.

She righted the steering wheel, surprised her heart hadn't leapt right out of her chest. "I—I thought we should go to Kenny's, see if we could find any clues to where he took Springer."

"You are planning something. Tell me!"

She was trying to come up with a plausible story when, very

abruptly, a black helicopter lowered and hovered about two hundred yards dead ahead of them.

He jammed the gun harder against her temple. "What have you done?" he screamed.

"Nothing—I haven't done anything," she yelled back, slamming on the brakes.

"No, no!" he continued screaming, waving the gun now. "Go around, go around!"

"I can't—there isn't enough room." She was shaking so hard she could hardly grip the wheel. So much adrenaline had pumped into her system over the last hour or so, she was sick to the point she honestly thought she might throw up right there in the truck.

"I said go around!" he barked as she continued to slow down. "They will move—they will not chance hurting you."

She didn't know what to do—then she drew close enough to see that Rafe was in the passenger seat. If she was close enough to see him, he was close enough to see her. She had no idea what he thought was going on, but hopefully the gun being waved around at her had given him a good clue as to which side she was on.

She knew what side she was on. And vowed to make sure he never doubted it. If she lived long enough.

JuanCarlo was still screaming threats and obscenities, and it was like everything was happening in slow motion. She kept her gaze locked on Rafe.

He pressed his hands in a downward motion. He wanted her to stop.

So she did.

Hard.

Chapter 29

Rafe lost another lifetime when he saw the gun pointed at Elena's head. He never wanted to relive the emotions he'd experienced in the past few hours, but he most definitely would choose them over this.

He knew who was in the passenger seat. He'd figured it out when he'd contacted Charlotte Oaks a little over an hour ago and asked to speak to him, only to be told that JuanCarlo had disappeared three days ago and nobody knew where he'd gone.

JuanCarlo had fielded Kate's initial call, and heard about Rafe's recent follow-ups when the trainer he'd spoken with had mentioned it to him and speculated about what Elena could have done to warrant such interest. JuanCarlo had done some checking on Trinity, and decided to look into it. He was crazy, but his instincts were solid. He'd been the one to hire Johansson. As Rafe had speculated once he'd uncovered Johansson's other line of work, he hadn't been working in his capacity as an insurance investigator—that had been his cover story to get close. He'd apparently called first, using a made-up name, as a prospective client for Trinity, but Mac had filtered him out as someone looking for a handout. Then he'd contacted Kate, with a different name, acting as a parent needing help for his child, and she'd invited him to bring his child to see the camp and talk with her about his needs. He'd shown up without his supposed special-needs child, claiming he wanted to see for himself before bringing his son. It was hard to say how he'd have learned about the pregnancy, but with no one knowing what was going on, it likely had been revealed innocently enough by one of the barn helpers.

Kate said she didn't recognize Johansson when he stormed her office the day before, but he'd been wearing aviator sunglasses and was waving an insurance card around, so she hadn't put the two together.

What Rafe didn't know was why he'd been killed, or what had made him turn tail and race off the day before. He prayed he'd have the chance to find out.

He pushed his hands down, signaling Elena to stop, and braced himself for what was to come next.

Each second of the next twenty seemed to stretch beyond infinity and back, even as it was happening so fast, he hardly had time to think. Only react. He'd already radioed Mac and sent up a silent prayer that his partner got there in time for backup. The pilot gave him a thumbs-up and shifted the chopper so the open door on Rafe's side faced the swerving front end of Elena's pickup truck . . . and the waving muzzle of JuanCarlo's gun.

The pilot had to make dipping adjustments as the truck's brakes locked up, and it slid almost sideways directly at them. Rafe motioned for Elena, who was fighting the wheel with all she had, to exit out of the driver-side door, which was presently aimed right at him.

He could hear the squealing tires even over the chopper noise, and smelled the burnt rubber as the truck completed a spin, putting JuanCarlo facing him. He prayed JuanCarlo would change targets, trading Elena for him . . . but he was too smart for that.

The truck finally stopped when the tires hit the soft sand on the side of the road, rocking dangerously onto two wheels before settling right-side up.

Rafe signaled the pilot to land and was out the door, gun drawn, before JuanCarlo could get his door open.

"Put the gun down," he shouted.

JuanCarlo just laughed, then dragged Elena across his lap by her hair and shoved her out the door in front of him, keeping one arm around her throat, the other holding the gun to her head.

I'll kill him, Rafe decided. Just for that.

"It's over, JuanCarlo," he told him. "You're stuck. Deal with me now, before everybody I've radioed shows up, and you'll do a lot better. Once you're outnumbered with guns, I can't make any promises. We know about Johansson. We found Aaron. There's a lot of trigger-happy people out there just dying to talk to you."

"Then die they will. I'm no idiot."

Rafe opted not to comment on that. He tried not to look at Elena, to keep his focus exclusively on JuanCarlo. It was his only chance at getting through this without losing his edge.

"You tell me where Springer is, and we'll cut a deal on the baby. We don't want him. He's already caused way more trouble than he's worth to us. Everybody wins."

"No!" JuanCarlo shouted. "Everybody has already lost."

"Why'd you torch the stables?"

"Revenge," he spat out, surprising Rafe that he'd responded.

So he pushed some more. "You wanted something you couldn't have. What wouldn't Gene give you?"

Elena mouthed the word *Kami*, despite having her windpipe all but crushed under JuanCarlo's forearm.

Rafe hadn't seen that one coming. *Shit*. JuanCarlo and Kami Vondervan? Oh yeah, this had gone way south. This was no rational assault for the intent of getting rich that had somehow gotten out of hand. This was obsession. And JuanCarlo had killed for her now, so there would be no bargaining.

"You killed Geronimo to get back at Gene? What did he do to you?"

"He didn't care about that goddamned horse. It was a token for him, a token!" JuanCarlo shouted. "Something to keep her happy, to keep her quiet."

To keep her from you, Rafe thought. So Gene had given Geronimo to Kami as a present. Now JuanCarlo wanted to give her his only heir as a way to woo her back. Christ.

"You can keep her happy with the baby, isn't that right, JuanCarlo? I can help you with that. All I want is what is mine. And that is the woman you're holding. Anything else is yours. I can make that happen."

He jammed the gun harder against her head and JuanCarlo's finger twitched on the trigger.

"You must think I have lost everything if I would take such an offer."

"You don't have much at the moment," he told him. "I'm the only one who knows where her horse is." A lie, and he hated giving her that hope, but there was no other way. "You take her out, and I have nothing left. Then I won't care. I'll just start shooting and we'll see where that ends up. Either way, you'll never get that horse. You can only get the baby going through me."

"Or me."

At the sound of Mac's voice, behind and above Rafe, coming from what could only be a perch atop the chopper, Juan-Carlo looked up.

And his hand holding the gun dropped.

That split second was all the time Rafe needed.

Chapter 30

It all happened so fast, they had to explain to her later what had happened.

Mac had taken out JuanCarlo's knee.

Rafe had blown off his elbow.

All she knew was that JuanCarlo had dropped to the ground howling, taking her with him, and she'd scrambled from his suddenly lax grasp and half stumbled, half crawled across the pavement and into Rafe's arms.

That had been three days ago. At some point, she figured she'd stop shaking every time she thought about it.

Rafe must have felt the tremor, because he squeezed her hand.

She was sitting next to him in the helicopter as they headed south to North Carolina. He didn't much like her being beyond arm's length these days. As it turned out, she was perfectly fine with that.

"I hope we get there in time," she said, hating the waver in her voice. The past three days had been like three centuries.

After surgery on his arm and leg, JuanCarlo was presently sitting in a jail cell, but the story was all over the media and likely would be for weeks to come. And again, later, much later, when he went to trial.

She was just happy being high above the earth, temporarily away from cell phones, reporters, and a replay of the nightmare of media attention after Geronimo died. Only this time the focus was on her.

Rafe had already lined up an attorney. They'd already spoken to Gene and Kami, and he'd been so thankful to find out that Geronimo had an heir, he'd very willingly worked out a deal with her. Turned out the horse had been far more than a token to him. It had been something special he'd always wanted, and a gift to his wife as a promise to be a better husband.

Given the way the Vondervans had been clutching each other's hands when they'd all met face-to-face, she hadn't doubted he'd turned over a new leaf. She'd hardly recognized him, in fact. Apparently it had taken almost losing a second wife to make him realize what was important.

Now they'd have the baby . . . and Elena would get her freedom. All they had to do was get to Kenny's cousin's farm in North Carolina in time to see the baby being born.

"I still can't believe what Kenny did, to keep her safe."

Johansson had tracked Springer to Kenny's but Kenny had turned him away. Which was why he'd stormed Dalton Downs a few hours later. In that time, Kenny had trailered his horses to a neighboring farm a few minutes down the road, then loaded up Springer and taken her out of state until he figured out what was what.

It turned out that Johansson was the one who'd gotten greedy. Once he'd figured out the paternity of the baby, he'd tried to stick it to JuanCarlo, playing middleman for a fee. A much higher fee than they'd originally agreed on. Only Kate hadn't let him talk to Elena, and Kenny hadn't let him near the horse. So he'd left Dalton Downs, apparently heading back to Kenny's, with some plan in mind. Only he'd seen JuanCarlo in the Charlotte Oaks truck, heading the opposite way on the one-lane road, and pulled a one-eighty, apparently deciding to beat him back to Dalton Downs. Only JuanCarlo had put an end to that plan with a bullet in Johansson's head.

Then he'd staked out Dalton Downs until he could get Elena alone . . . and the rest had happened from there.

It was the media story of JuanCarlo's shootings and arrest that had finally brought Kenny out of hiding. After a very relieved reunion over the phone, they'd told him to stay put. Springer had been having some continued problems, which all the traveling had only exacerbated, plus they hadn't talked things out with the Vondervans at that point.

Now things looked like they would be settled amicably . . . and, other than the media, the worst was over . . . and then Springer had gone into early labor.

Now they were flying south, with Elena squeezing the life out of Rafe's hand, willing the damn bird to fly faster.

"Almost there."

"What if—"

"Don't. Positive thoughts only."

She nodded, then squeezed her eyes shut as the pilot dipped down suddenly, heading toward a big square marked with hay bales in the back of what appeared to be a pretty decent spread.

"I'll never get used to this thing. It's just not natural," she told him, still queasy at being this high in the air. A first for her.

Then they were landing, and Rafe let her go, right on her heels as she sprinted to a waiting farm hand and he directed her to the barn where Springer was trying to give birth.

She entered the darker interior on a skid, willing her eyes to adjust faster so she could find Kenny. It was the sounds of her horse in distress that pointed her in the right direction.

Ten seconds later, she was pulling on shoulder-long rubber gloves and after a loud, smacking kiss on the top of a crouched Kenny's head, got right in next to him and helped her horse give birth forty-five sweat-drenched minutes later to what turned out to be a very beautiful little colt. Not that she was biased or anything.

Once the event was safely over, Rafe pulled her back against his chest, wrapping his arms around her as she stood, tears streaming down her cheeks, watching while Kenny helped Springer with the afterbirth and got her cleaned up. "She's going to be okay," she said, for what was probably the dozenth time.

"I know," Rafe said, awe and wonder clear in his tone. "You might not like flying, but what you just did . . ." He trailed off and pressed a kiss to the side of her temple.

She winced automatically. She was still sporting a pretty good bruise there from JuanCarlo's gun muzzle, but at the moment there was no pain in her world.

"Sorry," he said, immediately soothing the tender spot.

"Right now, life is perfect. There is absolutely nothing to be sorry about." She turned into his arms. "Except what I just realized I am doing to your very expensive shirt."

"I'll live," he said, not flinching in the least when she pressed her birthing-covered overalls against his chest and plastered a kiss on his mouth. When he lifted his head, he looked down into her eyes, and said, "I'm pretty much only interested in seeing you smile at me the way you are right now for as long as humanly possible."

She kissed him back, then they both turned to look at the baby, who was trying hard to stand on very wobbly legs. She laughed and cried at the same time.

"What are you going to name him?"

"Not my job. That's up to Gene."

"Oh, I don't know about that," came Gene's booming voice from the aisle just outside the stall.

She looked up, trepidation filling her as she looked at her former boss. "You just missed it." The Vondervans had flown their own helicopter down. "I'm so sorry."

"She healthy?" he asked, motioning to Springer.

"Yes, she'll be fine."

"And he's okay?" he said, pointing to the baby.

Elena nodded, her throat closing over as the emotion of the

day caught up with her. She couldn't stop the tears from continuing to leak out.

"Then it's all good," he said, tugging Kami into view for the first time. "Look at him, honey. Just look at him. That's our future right there."

And the gruffer note in his always gruff tone told Elena just how moved he truly was. Then he shocked her by looking up at her . . . and offering her the entire world on a platter.

"I have a name already waiting to be registered, but there is something else I'd like you to consider," he said.

She swiped at her face with the shoulder of her t-shirt, but it did little to clean up the now tear-streaked muck. "I'm just happy he's okay," she told him. "I'm so sorry about everything, I—"

"I believe we've covered all that." He'd already made it clear he wasn't much for overt emotion, so she did her best to get herself under control.

"What was it you wanted me to consider?"

"Coming back down to Charlotte Oaks and helping out with his training. See what he's got."

Elena knew she couldn't have heard him correctly. She felt Rafe's arm tighten reflexively around her shoulder, but he said nothing. She looked from him, back to Gene, but she wasn't dreaming this.

"I—I don't know what to say. After what I did—"

"What you did was give me a dream. Don't much care how it happened. All things happen as they do for a reason." He looked at Kami then, and there was no mistaking the emotion on his face, or hers. He looked back at Elena, his voice a little rougher when he continued. "Don't mistake this offer. The world is going crazy with this, and me making you this offer sums up as nothing else could where I stand on this issue. I want peace and quiet as soon as possible. I know of no better way to end the speculation than making a very public show of putting this all to rest." He drew Kami closer. "The only time I want that little fellow to garner global attention is when he's winning the triple crown."

"Mr. Vondervan—Gene," she corrected, as he'd demanded early on. "I—I'm not sure, I—"

Rafe pulled her aside then, and spoke over her. "It's been a long couple of days. Can you give her a little time to consider this?"

Not surprisingly, Gene seemed rather taken aback by that, and Elena started to step in to smooth things over. Then Gene looked between the two of them, and said, "Take all the time you need. We're staying local at least for the next few days. You?"

"We're staying here," she said, "but I won't need that long to give you an answer." She looked up at Rafe, and knew without question what her response was going to be. But she needed to talk to him about it first. If she was going to make this big a life-altering decision, then he had a right to know what it was she wanted before she did it.

It was much later that evening, but she finally had time alone with him. They were standing at the stall door, watching mother and baby. Elena was showered and presentable this time. Rafe was effortlessly perfect as always.

"Elena, we have to talk about this."

"I know. That's why I brought you out here." She turned to face him, but he spoke before she could start her little speech.

"This is a huge thing, what he's offering you. Regardless of his motives, given what you've told me about the racing world, you won't likely have this big an opportunity again."

"Never, actually, given that what I've done is now being very publicly analyzed and dissected. I'm the most reviled person in horseracing."

"Ah, you're being harsh." He smiled a little. "It's about fifty-fifty, the love and the revilement."

She smiled, too. "Well, then, maybe by the next millennium, someone will trust me around their plow horse."

He laughed, and brushed the hair from her face. She'd left it down on purpose, knowing he liked it that way. It felt good, actually. Her scalp was still sore and the braid she'd put it in this morning, in anticipation of the birth, hadn't helped matters.

He traced his fingers across her cheek, then down along her nose, and across her lips. It made her sigh and tingle all at the same time.

"You should do this, Elena. Show the world what you're made of."

"The only person I'm wanting to show that to is you."

His eyes went darker as his pupils expanded in a physical response to her declaration, but he kept his touch light, and his voice steady. "I already know."

The look in his eyes made what she had to say even harder. He wanted her, but she could see the noble gesture, just waiting to be made. Stupid man. She took a little breath to get steady before she told him what she wanted to say, needed to say.

"Elena—"

"Rafe—" They spoke at the same time, but she went on first. "Hear me out. I've made my decision, but I want to explain it to you first, before telling Gene, aka the entire world."

"I wouldn't be surprised if he holds a press conference outside the stall here." At her alarmed look, he tugged her closer into his arms. "I'm kidding. And I'll also make sure we let him know that's not going to happen. Just in case he is planning such a thing."

"I don't think he'll need to make an announcement."

Rafe's smile faded. "Elena, if you're deciding against this, and I have anything to do with that decision—"

"I am turning him down."

"It's not an either/or decision, you know. If that matters."

That stopped her. "What did you just say?"

He cupped her cheeks, tilted her face to his, and looked into her eyes. "I said, you don't have to choose me over the horse, or vice versa. If that's what you're doing."

"Not entirely, but—"

"If you want both, we'll make it work. I don't have to be in Dalton Downs. And for that matter, the baby doesn't have to be at Charlotte Oaks."

"Gene would never—"

"You don't know that. Until we try. Either way, we'll figure something out. That is, if you want both."

Now she reached up and held his face, and the look in his eyes almost undid her. Like it was okay for him to be making all the moves, but her touching him, taking him, making the gesture, somehow made it harder on him.

"I want you," she told him, and the undeniable relief she saw in his beautiful face told her just how worried he'd been. And gave her everything she needed to know. "And I want what Dalton Downs has to offer."

"But racing—"

"I've done what I can do there. And if I hadn't, these past few days would have done it for me. I—I want to go home. And the only place that calls to me is Dalton Downs. And you." She held his face even more tightly when his eyes grew glassy. "I'm making a difference there. A greater one than I'll ever make in racing. And I want to make a bigger one. I want to talk to Kate about taking on more Bonders. About working with more Traceys. But I don't want any of that if I have to stare up at that pool house, and know you're in there . . . and I'm not." She smiled. "I'm a package deal, however. Love me, love my horse. And we both know she's a wanton hussy who gets into trouble when you least expect it."

He wrapped his arms more tightly around her. "Maybe we'll get her her own guy, and have our own little wild offspring. This one seemed to go okay. Could she do that again? Planned this time?"

Now it was her turn to get glassy-eyed. "She could, but you don't have to—"

"I'd love to. Deal?"

Her throat tightened against unshed tears. "Deal."

He kissed her then with such intensity, she got dizzy. Dizzy in the best possible way. "Ah, *mi mijita*," he said gruffly, when he finally lifted his head. "I'm still willing to talk to Gene, too. We have the room to build a track. Maybe you could—"

"I know what I want," she said, her gaze never wavering from his.

He grinned. "Well, then, you're about to get very, very lucky."

Springer chose that moment to lift her head and look in their direction. She grumbled, almost as in warning, which had them both laughing.

"Don't worry," Elena told her dearest friend. "I'll be careful." She squealed as Rafe scooped her up and carried her out of the barn, then thrilled at the wicked grin on his face as he kicked open the door to the little travel trailer they'd been given to stay in for the duration.

"Maybe," he said, before tossing her lightly down on the bed and following right down after her. He swiftly divested them both of their clothes, pulling her immediately under him, both of them grinning like loons.

"Maybe not," she said, knowing she'd never tire of feeling his weight on her.

He nipped her earlobe and looked down into her eyes, already lifting her hips even as he slid deep inside of her. "Yeah," he said. "Maybe not."

If you liked this book,
you've got to try
STRONG AND SEXY
by Jill Shalvis,
new this month from Brava . . .

"Why do you look so familiar?" His mouth was close to her ear, close enough to cause a whole series of hopeful shivers to rack her body. He was rock-solid against her, all corded muscle and testosterone.

Lots of testosterone.

"I don't know," she whispered, still hoping for a big hole to take her.

"Are you sure you're all right?"

"Completely." Except, you know, not.

"Because I can't help but think I'm missing something here."

Yes, yes, he was missing something. He'd missed her whole pathetic attempt of a kiss seduction, for instance. And the fact that she was totally, one-hundred percent out of her league here with him. But his eyes were deep, so very deep, and leveled right on hers, evenly, patiently, giving her the sense that he was always even, always patient. Never rattled or ruffled.

She wanted to be never rattled or ruffled.

"Am I?" His thumb glided over her skin, sending all her erogenous zones into tap-dance mode. "Missing something?"

"Yes. N–no. I mean . . ."

He smiled. And not just a curving of his lips, but with his whole face. His eyes lit, those laugh lines fanned out, and damn, that sexy dimple. "Yeah," he murmured. "Definitely missing something."

"I'm a little crazy tonight," she admitted.

"A little crazy once in awhile isn't a bad thing."

Oh boy. She'd bet the bank he knew how to coax a woman into doing a whole host of crazy stuff. Just the thought made her feel a little warm, and a nervous laugh escaped.

"You're beautiful, you know that?"

She had to let out another laugh, but he didn't as he traced a finger over her lower lip. "You are."

Beautiful? Or crazy?

"You going to tell me what brought you to this closet?"

"I was garnering my courage."

"For?"

Well wasn't that just the question of the night, as there were so many, many things she'd needed courage for, not the least of which was standing here in front of him and telling him what she *really* wanted. A kiss . . .

"Talk to me."

She licked her lips. "There's a man and a woman in that first office down the hall. Together. And they're . . . not talking."

"Ah." A fond smile crossed his mouth. "You must have found Noah and Bailey. They've just come home from their honeymoon. So yeah, I seriously doubt they're . . . talking."

"Yeah. See . . ." She gnawed on her lower lip. "I was hoping for that."

"Talking."

"No. The *not* talking."

Silence.

And then more silence.

Oh, God.

Slowly she tipped her head up and looked at him, but he wasn't laughing at her.

A good start, she figured.

In fact, his eyes were no longer smiling at all, but full of a heart-stopping heat. "Can you repeat that request?" he asked.

Well, yes, she could, but it would make his possible rejection that much harder to take. "I was wondering what your stance is on being seduced by a woman who isn't really so good at this sort of thing, but wants to be better . . ."

He blinked. "Just to be clear." His voice was soft, gravelly, and did things to every erogenous zone in her body. "Is this you coming on to me?"

"Oh, God." She covered her face. "If you don't know, then I'm even worse at this than I thought. Yes. Yes, that's what I'm pathetically attempting to do. Come on to you, a complete stranger in a closet, but now I'm hearing it as you must be hearing it, and I sound like the lunatic that everyone thinks I am, and—"

His hands settled on her bare arms, gliding up, down, and then back up again, over her shoulders to her face, where he gently pulled her hands away so he could see her.

"I saw the mistletoe," she rushed to explain. "It's everywhere. And people were kissing. And I couldn't get kissing off my mind . . . God. Forget it, okay? Just forget me." She took a step back, but because this was her, she tripped over something on the floor behind her. She'd have fallen on her ass if he hadn't held her upright. "Thanks," she managed. "But I need to go now. I really need to go—"

He put a finger to her lips.

Right. Stop talking. Good idea.

His eyes, still hot, and also a little amused—because that's what she wanted to see in a man's eyes after she'd tried to seduce him, amusement—locked onto hers. She couldn't look away. There was just something about the way he was taking her in, as if he could see so much more than she'd intended him to. "Seriously. I've—"

He turned away.

Okaaaay . . . "Got to go."

But he was rustling through one of the shelves. Then he bent to look lower and she tried not to look at his butt. She failed, of course. "Um, yeah. So I'll see you around." Or not. Hopefully not—

"Got it." Straightening, he revealed what he held—a sprig of mistletoe.

"Oh," she breathed. Her heart skipped a beat, then raced, beating so loud and hard she couldn't hear anything but the blood pumping through her veins.

His mouth quirked slightly, but his eyes held hers, and in them wasn't amusement so much as . . .

Pure staggering heat.

"Did you change your mind?" he asked.

Was he kidding? She wanted to jump him. *Now.* "No."

With a smile that turned her bones to mush, he raised his arm so that the mistletoe was above their heads.

Oh, God.

"Your move," he whispered.

She looked at his mouth, her own tingling in anticipation. "Maybe you could . . ."

"Oh, no. I'm not taking advantage of a woman in a closet, drenched in champagne." He smiled. "But if she wanted to take advantage of me, now see, that's a different story entirely."

He was teasing her, his eyes lit with mischievousness and a wicked, wicked intent.

"I'm a klutz," she whispered. "I might hurt you by accident."

"I'll take my chances."

She laughed. She couldn't help it. She laughed, and he closed his eyes and puckered up, making her laugh some more, making it okay for her to lean in . . .

And kiss him.

Don't miss
the newest title
from Kathy Love,
ANY WAY YOU WANT IT,
available now from Brava . . .

"I had a woman read my tea leaves today, too." As soon as the words were out of her mouth, she knew that wasn't it.

And unfortunately, Ren's interest was piqued.

"Oh yeah. And what did you find out? Something about having a wild fling with a long-haired, white-eyelashed musician?"

From her violent blush, Ren realized his flirtatious joke had been dead on. Well damn. He had to find that tea leaf reader and give her a big kiss.

He studied Maggie. Had she revealed she wanted him to the fortune teller? There was something thrilling about the idea that she'd made it clear to someone else that she wanted him. Even after his brush off. He didn't deserve one, but he was damned glad he was getting a second chance with her.

And a wild fling was exactly what he wanted, too. Man, this all seemed to be falling into place so easily. There *were* brief times in his existence when he didn't feel quite so cursed. This was definitely one of them.

Of course, he still sensed some reservations in her that he would have to get around. Actually, two distinct feelings swirled around her like a cocoon, one real and one manufactured.

Her announcement had her embarrassed, and she'd also had too much to drink. He could take care of her embarrassment; she had nothing to be ashamed of, period. But he did not want sex with this woman to be the drunken variety. He should have realized that alcohol would affect her more in his presence.

Humans always got more drunk, more tired, more overwhelmed in his presence. A side effect of his nature. Even when he wasn't trying, he still stole some of a human's energy, which brought their natural tolerance down. It was part of being a lampir that he couldn't totally control.

He did not want Maggie drunk when he was with her. He wanted her fully aware of him when he ran his hands over her soft skin, kissed her, and entered her curvy little body.

His cock pulsed against the material of his jeans as if cheering at that idea.

And Maggie was so worth cheering about. Her energy snapped between them. So alive, so powerful. She had a wholesomeness that radiated from her and filled him. He liked that feeling. Wholesomeness. When had he ever known that feeling?

He started to reach out to tuck one of her flyaway waves behind her ear, but stopped himself. She was too uncomfortable now. He needed to give her time to settle down again before touching her, even in the most innocent way.

Instead, he pushed away her drink. "I think you've had enough Impaler for tonight." God, no double entendre there.

She didn't argue. "I think you're right."

"Do you want to get out of here?" he asked, needing to take her somewhere where he could touch her. Not that Sheri would think twice if he decided to make out with Maggie right where they sat. Hell, he'd done more than that at this very table. But Maggie wasn't like the women he was used to. She needed seduction, not the usual inelegant groping he'd become accustomed to.

"I think that's a good idea," she said.

He noticed that her eyes tracked the features of his face as if they were moving. Oh yeah, she'd drunk too much—and he'd taken too much of her energy too. It was so damned hard not to.

"Fresh air might be good," she said, still looking a little disoriented.

Ren nodded, and immediately regretted the action as she nodded in response, trying to focus on him.

He waved to Sheri, thanking her. Maggie thanked her too, her voice sweet and only a little slurred.

"Maybe we should walk around for awhile," he suggested.

"I think that's a good idea." This time *that's* was only slightly slurred.

He took her elbow. She allowed the touch, even leaned into it. He liked the feeling of her against his side, warm and soft. He focused on giving some of his energy back to her. Another trick a lampir had. He constantly took energy from those around him, but he could also give it back. That made him less of a leech, right?

They stepped out of the bar and he headed left onto Bourbon, only to take the next side street off it. The smells of Bourbon did not even approximate fresh air. Between the odor of beer, trash, and other disgusting things, it was not the place to sober up someone who was a little tipsy.

He walked slowly, not pushing her into conversation, in case she didn't feel quite up to it. But once they were away from the music blaring from within the bars and the air was a little less aromatic, she spoke.

"I already feel better. Thanks."

"Sure. Not like I haven't been there." It took him a lot more than three tumblers of wine and a half an Impaler to get there, but he did understand. And yes, he had been counting her drinks. He'd been aware of everything she'd done since she'd walked into the bar tonight.

They reached Jackson Square, and he gestured to benches lining the outside of the wrought-iron fence. "Want to sit?"

She nodded.

Once they were settled, she turned to him, her big gray-green eyes regarding him solemnly—and more focused.

"I'm sorry I told you about the—thing at the cemetery and the tea leaf reading."

He wasn't. He liked both announcements, a lot.

"Well," he said slowly, "technically you didn't tell me anything about the tea leaf reading. And I really liked what you had to say about the cemetery tour."

The dim light couldn't hide Maggie's blush.

"That was a really good story," he added when her gaze dropped to her hands folded on her lap.

"I don't think blurting out that I wished to have a wild fling really constitutes a story."

Ren smiled at that. "Oh, I don't know, I think there's a story there. And frankly, I'm really hoping that I get to be an integral part of it."

Her head popped up, surprise clear in her wide-eyed expression. How could she possibly be surprised by that? Did she still doubt that he wanted her? Silly woman.

"Ren," she started, and the slow way she said his name didn't make him think he was going to like what she had to say after it. So he did the first thing that came into his mind.

He kissed her.

Tensions are running high
in Charlotte Mede's
EXPLOSIVE,
available now from Brava . . .

"What exactly is the nature of your agreement with de Maupassant? Is it money? The promise of notoriety?" Devon turned her head sharply to look up at him, absorbing the stark lines of his face, the wide mouth above the strong jawline. She pivoted gracefully in his arms, holding herself stiffly as though more conscious than ever of a confused up-surge of unwelcome sensations, of fear and desire. Blackburn felt her invoke her steeliest reserve.

"My relationship with Le Comte has nothing to do with us."

"He has everything to do with us," Blackburn muttered. "He's thrown us together quite deliberately. And he's prepared to give you access to the Eroica, despite your denials," he said just as the orchestra struck up a lively minuet.

"It's not that easy." Her mouth was set in a firm line. "I don't want or need your offer of money, or anybody else's for that matter."

"Don't take me for a fool, Mademoiselle. And I won't take you for the innocent that you pretend to be," he said in a softly uttered threat. "You know how to play Le Comte for a puppet, and you know exactly how to convince him to relinquish the score to you."

The confusion and embarrassment clouding her eyes was a

fine bit of acting, he thought, looking at her drift away from him a few steps, in perfect time with the music's rhythm.

"Tell me, is Le Comte sparing with the purse strings?" he continued ruthlessly as his strong arms propelled her back toward him. "One should think those emeralds around your lovely neck would keep you satisfied. Or are you trying for diamonds?"

"Stop it," she whispered under her breath, then in the next instant lifted her gaze to him boldly as though changing her mind. "Rubies, actually," she said with a brittle voice. "I'm trying for rubies, if you must know."

He didn't like the answer or her bravado. "Then perhaps we should turn up the heat."

She gave him a mockingly sweet smile, for his benefit or for their audience, he wasn't sure. "And how do you propose we force Le Comte's hand?" she asked.

"With the utmost discretion, of course," he said, fooling neither her nor himself. "As strategies go, you of all people must know how potent the combination of seduction, jealousy, and deception can be, Mademoiselle," he explained, his voice rough velvet as he led her from the center of the ballroom to the protective shadows of a grouping of leafy plants.

She was a tall woman but he still towered over her, backing her into a corner. In the wavering candlelight, he thought he glimpsed uncertainty and fear in her eyes as she refused to lower her gaze, staring steadily, courageously into his face. Vulnerability was difficult to feign and for a moment, Blackburn questioned his own powers of observation. He watched the tip of her tongue slide from her lips, the gesture deliberate, he didn't know. All he knew was how his body reacted with a blast of heat.

As though to make it easier for her, his shadowed face moved fractionally closer as he slid his fingers deep into the mass of her hair to tilt her face upward. It was just one way to fight the battle, he persuaded himself, before taking her face in both palms. Her mouth trembled beneath his, moist, pliant, and intensely female.

The tension eased out of her by slow degrees as his lips brushed lightly against hers. Instead of drawing away, Devon drew unconsciously closer, her lashes lowered, closing her eyes. He teasingly nipped her lower lip, his tongue licking inside. She surrendered her mouth, opening to the voracity of his deepening kiss while the strains of violins and the protective covering of fronds receded in the distance.

More insistent and demanding, the pressure of Blackburn's lips increased in a velvety heated stroking as his tongue suggestively explored, caressing her sweetness, tasting her mouth with a lazy greed. Slow and inexorably consuming, his mouth devoured hers until she gasped for breath. He heard her groan as she pressed her breasts against him, oblivious to the sharp edges of the pilaster biting into her back, sighing against the succulence of their hot, ravenous play.

"We should have done this from the very first," Blackburn whispered roughly, and plunged again for her pliant tongue as his hands stroked their way down her back and to the sides of her breasts.

Against his mouth, she whispered, "This makes no sense . . ." But she wound her arms around his neck, shuddering at the feel of his palms molding her breasts. She sank into his kisses, long, leisurely, wet incursions that left her so weak he had to hold her up in his arms.

As if he had all the time in the world, and as if a good number of Le Comte's guests had not spied their impromptu rendezvous, Blackburn traced a voluptuous trail along her parted lips, her smooth cheek, the curl of an ear, the highly sensitive, he discovered, curve of her neck. He moved his mouth to the softness of her shoulder and felt Devon shiver at the touch of his mouth, his teeth, the soothing stroke of his tongue.

No longer distant nor in complete control of the encounter, Blackburn felt himself become harder, tauter, his body contemptuously mocking his attempt at detachment. Her skin was like rich cream beneath his lips, her body sinuously lush as it melted into his. She drew a shuddering breath and, against his will, his hard fingers slid from her breasts to the back of her head where they tangled in her thick hair. His mouth, a hot brand, closed over hers once again.

His eyes closed in self-defense and he immediately saw her naked beneath him, warm and soft and ready. He groaned against the tidal wave threatening to overtake them both. Her open and ardent sensuality startled him like nothing had in a very long time, and he had drunk from the very depths of decadence, manipulating, controlling the most sophisticated of carnal games.

He forced his eyes open, pulling back and releasing her by slow degrees with small kisses, erotically tugging at her lips, willing himself to ignore the clamoring of his heated blood, willing his erection to subside. She was just another of de Maupassant's women. His pulse slowed, he tensed and ice water began to replace the blood in his veins.

The objective was to have her secure the Eroica, at whatever cost.